The Other Woman

The Other Woman

A Novel

Aria Devi

Also by Aria Devi

The Velvet Clover

Wanter Dynamics & The Love We Are

To the woman who has chased love down a complicated path—may you find the strength to choose yourself.

Trigger Warning

This book touches on sensitive themes, including mentally abusive relationships, divorce, postpartum depression, and discussions of plastic surgery. Please read with care.

Chapter One

Anxiety pressed against my chest, relentless and heavy. I sat at my desk, the buzz of the city alive outside the windows —taxis honking, voices rising, the pulse of New York never ceasing. Inside, the atmosphere felt just as oppressive. The manuscript stared back at me, its deadline hanging over my head like a guillotine. Tomorrow morning. I had until tomorrow morning to finish this edit.

It had been one year since I'd landed this job at Regent House Publishing, and I'd poured every ounce of myself into proving that I belonged here. A year of late nights, early mornings, and going above and beyond on every new project that came my way. I worked hard to meticulously proofread my colleagues' manuscripts (to help them, of course, but mostly to hone my own craft). I had taken on any extra projects that needed more eyes on them, and I had spent time supporting several of the senior editors with their overflowing work-loads while asking for no additional pay. I was desperate to prove that hiring me wasn't a mistake.

A few days ago, Regent's executive editor and my mentor,

Willow Brooks, had pulled me aside in the hallway, her voice almost conspiratorial.

"I wanted you to hear this from me first," she said, scanning the hallway before she spoke. "The merger's official. The transfers from Chicago are going to be coming in the weeks following the Gala. Expect changes in leadership, and a senior editor spot to open up. This could be a great opportunity for you to gun for that position. I recommend volunteering your extra time to other divisions, asking if they need support on any projects, seeing how you can lend a hand."

This was the opportunity I had waited for all year. The one I had worked hard to be prepared for when it did come.

After Willow shared the news, I couldn't help but notice that upper management had been keeping a closer eye on the junior editors, even before the announcement was officially made. They must have been sizing up who might be the right fit for the role. I wanted it. Not just for the title or the paycheck—though I wouldn't complain about those benefits—but because winning was who I was. My career had always come first, and this was my chance to prove, once again, that no one wanted it more than me.

I barely registered the sound of Izzy's boots clicking against the floor before she perched herself on the edge of my desk, one leg swinging lazily. "So, Bathtub Gin after the event tonight?"

I blinked up at her, disoriented. "What?"

She rolled her eyes. "Bathtub Gin. After the Gala? That prohibition-style speakeasy in Tribeca. Drinks. Socializing. *Fun.*" She said the last few terms as if they were foreign concepts to me.

I sighed, forcing my eyes back on the manuscript. "I really need to squeeze in time to finish this developmental edit. If I can't finish it by the end of the day today, I'll need time after the Gala to work on it," I muttered under my breath, typing a comment with more force than necessary.

I'd been looking forward to the Regent House Publishing Gala all year. Izzy told me it was an incredible event, but I needed all the time I could get to hit this deadline. Ideally I would knock it out and be able to put all of my energy into impressing the managers and executives at the event. I figured since I knew about the position before the other junior editors, I could go early and schmooze some of the key decision-makers. The last thing on my mind was going out to a Manhattan club afterward.

Izzy, of course, didn't take the hint. She rarely did. Her blonde bob was still damp from what I assumed was a late morning shower. While I was buried in edits, she was probably juggling schedules or making reservations for Theo and Willow at their favorite restaurant for lunch. Izzy never dealt with late nights or frantic deadlines. The life of a personal assistant must be nice.

Sometimes, I was jealous of my best friend and roommate. At this point, we were more than that—we may as well have been sisters. Although I was sure she had her own share of work stress, her life seemed to be somewhat carefree. Being the assistant to the executive editor and the chief creative officer must have its own set of challenges I wasn't aware of, but she did her job with ease and always seemed to have time for fun.

"Come on, Sarah," she scoffed. "There's no way you're going to be sober enough or have the energy to edit after the party." She inspected her nails, as if this whole discussion was a formality she'd already won.

"Iz, I need to focus," I reiterated, my eyes glued to the manuscript. "I'm really stressed about work." I gestured to my computer and the various notes littering my desk. "Willow told me about that senior editor position that they are opening up and announcing at the Gala, and I told her I would take on this last-minute project to show her I was serious."

Izzy gave me a sympathetic look, but I could tell she wasn't going to back off. "Right, Willow told me about that. It *is* a perfect opportunity for you. But you've been pushing yourself so hard. You're going to burn out if you don't slow down. At the very least, decompress by having one fun night out in the city." She leaned in and whispered so the other junior editors around us wouldn't hear, "Plus, you won't be very effective as a senior editor if you are completely burned out from overworking to get the promotion."

I shook my head and exhaled, finally looking at her. "Thank you for your concern, but I don't really have a choice here. It won't be forever that I have to work like this, but I really want this promotion. It's my opportunity to prove that I'm ready for more—more money, more responsibility . . . everything. If I don't get it, I feel like I'll be stuck as a junior editor forever. Who knows when the next position will open up."

Izzy slid off the desk and leaned in close, her eyes narrowing at me. "Sarah," she began, lowering her voice as if she were sharing a secret. "You're one of the company's shiny new stars—everyone can see it. All the messy drafts you have turned around, and remember when you fixed that disaster of a manuscript overnight? No one asked you to do that; you just took initiative. The times I have seen you help other editors in the bullpen, not because it is your job to do that, but because you wanted to help them and get better yourself. You're the one everyone's watching."

I paused, feeling a flicker of pride despite myself. "Thanks, Iz. That is sweet of you to say, but none of that changes the fact that I need to finish this edit by tomorrow. It's not like it's going to get done by itself," I said, trying to move my focus back to my work.

Izzy raised an eyebrow. "You'll finish it before the Gala, no problem. Or you'll wake up early and knock it out before work. You always do." She shrugged it off like it was nothing.

I sighed, rubbing my temples, knowing she was right, but still feeling the weight of the deadline, the weight of the promotion looming. "I just really don't want to mess up this opportunity."

Izzy stood, gesturing around the publishing office like a Broadway performer on stage. The bullpen buzzed with activity. Desks were cluttered with laptops, glowing screens displaying marked-up documents, headphones tangled beside cold coffee cups, and sticky notes clinging to every available surface. Floor-to-ceiling windows framed the New York skyline, casting natural light onto the sleek, minimalist

4

furniture, while whiteboards and pinboards lined the walls, scribbled with timelines, editing deadlines, and motivational quotes. The smell of coffee lingered. Editors were hunched over their computers like zombies, and Izzy's grand gesture pointed out Phillip, another junior editor, who looked like he was sleeping with his head resting in his hands.

"Look at him," she said. I popped up out of my seat just enough to see his eyes were, in fact, closed. Most likely napping. "Most of these people don't do a sliver of the work you do. You don't have much in the way of competition. And of those who are your competition, few of them have your eye for detail, your drive and leadership potential."

I leaned back in my chair, letting her words sink in as I stared at the red markings across my digital manuscript. Izzy, ever the master of persuasion, stood there with a glare that screamed, *Give in already.*

"Izzy's not wrong, you know," a voice said before I could answer.

I whipped around in my chair. Theo had a way of appearing out of nowhere. Today his hands were in his pockets, and his last few strides toward my desk were casual. His black hair and well-groomed beard streaked with a copious amount of gray strands gave him a look of a new age philosopher, which he totally was. Despite the company's business casual dress code, he always managed to get away with wearing a white T-shirt and jeans, a small rebellion that somehow suited his position as chief creative officer. He offered one of his rare toothless smiles.

"You've been putting in a lot of effort, and it has shown," He narrowed his eyes, like he could see the dark circles hidden under my double-layered concealer. "And honestly, it looks like you need a night away from that desk and any type of words on paper." He smirked, like he had been where I was, once upon a time, when he was a junior editor.

Even though Izzy had always insisted that Theo and Willow were like family to her—and, by association, me—I still couldn't shake the nerves that always seemed to creep up whenever they were around at work. When the four of us were at lunch together, or hanging out on the weekends, it was relaxing, but in the office . . . Despite having been personally and professionally mentored by them for nearly a year, Theo's presence still made me feel like I needed to sit up straighter, and Willow's made me feel like I needed to quadruple-check my work.

Within that agreement to teach me what they knew, there was an expectation that I would commit to working harder and smarter than anyone in the office, study more to advance my craft, be coachable when they gave me advice, whether it be personal or professional—they believed one had a heavy influence on the other, which made total sense to me—and strive for opportunities that arose to advance my career.

And that was just what I had wanted. What I had asked for. People who could challenge me and push me beyond what I thought I was capable of, in *every* area of my life. Theo, Willow, and Izzy had truly become my New York City family. But just like family, they were fiercely protective and sometimes hypercritical, always quick to celebrate my wins but never letting me forget that I could do better.

I swallowed, forcing a smile and pushing the swirling energy down from Theo's presence. "I'm just trying to stay on top of my projects," I said, avoiding his gaze, hoping he didn't catch the hint of uncertainty in my voice.

Trailing behind him was, of course, Willow. They were never more than a few seconds apart. Willow, not only the executive editor of Regent House, but Theo's wife, approached like a storm front about to deliver one of her trademark doses of tough love.

"Sarah, don't listen to Theo *or* Izzy," she began, her tone sharp and hushed so as not to spoil the news to the office. "The senior editor position will require laser-focus and no distractions." She paused, giving me a look that felt like a challenge. "You have incredible skills when it comes to your personal production, but it's not just about proving you can *do* the work. This isn't just about delivering edits. It's about demonstrating you can handle more responsibility. Leading a team, managing tough deadlines, making decisions with confidence. We see all you have been doing to go above and beyond. But this role requires a different level of leadership. Not just self-leadership. Theo and I are here to show you the way, but you going out to the bars probably won't help much," she said, shooting her husband a look of disdain for even recommending it.

I nodded, my back straight, doing my best not to absorb the intensity of her energy. Despite my fear response, I was equally grateful she was willing to tell me the truth of what it would take, reminding me that going out may not be the best choice, even if it was momentarily tempting.

"Totally understood, Willow," I said militantly. Willow was one of the prime decision-makers for the senior editor promotion. But she couldn't just promote me because she liked me. She had to back up her choice for the promotion with proof they deserved it. I had to earn this just like anyone else.

"Leadership of others means leading by example. If you would be okay with all your junior editors going out and getting drunk after the Gala, needing to recover all weekend, only to show up Monday hungover, which ultimately affects team performance, then by all means . . . go for it." Her frosty tone moved to one of a nurturing mother. She tucked her bright red hair behind her ear. "I trust you will make the right choice on this one," she said, glancing at me, then sidelong to Theo and Izzy, not hiding her annoyance at them both.

That was Willow. She would go from hot to cold, fire to ice, in a split second. Professional to personal like it was nothing. Her delivery wasn't always wrapped in sugar and spice and everything nice, but her intentions were always to improve the entire Regent team– including me. That was her job after all.

I forced a grin, glancing around my desk like I was looking for a microphone. "Seriously, have you two bugged this place?" I clenched my jaw, determined not to let them see my nerves. Humor was my favorite mask, a quick fix to cover the cracks when nerves and insecurities started to show. Willow raised her eyebrows, awaiting a real response. She knew this about me better than anyone.

I never thought I'd find myself in a dynamic where two people could shift seamlessly from the easy comfort of friends hanging out to complete and utter terror as bosses—all within seconds.

"Thanks for the advice, both of you," I finally said, glancing between them. "Theo, you're right—I could use a night off. Willow, I can't argue with you about drinking. Probably not the best move if I want to be on my A-game while working for the promotion."

Inside, my stomach was twisted into knots. Willow knew my deadline—she probably knew exactly how much work I still had left on it. Her ability to read me like an open book was both a gift and a curse.

They shared a glance, smirks flickering at the corners of their mouths.

It wasn't the first time we'd had conversations like these. Even before the promotion was on the table, there were weekly reminders to stay focused, daily nudges to take on responsibilities like a leader would around the office.

I'd had a conversation with Willow one evening, when the topic of my career ambitions came up. "I think it might be best to pause dating for now," I had said. "At least until I'm further along in my career." At the time, I'd told myself it was about focusing on work— but, truthfully, that night I wasn't feeling particularly confident. Deep in my luteal phase, I couldn't shake the nagging voice that whispered no guy would ever be interested in someone like me—someone so consumed by her career. Saying it out loud to Willow felt like a way to hold myself accountable, to make the choice seem deliberate. At least if I ended up old and alone, I could pretend it had been on my terms.

Willow hadn't even blinked. She'd nodded, as if I'd just made the most logical decision in the world. "Guys your age are nothing but a distraction," she'd said, her tone blunt. "Focus on your career now, and you'll have time for everything else later. Trust me, you don't want to date seriously when you're this young anyway—you're still figuring out who you are. Over the next five years, you'll grow so much, and when the time is right, you'll attract a man who truly deserves the incredible woman you've become."

Though the conversation had been a serious one, it had become a running joke between the three of us. The no-dating rule. Sarah wouldn't date until she was at least a senior editor.

At first the rule was effective. It kept me from feeling shameful that I was never being asked out on dates. But as time passed, and I did get asked on a few . . . the rule wasn't as airtight as I intended. When men asked me out, I wanted to say yes. I hated to admit it, but I liked the attention.

After some time, I decided (independently, of course) that first dates didn't count. At least, not to me. A quick drink or dinner with someone I'd just met wasn't really "dating." It was . . . casual. I was sure it wouldn't affect my career negatively to have a little male attention every once in a while. If anything, it motivated me. Plus, it wasn't like these dates were happening every week. *Maybe* every three or six months. I saw it as a way to unwind every now and then. No strings. No mess. No expectations. A little male adoration. No harm, no foul. And as long as the rule kicked in after the first date, it could still be my reason for being single, focused, and alone. This way, I didn't risk any of the guys becoming a distraction but could still show myself that I wasn't totally undesirable on the dating market.

Once in a while, though, as I sat alone at my desk after another long day, I couldn't help but wonder. What was it all for? The promotions, the recognition, the success? Yes, it was everything I wanted, but . . . *alone?* At the end of the day, when the lights were off and the office was clearing out, I was just another person in a city that never stopped moving. Chasing. I hated to even think about it, but sometimes it all felt . . . meaningless.

"I'll stay focused. I promise," I said, bringing myself back to the present, forcing a smile that I hoped looked more confident than it felt.

Izzy, who had been lounging against the corner of the desk the entire conversation, her arms crossed casually, gave me a knowing look.

As if the sight of Izzy looking relaxed set her off, Willow shot her a look. "Izzy, did you call Greg for me yet to ask him about the press event next week?"

Izzy, clearly caught off guard, stood from the desk. "Oh, right. Totally spaced on that." She glanced at me again before flashing a sheepish grin at Willow. "I'll do that right now," she added, spinning on her heels and rushing to her desk, conveniently located right next to mine. She snatched up the phone with a dramatic flourish to call whoever Greg was.

"Good," Willow said. She was looking at Izzy, but her words were directed to me. Her tone softened slightly as she focused on me, though her fiery red hair still flared like an extension of her unyielding presence. "For God's sake, you're only twenty-three years old, Sarah. If I had found this profession as young as you and I had been as focused as you, I wouldn't have wasted a second on any of the distractions. None of them are worth it. By the time you are my or Theo's age, you will be so insanely rich and successful. Just don't listen to anyone who doesn't have the result you want." She glanced at Izzy, and I couldn't tell if she was insinuating that Izzy was a bad influence or if she was checking in on the progress of the phone call with Greg. For good measure, she shot Theo another look that screamed, *Shame on you, again, for suggesting she go out.*

Theo pursed his lips, raised his brows, and shrugged. He looked at me in silent communication, *You know how intense Willow can get. If you need a break, take it.*

Theo and Willow were a wild juxtaposition of personal and professional. I often wondered if how involved they were in my personal life was healthy, but most of the time I was lucky that they were interested enough to help and guide me on my path.

"So, I will see you guys tonight at the Gala?" I said trying to wrap up the conversation so I could get back to work.

Willow leaned against the edge of my desk, arms crossed, "Sarah, tonight at the Gala, you're gonna have to get in front of the right people. Specifically, the ones from Chicago who you don't know personally yet. The upper management that is transferring will be a part of the decision-making process for the senior editor position." She paused, making sure I was taking it all in. "You've got to be strategic. Speak to me or Theo when you can and we can point out who you need to meet. You most likely won't know who they are if they are from Chicago. I will find you at some point in the night and make sure you're staying on the radar of the higher-ups, make any introductions that I can."

I grabbed a pen and paper to take a few notes.

She leaned in a little closer, lowering her voice. "And, if the opportunity arises, drop in how you've led or taken charge in your projects. Make it clear you're more than just a hard worker. You've got to demonstrate that you're ready to lead teams and make decisions. That you understand the vision of where we are going as a company and how you will contribute to that direction. If you want them to take you seriously, you've got to make them remember you for the right reasons."

I nodded, scribbling as fast as my hand could move, feeling the weight of the task ahead.

Willow gave a look of approval. "You've got this, Sarah. Just make sure they walk away thinking, *That's the right person for the position.*"

I forced a polite smile and nodded to them both. "Understood," I said with confidence. They smiled, and I watched them as they walked away, moving on, no doubt to rattle some of the other employees. Once they were out of earshot, Izzy hung up the phone and gave me a wide-eyed glance. A beat later, we both burst into laughter—our usual post-Theo-and-Willow-debriefing routine.

I grabbed my phone and texted Izzy.

Me:

Aria Devi

> They may be like family, but sometimes they scare me. . . .

Izzy:

> Oh, they're scary. But they're the best at what they do, which is the only reason I've been their assistant for so long.

Me:

> Seriously, how do you survive them?

Izzy:

> A delicate balance of crippling anxiety and an unhealthy amount of caffeine, mostly. Sprinkle in a weekly therapy session.

Me:

> Well, I guess that means I'm not going to Bathtub Gin. 'Mom' heavily advised against it.

Izzy:

> Please. What's the point of having parents if you can't break their rules once in a while? Plus, you aren't required to work after hours anyway.

Me:

> Right, but the work needs to get done. You were just ordered back to work. Stop distracting me.

Moments later, Izzy replied with an emoji of a raised hand

waving goodbye.

Izzy:

> Bitch, you texted me. Plus someone in this
> office needs to be fun.

I rolled my eyes sitting back in my chair, staring at the screen, I felt the weight of the deadline back on my chest. I scanned the bullpen, wondering if Willow had mentioned the promotion to anyone else. Phillip was still asleep at his desk, while Mindy, another junior editor, chewed gum and twirled her black hair, her eyes glued to her screen. In the corner, the business development guys were up to their usual antics. Peter Harris, tall and athletic, shot paper into Jordan's trash can. I never understood how they got paid more than the editors when they barely did anything.

Just as the crumpled paper landed in the trash, I heard Peter yell, "Whoop, suck it. You can call me Daddy!" I rolled my eyes and shot him a glare before turning my attention back to my work.

Maybe Izzy was right—Phillip and Mindy certainly weren't my competition for senior editor. But the other candidates, especially the ones from Chicago, were. I still had to impress the higher-ups at the Gala if I had any hope of landing the position.

I leaned over my computer, determined to hit this deadline by tomorrow morning. The rest of today would be a sprint, but I'd get it done. Like Izzy said, I always did.

And with that, the responsible, driven part of me pushed the idea of going out and unwinding completely aside. It always did.

Deep down, the question from earlier lingered: *Would all of this be worth it if I ended up alone?*

———

Standing in front of my bathroom mirror, I straightened my blazer, smoothing the fabric around my waist and buzzing with anticipation for the Gala. The lines of my suit tailored at the waist, and I felt like I had achieved the perfect balance between fashionable yet professional. I went for an outfit that screamed, *I am senior editor*. I ran my fingers through my bleached hair, tucking a lock behind my ear before pulling the long pieces to the front and giving them a quick fluff. My look had come together nicely, nothing made me feel more in my power than a men's suit. It gave me an odd confidence that I needed to walk into any room and demand respect, no matter my age. Tonight felt like that type of energy was required.

Not only had my look for the night come together seamlessly, but I could also proudly tell Izzy that I finished my edits this afternoon with time to spare. I don't know if it was the conversation with Theo and Willow or the senior editor position dangling that created an extra layer of motivation, but I had never worked that efficiently. That quickly. But I had decided against going to Bathtub Gin after the Gala altogether. I wanted to be able to be completely focused at the Gala without the distraction of going out afterward.

The Regent House Literary Gala was the event of the year—an evening filled with the company's top executives, editors, and the full staff. The event was a gathering of everyone from all the offices, to celebrate the year's achievements. It was my first time attending, and the pressure I was putting on myself was overwhelming. Knowing everyone at the company would be there watching, assessing all of the junior editors to get a glimpse of who might be up for the promotion, was at the forefront of my mind. I was determined to put on a confident front and present a good first impression to those decision-makers I hadn't had a chance to meet yet.

Willow said the Chicago merger would be announced at the Gala. This meant more opportunities, yes, but also a lot more competition. Tonight would be my first chance to rub elbows with the new power players—those from Chicago who would likely have a say in my future here, and those that were now my competition.

This wasn't just a party—it was a proving ground. My chance to show that I belonged, to measure myself against the best, and to figure out how fast I needed to climb to secure the promotion.

I stared at myself in the mirror, adjusting my collar one last time before heading out the door to the Gala, a flicker of doubt crept in. *Did I really belong in that room?* Despite all the confidence I projected, all the late nights and relentless work I'd put in to build what confidence I did have, there was always a small voice that whispered I wasn't enough. I wasn't polished enough, I wasn't in the right circles, I didn't come from the kind of background that made it easy to belong in a room full of high-powered, skilled, and talented publishing mavens. I had earned my place here, but the fear that I didn't truly belong, that I was just pretending to be one of them, never quite left. It was a nagging sense of imposter syndrome that never seemed to go away. No matter how much I tried to fit into their world, there was a part of me that felt like I was always on the outside looking in.

I clenched my jaw. There was no time for doubt. I was here to make an impression and show I was the person for the job.

On the other side of our tiny Upper East Side apartment, Izzy lay sprawled across the couch, a towel wrapped around her, her fingers flicking her phone. The apartment was cramped, but cozy, with mismatched furniture and half-empty bookshelves that gave it a lived-in feel.

"Are you ready?" I asked, checking my watch. "I want to get there early, check out the setup, meet some important people before everyone else shows up."

Izzy continued to stare at her phone, her expression flat. "Of course I'm not ready. You know me. It only takes me ten minutes to jump in the shower and put on a dress. I just got back from setting up. Willow told me I needed to come back to shower and get 'fancy.'"

I couldn't help but laugh. "Only you could get ready in ten minutes and look just as fabulous as everyone there."

Izzy shrugged, still absorbed in her phone. "What can I say? Many years of practice."

I was the exact opposite. If I wanted to be anywhere on time (and I always was) I had to be prepared and organized—and I needed at least an hour for hair, makeup, and to put together an outfit that was suitable. But Izzy? She'd always been the last-minute wild card and usually prioritized a pre-event nap over getting ready.

"How do I look?" I asked.

She looked up from the screen lighting her face, "Holy shit, you look hot."

I did a quick turn, raising an eyebrow. "Thank you. It's my favorite suit. But I am hoping I don't look too much like I raided a guy's closet."

Izzy laughed, throwing her head back. "Honestly, that's exactly why you look so good. It's bold, and you're owning it. The perfect balance of tomboy chic. Very you." She leaned back on the couch, giving me a teasing look. "You always pull this stuff off. It doesn't hurt that you have legs for days. If I wore that, I'd look like a toddler playing dress up in her dad's suit."

I rolled my eyes, threw on my long, floor-length wool peacoat, and grabbed my keys from the counter. "By the way, I finished my edits, but I don't want to go out tonight. We should really maximize the Gala as much as we can."

"I knew you would finish them!" She cheered. "You are a machine!"

I smiled as I grabbed for the door handle. "Don't be late!" I called over my shoulder.

"Wouldn't dream of it." Izzy shouted as I closed the door behind me.

I darted down the stairs (as much as one can dart in four-inch heels) and out into the street, raising my arm to hail a cab. Tonight was the night—no distractions, complete focus on making the right impressions with the right people. If I played my cards right, this could be one giant step for my career. One that set me on a solid path to success and senior editor.

Chapter Two

The taxi dropped me off somewhere near Wall Street. To be honest, navigating south of Houston Street without Google Maps always left me disoriented. The biting winter air sliced through my coat as I ran toward the venue, bracing myself against February's bone-chilling cold, silently cursing myself for not wearing more layers. Once inside, the heavy glass doors swung shut behind me, and the warmth was immediate, thawing my skin.

The sight before me was nothing short of cinematic. Towering marble walls rose in pristine grandeur, their surfaces polished to perfection and bathed in the golden glow of antique sconces. A vaulted ceiling stretched high above, with gold accents and hand-painted murals that could compete with the Sistine Chapel. The faint scent of aged wood hung in the air. It wasn't just a ballroom—it was a masterpiece, a place that seemed to demand reverence.

I made my way through the lobby and reached the room where the event was being held, I paused, allowing myself to dream for a moment. I stared at the stage. I could almost see myself up there one day, receiving awards for my editorial work or delivering speeches, maybe even running the place altogether. The thought sent a thrill through me. Tonight wasn't just about imagining that future me—it was about stepping into it and acting as if I already was that woman.

I checked my watch, and with some time to spare, I stepped into the bathroom to freshen up. I pulled out my pink lip liner and gloss combo, leaned close to the mirror as I carefully overlined my lips. I adjusted my blazer one last time, brushed a few strands of hair back into place, and took one last look in the mirror. Satisfied, I turned and pushed open the heavy bathroom door with my back, shoving my lip products into my pocket, one hand clutching my phone, my peacoat in the other.

And then it happened. A sudden jolt.

I collided with something—or someone—with enough force to knock me off balance. My heels slipped on the polished marble, and I barely caught myself before hitting the floor. At the same moment, a cold splash of champagne hit me square in the chest and down the front of my jacket, seeping into the fabric.

My heart sank as the stain set into my suit. Thank God it wasn't red wine.

"I'm so, so sorry!" I blurted out, my words tumbling over each other as I regained my balance. "I didn't see you there."

She stood before me like a statue—impeccably dressed in a gorgeous black ballgown, her bleached hair almost the same color as mine but straight as a board. She looked like a doll, her face perfect, her lips filled with what looked like multiple syringes of filler. Her air of authority was so palpable that that alone had practically knocked me back. My stomach twisted as I braced for a scolding, but at the same time, a wave of relief flooded through me. I didn't recognize her, meaning she wasn't one of the Manhattan executives, not someone whose name I needed to know or needed to impress.

Her narrowed eyes scanned me, sharp as daggers, before she rolled them in disdain and walked away without a word and an empty champagne flute.

My eyes went wide in shock. Did she really just completely ignore me and walk away? Once she was out of earshot, I muttered,

"Nice to meet you too, bitch." Under her wordless scrutiny, I felt about two inches tall. But it seemed she was just another guest with a bad attitude. Thank God.

Champagne was dripping from me, so I scanned the room for help. A waiter—there! I spotted one standing by a high-top cocktail table. I hurried over, heat rising to my cheeks.

"Excuse me, could you please get me some napkins?" I asked, tapping him on the shoulder.

When he turned, I froze.

Light blue eyes locked with mine, playful and piercing, as a lazy grin spread across his face. His tuxedo looked crisp, tailored to perfection, and his relaxed confidence radiated in the moment. He was tall, broad-shouldered, the kind of good-looking that made me feel self-conscious just standing next to him. His thick blond hair was neatly styled, like a more polished version of Dash from *The Incredibles*. His perfectly trimmed beard was the first I'd ever seen that made a man look even more put together.

"Sure," he said with a small chuckle, his voice deep, smooth, and tinged with amusement.

I blinked, momentarily stunned. Was he . . . making fun of me? Were waiters allowed to do that at events like this? His gaze flicked down to the champagne visibly soaking my suit, like he was assessing the scene before taking a course of action. He backed up with a slow, deliberate once-over. Not judgmental. Not pitying. Just . . . amused.

Before I could think of anything to say, he asked, "Think you'll survive for a minute while I go fetch napkins?"

I scoffed, crossing my arms. "Uh, yeah, I think I'll manage."

He smiled and turned on his heels. As he walked away, I shook my head, trying to compose myself, still slightly annoyed and offended. But he was insanely handsome. I shook it off. *He's just a cater-waiter, and you're here to network, not . . . whatever that is.*

A few minutes later, he returned, handing me a neatly folded stack of napkins. "Here you go," he said, his smile teasing. Then he leaned in slightly with his upper body, as if he were telling me a secret. "Though, full disclosure, I skipped the napkin retrieval module in my training, so if my service isn't up to snuff, my apologies."

I let out an involuntary laugh, surprised by his charm. "What kind of waiter skips napkin retrieval? Isn't that like the entire training?" I asked, tilting my head, as I grabbed a few of the napkins and started to blot the champagne that was soaking deeper into my suit by the second.

He grinned and took a small step closer. "Do you mind?" he asked, pointing at the lower half of my jacket. "The last thing you want is this to set in."

I shook my head. As I focused on the chest area, he started to dab at the bottom of my jacket with his napkin.

Finally he said, "Let's just say I'm more of a cocktail guy. I suppose expanding my skill set might not be a terrible idea, for situations like these." Was he *flirting* with me?

"Maybe we can team up," I joked, raising an eyebrow but still focused solely on my jacket. "Spill recovery for beginners. You'd make a great first student for my class."

He chuckled. "I don't know. Something tells me you'd make a pretty tough instructor."

His gaze held mine for a moment too long, my breath catching. I suddenly became hyper aware of his hand at the base of my jacket. It had made us stand close enough that I could almost feel the heat coming off of him. Time seemed to freeze, everything moving in slow motion—like one of those movie moments when the two main characters meet and the world fades away.

The moment broke when I saw the growing crowd behind him. I stepped back, pulling the jacket from his hand. "Well, you better get back to work." I tried to sound indifferent, but my tone bordered on flustered. "Those drinks aren't going to pour themselves."

"Or spill themselves," he shot back, his eyes sparkling.

I narrowed my eyes, lips pressed together, and let out a quick click of my tongue. "Too soon."

"Fair enough," he teased, leaning casually against the table. "So, you are kicking me to the curb already?"

"Just trying to keep you out of trouble with your manager. I am sure they would prefer you were actually doing your job that you were trained for."

He grinned, his posture shifting as he straightened his jacket. "All right. But don't think this is the end. I'll be around."

As he turned to leave, he looked back with a grin. "Oh, by the way, you know, the cater-waiters . . . They wear coattails on their jackets. But the guests at events like these don't. It's all about the tail," he said with a wink.

I froze, my eyes going to his jacket. No tail present.

My stomach sank. Shit. "Oh . . . you're not . . . uh, the help?"

He grinned, clearly enjoying this. "Well, it's 2019. They don't call them 'the help' anymore," he teased. "And, I am afraid not. But hey, you're not the first one to mistake me for a cater-waiter. No harm done."

"I—uh—" I stammered.

He put his hand up to stop me. "Happens more than you think. Just part of the job . . . or lack thereof," he said, his eyes locked on mine.

I struggled to recover and let out a nervous laugh. *Say something funny. . . .* "Typical. I always seem to be chasing the wrong tail." *Why the hell did I just say that? I sound like a creep.*

He let out a deep belly laugh. It was warm and felt like Christmas.

Grateful that my terrible joke landed, I immediately turned mortified at the whole interaction. "Well . . . um—enjoy the event. And thanks for the, uh, napkins," I said, pointing and looking down at my still damp jacket.

He winked. "Anytime."

As he turned and disappeared into the crowd, I exhaled shakily. Relief flooded me once again. He wasn't a cater-waiter, but I didn't recognize him either as one of the executives from my quick earlier

Aria Devi

Google research. That made me two-for-two on career-ending, embarrassing disasters averted for the evening.

After *that* interaction, it was probably best to steer clear from any semblance of flirting for the night. I didn't have time for any more embarrassing run-ins. My career goals were clear—laser-focused, rigid, in fact. I reminded myself that I would have time for all the flirting I could ever want or need in the future, there was no room for that tonight.

I shook my head, determined to move on. The night was far from over, and I needed to stay on track. *Senior editor. Senior editor.* This was the single and primary goal. Everything else could wait. No more flirting with cater-waiters or champagne mishaps tonight. I had hit my limit of horrifying moments for the year.

Chapter Three

As guests arrived at the venue, the night carried the unmistakable energy of the city—the kind of event where you either belonged completely or felt like an outsider. Right now, after my last two interactions with guests, I felt like I was somewhere in between. My earlier run-ins had completely thrown me off. I tried to shove them to the back of my mind, as I had bigger targets to focus on this evening. As the room filled with guests, champagne glasses in hand, a small trace of it still visible on my coat, the evening was officially about to start.

The stage lights dimmed, the crowd grew silent. My skin tingled with goosebumps. I couldn't believe I was at the event I had looked forward to all year. Since I was a young girl living in Idaho, I dreamed of working in a New York City publishing house, attending events like this. Rubbing elbows with people at the top of their game. And here I was. It was surreal.

The emcee ran up on the stage, voice booming over the chatter of the room. He was dressed in a gorgeous tux, his shoes polished to a mirror shine. With his slicked-back hair, he looked more like a game show host.

Clusters of people turned from their cocktail tables toward the stage as he spoke.

"Good evening, everyone. Welcome to the annual Regent House Publishing Gala. We are honored to have all of you here tonight to celebrate the past year's wins, announce exciting new opportunities and changes within the company, and, of course, give you all a chance to connect outside of the office."

The announcement of the open senior editor position was coming. The merger. A cocktail of nerves, excitement, and anxiety stirred in my gut.

"Now, all of that is coming—but not from me." The emcee grinned. "I, for one, can't wait to get off this stage and welcome the woman who is the driving force behind so much of what you see here at RHP. She is truly one of the most inspiring and motivating leaders we've had the pleasure of working with. She's here to officially open the event and share some incredible things coming down the pipeline for 2019.

"Without further ado, please welcome our youngest-ever executive vice president of Regent House Publishing, based in Chicago—"

Like some cosmic twist of fate, she walked onto the stage—the woman I had quite literally bumped into outside the ladies' room less than an hour before.

I barely registered the name. My mind was still catching up, my thoughts a blur. My heart dropped past my stomach and into my feet.

She strode across the stage with a charming smile and unshakable confidence, owning the spotlight like the stage had been built just for her. Everyone applauded, cheered, and whistled. I couldn't take my eyes off her. She was absolutely mesmerizing.

Striking, dressed in the silk-and-lace black gown I had seen up close and personal less than an hour ago. I shuddered at the memory of her earlier icy glare. On stage she exuded complete elegance and authority. She moved in a way that seemed designed to grab the attention of every man and woman in the room. I couldn't help but once again gawk over her features. Her platinum blonde hair, perfectly straight, framed her cheekbones and jawline so sharp and flawless they could've scratched a diamond. It was the kind of beauty that only the world of the elite could breed—that or a lot of cosmetic surgery—the kind of beauty that seemed too perfect to be real, and certainly too flawless for someone like me to get anything more than a cold shoulder by the bathroom.

Standing at center stage, she spoke, "We are here tonight to connect, to celebrate, and to honor innovation and creativity." Her voice was smooth. "At Regent House Publishing, we are in relentless pursuit of excellence and integrity. We don't just curate words on a page—we shape minds, influence thought, and are here to change the world through story. Before I started at RHP, I was a young woman from a small town. . . ."

The resemblance was hard to ignore—the hair, our features, even our body structures, tall and strong, the determination and hunger to succeed. As she spoke, the familiarity only grew. Our upbringings, our backgrounds, it was like hearing my own story echoed back to me. Both small-town girls who had moved to the city to find something more. With nothing but ambition, trying to make a place for ourselves in the publishing world. It was as if everything she had achieved, everything she had worked for, aligned with all of my goals and ambitions yet to come. For her, all of it had already come to fruition, while I was struggling to keep up, years behind her. She was who I had always imagined I could become, the one that had 'made it.' Standing here, watching her, I realized that despite all my ambition, all my struggle, I was still miles away. Years away from her. From that version of myself.

From where I stood, in my men's suit—a pang of envy twisted in my chest. She was like a walking mirror of everything I wasn't . . . yet. Everything I was trying to be: polished, poised, powerful.

But maybe that was why I was here—to prove, like she had, that I could belong too.

Growing up, I watched my parents work so hard just to make

sure we had what we needed. My dad would say, "If you want something, you have to work harder than everyone else to get it." And I had. I worked my ass off to get a scholarship, worked my way into the publishing industry, and finally landed this job through Theo and Willow, in a city that still sometimes felt as foreign to me as the skyscrapers towering over it.

I told myself I was chasing the dream—to one day become a senior editor. That title had felt like the ultimate prize, the proof I'd finally made it. But seeing Jane on that stage, announced as executive vice president like it was nothing, made my dream feel . . . small. I wasn't even close. For the first time, I wondered if I ever would be.

"Jane," a voice whispered in my ear, making me jump.

"Jesus Christ!" I turned to the side, searching for the source of the mental interruption. Izzy was sitting next to me, as if she hadn't just sat in our apartment wrapped in a towel less than an hour ago. "Iz, don't do that! You scared the hell out of me," I slapped her arm. Once my heart rate settled, my curiosity piqued."Who?"

"Her!" Izzy pointed to the woman on stage. "She has been between New York and Chicago for a few years. With the merger she is officially going to be moved to our floor in the Manhattan office." Izzy had this uncanny ability to know the inside scoop on everyone without ever really interacting with them.

"Wait . . . *that* is Jane?" I asked in disbelief. Izzy nodded.

I recognized the name, of course. I had heard people mention Jane around the office. But, I wasn't familiar with many people from the Chicago offices. I had just gotten the hang of most of the employees in Manhattan. The youngest EVP. I never would have guessed she would look like *that*. The way people spoke of her, I assumed she would be in her fifties at this point.

"And now, I am eager to make an exciting announcement—well, actually, two of them," Jane continued, all my attention being brought back to her. This was it. I braced myself for the audience reaction.

"As part of an exciting new phase for Regent House Publishing, we're entering a partial merger with our Manhattan and Chicago divisions. Some of our incredibly talented employees and executives, including myself, will be transferring to our Manhattan office. This transition also means that a senior editor position is now open for one junior editor. For those of you who are interested, please reach out to the executive editor at your location to learn more about what we're looking for in that role. The announcement for who will be the lucky new senior editor will be made at next year's Gala."

I glanced around while people cheered, presumably excited about moving to New York. Some of the older employees had looks of disdain for any sort of change. I searched the room for the junior editors I worked with to see their reactions. Some of them perked up; some of them couldn't seem to care less. I looked around to see if there was anyone else who seemed like they might be running for it.

As I turned, I felt it—a subtle chill that had nothing to do with the temperature of the room. I scanned the crowd, and my eyes fell on him. *He* was looking at me. Those same blue eyes from earlier. The not-so-cater-waiter standing there, tall and proud, with a slight smirk across his face. As our eyes met, I couldn't help but blush. I smirked and acted like I hardly noticed, continuing my scan of the room, turning back around, forcing my gaze back to the stage. Back to Jane.

As Jane spoke, the earlier tension from our hallway mishap lingered in the back of my mind. Her voice was calm, powerful—certain and unwavering, as if nothing could rattle her. I leaned forward, drawn in by her confidence, trying to push aside the lingering discomfort from earlier.

I could imagine myself following in her footsteps. If she could do it—speak with such confidence and authority, becoming the youngest EVP ever—why couldn't I? If we had such similar upbringings and backgrounds, I didn't see what would stop me. Jane, while feeling in many ways like an unattainable figure, was also proof that someone like me could get to the top of this industry. She wasn't just someone I could look up to—she was proof that women like me could succeed in this world.

"She is amazing," I whispered to Izzy, who nodded absently.

My eyes drifted to Theo and Willow nearby. They stood together, as always, impeccably dressed. Tonight, their coordinated orange and navy outfits looked as chic as ever. I couldn't help but look at them and want that lifestyle–theirs and Jane's. I was still living paycheck to paycheck in a city that was unforgiving, but I couldn't help but wonder if having Jane in my corner as well as them would give me extra momentum to change that.

I caught their attention and whispered, "Will one of you introduce me later?" with a nod toward Jane. If Willow could get me in front of her, maybe I could smooth over the earlier mishap—and who knows, maybe she'd let me into her inner circle, consider mentoring me, or at least offer some high-level advice for someone aiming for the promotion.

Theo and Willow exchanged a look. Theo's eyebrows raised. Willow gave me a thumbs-up and came closer. Leaning in, she said, "I will come grab you later when she is off stage and available for introductions."

I buzzed with excitement. This could really get me ahead for the promotion.

As Jane finished her speech, the applause swelled around me. I clapped my hands harder than anyone else's. Despite my earlier embarrassment, despite feeling so far beneath her, despite all of it, her words and energy on stage lit a fire inside of me. An odd dichotomy of possibility. Jane had become my standard of what was possible. I had to meet her.

But as the applause died down, I found my thoughts drifting back to him—the cater-waiter. His icy blue eyes lingered in my mind long after our interaction. I tried to shake the thought, but each time I scanned the room, I could feel his gaze on me, as if he was watching from somewhere. Or maybe I was just secretly hoping he was. I couldn't shake the urge to know who he was, what he was doing here, and most importantly, where he worked.

It seemed there were two connections I longed for tonight.

————

As the night continued, the focus shifted to networking. Izzy and I stayed close, navigating the room side by side. Izzy had a way of making me feel at home in this high-powered world, so keeping her within eyeshot at events like this helped. It made me feel like I was already part of an inner circle. Having been at Regent for years, she knew everyone and moved through the crowd like a pro, as if she were the prom queen.

While she worked the crowd with ease, I concentrated on making strategic connections—opportunities that could bring me closer to the senior editor position.

I carefully scanned the room, identifying potential competitors vying for the attention of higher-ups. Taking Willow's advice seriously, I made it a priority to introduce myself to every key player I noticed another junior editor engaging with. It pushed me out of my introverted editor comfort zone. I just kept telling myself that becoming senior editor would make it worth it. With a firm handshake, a practiced smile, and thoughtfully crafted questions, I made sure to signal that I was serious about advancing within the company.

After about an hour of mingling, it finally felt like an appropriate time to pull Izzy away and tell her about my "not-so-cater-waiter." I needed to know who he was and where he worked. If anyone would know who he was, it would be her.

"Iz, I met this guy. I need you to help me find out who he—"

Before I could finish, someone gently squeezed my arm from behind. My stomach dropped. Please, let it be anyone but him.

"Sarah?" It was Willow. Her presence alone made me jump to attention.

I plastered a smile on my face as I turned. "Hey, Willow, how's it goi—?" I asked, immediately regretting the small talk. Willow didn't do small talk—only big talk.

She interrupted, "I have some people I want you to meet." Without waiting for an answer, she turned and started walking, assuming I would follow. My heart raced at the thought of meeting more people, but I jogged to catch up, holding up a finger to let Izzy know I'd be back with details shortly.

My mind was racing as we approached a small group of seven or eight people—executives, VPs, and C-suite members from various Regent House Publishing offices. Willow, always confident and commanding, stepped forward.

"Excuse me, everyone," her voice cut through the chatter, drawing their attention. "This is Sarah Jones from the Manhattan office—our newest rising star, whom Theo and I are personally mentoring." She glanced at me with a look of pride as if daring anyone to question her endorsement. My own pride swelled. This was her way of putting me on the map with the executives, showing them that I was a serious contender for senior editor—the one she believed in. "She's working for the senior editor position we just announced, and I thought it only fitting to introduce her to you."

The group's attention shifted to me. Judgment in their eyes, like they were sizing up every gesture, every movement, every hand shake. Competition for the role had been palpable since it was announced. Willow's introduction wasn't just about showing me off; it was about positioning me as the obvious choice, a huge leg up for me.

One by one, I shook hands with each member of the group, offering my most professional smile, doing my best to stay calm. After a few handshakes with some individuals who seemed less than inter-ested by my presence, my eyes landed on her—her eye contact stop-ping me in my tracks. She looked like me, only ten years older and infinitely more polished. Jane. She gave a polite nod, her gaze lingering on me a moment longer than the others'. Was that a look of approval? Intrigue? I couldn't tell.

The look was a one-hundred-and-eighty-degree difference from the death stare she'd given me earlier, like the woman outside of the bathroom and this woman in front of me were two separate people.

"We are excited to see what you bring to the table, Sarah," Jane said, her voice oddly sincere. "If there's anything I can do to support you, please don't hesitate to ask."

I heard the words, but I couldn't help but feel an incongruence behind them. It was the kind of thing everyone said, the polite, obligatory line that sounded good but rarely meant anything. Still, I nodded, forcing a smile. At least she said something. I guess that was more than I could say for the others.

Willow cut in, "Sarah, you saw Jane earlier on stage. Like she mentioned, she'll be transferring to our floor soon. She's been working intermittently between the city just a few floors below us and the Chicago office. I'm not sure you two would have met yet, but you can certainly learn a lot from her."

"Actually, we did . . . meet," I admitted. "We had a little run-in outside the bathroom. I am so sorry about that, by the way," I said, grimacing, praying my apology might soften the tension.

Jane stared at me, her expression unreadable, but then her voice shifted, just slightly. "It's no big deal, Sarah," a hint of warmth cutting through her otherwise stoic tone. It was enough to give me a spark of hope.

"It's so incredible to meet you," I said, perhaps a little too excited. "Hearing your story on stage was extremely motivating. I see a lot of myself in the younger version of you. I have similar aspirations and a similar background. I would love to be able to learn from you once you transfer. If I can help with any extra work or projects, I'm all yours—no questions asked." The words tumbled out faster than I'd planned, but I had to recover from the earlier fiasco somehow.

Jane tilted her head slightly, her eyes narrowing just enough to make me wonder if I'd said too much. Before I could gauge her reaction, a sleek-looking assistant materialized at her side. "Jane, they're ready for you," the assistant—I assumed—whispered loudly in her ear.

"Excuse me," Jane said, offering a polite smile to the group before turning to leave. She didn't address my offer, leaving me standing there with my heart still racing.

I watched her disappear into the crowd, every bit as poised and untouchable as I'd imagined. Shaking her hand, standing in the same circle as her—it was surreal, like meeting a celebrity.

Willow, still at my side, said, "Keep at it. You've got her attention now. Great job planting the seed."

I nodded, the wheels in my mind turning. I had to follow up with Jane. Somehow. I was sure I would have an opportunity to catch her on the office floor in the coming weeks. A small sense of relief washed over me, knowing I still might have a chance to salvage this.

Jane's leaving caused a ripple effect, pulling Willow and a few others into side conversations. I turned back to finish shaking the remaining hands, finally coming to the last one.

A large hand closed over mine, and a jolt of energy shot up my spine. I looked up—and froze. *Jesus Christ. You have got to be kidding me.* The cater-waiter, sans coattails. This time, my heart dropped straight through the floor and into hell.

Something flared inside me—anxiety? Panic? He stood there, impossibly calm, one hand in his pocket, his eyes fixed on mine with a smile so genuine it made the room blur. The room, the crowd—everything disappeared. It was like we were the only two people in the room. Just us. A quiet, undeniable connection pulsed between us.

With his hand wrapped around mine, it felt right, like it was meant to be there. My knee-jerk reaction was to pull it away, but his grip was strong, firm—like the hands of the men from my hometown who had worked the fields and ranches, calloused and rough. I wanted to pull away, but I hated to admit it only drew me in that much more.

"John Reynolds," he said, his voice deep and soft, like warm honey. "VP of Acquisitions, from Chicago. Pleasure to meet you, Sarah." A knowing grin tugged at his lips.

His words lingered in the air. Time slowed, the sound of clinking glasses and distant chatter fading into static. My stomach tightened like I'd had the wind knocked out of me. Two colossal mistakes—back-to-back—on the night that was supposed to set me apart. Mistaking Jane for some random guest with an attitude and running into her? Bad enough. But this? Mistaking *him*—John Reynolds—for a damn cater-waiter? And worse, calling him 'the help'? *The help.* No. No. No. No. No.

I wanted to disappear, to vanish into thin air. *Important,* my brain screamed. *He's someone important.* Important, yes, but also devastatingly handsome. And I'd just humiliated myself beyond repair in front of him.

I could cry later—Izzy would let me vent about this disaster while shoving a pint of Ben & Jerry's at me. But right now? I couldn't let them see me unravel. I fought the instinct to shrink away, forcing myself to stand taller even as my skin burned with humiliation. Why hadn't I done my research? I should've memorized every executive's face, stalked their Facebook profiles if necessary. Stupid, stupid, stupid.

I swallowed hard and pulled my hand back, biting my lip to stifle my own self-loathing. Forcing a smile, I glanced around the remaining group and then back at him. With that look, the group dispersed. But John's piercing gaze hadn't left me, and that damn smile—wasn't helping anything. If anything, it was making this worse. My pulse quickened, my thoughts spiraling as the air between us grew thick.

There was something about him, something magnetic that made me feel completely out of control. My breath hitched as the pull between us intensified. I scrambled for something to say, *anything* to salvage this. Maybe an apology? Or some witty remark to prove I wasn't a total idiot? Or, hell, even a casual, "Want to grab coffee sometime?" to smooth things over?

But nothing. Not a single coherent thought made it to my lips. My mind was too tangled in the force of his presence, and before I knew it, the moment slipped away. I was left standing there, utterly captivated and entirely speechless, as he tilted his head, that damn smile still in place.

"Well," he said, his voice low and steady, "I guess we'll be seeing more of each other."

And just like that, he turned and walked away, leaving me standing there with my stomach in knots and my heart no longer in hell, but somewhere in my throat.

Chapter Four

Izzy flopped onto the couch next to me, shoving a pint of Chunky Monkey and a big spoon into my hands, her eyes wide with a mix of curiosity and disbelief. "Okay, what the hell happened? I leave you alone for one night—no, not even a full night, *part* of the night—and shit hits the fan? I swear, sometimes you are like a puppy that chews up the couch cushions the second I turn my back," she said, shaking her head with a sarcastic tisk.

Thankfully, I'd wrapped up my edits earlier in the day because, after tonight, there was no way I'd have the mental bandwidth to finish them. Skipping Bathtub Gin had already been my plan, but tonight's semi-disaster gave me the perfect excuse to dodge Izzy's peer pressure. I'd told her there was far too much to unpack for the loud, dimly lit Tribeca speakeasy. What I needed was the comfort of our apartment, a warm blanket, and, most importantly, ice cream.

I was still buzzing from the night. "It was . . . something," I started, my voice a little hollow. "Jane was inspiring, I guess, and thanks to Willow, I did meet some important people—"

"Sarah," Izzy interrupted sharply, "spare me the networking spiel. I want to talk about those deer-in-the-headlights eyes you gave

John Reynolds. I saw you from across the room. You looked like you'd seen a ghost. And let's not forget the *come-fuck-me* eyes he gave you right back. Don't think I didn't catch all of that when Willow introduced you to Jane and the other bigwigs."

My cheeks flushed, but I forced my expression to remain neutral, unwilling to show how surprised I was to get someone like John Reynolds's attention. This feeling was buried deep underneath the humiliation, of course.

The idea of John Reynolds—handsome, charming, and powerful, certainly no cater-waiter—showing any sort of interest in me, stirred something I wasn't sure I wanted to acknowledge to Izzy, or myself. I wasn't here to be distracted by men, but the thought of his attention on me made it hard to think straight. I held back a smile, trying to sound nonchalant.

"It's probably not what you are thinking," I muttered, though my heart was pounding a little faster than I cared to admit just thinking about him. "But . . . *he's* the guy I was trying to tell you about before Willow pulled me away. I thought he was a cater-waiter—"

Izzy raised an eyebrow and leaned in, "You thought *John Reynolds* was a *cater-waiter?*"

"Well, I didn't know who John Reynolds was. I know who he is *now*. I definitely know he is *not* a cater-waiter. But there's more. When I got there early, I was coming out of the bathroom and . . . I ran into Jane."

Izzy raised an eyebrow, clearly intrigued. "Nice, how was that?"

"No, I mean, I *literally* ran into her. I bumped into her coming out the door, and she spilled all her champagne on me."

Izzy gasped, her hand flying to her mouth. "No way."

"Yes. But I didn't have any idea who she was. I apologized profusely, but she didn't say a word. Just rolled her eyes and walked off like a total bitch. I was absolutely mortified." I covered my face with my hand, still seething in embarrassment.

Izzy stared at me. "You really didn't know who she was?"

"No. I had no idea. I had only heard her name in passing, like twice. I assumed she was . . . old. I didn't think our executive vice president would look like a Barbie. In my head, I pictured more of an older Jackie Kennedy, rather than a Marilyn Monroe in her prime."

"I mean, I guess that makes sense," Izzy said, trying to make me feel better for my cringe-worthy evening. "I didn't know what anyone looked like from Chicago until I went to my first event either. But Jane has had one of the most successful careers in publishing history—not just for her age or as a woman, but for anyone. I can't believe I haven't mentioned her to you. I just assumed you knew her by now." Izzy leaned in with her own spoon to take a scoop of my ice cream. "Wait, so you don't even follow her on Instagram?"

"I . . . don't?" I shrugged, somehow feeling even worse now. Did I just totally fuck up any chance I had at the promotion? I could feel impending doom lingering over me like a storm cloud.

I winced, a mix of shame and frustration bubbling up inside me. I should've known. *I should've known.* Such a rookie move not to do deep research before the event. Jane wasn't just another executive— I'd been so focused on myself and my work that I missed something as simple as that. Maybe this was what Theo and Willow were talking about when they said that thing about not only being a good solo producer, but seeing the bigger picture of the vision of the company.

Izzy shook her head, tapping away at her phone. "I'll send you her profile. She has a massive following, seriously—she's like a mini celebrity. She would be a good example for you to look after, given your goals."

"Thanks," I said, trying to steady my voice. "I'll check it out. And maybe I can figure out a way to make things right with her."

Izzy didn't comment, pursing her lips with sympathy. It was clear she knew I was spiraling. "So, where does John come into all of this?"

"Right." I brought the conversation back on track. "So, after getting dagger eyes from Jane and having her champagne all over my jacket, I found this guy who looked like he worked at the hotel. I asked him for some napkins, and he went and got them for me."

"And the guy was John? Why would he do that if he didn't work there?" Izzy asked.

"I didn't know he didn't work there," I said, my voice tight as I rubbed my temple, still cringing at the memory. "I was treating him like a waiter, and he was just playing along, I guess. Or maybe he felt sorry for me, like I was some girl that couldn't handle her liquor before the event." I let out a shaky breath. "Anyway, we stood there flirting—I think it was flirting—and we had a quick conversation. As he was leaving, he mentioned something about how the waiters have tuxedos with tails on the jacket, but the guests don't. And he didn't have a tail on his jacket."

"Of course. You can always tell who the waiters are by their coat-tails," Izzy said, as if it were obvious, as if I should've known.

"Yes, Izzy, a 'black tie event tidbit' that everyone at Regent House Publishing seems to know but me," I said sarcastically.

Izzy was the kind of person who knew random facts about every-thing, even though she'd never watched Jeopardy a day in her life. If she ever did, she'd win by a long shot. She knew things like the proper way to cut a mango, how to keep houseplants alive for years, and the quickest way to fold a fitted sheet. She had picked up a lot of random, seemingly useless knowledge in her almost thirty years. And every once in a while, it actually came in handy.

"But that's not the point." I shook my head, refocusing my cham-pagne-soaked brain. "The point is, after that, I saw him staring at me when Jane was speaking, and a few other times throughout the night. I literally couldn't stop thinking about him as I was networking. Then Willow pulled me over to the group and I shook his hand . . . It was one of the most intense experiences I've ever had."

"And that was when you learned he wasn't a waiter?" Izzy asked, trying to piece together my story.

"Exactly, and I don't know what was going on between us, but there was definitely something there," I admitted.

Izzy gave me an almost amused look, "You're still thinking about him?" Her tone was bordering sympathetic.

I nodded, a little too quickly, looking away, suddenly self-conscious. "I—yeah, I guess. It was just . . . different, you know?" My words trailed off. The way he looked at me, it was like he was seeing right through me, or maybe right into me. I couldn't tell.

Izzy raised an eyebrow. "Sounds like more than just a handshake."

I let out a breath, rubbing my temples, the pint of ice cream resting between my thighs. "It was like everything else in the room just disappeared. It was wild. Then, after the handshake, he didn't let go right away. Like he was waiting for something. I don't know. I was so thrown off by the fact that he works at Regent, that I didn't know what to say."

"Wow, you're really shaken up by this."

A part of me wondered if she thought I was totally pathetic, thinking someone like John might be interested in a measly young junior editor like me.

"Shaken up, freaked out . . . I don't know," I muttered. "But I definitely haven't forgotten it. I think he mentioned that he was a VP or something? What do you know about him? Is he a creeper?"

"No, not a creeper at all. John is great. He has a great reputation at RHP. I hear Corporate's transferring him to the New York office soon too."

I blinked. "Wait, he's transferring to the Manhattan office?" I leaned forward, my voice a little too eager.

A rush of both excitement and dread flooded me. Moving to the New York office meant he'd be closer. I suddenly wondered if I'd ever cross paths with him again, if I should've done more to recover from my first impression.

"He's a total hunk. Women fawn over him, especially now. I mean, he looks like a clean-cut, sexy Nordic viking, for God's sake."

As Izzy snatched the ice cream from me, I grabbed my phone and started scrolling through Instagram, looking for his profile. There he was—John Reynolds, effortlessly cool in tailored suits, professional, his charming smile and blue eyes lighting up the screen.

"Should I follow him?" I asked, my heart racing with a mixture of excitement and apprehension. Why did this feel so risky? So forbidden?

"Hell yes, you should! He's hot—like a real man, not some little boy you've been guilty of going on first dates with. And he's loaded. He's been making a shitload of money since he was in his twenties. At the very least, he could take you to a nice dinner for once. Go for it."

"Okay . . . I highly doubt it would lead to a date. He works at Regent. But I'll follow him on Instagram. No harm no foul, right?" I shrugged, trying to act reluctant, playing it cool, but the butterflies in my stomach refused to settle. He was a VP at Regent—successful, wealthy, definitely not a cater-waiter. I shuddered at the memory of asking him for a napkin. How could I not have noticed that he didn't work there? There was no way this would progress past a friendly work connection . . . even if secretly I wanted it to.

There was something about him. I couldn't put my finger on it. Something familiar. I'd never felt that way shaking someone's hand. Hell, I had never even felt that way on any of my first dates I had ever been on. You could hardly say men were on my radar, but he was.

I continued to scroll through his Instagram, a new nagging thought crept in. Was there a corporate policy about dating coworkers? Did Regent even have one? I didn't remember seeing anything in the employee handbook, but I'd also never really cared to check. Now, though, the idea of navigating any kind of romantic connection with someone in the same industry—let alone someone as high up as him—felt like an entirely different challenge. I was getting way too ahead of myself, but my mind wouldn't stop.

Izzy polished off the ice cream and went to the bathroom to start her nighttime face washing routine.

Whatever. I'd follow him and leave it at that—doubtful anything would come of it. My finger hovered over the follow button. Was I really about to do this? But as soon as I thought about it, my finger took over and clicked the button. A wave of heat washed over me, and suddenly I was sweating. Maybe it was the champagne, or maybe it was just the memory of him standing there in front of me staring into my soul.

As a distraction from my risky behavior, I opened the message from Izzy, Jane's Instagram account she had sent me. As I scrolled through her photos, a surge of motivation hit me. Jane was stunning—smart, driven, ambitious, and effortlessly fashionable. She literally was a woman who had it all. Each post exuded confidence and showed not only her impeccable style, but her intellect, passion for her work, and leadership ability. Some of her captions even mentioned her strong faith, which made her seem even more grounded beneath all that je ne sais quoi. I really hoped Izzy was right and she'd be transferred to our floor with the merger. It would be so cool if I could get in her good graces and learn from her.

I scrolled back to the top of Jane's account to follow her—and my stomach sank. Her username—it couldn't be. There was no way. Had I really had that much champagne? It read: @itsjanereynolds. *Reynolds.* Jane Reynolds. As in . . . *John Reynolds?* My heart raced, fear washing over me like a wave. The potential realization hit me hard. It couldn't be. I sat frozen, staring at the screen.

"Izzy!?" I yelled, my voice cutting through the silence.

She looked up from the bathroom sink, where she was washing off her makeup, her face covered in bubbles and mascara streaked down her cheeks.

"What's wrong?" she replied, still scrubbing her eyes.

"Are John and Jane . . . *siblings?!*" I blurted, my mind trying to process what I was seeing. They did kind of look like they were related. Both blonde hair and pale skin. The pieces of the night were starting to make less and less sense with every passing second.

Izzy blinked, caught off guard. "No, why?"

"They have the same last name." I almost laughed at myself for not putting it together sooner.

Izzy let out a small laugh, shaking her head. "No. Sarah, they were married."

I froze. My mind racing to catch up to her words. *What?*

Married? "Wait, why didn't you say that earlier?" my voice rising to a shrill tone. A surge of frustration and embarrassment washed over me, my stomach sinking at how badly I'd missed the obvious. How had I not connected the dots sooner?

Izzy shrugged, clearly confused. "Well, it's not exactly a secret. People talk about them at Regent all the time, especially with all the office drama since the split. They've been trying to keep it under wraps, but it's been a huge deal. A lot of people who have been around for a while know Jane and John, and their history is pretty hard to miss. I'm sorry, I just assumed, after Jane was announced tonight, that you'd put it together—they're both Reynolds."

My eyes wide as I stared at Jane's profile photo. I hadn't heard her name because I was too distracted seeing the woman I had had a champagne run-in with earlier up on stage.

John and Jane were married?

I finally looked at Izzy. Water and mascara were now running down her neck. She studied me with raised brows.

"Okay . . ." I said. "Moving forward, let's just assume that moving forward I know nothing and you need to disclose everything that you know about these people, deal?"

She nodded. "Sorry, Sarah, I will. I just thought you knew." She shrugged and turned to finish washing her face.

My phone buzzed with a notification. I glanced down, and a wave of unease washed over me—one new follower.

John Reynolds.

Chapter Five

I woke up with a hangover that wasn't just pounding in my head —it was making me question all my life choices. Reliving last night felt less like a memory and more like a highlight reel of bad decisions, leaving me nauseous and deeply regretting all of it. It was time to chug some water, down a shot of espresso, and get to work. I'd already put too much energy into this John and Jane Reynolds situation; it was time to pull myself together and refocus on what mattered, getting the senior editor position. I didn't have any room for drama in my life.

When I arrived at Regent, Willow called me into her office. It was Saturday, and I had come in to get ahead on my workload and get Willow my manuscript—I figured, now that everyone knew about the position, it was really time to go the extra mile. I assumed the office would be empty, especially considering how many people would be nursing hangovers after the Gala.

I rounded the corner, the morning sun streamed through the windows, casting a glow over the wood furniture. I loved being at Regent when no one was there in the morning. I could think more clearly.

Willow's office was stunning—like something out of a catalog, sleek and sophisticated. As I walked toward the door, glass walls exposing her office, I wasn't alone. Jane Reynolds, of all people, was on her way out.

My pulse spiked so fast it made me lightheaded. Of course she was here. As if the universe hadn't toyed with me enough last night. I wasn't prepared to win her over. In fact, I had nothing prepared. And honestly, after finding out about her and John's history, I felt confused, guilty as to how I could even ask her to mentor me. *'Hey, I have a crush on your handsome husband. Oh, and by the way, will you mentor me?'*

Instinct kicked in—I veered sideways, considering if I should duck behind a nearby desk or bookshelf. Too late. She looked up, her green eyes locking onto mine. I froze, gripping my notebook like a lifeline.

Did she recognize me? Did she even remember me?

I walked up and stood in the door frame. "Morning," Jane said, shooting me a quick glance before returning her attention to Willow.

I swallowed hard. "Morning Jane," I managed to get the words past the lump in my throat, my tone painfully try-hard.

"Thank you for your time, Willow," Jane said. I was just grateful the attention had shifted away from me.

"I'm looking forward to being office neighbors now," she added, her smile wide and confident—like she owned the entire building.

Willow smiled warmly. "Me too. Jane, you remember Sarah from last night, don't you?" Willow was doing her best to continue to position me as the obvious choice for the promotion. Unfortunately, this time, redirecting the spotlight back to me wasn't as ideal. Willow gestured for me to join her, shuffling through a stack of files on her desk.

"Of course," Jane said, raising a brow. "I guess we'll be seeing more of each other." Her voice carried just the right balance of warmth and authority, making it impossible to tell if she was being friendly or putting me in my place.

Jesus. I couldn't imagine what she would have been like if I'd been the one to spill my champagne on *her*. Or maybe she was always like this. Hard to read, never knowing if you were going to get Nice Jane or Ice Queen Jane. Part of me wanted to ask her a few questions while I had the chance—if I was in her line of fire, I may as well get some tips—but being in her presence was so intense that I chickened out. I needed to be more mentally prepared than this to approach her about anything work related.

I scanned her while she looked at Willow. This woman really did have it all. Poise, power, John. The realization hit me like a cold wave, leaving a sinking weight in my chest. Jane lingered for a moment, as if expecting me to say something—this was my chance. But before I could find the words, she gave a curt nod, said goodbye, and strode off toward her new corner office, just down the hall from my tiny desk.

I hadn't thought of my desk as pathetic until now. But standing there, watching her walk toward her office with "Executive Vice President Jane Reynolds" on her door, reality hit hard. Her office could easily fit my entire apartment inside it.

A familiar jealousy surged through me, bitter and sharp. It wasn't just about the office or John—it was her. The way she moved, the way she spoke, the way she commanded the room with confidence. Effortlessly. She was untouchable, the embodiment of everything I aspired to be but secretly feared I might never have the courage or skillset to become.

My chest tightened, my breath grew shallow. Could I ever compete with someone like her? Do what she had done? Would I always find myself in the shadow of someone like her—not just in the office, but in every corner of this world—no matter how hard I worked? The thought gnawed at me.

Izzy and I had stayed up another hour last night. She'd filled me in on the Jane and John drama. I spent the first fifteen minutes in disbelief. And another fifteen in disbelief that their names were Jane and John.

"Are they really Jane and John?" I asked her, laughing in spite of myself.

Izzy rolled her eyes. "I know, right? It is like they were named by a really lazy author."

"Or maybe they are both in the witness protection program. Or like Angelina and Brad in *Mr. and Mrs. Smith*. Maybe they're spies," I teased, raising an eyebrow, feeling like the only way not to die of embarrassment was to make a joke. "Secret agents living undercover as perfectly normal office people."

They'd married young—high school sweethearts who'd both started at Regent right out of college, together. By their early twenties, they'd risen to management positions, even breaking a few company records—a classic power couple.

From the outside, it seemed that the more successful they became, the less they were seen together socially. Izzy told me they'd been the perfect couple for years, but about a year or two ago, they started living in different places and doing fewer conference calls together. John was in the Chicago office, while Jane was spending more and more time in Manhattan.

Apparently, everyone at Regent was dying to know what was going on, but Jane had built such an impenetrable wall around herself that no one dared ask about her personal life—it felt too intrusive, and a bit inappropriate. Izzy and I came to our own conclusion that they were probably separated. Neither of them wore their wedding rings on Instagram. Hence why Izzy didn't tell me all of this information to start. Based on her thorough research, Izzy had predicted they were in the midst of their divorce. I imagined it could get messy with all that money involved.

I had made up my mind after that—I wasn't going to get involved with John. Not after finding out he was married. No matter how handsome or charming he was, or how my body seemed to react in his presence, it wasn't worth the risk. Even a harmless conversation could spiral into complications that might derail my career, and I wasn't sure I trusted myself to keep it harmless. Besides, I already had enough to juggle without adding office drama or personal entanglements to the mix.

But Jane? That was a different story. Pursuing her as a mentor felt like the smarter move—the kind of opportunity that could actually change the game for me. If I could keep my distance from John, I'd have a much better chance at earning Jane's respect. Her guidance could be the missing piece, the advice I needed to land the senior editor position and potentially grow my career beyond that.

"Did you finish that manuscript?" Willow interrupted my train of thought. Her look was sharp, like it was a test to see what choice I made last night.

"Happy Saturday, Willow," I said, leaning against the doorframe. "Yes, I do. I finished it yesterday before the Gala. I'll grab it for you."

"Wow . . . really?" Surprise laced her voice. "Great work, Sarah."

"Yes, ma'am. Thanks for the advice about staying in last night—definitely the right call. Oh, and for introducing me to Jane. She seems incredible." I was testing the waters, fishing for more insight. Sure, I wanted intel on Jane to prepare for when I asked her to mentor me, but a small part of me couldn't help hoping John might slip into the conversation. Even if I wasn't going to pursue anything with him, I still wanted to know the details.

"Oh, definitely. She was impressed by you. You will want to stop by her office during the week and offer support again."

"I can do that. I'll have some project ideas ready too," I replied. "You two seem like pretty close friends."

"We have known each other for nearly a decade. It's good to see her having fun again." She looked toward Jane's office. "She's finally in her mid-thirties, looking better than ever, and it looks like she's ready to dive back into the dating scene where she belongs."

The dating scene? I fought to keep my expression neutral. "What do you mean?" I asked, trying to sound casual, but the question barely passed my lips before a thousand thoughts flooded my mind. Was she talking about John?

If Jane was getting back into the dating game, could that mean . . .

47

he was available? Was there actually a chance they were already separated, maybe even divorced already? That could change things . . . maybe? I forced myself to focus on the conversation, but my mind was spinning.

"Well, it seems like she and John haven't been living together for a while. I saw her pretty close to one of the guys who works in the office last night. Peter . . . that kid in business development." Willow waved her hand dismissively like it wasn't a big deal. "They seemed to have been seeing each other for a while. I try my best to stay out of office politics."

"You didn't ask her about it?"

"No. Theo and I have been friends with Jane and John from before Regent. We would never pry. They have always kept their relationship very private, even from us. I don't know the details. They haven't officially announced anything about their separation."

Willow usually kept her opinions to herself, but I could tell she was excited for Jane—as a friend. This change seemed to be a welcome one. But, why?

I leaned forward, sensing an opening. "So, she and John . . . they're not together anymore? Are they separated?" I asked, hoping it would sound casual. John and Jane had kept things quiet, probably to avoid causing a stir in the office.

"I wouldn't assume that," Willow replied. "But they haven't lived together for almost a year. It's complicated, like everything in this business. They have to manage their images, you know? They're like publishing celebrities in a way."

"Publishing celebrities?" I echoed. Izzy had implied the same thing last night.

"Yeah," Willow shrugged. "People in the company look up to them—John and Jane are at the top, a lot like Theo and me. They've built a brand around themselves within the company. Their relationship, their personal lives . . . it all becomes a part of the public narrative. So, they have to handle everything carefully, especially if they want to keep their status intact." I could tell she was only sharing this because she knew one day I may be in a similar position within the company.

Willow raised an eyebrow. "Either way, it is really none of my business." Willow's eyes pierced me, shifting from friend to mentor in an instant, like she remembered who she was talking to. "It's none of your business either. Office drama is a complete waste of your valuable time."

"Totally. Interesting. I was just curious because I met them both last night and I would have never guessed they were together," I said, trying to sound nonchalant and naïve, as I processed the new information. "I'll email you the manuscript now," I said, scrambling to regain my composure, my mind racing with questions from what she just shared.

Willow returned to the papers on her desk, seemingly oblivious to the storm brewing in my mind. A mixture of hope and fear swirled through me.

I left Willow's office, my thoughts spiraling. Had I made the right decision, ruling out anything with John just because he was married? What if Jane had moved on with Peter—was there a chance for something with him, then? But the very thought made my stomach turn. Guilt crept in, and I couldn't escape the nagging feeling of betraying Jane, of crossing a line I'd promised myself I wouldn't. I couldn't ignore the strange pull I felt toward her. She had everything I wanted —career, success, confidence. And here I was, considering stepping into her world in a way I knew wasn't right.

Sarah, stop, I scolded myself. *Focus on your work. No distractions. No dating. You promised Theo, Willow, and most importantly, yourself.*

As I walked down the hallway, my mind drifted back to Jane. She could help me climb the ladder faster than I ever could on my own. Maybe it wasn't about pursuing John, but about growing closer to Jane. I could use her as a guide, without crossing any lines. The more I thought about it, the clearer it became. I needed to prove myself— not just as a junior editor, but as someone who could handle the demands of this career without getting sidetracked by personal drama.

I wouldn't step into Jane's world with any ulterior motives. I had already decided I wasn't pursuing John—not with his marriage. And that decision stood. This was about my future, my career. And if keeping my distance from John was the only way to stay focused, then that's what I'd do.

Chapter Six

A few hours later, Izzy and Theo wandered into the office, the usual Saturday lunch crew. Theo was here for lunch with Willow, and Izzy tagging along was nothing new—they'd been doing this for years. I glanced up from my desk as Izzy walked in.

"What's up?"

Izzy shrugged. "Theo asked me to join for lunch. He said the invitation is open to you as well."

Usually I would join, but today I was too focused on getting ahead of my work and proving my commitment to the promotion.

Twenty minutes later, Jane, Theo, and Willow made their way through the near-empty bullpen, stopping in front of our desks.

"Are you two coming to grab a bite with us?" Theo asked.

"That's why I am here," Izzy said. She closed her browser grabbing her bag. For her, lunch with Theo and Willow wasn't optional—it was practically laced into her job description. She ran their entire lives. We used to joke that they'd probably lose their heads without her. If she wasn't there, no one would remember to sign the check or save the receipt for taxes.

"Thanks for the invitation, but I am going to work through lunch." I gestured to my computer screen. I didn't mind working Saturdays; it was a time when I could get lost in the work without the usual distractions. Having the three most important people in the office see my dedication was just icing on the promotion cake.

"See? This is why you're going to run this place someday," Theo said, giving me a high five. "Working on a Saturday, no lunch break? That's badass, Sarah." Theo was a master at what he did. As chief creative officer, his job wasn't just to come up with new ideas—it was to keep us fired up and focused on our work, day in and day out. And when it came to that, he was the best in the business.

Willow and Jane smiled in agreement. Jane looked me up and down like she was scanning me through my desk. Her presence in this moment, seeing the extra work I was putting in, was reassuring and nerve-racking all at once. Something about her made me question everything I was doing. Despite her smile, I couldn't read her. Something about her made me want to work hard to get her approval.

With her phone in one hand and designer purse in the other, dressed in an outfit that outshone nearly everything in my closet, she carried herself like a celebrity—like there were different rules for people like her. Rules that were all too real for me but vanished in her version of reality. For a moment, I considered joining them for lunch, to soak up any insights or stories Jane might share. But I stayed planted in my chair, knowing this was where I needed to be if I was going to prove I was ready for senior editor.

They waved goodbye as they headed to the elevator, and as the group disappeared, likely to a five-star lunch, the office settled into a quiet calm. A flicker of envy poked at me, but I turned back to my tasks, determined to remain productive. I would have almost an hour of silence—just me and my work, no distractions, no noise.

Just as I was getting into the flow, the door swung open. When I looked up, I saw John Reynolds stepping onto the floor, commanding attention in the otherwise empty bullpen. If there had been anyone else around, they would have been drawn to him immediately. He scanned the room . . . before landing on me. He smiled at me and my heart skipped a beat.

Are you kidding me? I clenched my hands and took a sharp inhale as I tried to keep my eyes glued to the screen in front of me. Of all the moments for him to walk in, it had to be now. When I was all alone in the office. Right after I'd promised myself I wouldn't get involved. A rush of nervous energy coursed through me, and I could feel my cheeks flush.

The office was eerily quiet, and I couldn't ignore the fact that we were the only two people here. I couldn't *completely* ignore him, could I? I reminded myself of what I'd just resolved: no distractions, no dating, no going behind Jane's back. Especially not with him. My stomach churned. What did he want? Why was he even here?

I forced myself to stay seated, determined not to let him see how much his presence rattled me. *This is just another test, to show how badly you want senior editor. Stay professional. Stay focused. Do not let him derail you.*

"Hey there," he said, strolling over with that confident, relaxed walk. When he reached my desk, he looked around and joked, "Did you fire everyone? I didn't realize they had put you in charge already. Fast work."

His grin nearly made me gasp. *Breathe. Play it cool. Act unattached.*

"That's nothing. You should have seen the chaos an hour ago. The team was rioting. There were fires everywhere," I said stoically, my voice as dry and barren as I could manage, barely looking away from my computer screen, hoping to communicate that I wasn't interested.

"Tough boss," he said. I could almost hear him smiling, clearly amused by my attempt at indifference.

"Maybe now you'll think twice about moving here," I said, raising my eyebrows.

As soon as the words left my mouth, I realized that I probably wasn't supposed to know that. Damn Izzy and her inside information. Of course the merger was happening, but not everyone from Chicago would be transferring. It was like one of those moments on a first date when you'd online stalked them enough to know their third aunt's name, and when they mentioned her, you accidentally asked if it was Aunt Jeanie or Tammy. As if you hadn't just spent hours before the date studying his astrological chart to find out he too was an Aquarius.

John's lips curled. "Oh, I wouldn't let a little thing like that put me off. Word is you're one of the up-and-comers around here."

"Well, if that's the word on the street, I should ask for a raise," I said, finally pulling my eyes away from the screen. I tried to drain all emotion from my expression, keeping any trace of interest buried deep. I couldn't trust myself around him. I could feel the floodgates threatening to open—smiling, flirting, being cute—but once that door opened, there'd be no going back.

"It's Saturday," I said, trying to recover. "Aside from a few of the managers, it's usually pretty quiet around here on weekends." I narrowed my eyes on him, as if somehow not letting him see my fully dilated pupil would put a much-needed distance between us. "What floor will you be working on, anyway?" I asked, doing my best to shift the conversation away from myself.

"Not sure yet. I'll probably be one of the last to transition. Still have a lot of loose ends to tie up in Chicago." He leaned in, lowering his voice like he was about to share a secret. "You're the *only* one here on a Saturday afternoon," he said, part question, part observation, scanning the empty office before leaning against my desk with his arms crossed. Confidence radiated from him like blinding sunlight.

I waited for the rest of his question. When it didn't come, I furrowed my brow, resisting the pull of his energy. "And?"

He ignored my response, standing up and pacing around the office. He leaned into a few of the open office doors, peeking inside. "Maybe I'll request this floor. It looks nice, spacious—good windows.

Who knows? Maybe I'll even pick up a few tips from you when I'm not playing cater-waiter."

A grin tugged at the corners of my lips despite my attempt to hold it back. "Wait . . . I never would have guessed you have even *more* skills beyond serving drinks and fetching napkins. Color me impressed." It was like the words slipped out before I could stop them.

There was a flicker of amusement in his eyes, and I suddenly felt a rush of heat rise to my cheeks. Did I just . . . flirt? Shit, it was like I couldn't control it. I quickly dropped my gaze to my computer screen, hoping to mask the slip.

John chuckled. "Hey, don't underestimate multitasking. I could carry a tray and close a deal at the same time if I had to."

"Unlikely. It has actually been scientifically proven that men can't multitask. It is called singular focus," I said opening up my calendar, acting like I was checking it for a meeting that didn't exist.

Just like the night prior, there was something about his presence, like our bodies were opposite ends of a magnet, drawing our energies together. It was like the air in the room shifted, and I felt this sudden awareness of him, of us, of the space between us. The electricity between our bodies. The memory of shaking his hand flashed in my mind. I shook my head to clear it.

He looked at me with the amusement of a wild animal in captivity, making his way back to my desk. Yet there was something in his gaze that suggested he knew exactly what was going on in my mind. It was as if he could see through my attempts at distance, reading my thoughts like a book.

I was doing my best to sound detached—sarcastic—hoping that would show him I wasn't interested. "Honestly, I'm not sure you're ready for the pressure of this office. Chicago is a minnow pond compared to Manhattan."

"Well," he said, leaning in slightly, "maybe you'll be the one to keep me on my toes, boss."

My heart raced, but I kept my voice casual. "As Theo Brooks always reminds me when I'm talking too big of a game for my own good . . . we'll see."

He smiled and let out a deep laugh. I couldn't help but let the smallest smirk spread across my face. I did my best to fight it by biting my lip. There was a moment of stillness, silence, our eyes locked on each other. Then I remembered he had followed me back on Instagram last night. I immediately felt self-conscious. Had he looked at my page like I had stalked his? Had he read my posts? Did he know things about me? Why *had* he followed me back so quickly? I doubted a married man would do that. For the first time ever, my heart pounded so intensely it flooded into my cheeks.

"So, why are you here?" I asked, trying to fill the deafening silence.

Before he could say, the elevator doors opened, signaling the return of the team. Jane, Theo, Willow, and Izzy entered, their laughter filling the office. John straightened and gave me one last playful smile and a wink before turning around and nodding to them, giving them all a wave.

"Looks like I'd better get out of the way before they all put me to work," he said under his breath to me before they were in earshot.

"Careful," I whispered as the group approached. "*We* just might." My stomach tightened as I said it. What was I doing? Flirting. I was flirting with John Reynolds—Jane's John—while she was just steps away? I was a terrible person. He stepped toward the group, his charm dialed down. The moment long passed, but the heat still clung to my cheeks.

Jane's eyes darted between us as she approached my desk, her smile changing to a sharp stare in my direction. I couldn't help but wonder if she was glaring—though her Botox probably wouldn't allow for that kind of scornful look. I acted like I was focused on my manuscript, but I still caught the interaction. A subtle tension filled the air as she exchanged a quick glance with John, her demeanor instantly shifting the energy of the whole office. She didn't say anything, only gesturing her head to her office as if to say, *My office, now*. Without missing a beat, she walked past my desk, and John followed her lead.

The soft murmur of their conversation drifted into the hallway, but I couldn't help wondering: Were they still together? Separated? Divorced? And why did I care so much? The questions gnawed at me, though I didn't want to admit it. As the door closed behind them, I found myself staring after them, curiosity getting the better of me about what was really going on behind closed doors.

Theo and Willow returned to their offices, and Izzy sat back down at her desk to wrap up what looked like a few admin tasks.

I glanced down at my desk, trying to regain focus, but the questions kept swirling in my mind, too persistent to ignore. I had told myself I wouldn't pursue John—that I wouldn't risk a valuable mentorship with Jane, or jeopardize my reputation by getting involved with a married man. I had promised myself I wouldn't break my no-dating rule. And I meant it.

But now? Now, I wasn't so sure.

There was something about John—something I couldn't explain. It wasn't just his charm or the way his smile seemed to disarm me completely. There was something there. Like some invisible thread had tied us together, pulling me closer no matter how hard I tried to resist. It was reckless, dangerous. There was a part of me, a small, quiet part, that longed for the connection. A connection I hadn't even realized I'd been searching for, didn't even know existed until now.

I shook my head, rubbed my temples, frustrated with myself for even considering it. What was I doing? The thought left me more confused than ever, torn between the promise I'd made to myself and this strange, undeniable feeling that I couldn't seem to shake.

And as I stared blankly at the manuscript in front of me, I couldn't help but wonder if this was the moment everything in my life was about to change.

———

The next day, I took a full day off—something I rarely did. I usually worked a bit on Sundays, but after the whirlwind of the Gala, I needed an emotional reset. Izzy and I stayed in our pajamas, lounging in bed and unwinding from the week while preparing for the one ahead. With the shades drawn and *The Wolf of Wall Street* playing on my laptop, we vegged out until the sun started to set. Eventually, hunger set in, and we dragged ourselves out of our cave for a ramen run.

Before we left, I snapped a photo of Jordan Belfort's infamous yacht scene from *The Wolf of Wall Street* to post to my Instagram stories, secretly hoping John might see it. What guy wasn't obsessed with this movie? I added the caption:

Sunday Night. Favorite Movie of All Time

As soon as I hit "post," I felt lame. I also felt complete exhilaration. Was I really posting this just to get John's attention? Shame washed over me. Virtually flirting with a married man—especially one I would be working with—wasn't just risky; it could ruin everything I'd worked for. And yet, I couldn't help myself. Every cell of my being wanted him to see the post and strike up a conversation. Just to test the waters. To see if he actually was interested in me or if he was just a flirt. I hated how easily he got under my skin, how I was letting my own values and the small amount of loyalty I did have toward Jane slip for a fleeting moment of validation from a man. It was like the second I thought of him, I was tempted to throw all of my rules out the window.

I didn't know what to make of John yet. He was flirty, but also . . . married? His reputation was impeccable around Regent. From what I gathered on Instagram, he seemed wholesome. From a small town with a long list of siblings. But what was his deal with Jane? Why would he flirt with me at the Gala and yesterday in the office if he wasn't interested? It would be just as risky for him. I couldn't imagine why he would—unless he was available or felt some small amount of attraction towards me.

We were walking back from our ramen stop, full and satisfied, when my phone buzzed. I scrambled to grab it, and Izzy, confused by my reaction, asked, "Who is that?"

I opened the Instagram app, and there it was, a direct message from none other than—drum roll, please—John Reynolds.

"Izzy!" I slapped her arm in excitement. "It's from John!" I shoved my phone in her face.

Still in her ramen-belly haze, Izzy squinted at the screen and read his message aloud, doing her best impression of John's deep voice.

One of THE BEST movies ever made.

She adjusted back to her normal tone. "Damn, and he sent the prayer hands. Okayyy, girl." She seemed half surprised, half impressed.

I grabbed the phone back, my heart racing. John Reynolds had just messaged me. "Should I 'heart' the message and not reply? Or should I reply and 'heart' the message?" I muttered to myself. "What am I even trying to communicate? You're hot. I may have a crush on you. I have already decided not to pursue you, so please leave me alone. You may be married to my role model, and I'm trying to figure out if you're just a player. Or leave me alone. I am not interested. I need to focus on becoming senior editor. . . ."

"Okay, slow your roll, SJ. You're way overthinking this." Izzy grabbed for my phone, but I held it out of arm's reach. "He is a guy. Just say something flirty or send him a picture. Men are all visual."

"Ew," I said. "I am not good at flirting over text."

Izzy raised an eyebrow. "Please. Sarah, you just flirted with him like a *pro* at the Gala—and based on what you told me, you did just fine in the office too. Don't try to act like you don't know how to work it."

"I can in person, but texting feels weird," I said, feeling like a giddy schoolgirl. As much as I tried to convince myself I wasn't interested, the excitement bubbled up uncontrollably. I typed,

> It really is . . .

Detached and cool. Mysterious.

The words felt innocent, but my heart wasn't lying to me—I'd completely gone against my own rule. When we had a phone between us, all the feelings I wanted to let out in person felt free to roam.

A married man wouldn't interact with a random girl from work on social media—especially not someone like John. Meaning he had to be available, right? From all my research over the past twelve hours, he was known as nothing more than a loyal and loving husband, when they were together. You could see it in their old posts and videos. He was head over heels for Jane—awestruck, despite the decades they'd been together. They'd been a power couple. But in their more recent content, that seemed to be changing. More and more, John and Jane seemed to be sending signals that they were . . . available.

Of course I did wonder what could cause them to go from in love to separated to potentially divorced, but those answers weren't online. Only John or Jane could tell me that.

I wanted to stand in my resolve to not entertain anything with John. And yet, as much as I told myself I wanted to stay away, a part of me . . . my heart. My heart couldn't stop feeling what it was feeling. My mind couldn't stop wondering what it was wondering: *What if what I am feeling for him was real? What if the attraction between us, this pull I feel when he smiles at me, was something rare? What if he feels it too? What would make it something worth exploring and risking things at work?*

It didn't help that every time I considered staying out of it, the idea of pursuing whatever this was with John felt almost . . . necessary. Like I was missing out on something that was more important than I realized. I had always prided myself on making smart deci-sions, the kind that wouldn't jeopardize my career. I sounded crazy. We had only had a few brief interactions. But with John, it was . . . different. With John, the lines didn't just blur—they seemed to vanish altogether. It was like I had to consider something more, something I'd never felt before. Like all my rules *wanted* to go out the window for him.

I didn't want to admit it, because it sounded insane, but the truth was, if I knew John was available—if I didn't have to worry about Jane —I'd go on a first date with him. Hell, dare I say, I'd go on a second.

But that was the part I couldn't let myself ignore. The question of what this would mean for Jane—and for me.

I couldn't figure out if I was losing my mind or if this was a once-in-a-lifetime feeling I was experiencing. What if this guy was my soulmate and I just ignored him for the sake of my career? I might always regret that. Either way, the questions kept lingering: *What if it was worth it to pursue things with him? What if I could have a happy relationship* and *a successful career? What if, like Jane, I could have it all?*

————

It was 2 a.m. We'd watched three hours of Jordan Belfort's absolute insanity before Izzy passed out in my bed next to me, and John and I were deep in an Instagram conversation. I couldn't tear myself away from my phone, trying to ignore the fact that it was now Monday and my alarm was creeping up on me like a sketchy guy at a bar who couldn't take a hint.

John had responded immediately to my message about the movie. Of course, the conversation eventually veered into flirty territory, but it was still a relatively tame exchange, with Izzy guiding me through the whole thing. Like I told her, flirty texting wasn't my forte. I was more of a "direct communicator" (according to my coworkers).

Until Izzy fell asleep, it was basically her holding my phone and replying on my behalf. I saw it as an opportunity to learn from the queen of flirty texting herself. She'd tell me what she was typing, I'd take mental notes, and she'd send it before I could change my mind or tell her not to. I almost had a heart attack when she mentioned something about me visiting him in Chicago one day. John didn't take the bait. I think we were both trying to figure out the situation. Feel each other out. How much could we trust each other not to completely ruin the other person's career by exposing our late night conversation. Until I found out if his marriage was really over, we'd both have a lot to lose by even messaging each other. But I figured, if he was willing to risk it, so was I. There was clearly some mutual unspoken trust. I figured I could just delete the conversation later if I needed to.

Once Izzy was asleep, I flew solo. The conversation shifted to discussing our families, our upbringings, and our careers, much more my territory. Izzy had practically nailed down every detail about him when she told me about him after the Gala, so I had to pretend I didn't already know about his full history with Regent House—or many of the details about his relationship with Jane, for that matter.

I did, in fact, learn that he was thirty-two, which meant there was quite an age gap to consider, if it ever got to that point. Jesus, I was getting ahead of myself.

When the clock struck 3 a.m., I figured it was time for Cinderella to call it a night. I didn't want to seem too available.

> Well, Mr. Reynolds, I am turning in for the night. Let's do this again sometime. Sleep tight.

He replied right away,

> Good night, Sarah. Don't let the bed bugs bite. I'm looking forward to it . . . more than you know.

I drifted off to sleep, and for the first time in a long time, I fell asleep with a smile on my face, not thinking about work or the stress of my job. I fell asleep excited to wake up and start the day, even though I knew better than to expect anything more. The attention John had given me tonight, the connection we had, made me feel something I hadn't felt in a long time, if ever. I felt alive. I felt seen. I didn't know what would happen between us, if anything. But that feeling alone was enough, for now.

Chapter Seven

On my way to the office, I'd downed a coffee the size of my head. My alarm had felt like a foghorn, punishment for last night's late bedtime. The morning passed in a haze of emails and edits, rinse and repeat until 2 p.m.

That afternoon, my phone dinged—the cursed sound that had become my own Pavlov's bell. Trained to salivate and leap at every Instagram notification, I hoped it was a message from John. My arms were full with a stack of client proposals—projects I'd taken on to help Phillip, who was drowning in work—and a few slush pile manuscripts from up-and-coming writers. But I couldn't wait until I got back to my desk to check the message. My heart raced as I freed one hand, fished my phone from my pocket, and watched the screen light up.

I read the message. *No. Freaking. Way.*

I froze for a moment before running to my desk and throwing the papers on top, not caring where they landed. Trying to look composed, I hurried over to Izzy's desk. She looked very well rested after falling asleep last night, leaving me to flirt for myself with John.

"Look at this," I said, thrusting the phone at her. Her eyes went saucer wide as she read the screen, her jaw dropping. I nodded, grinning like a maniac, my excitement barely containable. Why was I so giddy when it came to this guy?

Before I could break out in complete high school cheerleader energy, Jane stepped out of her office and into the bullpen. She walked across the floor like she owned the place—which, to be fair, she kind of did—pausing only to talk to her assistant who had pulled her away at the Gala, Jenny, before going back into her window-walled office.

Her presence brought me back down to earth. Hard. I sat back down at my desk. The thrill of getting a message from her husband—or most likely ex-husband—was doused with the cold reality of who she was. She was a walking reminder of the focus and determination I needed to achieve my own goals. Also a reminder that I needed to find a way to get in her good graces.

I shook my head. I hadn't been thinking straight. "I need to have an early night tonight," I muttered to myself. I had a big week ahead with these extra projects. Every week would be a big week until I found out who got the position as senior editor. A never-ending rat race to secure the position.

But first, the message. My fingers itched to open it again. Glancing up to make sure Jane was out of sight, I held the phone under my desk to reread the message.

John Reynolds:

> So, when you said that thing about coming to see me in Chicago, were you serious . . . or were you just kidding around?

My cheeks burned, taking everything I had not to break into a full-on toothy smile. I had opened the floodgates by flirting with him, and now it felt impossible to close it. Suddenly, my rules flew out the window. I wasn't even considering the link between him and Jane. They felt like two separate entities. Like my flirting with John had nothing to do with Jane. Or at least that was the way I would be able to justify it. Complete compartmentalization. I felt safe knowing that he was willing to say what we were both feeling. I felt like I could trust him because of it. My answer came quickly.

> Of course. How else are we going to catch you up on all your subpar cater-waiter skills? Name the time and place.

While I wanted it to come off as a flirty joke, was it too forward? Was he seriously asking me to fly to Chicago on a whim? Was this how wealthy people operated—expecting you to uproot your life to fit into theirs? I glanced at Izzy for support, hoping she'd help me decode this invitation.

As I raised my head, there stood Jane, looming over my desk. It was as if the air had been sucked out of the room. My smile turned to stone, my face freezing as the reality of the situation hit me.

"Oh, hey, Jane!" I blurted, my voice unnaturally high. Her brows raised at the pitch—well, as much as brows could with ninety units of Botox. "I was just . . . finishing up the edits from that new thriller, *Voices in the Dark*," I said, dropping my phone in my lap under the desk, putting my hands on my keyboard, praying she hadn't seen my screen with her husband's name on it. Damn me for wanting to save a few bucks at Verizon when they offered me that privacy screen. "And, um, brainstorming marketing angles for the upcoming meeting. You know, just trying to help out wherever I can." *Stop talking. You sound like an idiot.* "Anyway, how's the office treating you? It looks amazing."

"Hi, Sarah," she said coolly, brushing off my ramblings like lint from her jacket. "I'd like you to sit in on the meeting with Gabriel Stone next Monday at 2 p.m. To learn."

It wasn't a question, though she softened it as if it were.

"Oh. Really? Wow. Junior editors don't usually get invited to those," I stammered. *Obviously she knew that or she wouldn't have invited you.* "Are you sure? I mean, thank you! Yeah, I'll be there."

"Yes, you will," she said with a faint smile, the kind that felt both approving and slightly dismissive. "This is a pre-meeting with Gabriel because, as one of our highest-profile clients, we always do a strategic session before handing things off to marketing. This will be a great opportunity for you to learn how we position authors at this level and help shape the direction for their success."

"Amazing," I said, writing a few notes on the sticky note in front of me. "That sounds wonderful. Thank you for thinking of me, Jane."

She raised her brow, turned on the heels of her twelve-hundred-dollar, red-bottom, Louboutins, and strode back toward her office, tossing her hair over her shoulder. Midway there, she paused and turned back around. "Oh, and Sarah," she called back to me.

"Yes, Jane?" I said, half standing from my chair like she was royalty and I was a common peasant.

"You should really turn that thing off. Audible notifications are *terrible* for your nervous system."

I barely had time to process her parting remark before my phone dinged again. This time, rather than salivating, I seethed at the sound. My stomach turned. I held up my phone while I turned it on silent. "You got it," I said, forcing a smile as she returned to her office.

As soon as she did, I scrambled to unlock my phone.

John Reynolds:

> Actually, I changed my mind.

Changed his mind? About what? Did he not want to see me now? *Jesus, you take three minutes to respond these days and they lose interest. . . .*

Another message came in.

> I'm in NYC for two more days. Let's meet tonight instead. It's not very gentlemanly of me to expect you to fly across the country for a first date. L'Artusi at 8 pm?

The words, "a first date," blared loud in my mind. As if they were

67

bolded and italicized. It was all I could see. He was asking me on the first date. My heart pounded in my chest. Tonight. In person. Thrill and horror hit me at the same time. A familiar sense of hesitation crept in.

Was this reckless? Brave? We had a connection—something I'd never felt before. I guess, if nothing else, spending time with someone like him could only be good for my career. Right? I could learn a ton, ask him questions as a mentor. I could at least get some answers about what is going on between him and Jane. But, then again . . . not pissing Jane off further would be even better for my career. I was in the middle of an impossible choice. My career and my heart's desire.

I glanced toward Jane's office again. Her presence loomed even when she wasn't looking. Was I really going to do this? Was I insane? Suicidal?

Izzy's eyes caught mine. She arched an eyebrow, her expression a perfect mix of *What the hell are you waiting for?* and *Go for it!*

Izzy's unspoken encouragement pushed me past the hesitation. It wasn't just about the thrill or the attraction; it was something more. I knew it. I could feel it. I wouldn't have acted on it if I wasn't sure it was something more. Maybe it was the feeling that, for once, I deserved to follow my heart. To take a little risk. To break my rules. That feeling, the idea of being alone forever, twisted in my gut. The more I felt what John had awoken in me, the more I didn't just want a successful career. I might actually want someone to share it with.

I couldn't play it safe forever, especially when it came to relationships. It's not like I would be a desirable candidate forever. I probably had six good years left before I started to be considered old. What if this was my only chance at a relationship with someone I was truly compatible with? If I was going to take the leap into something with someone (at least a first date anyway), why not start with him?

I bit my lip, my fingers hovering over the keyboard. A deep breath. Type. Send. Before any doubt or my better judgment could creep in.

See you tonight.

Chapter Eight

I spent far too much time staring into my closet stuffed full of clothes, but still felt like I had nothing to wear. I'd pull out something, hold it up, and compare it to the dresses Jane wore at the office or on Instagram—ones that likely cost more than my entire wardrobe—only to spiral into self-doubt. From what I knew about John, his cufflinks or pocket square would probably cost more than my entire outfit for the evening.

After twelve or so outfit changes—three of them borrowed from Izzy's closet—I veered away from my usual suit and settled on a simple red top, black leggings, and a leather jacket. I'd read once that men were more attracted to women in red, so I figured it could only help my case and make up for my lack of style. Most days, I stuck to a two- or three-piece suit for the office, so venturing into dinner-date territory felt like navigating a foreign land. I didn't want to overdress in case he wasn't serious about this being a date—although I couldn't imagine him joking about that—but I also couldn't risk being too casual and embarrassing him if he showed up in a suit.

The subway ride to the West Village felt endless, two lines and a twenty-minute walk to the restaurant. It was like traveling to another planet from my apartment on the Upper East Side. But I couldn't complain—John had chosen one of my favorite restaurants in Manhattan.

I deliberately planned to arrive a few minutes late to avoid appearing overly eager, a move that went against my father's deeply ingrained "fifteen minutes early or you're late" mantra that I heard thousands of times growing up. Being three minutes late almost tore my soul in two.

As I rode the subway, I gave myself a mental pep talk. *You can do this. You're a beautiful, confident, independent woman. Your career is just getting started, and that's your focus. You don't even need this guy. Worst case, you find out he's still married and a total piece of shit, and you go home like nothing happened. Hands wiped clean.*

Halfway down the 6 South subway line, John texted:

I'm here.

Shit. It was 7:45 p.m. He was exactly fifteen minutes early. Maybe he grew up with the same rules about time. After all, small-town roots were small-town roots. My stomach churned. Great, now he was going to think I was *that girl*.

When my stop finally came, I sprinted the last few blocks to the restaurant—avoiding the scattered ice patches on the ground—grateful I hadn't worn heels. I couldn't quite remember John's height, since the only times I'd seen him were either distracted and champagne-soaked or sitting behind my desk at the office. I didn't want to risk towering over him in heels if he was shorter than I remembered.

Before I went in, I sent a quick text to Izzy:

I'm going in. Wish me luck.

Her reply came instantly, as if she'd been waiting for it:

You got this, Mrs. Reynolds!

71

Her words made me smile—and triggered a swirl of emotions I didn't have time to unpack.

I rushed into L'Artusi's at 8:01 p.m. sharp, feeling like I'd kept him waiting for *hours*. The lighting in the restaurant was so dark I wasn't sure I'd even recognize him. I hurried to the hostess stand, trying to appear composed despite my three-block dash in the winter air.

Suddenly, a hand, his hand—at least I hoped it was his—rested on the small of my back. I turned around and there he was, towering over me. He had to be at least six-foot-three, with a smile so warm it could've melted the chill of winter off of me. His blue eyes pierced through the dim room, looking at me in a way that felt . . . familiar. Like we had lived a thousand lives together. Time stood still as his energy enveloped me, kinder and gentler than I'd expected, than I'd remembered. His charming self was dialed down. Like he wasn't putting on any show.

He gestured to the phone held to his ear, mouthing, *"Almost done."* Then he leaned in and gave me a hug—a moment longer than necessary for a casual greeting. Like being reunited with someone after years, even lifetimes, apart. That sounded crazy. It was odd but felt good. Right. My nerves vanished, replaced by a deep sense of ease.

John motioned for me to sit on the couch by the hostess stand while he finished his call. I sank into the cushions and scrolled through Instagram while sneaking glances at him as he paced back and forth. His freshly shaven face made him look younger than I remembered. I couldn't believe I ever thought he was a waiter. He looked like something out of a Greek myth—big muscles, a smile that made me weak, and a perfect head of hair. Then there was his style. Who didn't love a man who knew how to dress himself? He wore all black, a button-down shirt with the sleeves rolled up, the top button undone, as if he'd just come from a high-level meeting.

Out of curiosity—and, admittedly, a bit of paranoia—I checked Jane's profile. Based on her stories, she was having dinner with a friend in Soho, a little too close for comfort, but far enough away from here that there was no chance of a run-in. Her hair was slicked back, and she wore a small silver top and a fur jacket that screamed chic and glamorous. I screenshotted the outfit for later. *Note to self: Step up your fashion game. Another note: Don't come to the West Village with John again. Too risky. Stay uptown.*

"All right, man, I gotta go. Going to dinner," John said into his phone, glancing at me with a smile that made my heart skip a beat. His laugh—a real, guttural sound—sealed the moment. It was one of the best sounds I'd ever heard.

When he hung up, he came over with his arms outstretched for another hug. "Sorry about that. My buddy Andy wouldn't let me off the hook. He *loves* to talk."

"No worries. I am so sorry I'm late," I murmured into his chest as we hugged.

"Don't worry about it," he said, pulling away with a smile. "I grew up with a dad who had to keep seven kids in line, so if we weren't fifteen minutes early, we were in big trouble." His tone was easy, unwavering. I smiled at the similarity.

He leaned back slightly, still holding on to my hand as we parted, as if giving himself a moment to really take me in. "Sarah, wow," his voice dipping just enough to send a rush of warmth to my cheeks. "You look . . . amazing. Absolutely incredible."

Feeling a mix of nervousness and playfulness, I took a twirl. "This old thing?" I teased, confident that my smile betrayed how much his words meant to me.

As I came back around, he gripped my hand gently, steadying me. His eyes traveled over me, lingering for a beat too long, and his lips curled into a slow, genuine smile. "I don't think I was prepared for you tonight," he added. My knees went weak at his words. It dissolved any sense of insecurity I felt earlier about my outfit choice.

We sat side by side at the bar. My mother had always told me to sit next to a date, not across from him, so it felt like the two of you were against the world. Less direct focus and pressure on each other.

I always thought it sounded cheesy, but tonight I was willing to give it a try.

"What can I get you two started on tonight?" the waitress asked, holding up her notebook.

"What would you like?" John asked, his tone suggesting he expected me to tell him my choice so he could order for us—a chivalrous gesture I found surprisingly endearing.

"Classic martini. Gin, dry vermouth, lemon twist," I said.

He repeated the order to the waitress, adding his tequila soda and half the appetizers on the menu, rattling them off with the ease of someone who didn't have to check prices on the menu. "Anything else to start?" he asked, turning back to me.

"That should do it . . . for now," I teased.

He grinned and turned his chair slightly toward mine. Our knees almost touching, the energy between us felt electric. My breath quickened as I tried to concentrate on the menu, but all I could feel was the magnetism pulling me closer.

What the hell was this feeling?

As I studied the menu for a few minutes, his knee brushed against mine. The electricity between us was undeniable, but something deeper churned inside me. Was this just insane chemistry? Was I being flat-out reckless? A physical attraction that had no depth beyond it?

I was drawn to him, in a way I couldn't explain, but the more I tried to rationalize it, the more confusing it became. My common sense screamed at me—this was odd, risky for my career. He was married, for God's sake. Even if he was separated, he was still *married* to Jane. Legally bound. If she found out, she could totally ruin my career, and rightfully so. Everything about this felt like I was walking a fine line between something amazing and something I might completely regret.

Was I really about to lean into this, fully aware of what was at stake? As the thought crossed my mind, it felt less like a choice and more like something I'd already chosen—like I'd crossed the line without realizing it, already deep in without any way of pulling back. I was here, with him, on a date. And the moment I looked at John, once again, all the fear melted away. Like that part of my life, my career, things with Jane, didn't exist at all.

———

Halfway through my martini and all the way through John's tequila, barely making a dent in the countless appetizers he ordered, I found myself admiring him.

He wasn't only incredibly handsome. He also listened—fully present, his focus unwavering. He had an ease about him, a confidence that didn't come off as cocky but, rather, assured. In a world where so many people were trying to be everything, he seemed perfectly content in his own skin. He was kind. Honest. He was . . . flat-out *genuine*. We talked about work, and our dreams, and I was surprised by how much I learned from him. It felt like I could tell him anything—no judgement, just real, unfiltered conversation.

Our conversation flowed easily, but my thoughts continued to nag at me: *Was he actually interested in me? What about his divorce? What about Jane? What is this?*

"So, Sarah," he said, taking a final sip of his tequila before signaling the waiter for another round. Why did my name sound so much better when he said it? "I'm curious—why did you get into publishing in the first place? Seems like you could do anything with your enthusiasm and work ethic."

Was this an interview or a date?

"Interesting question . . ." I said. My knee once again brushed against his, straightening my spine and making me realize how much I'd been slouching. Yikes. I bet Jane never slouched. He smiled and waited patiently for my answer.

"Well, growing up, I always kind of felt like an outcast, like a lot of kids do, I am sure. I played sports and instruments, I was in all the clubs, but I never really fit in with the jocks or the nerds. I was some-where in between. Like I was a misfit."

He nodded. Why was I telling him all of this? He just felt so . . . so safe. Like I could tell him anything.

"On weekends, instead of hanging out with friends, I'd ask my mom to drop me off at the bookstore. I'd spend hours there, picking up a stack of books and getting lost in them. Learning about every-thing that sparked interest. I didn't have much money, so I couldn't buy the books . . . so I learned to read quickly. I'd save my allowance, and as soon as I was old enough to get a job, I did—just so I could buy the books rather than having to sit in Barnes & Noble for eight hours at a time. I felt like I could be myself there." I laughed at the memory. "I devoured them, but more than that, I admired the authors. I imag-ined what it took for them to write a book, the hurdles they had to overcome to get their message out, the courage it took to publish. I looked up to them. They were like my role models."

I paused, offering him the space to speak, but he just listened, fully present. I felt exposed sharing all this, but his calm presence made it comforting.

"As I got older, when people asked me what I wanted to do with my life, I always wanted to say, 'I'd like to stay in my room all day and read.' Of course I never did. Sometimes I even wondered if maybe I could write one myself. My parents told me it would be better to have a more 'stable' job, so I figured reading books alone in my room wouldn't be a viable option. Editing and Publishing was the closest I could get to it."

John smiled, still listening. Like he really wanted to learn about me. About what I wanted and desired. So I kept sharing.

"Moving to New York was kind of taboo. Everyone in Idaho thought it was a wild jungle out here, which it is. But, once I decided publishing was the path, I wanted to be the best at it. Just like in sports or instruments, I applied the same level of discipline. So I grad-uated from college, and when I moved here, I met Izzy. She intro-duced me to Theo and Willow. We all meshed, and I think they saw potential in me. They helped me get the job at Regent, and here I am. That's it, I guess."

He leaned back in his seat. "Wow," he said, his voice laced with awe. "That's incredible, Sarah. What an inspiring story. Have you recently considered writing books of your own?"

His curiosity caught me off guard. I hadn't asked myself that question in years. It had been a childhood dream. Nothing I'd considered recently. This guy really knew how to dig deep. No wonder he was so great in Acquisitions.

"Since I started at Regent, there hasn't been any time for anything but work. But . . ." I paused. "If I'm *honest*, I'd say . . . sure. Maybe someday. Way far in the future once I don't have to worry about paying my bills each month, maybe."

"I hope you're always honest with me," he said, his lips curling into a half smile.

I rolled my eyes. "Ha ha. Very funny."

"Well, your trajectory is super impressive. I am confident you will get there. To be a senior editor *and* write your own books one day. If there is anything I can do to help you, any introductions I can make, I am happy to."

When he said the platitude, just like Jane had at the Gala, it felt different. Genuine, like he really wanted to help and support me achieving my goals. It was so refreshing to have someone ask me about my dreams, ones I had even forgotten about. It made me feel important. Most first dates involved me asking the questions and the man telling me all about how amazing he and his career were without any questions about me, let alone my career.

Time seemed to stretch as we talked, the hours passing like minutes. We exchanged notes about music, hobbies, movies, and books. The conversation felt effortless, yet there was a weight to it—a connection I hadn't expected. Before I knew it, it was eleven.

We approached the dessert menu. I was two martinis deep in liquid courage and decided it was time to ask the question that had been nagging at me all night. Before I could get too deep, I needed to know the truth. "So, Mr. Reynolds," I said, clinking my glass with the tip of my knife. I had to ask. I wanted nothing more than to keep things light on this amazing night, but I couldn't avoid the inevitable conversation—even though I feared the truth might break me.

"Yes?" he said, leaning in close enough that our shoulders grazed one another.

"I hate to ask about the 'ex-files' on a first date, but I feel like it's something we should probably talk about sooner rather than later. With all the crossovers in our worlds—both of us at Regent, you're possibly relocating to the New York office—"

"I *am* relocating to the New York office," he corrected.

I nodded, holding back a smile. "And with you being friends with Theo and Willow Brooks . . . They're my mentors." I was rambling, trying to avoid the question I really needed answered. *Ask it, already.* "Are you and Jane still married? Or . . . together? What's the deal with that?"

I held my breath, the weight of my question hanging between us. Would he answer? Overreact? Or would this be the end of the evening?

John let out a soft laugh that eased the tension, placing his hand on my knee. The warmth of his touch sent a jolt of electricity up my spine. He looked right at me, so he must have felt something too. I could feel anxiety tightening in my throat, I swallowed hard.

"Yes," he began, his eyes dropping to the ground as if the right words might be written there before looking back at me. "I'm so glad you asked. Thank you for that. It's . . . complicated, especially with the business. We've been trying to figure out the best way to tell the company without it becoming a distraction. People love drama—it's like fuel for procrastination."

He let out a deep breath before continuing. "We're separated. We have been for almost two years. She lives here in Manhattan full-time. I've been staying at our place in Chicago. We haven't lived in the same place since the split."

I stayed quiet, nodding, hoping the silence would draw more out of him. My mind was racing. Separated but still married?

He continued, "The divorce is in progress, but it's moving slowly. All our assets are intertwined, and have been for the last seven years. Untangling everything is taking longer than I'd hoped." He hesitated, his voice softening as he looked up, probably reading the confusion—or perhaps the nausea—on my face.

"I know it's not ideal," he admitted, his eyes searching mine. They held a quiet, resigned pain, the kind that comes from enduring too much for too long. "But in my mind, we haven't been married in a long, long time. It is all just a legal formality at this point."

I could feel his hurt, see the weariness etched into his expression. I was frustrated, not only because I had no idea what role, if any, I was meant to play in all of this, but also because he was stuck in a situation that seemed impossible to escape. His tangled mess wasn't just about the logistics of a divorce or a business deal—it was the emotional weight of being in something he couldn't easily untangle. And here I was, caught between wanting to help and wanting to run from the mess altogether. What was even worse was that I *chose* to be here. That a big part of me wanted to be here.

I tried my best to not make this about me. He seemed like a man desperate for freedom, not just from a marriage, but from guilt. The guilt of having a failed marriage. I could see a plea for acceptance, for someone to see beyond the mess and still choose him. Seeing this side of him made me like him even more. That he was willing to share this with me gave me certainty that he felt things for me.

I put my hand on his. "It must be so much to go through. I'm sorry you have been dealing with all this—especially with the company and the pressure of being the 'power couple' and all." I was careful not to let my feelings take over the moment. I didn't want to make it about me, about how much I enjoyed being with him, how deeply I already felt connected to him. How badly I wanted this first date to become a second, third, and fourth date. How much I wished there were no ties or complications with Jane. No one, especially someone as kind as him, deserved to go through something this challenging.

"How long do you think it will take to finalize everything?" I asked, trying to sound neutral, though my heart was anything but.

"As far as I can tell, it shouldn't be more than a few months," he replied. "I'm hoping to have it all done by the end of Q2." He exhaled, and for a moment, I saw a flicker of the man he wanted to be—confident, capable—but it quickly faded under the weight of vulnerability. It was surreal to see him like this: the charming, confident man I'd met suddenly fragile, exposed. I wondered what kind of dynamic was at play between him and Jane? It seemed like he had been really torn down. He hadn't said anything bad about her.

"If I had to guess," he said, "it should all be resolved within ninety days at the latest."

I could feel the words slip out before I had a chance to stop them. "I can do ninety days," I said, trying to inject some levity into the conversation. The moment the words left my lips, I realized how presumptuous it sounded, as if I was already planning out our future. My cheeks flushed, this time with mortification.

John smiled and cleared his throat, his fingers tapping lightly against the rim of his glass, as if searching for the right words.

"I . . . I didn't expect that," he said quietly, his voice a little lower. His gaze softened, and for the first time, I noticed the edges of uncertainty there.

As I waited for him to say more, I reminded myself that he wouldn't be here with me, risking both of our careers, if he didn't want to get to know me. There was an undeniable connection, one that I hadn't imagined and certainly wasn't looking for, but now that it was there, I could feel it pulling at me. So, while I was mortified, I also couldn't ignore the sense of certainty deep down that we'd both be walking into this, whatever it was, together.

He finally spoke again, "I mean, I wanted to be really open with you about all this, so you could make your own decision and not be kept in the dark, but I wasn't sure how it'd sit with you, or if you would want anything to do with it. Or anything to do with me."

I could see the flicker of fear, the kind of fear that comes from showing someone your raw, unpolished self and hoping they don't turn away. Underneath it all, we were both little kids, vulnerable, secretly wanting to be chosen by the other.

I remained silent. Then he showed a small smile. "But, uh, thank you. For being . . . well, *willing* to be part of this mess. I wasn't sure if I'd ever find anyone who could handle it."

His vulnerability hit me harder than I expected, and I found myself reassured, even as my own heart skipped a beat. It was strange —real, even—seeing him like this. And despite everything, I didn't want to back away. Quite the opposite. Something about his honesty drew me in, deeper than I'd ever thought I'd go.

"I can handle it," I said, smiling. "But, can I ask . . ." I began, choosing my words carefully. "Does anyone know about this? I promise I won't say anything, but do you have support? Someone you can talk to?"

John hesitated, the question clearly hitting a nerve. Who had he confided in? Maybe his friend Andy that he was on the phone with earlier? Certainly not anyone at Regent—that would be career and social suicide. His family? Doubtful. Divorce wasn't exactly celebrated in traditional households like the one he came from.

When he replied, shame laced his look. "Actually, you're the first person I've told."

My heart cracked open for him. In two years, he hadn't told anyone about this? How awful that must have been. I reached out, taking his hands in mine, giving them a gentle squeeze. At that moment, living in his eyes, I saw my dad.

A memory flashed. I was three years old, leaving his house with my mom and sister. As we drove away, he stood at the door, crying, waving as we left. The finalization of their divorce, the one he had never wanted, but my mom insisted on, had torn him apart. It broke

Aria Devi

my heart, seeing how much it hurt him. Tonight, I saw that same pain, that same look, in John's eyes.

"I'm here for you if you ever need to talk. Your secret is safe with me."

Our eyes met, and I could see a sliver of gratitude. He looked at me as if I had just given him something priceless, like I had helped fill a void he hadn't even known was there. A supportive ear and a judgment-free space.

For a moment, there was only silence between us, thick with unspoken emotions. Then, without warning, he tightened his grip on my hands and leaned in. The distance between us vanished, and his lips found mine.

The kiss was tender and soft. A quiet surrender that seemed to hold all the questions and answers we couldn't yet put into words. His lips were warm, hesitant at first, then full of a need that had been building between us. It wasn't rushed; like the world had slowed down just enough for us to remember the depth of our connection. Everything else faded away. It wasn't just a kiss—it was the beginning of something we couldn't deny, something we both desperately needed and wanted.

It was . . . sweet. Really sweet. I wanted more of it. All of it.

———

After he paid (what I assumed to be) the astronomically sized bill, we walked out hand in hand, our hearts completely consumed by one another. Only then did it hit me: He hadn't said a word about why the marriage hadn't worked or what had gone wrong. Just like he hadn't said anything bad about Jane. I respected that. Izzy told me before I came tonight that how a person talks about their ex is a reflection of how they'll talk about you when or if it ends. "It will tell you everything you need to know," she had said.

The fact that he didn't try to disparage her made me think he was really as nice as he seemed. Jane was crazy to have let him go. I

82

didn't dwell on it too much, though. Answers would come eventually. For now, he had told me something he hadn't told anyone else, and that was enough.

As we walked, still, my no-dating rule weighed heavily in the back of my mind. Would this be the first and final date? It wasn't like it had officially gone out the window, but here I was, toeing the line— or maybe I'd already crossed it. And Jane . . . what would she do if she ever found out I went on a date with her husband? That I *kissed* him? She could *never* find out.

At this point, I just hoped this whole night would stay buried, hidden from the one person it could hurt most. I didn't want to think about how it would be at the office tomorrow. I didn't want to think about what would happen next between John and me. I didn't want to think about any of it. It was good to feel free of all those questions, for now.

Tonight wasn't about what Jane would think or how all of this would affect my job—it was about *him*. About *us*. And somehow, focusing on that made ignoring all the consequences a little easier.

Chapter Nine

Since I was already miles from home, I figured I could walk John back to his hotel and catch the subway from there. We were having such a fun time, despite it being freezing cold, I didn't want the night to end quite yet. I used to use the check arriving at the end of a first date as the perfect excuse to make my exit, retreat home, and slip into sweatpants for an early night. But not tonight. I never wanted this night to end.

The winter air carried the scent of damp stone, coffee from nearby cafés, and the faint warmth of wood smoke curling from chimneys. Walking through the cobblestone streets of the Meatpacking District back to his hotel made me glad, once again, I'd left the heels behind. *Of course he was staying in the Meatpacking District*, one of the most expensive areas in the city. As we walked, it felt like we were old lovers—hugging, stopping every few blocks to kiss, holding hands—a built-in familiarity and comfort, as if we'd been reunited after a lifetime apart. I'd never felt so comfortable with anyone, especially not so quickly. Maybe this was what all those people meant when they talked about soul mates.

We passed the brownstones, each one over one hundred years

old, and I couldn't shake the feeling that I was on the set of *Sex and the City*. I was Carrie Bradshaw—a just-over-broke girl working in publishing scraping by, and he was my Mr. Big: much older, towering over me, mysterious, sexy and technically previously committed. John . . . he smelled like a warm mix of sandalwood and musk, earthy and comforting, lingering in the night air. I loved it. I loved this. It was like the reality of my life had completely fallen away, like I was in a fairy tale.

Ten minutes later, we arrived outside his hotel and faced each other, his arms wrapped around me, keeping me warm.

"Do you want to come up?" His voice was deeper, sexier than I remembered it being.

I shot him a playful "shame on you for even thinking it" look, shaking my head with a knowing smile—the kind that said, *I see what you're up to, mister.*

"No." He laughed, his head dropping back. "Not like that. I promise." He let go of me to extend his little finger. "I pinky promise."

"A man of his word? I guess we will see," I said, locking pinkies with him. Our eyes met. "No funny business."

"Cross my heart and hope to die." He made an X with his hands over his heart, then grabbed my hand. We ran inside like two giddy kids going to play together at recess.

———

The next morning, I woke up in a bed. In *his bed*. Or, his hotel bed. My date-night clothes were still completely intact. There was no sign of any funny business from my immediate assessment. We hadn't slept together, though we had. We talked. We laughed. We kissed. We kissed some more. A very PG-13 night. It was perfect. I wanted to wait for the next time for the rest—if, of course, there was a next time. I'd made that mistake before—one too many times on first dates —and I wasn't going to make it with John. With someone who could actually become something. I especially didn't want to be *that girl* with him.

Lying there, staring at the ceiling, I couldn't deny it anymore—the no-dating rule was gone, shattered. If he asked to see me again, I wouldn't say no. In fact, I would jump at the chance. I wasn't sure when I'd let go of it, but it was gone, and here I was, breaking my own rules like they never existed. It felt worth risking everything just to spend more time with John. The rest I could figure out later.

When I was with him, I was someone else—someone I didn't recognize—but I liked it. I knew this would affect my life, my work, my relationship with Jane. God, Jane. Did I feel guilty for being here? Of course. She was still in the picture, and always would be. I probably should have felt worse about sleeping in her husband's hotel room. But when I was with John, it was like nothing else existed. Like we were in a bubble, just us, untouched by anything outside.

It wasn't smart. I knew that. But for some reason, it felt worth it. Worth the guilt. Worth the risk. Because when I was with him, I felt something real, something I had never felt. And that was enough to make everything else fade away. For now, at least.

I scanned the gorgeous hotel room. God, this place was even better in the morning light. Bright. Everything was immaculate, from the scent of the sheets to the elegance of the decor. I could get used to this. I stretched out on the king-size bed, feeling like I'd woken up in a world where every detail was designed for pure pleasure and luxury. This was a different side of New York. I guess this was Manhattan when you had money. The hard carved marble countertops, the crisp white linens, the city below—it was the kind of luxury that felt so far removed from my cramped two-bedroom apartment, where the ceiling leaked every time it rained and the walls were thin enough to hear my neighbors' arguments.

As I slowly regained full consciousness, something felt off. I blinked into the morning light, and then it hit me: He was gone.

"John?" I called out. A long deafening silence was the only response. No answer. No sign of him.

Shit. *Shit.*

Was this it—the moment I'd always feared after a date? But this time it was with someone I actually liked? The realization slammed into me like a ton of bricks. Had I completely misread the entire night? I could handle the usual first-date exit, sure, but not from John. He was gone, and not even with the satisfaction of getting what all men wanted. There wasn't a trace of him. This might potentially be my rock bottom. Time to get the hell out.

Panic clawed at me as I scrambled to collect my things, desperate to escape with whatever dignity I had left. This place was massive— and where the hell was my purse? I searched under the bed, then the bathroom, each place more frantic than the last, my mind struggling to remember where my drunken self had tossed my things.

Fuck. I was going to have to face him at the office soon enough. I don't know if it would be possible to be more humiliated.

How could I have been so stupid? Last night, I was practically floating, thinking this could actually *be* something. The way he talked to me, the way he looked at me—God, it felt like we were meant to be. That sounded so naïve now that I was alone in this hotel room. No note. No hint of the guy who had made me feel so sure of myself just hours ago. I felt like an idiot. How could I have misread everything? The way he treated me, talked to me, made me feel like we were the only two people in the world—and now, this.

I wanted to scream. This wasn't who I was supposed to be. Not the girl desperately searching for her purse, scrambling to leave before she fell apart completely. After finally deciding to cave on her rule that would assure her career success, thinking *he* would be worth it.

I ran for the door, my mind jumping between waves of absolute shame and desperate attempts to pull myself together enough to make a clean getaway. I tried to remember what day it was, deeply regretting the three martinis that had me in a haze, maybe even a little drunk still. When I reached the door, I prayed that my bag would be there so I could get out—preferably without running into him in the lobby. I caught a glimpse of myself in the mirror: mascara smudged from my five-star sleep. Perfect. I was fully prepared for my "fifty streets up and seven avenues over" walk of shame.

There it was! I grabbed my purse. It was sitting right next to the door, thank God. I flung the door open—

There was John, standing in the doorway, holding two coffees, fumbling for his room key. He looked up at me, smiled, and said, "Good morning, sunshine. How did you sleep?" His tone was light. Not the tone of a man who was trying to escape from a date the night before.

I froze, my brain scrambling for a believable excuse as to why I was standing at the door ready to escape. He hadn't . . . *left me?* He had gone to get us coffee, no less? He glanced down at my purse, then back at me, his smile widening just enough to let me know he understood exactly what was happening.

"No way you're sneaking out on me," he said, shifting both coffees into one of his massive hands. "I got us coffee, and from the looks of it, we both need it."

My body relaxed just a little. He hadn't ditched me. I'd been ready to accept my worst fear coming true—finally letting my guard down and making an exception for a second date, only to be abandoned. I had convinced myself he'd regret last night, that I'd made a fool of myself. But here he was, standing in front of me with that smile, looking at me like he didn't want me to leave. Actually he looked like he wanted me to *stay*.

I stepped back to let him in. The room was still bigger than my entire apartment, but somehow, with him in it, it was warmer, cozier.

"I guessed an Americano with almond milk," he said. "Hope that was a safe bet." He was totally unfazed by the fact that I'd just been caught red-handed trying to sneak out of his hotel room. He was already dressed for the day, looking like he had a full nine hours of sleep. How the hell did he look so refreshed while I looked closer to a raccoon found in a trash can?

I narrowed my eyes at him before slowly reaching for the caffeine that was about to bring me back to life. Was this all some act? Or was last night as real as I thought it was, before he was nowhere to be found?

"Thank you. You didn't have to, but I'm glad you did."

I took a sip. "How did you know I like Americanos?" I asked, trying to sound casual, though the warmth spreading through me was anything but.

He shrugged, his smile turning a little smug. "Like I said, lucky guess."

"Hmm," was all I could manage. Instead of being offended by his presumption, like I would have with most men, I felt . . . seen. This was the kind of thoughtful gesture I hadn't realized I'd been craving. Like I wanted to let my guard down again . . . a little.

"Would you want to get some breakfast? I thought we could do that and take a walk along the Hudson," he asked, sitting on the couch, sipping his coffee.

My eyes narrowed, and I shook my head in disbelief. Who *was* this guy? What the hell was going on? He didn't kick me out, *and* he wanted to extend this already extremely long date? This was his last day here. And he wanted to spend it with me?

It was like everything I had experienced in the dating scene, my whole understanding of dating, all my rules, were being thrown out the window. Maybe all my terrible first dates had finally given me some good karma. The hopeless romantic part of me was head over heels. Of course I wanted to stay. We could lie in bed all day, make out, order room service, watch a movie, and fall for each other. Just like in the movies. I wanted that. I needed that.

But the responsible Sarah, the Sarah who was going to be senior editor, the Sarah who wants to be mentored by Jane Reynolds, slammed into me like an ice-cold wave. It was Wednesday. I had to go to work. Where I would see Jane, and be reminded that my career still needed to be a priority, my promotion. *That* was the priority. I was reminded that this—whatever *this* was—could unravel everything

I'd been working for. Reality was definitely not as fun as the fairy tale I had been living in last night.

Instead of letting myself sink into his arms and pretend I had no responsibilities for just a little longer, I forced a smile and said, "That sounds amazing. I would love to . . . but I really have to get to work."

"I totally understand," he replied. "It was worth a try to see if I could spend a little more time with you. Thanks for coming all the way out here, I know it was a long way from your neck of the woods." Spoken like a true Midwesterner.

"You're leaving tomorrow, right?" I wasn't sure what answer I was hoping for by asking the question.

I couldn't help but study him. He seemed . . . different. Like our conversations last night had opened something inside of him. I looked at his crisp shirt and expensive shoes, then back at my outfit from last night.

What was this guy's angle? Why was John Reynolds, VP of Acquisitions, so interested in spending time with me? It wouldn't be a status move for him. He could have anyone. To move from Jane to me? Why me? Compared to Jane, I was . . . horribly ordinary.

He took a step closer, and then his lips were on mine—a soft kiss that sent a jolt of warmth straight through my body, rivaling the piping hot coffee I had just drank. My chest tightened, and for a moment I forgot everything else.

"I do . . . leave tomorrow," he said as we broke apart, his voice deep and sincere.

I pulled away, the reality of my breath—less than fresh from sleep —making me self-conscious. I quickly wrapped my arms around him to avoid another bad-breath kiss.

"Okay," I said, my voice betraying none of the uncertainty swirling inside me. My heart was pounding, but I forced myself to keep my expression neutral. What did this mean? Was he going to forget all of this once he got back to his real life? Was this just another moment I'd have to leave behind, hidden away like the others before it?

I had this strange feeling. One that made my chest swell with something that felt like lust, but deeper, fuller. My mind was a tangled mess of certainty and doubt. Everything about last night, every word we shared, every look, told me it was real. It felt like home. I fit into him like pieces of a puzzle clicking into place. I couldn't deny it—he was the one for me, and somehow, I was the one for him. Despite all my doubting, my questions, I knew. There was a quiet confidence in me that this was what I'd been waiting for.

But then those "buts" crept in and clouded the clarity of my heart.

But we could never be together.

But he was married to Jane.

But he was a decade older than me.

But he lived in Chicago—for now.

I didn't know what that meant yet, but the fact that he was coming to New York could change a lot, couldn't it?

Once he moved here, we'd all be in the office together. Me, John, Jane, Willow, Theo, and Izzy. That alone would change everything. It would be all business. There was no way we could be lovey-dovey at work. Even after the divorce was final, I doubted Jane would approve of us being together. Even something as simple as going out for dinner in the city would always carry the risk of running into someone from work, making everything feel too exposed.

And yet, this part of me, this electricity I had been experiencing with him, felt so real. This desire that I had to be with him, to throw all my rules out the window, to risk not working with Jane if it meant I could be with him. I was willing to risk everything if it meant being with him. A microscopically small part of me still believed I could be with him *and* succeed in my career, maybe even still work with Jane and learn from her. And I wanted to hold on to that kernel of hope. No matter how small it was.

"I had a great time," I told him. "Thank you so much for dinner. I have to run so I can make it to work on time."

He nodded in understanding. He looked at me. Into me. Into my soul. Into my heart. As if he wanted to crack it open and live there with me. As if he wanted to say something but couldn't. As if circumstances limited his ability to fully communicate everything he felt.

Despite his inability to articulate (ironic for a guy in publishing), he grabbed my arms and pulled me into one final kiss. And boy, did we kiss. I kissed John like it was the last time I might ever kiss him. There was a chance that it might be. But deep down I knew it was only the beginning for us—at least I hoped it was.

I felt the words "I love you" trying to escape my body, like something possessed coming from deep inside me, but I stopped them before they reached my lips, saving myself from humiliation before eight in the morning. Our noses grazed, then I gave him one last look, my cheeks flushed, and grabbed for the golden handle on the door I'd almost escaped through minutes earlier.

As I walked quickly down the hall, I ducked my head like I was dodging bullets. John yelled behind me, "Hey, Sarah!"

I turned around and tried to change the look on my face from one of fear that this would be just another first date to one of casual confidence, as if nothing could rattle me. Like I assumed Jane would look.

"Next time I see you, I'd like to take advantage of those catering lessons!" He smiled and waved.

I felt a slight relief, relief that this might not be just a first date, that it would be one of many. At the very least, he just said he wanted to see me again. That was hopeful, right? I puckered my lips to give him an air kiss and winked. "You wish," I said as he stood there beaming, his smile so wide it took over his entire face.

"You little rebel," Izzy squealed, her mouth half filled with lettuce. She bribed me to tell her about my date—affair?—by promising to buy me lunch. I was only leaving the office, and all the work I had to get done today, if this food was free.

She oh-so-dramatically lowered her clear-rimmed glasses and gave me a suggestive look like I was Monica in the Lewinsky trial.

"Izzy, stop," I said, trying to hold back a smile. "Nothing happened!"

"Seriously?" Her voice now laced with disappointment. "You idiot!" She said, slapping my shoulder. "Why didn't you sleep with him? You had a golden, once-in-a-lifetime opportunity to bang John freaking Reynolds, and instead you turned into a nun—good old Mother Teresa—for the night? What were you thinking?"

"Iz," I replied, not able to hold back a smile, "I think this could really turn into something. And you know as well as I do that sleeping with a guy on the first date doesn't usually result in him sticking around for long. We've both seen that trope play out too many times, in books and in our own lives."

"Fair enough," she admitted. "But still. Come on. It's John Reynolds. Who cares if you only meet him once? That's like turning down Taylor Swift concert tickets just because they're in the nose-bleeds. It will still be a fabulous show from wherever you sit."

I raised an eyebrow. "Yeah, but sleeping with him on the first date is like sneaking into a concert and getting kicked out before the show starts."

Izzy stuffed another forkful of salad into her mouth. "Sometimes it's worth getting kicked out just to get the picture and say you were there."

"Funny." I scoffed. She never ceased to amaze me with her wit.

"Did you get any info on the Jane situation?"

"Some. Yes. They're over. Have been for a while. The divorce is just dragging on. He didn't say much about her, but my guess is she is afraid of losing all the money."

Izzy leaned in. "I knew it. Typical. Always about the money. So what's his deal? Did he give you the 'I'm just waiting for the paper-work to go through' line?"

I nodded. "Sort of, something like that. But it didn't feel like a line. He seemed . . . honest. Drained from it all. Tired. Like he'd been carrying the whole thing for so long."

Izzy rolled her eyes. "Please, they always look tired. It's their best move—to make you feel sorry for them. Next thing you know, you're playing therapist instead of their girlfriend. Or in your case . . . mistress."

I hesitated for a moment, feeling a sharp tug of defensiveness. "I don't think it's that simple," I said. Izzy meant well, but something about her tone rubbed me the wrong way. Maybe it was because I was already questioning my own actions, and hearing her talk about John that way made me feel like I didn't know what was really going on. "I felt something. It was real. He is telling the truth. You can't fake that. Plus, you know me. I don't *want* to date. But I have been thinking. What if he is the only love of my life and I miss it? If it is and I am supposed to end up with him, it wouldn't necessarily stop me from becoming senior editor."

"If anything, he could probably help me get there. Jane did it with John by her side. I figure I could do it too," I said, trying to convince myself, what I was doing wasn't morally grey. Izzy sat quiet, listening. Absently swirling her straw in her iced coffee, the ice clinking against the glass. She hadn't said anything yet, but her silence was louder than words.

I paused, my comment hanging in the air like a weight. My fingers toyed with the edge of my napkin. "I mean, if we did pursue things . . . she wouldn't know. No one would know, at least in the beginning." My voice was quieter now, unsure. I glanced up at Izzy, meeting her gaze. "I just mean he could give me some pointers and help me come up with some creative ideas to secure the spot, plus we could get to know each other and see if it is even worth it to try things."

I looked down at the table, avoiding Izzy's eyes. She sighed, pushing her drink aside, but didn't say anything right away. Instead, she picked up a sugar packet, folding it neatly in half and then unfolding it again, a nervous habit I'd seen her do before. I couldn't tell if she was stalling or choosing her words carefully, but the silence was suffocating.

"Given where their dynamic is as of now, us being together in any sense of the word would have to be hidden . . . from everyone."

"Damn, so you're *really* serious about pursuing this thing," Izzy said. "What's the plan? Are you going to tell him how you feel? Are you going to wait it out till their divorce is finalized? Are you still going to try to get mentored by Jane?"

All the questions I had been asking myself were thrown back at me. "This sounds really fucked up, but I don't think I want to wait until the divorce is over. I really like him, and I can tell he really likes me. I don't see why we can't at least get to know each other so that when the divorce is finalized, we can just *be* together publicly. Jane seems to have moved on to Peter, according to Willow. I don't see why John can't do the same. But for the sake of my career, and his, we would just have to keep it on the down low for now." I rubbed my forehead with my finger. "Jesus, what am I saying? What a love triangle, huh?"

Izzy leaned forward in her chair. "Love triangle? Babe, this is more like a love pentagon. You, John, Jane, his baggage, and that whole pile of money they're fighting over. What's one more corner?" she said. "But hey, at least you're not alone in the drama. You've got lots of company in the pentagon, right?" Her voice was light, but there was an understanding and support behind her teasing.

I threw my napkin at her. "Thanks for the vote of confidence."

Izzy cackled. "Hey, I'm just saying—if you're going to jump in the deep end and swim with sharks, at least make sure the water is filled with five-star hotels and good sex."

I rolled my eyes trying to hold back a smile. "Do you have any actual advice for me?"

Izzy raised an eyebrow, leaning forward a little. "If you're serious about John and want to keep it quiet, you're going to have to be really careful. You need to separate work and personal life completely. Compartmentalization is key."

I nodded.

"Keep your head down in the office. Make sure not to say anything about it to Theo or Willow. They can always smell a new relationship on me from a mile away. Make sure you focus on your career goals, and don't let your work slip until the divorce is finalized."

"First off, I would never let my goals slip," I interjected.

"Yeah, yeah," she brushed me off before continuing. "Make sure you're always showing Jane that you're loyal to her and the team. If you can handle the balance of keeping your relationship with John outside of work and proving your worth in the office, you could have the best of both worlds. Just don't let anyone see anything that could make them question your ability at work. Trust me, it can be easy to get sucked into a relationship bubble, especially if it is a secret." It was like she had personal experience with this. "Don't give them any reason to question you, and when the divorce is finalized, you may just be able to keep John and get the promotion, and maybe even have gotten some great mentorship from Jane."

I nodded my head, absorbing her wisdom. "Okay, I can do that. Stay focused at work, separate that from my relationship with John. Simple."

"And don't tell *anyone* at the office," she reminded me. "You trust too easily. I think it's that small-town thing you have going on. You cannot trust anyone. Especially the people who are gunning for the same promotion. You might think you can trust someone with the information, then next thing you know, they are outing you to Jane, Theo, or Willow and you lose your job completely."

I exhaled sharply, taking mental notes. "Okay, right. I'll keep that in mind. No telling anyone."

I hated keeping secrets. I hated hiding things. But if that's what I had to do . . . just until the divorce was over, if it meant feeling how I felt while with him last night . . . I could do that to protect John. To protect me. To protect us.

Chapter Ten

W hen I finally made it home after work, it was nearly nine. I was tired, but I needed to edit a manuscript that Willow had asked me to review. Awaiting me was *The Choice of a Lifetime* by one of the top authors at Regent, Clara Hawthorne. It was a big deal for me to get a chance to work on this project. And since Clara's books often explored the complexities of modern romantic relationships—a theme that felt all too relevant in my life since I met John—I was excited at the hopes that I could learn a thing or two.

I scrolled through the pages, landing on a page that read:

"In the great tapestry of love and ambition, choices are woven with threads of desire and fear. Each choice echoes the choices that came before it, whispering tales of what might have been, urging us to find our own way through the noise."

For some reason, my mother popped into my mind. Painstakingly beautiful. Irresistible to any man. After leaving my father for "greener pastures," she took us on a roller coaster ride of new homes every eight months and new boyfriends every eight weeks. An endless search for the same lasting love she had just left behind. As each man came and went, my mother—and, by default, my sister and I—felt the sting of a paper cut of abandonment, each one leaving a reminder that we were never quite enough to hold their attention for more than a season.

"Each choice echoes the choices that came before it."

Watching my mother chase fleeting romances left a mark on my heart that I didn't fully understand. I remembered how excited she would be with each new boyfriend, only to fade as the excitement wore off, like they became an old pair of shoes she had worn and was now bored with. With each of their departures, I felt that familiar sting of loss.

When I was a young girl, I promised myself I would never follow in her footsteps. I would never jump from man to man. I would stay in a relationship even when things were hard.

Sometimes I wondered if that was why I avoided relationships entirely.

"Choices are woven with threads of desire and fear."

When I came to New York, I threw myself into my career, keeping busy and pouring my energy into projects and deadlines. There was comfort in ambition—something I could control—while avoiding the messiness of love and the pain that I had seen come with it, time and time again. I resisted becoming my mother (don't we all). And I didn't want to mirror my father, relegated to being alone because my mom wanted someone new. I'd carefully crafted a life where I'd never have to worry about either, because my sole focus was on pursuing my dreams—on my career.

With John, though, it felt different. For the first time, the fear of becoming like my parents—of getting caught up in something messy —didn't seem to matter. Even though on paper, it looked just about as messy as it could get.

I knew how ugly divorce could be. I had seen it firsthand. Part of me knew that John and Jane's split would be just as complicated as what I saw growing up, even worse with the amount of money between them. Still, when I thought about being with him, it didn't feel like I was repeating their mistakes. It felt different. I didn't know how, but I knew that it would all turn out okay. There was a sense of peace and safety I felt with John. And I wanted to trust that, despite all the ways my mind was trying to convince me otherwise.

I was several chapters deep into editing when my phone buzzed and brought me back to the moment. I hadn't expected to hear from John after this morning, but I silently said a prayer to whoever was up there pulling the strings, asking for it to be him who had texted me.

John:

> Did you make it through the day without much sleep? Sorry to keep you out so late.

Seeing his name made me smile. He didn't need to text me, but he had. And for a moment, I let myself just enjoy that without over-thinking it.

Me:

> Can I tell you a secret?

John:

> Always.

I wasn't sure if what I wanted to say was too risky, as I'd only been on one date with him, but I shook my head, cringed, and hit send.

Me:

> I miss you . . . already. Is that weird?

Only a few moments passed before my phone rang. He was calling me.

"Hello?" I answered, trying to sound casual, feeling insanely vulnerable after revealing that I'd missed him less than ten seconds ago.

"I can't have you missing me," he said, his tone smug.

"Who is this?" I joked.

"That cater-waiter you hit on at the Gala the other night. The one who's head over heels for the girl he just met. Ring a bell?"

"Oh, yes I *think* I remember you . . . Mr. No Coattails, right?"

"For what it's worth, I miss you too . . . already," he said.

It was like a dream. Despite everything—Jane, the status discrepancies, his marital status—he called me. He wanted to talk to me *after* our first date. I was in unfamiliar territory, but I liked it.

"Maybe the next time you come back to New York, you can stay at my place," I said, testing whether he would bite on the idea of another date.

"I would love that. Sadly I head back to Chicago tonight, but I do owe you a trip up north on the island. What's your week looking like?" he asked. I couldn't tell if he was just asking about my schedule or if he was hinting at something else.

"Just a regular week. Friday is a work-from-home day, so I'll just be home. I am planning to work most of the weekend. Trying to secure that senior editor position, not sure if you remember Willow sharing that at the Gala when we met. Why?"

"Of course I remember. It's so awesome! I love that you're going for it. The senior editor role would be a perfect fit for you. I have no doubt you'll get it. Is there anything I can do to help you with that?"

I wanted to ask him a million questions, but I figured I could ask him the next time I saw him. I didn't want it to seem like I was using him for his industry knowledge. "That is so nice. I would love that. I will think about that and let you know."

"Please do. So hypothetically, how early could you leave the office on Thursday?" he asked.

"Probably around four depending on how early I can get a start that morning. Why?"

"Do you have a Delta Skymiles account?" he asked without answering my question.

"Uh . . . yeah, why?" I pulled up the number without asking questions. What was he planning?

"Can you give me that number, please?" he asked.

"Um, sure." I searched for the number in my categorized list of a million log-ins and passwords. "934105723, but why do you need my—"

"I am booking you on the last flight from LGA to Chicago on Thursday," he said with complete certainty.

"Are you serious?!" I let out a squeal of excitement.

"What's your email? I'll send you confirmation right now. You leave at 8:59 p.m. and land at 10:30 p.m."

"You seriously just booked me a flight to Chicago?" I asked. Was this a dream? Before John, I could barely get a guy to open a door for me. Now, here I was, days away from boarding a flight to see him in Chicago. What had I been doing dating twenty-something guys? Maybe I should've started dating older men years ago.

As the excitement hit a peak, a small weight settled in my stomach. I had plans. Plans to work a lot this weekend. Work I was determined to get done, with the new position on the line. A full weekend away would eat into all the extra hours I had planned to put in. Izzy's words from earlier at lunch rang on repeat. "Make sure you focus on your career goals, and don't let your work slip." But spending time with John in Chicago sounded amazing. I supposed I could work on the flights, plus I could always work while I was there. I was sure John occasionally worked on the weekends. If I wanted to have it all, I guess this was what that looked like, making both work.

"Yes, I did. Now make sure you're not late for your flight like you were for our date," he said.

I glanced at the phone screen as the flight notification came through my email. The idea of seeing him, of stepping into this whirlwind with him, had me beyond excited. For once, I was being pursued—like someone actually wanted me enough to make plans, to make it happen. To book a flight. While a sliver of hesitation hung in the air, I pushed it aside and said, "Thank you, John. I'm so excited to see you again."

"So am I. I can't wait for you to see where I am from. I am going to take you to all my favorite spots," he gushed.

I pulled up the email to add the flight details to my calendar when John interrupted me.

"Hey, just a heads-up," he said, his tone shifting to something more serious. "Don't put this on your work calendar. Jane, Theo, and Willow might see it. I'd rather keep this under wraps for now."

My stomach dropped—I hadn't even considered that. My fingers hovered over the save button as I realized how careless I'd been. "Of course. Thank you for the reminder—it's like you were reading my mind."

I needed to be more calculated, like Izzy had suggested. Secrets weren't my strong suit, I had to adjust. We said goodbye, and after we hung up, a laugh escaped me as I scrolled through the flight details again. I was going to Chicago.

I couldn't afford to mess this up. Every decision, every moment had to be deliberate—just like editing a manuscript. Every action needed precision.

I scrolled through the flight details to see if he booked me an aisle seat so I had space to stretch my legs and be comfortable during the flight. Plus I usually had to pee a lot. The booking confirmation read 'Seat 4A.' What seat was that? I pulled up the seat map to see he had booked me in first class.

Holy shit, he booked me first class!

I had never flown first class before. Having grown up in Idaho, I had never even been on a plane until I moved to New York. And once you lived in the city, there wasn't much reason to leave.

I opened my text thread with Izzy and sent her a message.
Me:

> I'm going to Chicago on a first class flight, compliments of John Reynolds!!!

Izzy texted back:

> No way. You better bring me back a souvenir.

Me:

> Done. Will you cover for me if TW asks where I am this weekend?

The guilt of asking Izzy to lie for me felt awful, especially if she had to lie to Theo and Willow. But I didn't have a choice. A lot of times on the weekends, the four of us would spend time together—grab dinner, or watch a movie at their place. I couldn't afford to have them question why I'd suddenly disappeared for the weekend.

Izzy:

> Of course, I've got your back. Just don't get yourself into any trouble out there in Chicago, all right?

I read her message and send a prayer emoji. I opened the text thread with John and typed:

> You booked me first class?
>
> 1. You didn't have to.
>
> 2. P.S. I am so excited that you did. It's my first time.
>
> 3. Thank you so much.

John responded:

> Nothing but the best for you.

Aria Devi

> First time, huh? I guess that means I have to make sure all your 'firsts' with me are just as memorable . . .

> Can't wait to see you.

My cheeks flushed:

> You're setting the bar high, Reynolds. Don't think I won't hold you to it. XX

A kissy face emoji popped into my inbox.

I smiled, setting my phone down as I paced the room, excitement and nerves buzzing through me. As much as I wanted to let myself celebrate, I couldn't ignore the weight of what lay ahead. If John and I were really doing this, I needed clarity from him as to what this all was.

Izzy covering for me this weekend and keeping it off my work calendar was a good start, but I'd have to navigate the rest carefully. Once I got there, John and I would figure it out together. Once the divorce was finalized, we wouldn't have to hide anymore. We could be out in the open. But for now, we needed a plan for what the next few months would look like, especially if it involved secret cross-country trips and taking me away from my work.

Chapter Eleven

T he day I was leaving for Chicago, I sat at my desk, eager for my time to leave the office, grab my bags, and fly to see John. But the more I daydreamed about him, the more Jane, of all people, consumed my thoughts. I found myself checking her Instagram obsessively, drawn to her in a strange, twisted way. She wasn't just the benchmark for success at work—now she was becoming everything I wanted to be in my personal life as well. It wasn't lost on me that I would be in what used to be her home, later tonight.

I glanced at her office for the hundredth time. She was in a meeting with one of the senior editors, Jackie. Her arms folded and leaning back in her chair. God, I wanted to be like her. I would kill for her job. Hell, I would settle to just be the senior editor in there with her, right now. I dreamed of having her confidence. Her looks. As pathetic as it may be, I caught my thoughts drifting to her all throughout the day. Asking myself, *How would Jane walk right now? Talk? Act in this meeting? How would she stand?* I would adjust accordingly. Closing the gap between my deficit and her awesomeness. I wanted her lifestyle, her fashion sense, her wealth. All of her connections.

Admittedly, I wanted her husband too.

Maybe there was some part of me that saw how John used to feel about her, and if I could just be a little more like her, then there was a chance that one day he might care for me just as much.

I forced my eyes back to my computer and cringed at the thought. I couldn't believe I was doing this. That I was about to jump on a plane to spend the weekend with her husband. I felt terrible, torn between my genuine feelings for John and my unsettling desire to become her. While Jane and I weren't friends, or even close colleagues, I felt an odd underlying loyalty to her. One that I was clearly ignoring. Despite that tug, that invisible bond, what I felt for John was clearly stronger.

I still fully intended to seek out Jane for mentorship once I returned; I figured next week's meeting she had asked me to sit in on was a perfect start. Clearly she saw something in me if she asked me to be there. There wasn't any reason I couldn't take advantage of the opportunity to learn from her and ask her a few questions. Compartmentalization was the name of the game.

I stole one last glance at her, telling myself it would be the final one for the day. I needed to focus—on work, on my trip, on anything but her. But as my eyes drifted over to see how she was handling the meeting, her gaze flicked up—locking onto mine. Like she had felt it. Felt me.

For a split second, I couldn't decipher her expression. Curiosity? Suspicion? Or maybe just a coincidence? My breath caught as she held my gaze a moment too long before turning back to Jackie, leaving me frozen, pulse racing, like she'd seen straight through me.

———

It was the first and only time I wished my flight was longer. I could get used to first-class legroom, hot towels, complimentary champagne, and great service. This was certainly my preferred way of flying.

I landed in Chicago, butterflies swirling in my stomach. John had promised to pick me up, but before grabbing my bag, I stopped in the ladies' room to freshen up. Under the harsh fluorescent lighting, I caught my reflection in the mirror, and insecurity hit me hard.

I ran my finger across my forehead, frowning slightly as lines appeared between my brows. Jane's face never moved. She was often expressionless, her Botox ensuring no trace of a wrinkle. For the first time, my ability to show expression was a flaw. I wanted my face to be frozen too.

My gaze dropped to my lips—thin and dry from the winter air. I bit them, fighting the urge to compare, but Jane's plump, syringe-filled lips flashed in my mind. Even my hair looked duller than usual. I put some oil on the ends and grabbed my phone to text Izzy before I could overthink.

Me:

> Botox date when I get back? My treat.

Not that I could afford it.

Her reply came almost immediately.

Izzy:

> Eh, no thanks. I got a headache last time.
> Sarah, you are beautiful. Your face is
> supposed to move. It's a good thing.

I stared at her response, caught between frustration and guilt. As if freezing my face would somehow make me senior editor. As if plumper lips or smoother skin would get me any closer to being like Jane—or to John choosing me.

But the thought lingered, stubborn as ever, even as I tucked my phone away and headed for baggage claim. I had barely known about

Jane for two weeks, yet I had spent most of my time thinking about her husband or comparing every inch of myself to her. I resolved to stop obsessing, determined to hold on to who I was before this insidious comparison took over. Since I was 800 miles away from her and the office this weekend, I was sure it would make it easier.

Outside the baggage claim, a Bentley convertible pulled past—it had to be at least a $400,000 car. "Jesus, there must be some major wealth in Chicago," I said to myself. I watched as it drove by, scanning the line of cars behind it for John. Then, someone yelled my name from behind me.

"Sarah!"

Please don't let it be someone I know, I thought, scrambling for an alibi. *Maybe I could say I was here for a project with the Chicago office.* I turned, bracing myself for impact. My heart skipped a beat as I did a double take. It was him—John. *Driving the Bentley.* Of course. My jaw nearly hit the concrete.

"Wow," I murmured, my stomach flipping with excitement—not just because it was him, but because I was about to ride in a car that probably cost more than I'd ever make in a year. This trip *was* full of firsts.

He stepped out, looking as handsome as always. He wore a baseball cap and dark sunglasses, a subtle attempt at keeping a low profile. Maybe he didn't want anyone to recognize him—or us. "Let me grab that for you," he said, putting my bag in the trunk. As he did, I caught a glimpse of him checking the surroundings, scanning the area. It was as though he was making sure no one could put two and two together.

As we got in the car, he took off his sunglasses and smiled. "I always run into people I know at the airport. We don't need any . . . attention right now." His tone was casual, but there was something protective in the way he said it. Like he was trying to shield us—me—from the world.

I couldn't help but smile back. "Got it," I said softly, and then, before I could say anything else, he leaned in and kissed me. Like it had been years, not days, since we'd shared a kiss. The weight of his lips, the reassurance in the touch, and everything about the moment felt more real than ever.

———

Chicago was more beautiful than I'd imagined. It wasn't New York, but it had its charisma—cold and snowy, but charming. We arrived at his apartment, and I stepped through the doorway. A knot twisted in my stomach. Correction: *their* apartment. The place that they had once shared, and had built together. Full of their memories.

John wheeled my suitcase in behind me. I inhaled the scent of pine and cinnamon. This was a home, not like my apartment that was filled with used furniture from the street corners and Facebook Marketplace. This place was for grown-ups. Grown-ups with money.

As I walked through the space, there was leather furniture, ornate rugs, furs draped throughout, music filling each room with an fancy sound system. I could see Jane everywhere in the space. Elegant decorations that made it feel like a warm embrace. Beautiful and (I assumed) expensive art hung in every room. Large windows opened to a view of Lake Michigan, as if the apartment floated above the water. Immaculate. The kind of home where no matter what you needed, they probably had it somewhere. Juicers? They had two. Massage table? Yep. First aid kit? Of course.

John gave me the grand tour, showing me his office. I couldn't help but notice that some of Jane's things were still there. Her desk was now just a place to store papers and miscellaneous junk. Her trophies and photos had been shoved underneath it, gathering dust.

We walked past the gym and multiple bedrooms before finally reaching his room.

"You can unpack your things here, if you'd like. Make yourself comfortable," he said with a smile as he gave me privacy and headed to his office to get some work done.

The more I looked around, the more I realized I was in way over my head. I couldn't shake the weight of their history woven into the space. It was beautiful, yes, but it also felt like a reminder of what I would never have with John. The life that they built together. He had already built a life up the first time, and while that might be a first for me, I would never share that first experience with him. The walls, the decorations, the furniture all held echoes of the life he had with Jane, and I was an intruder, caught between the past and the future, living somewhere in between.

In the bathroom, her vanity sat. An ornately decorated makeup table with a mirror and a chair upholstered in a chic, feminine floral fabric. Where, I assumed, she used to sit each morning and get ready. As if by clearing it off, he'd tried to erase any memory of her, acting like her things didn't exist for so long that eventually he didn't see any of it at all. I imagined many of the hall closets still held her clothes, the ones she never bothered to come back for. I couldn't dare look; it might ruin me. He had tried to hide her, just out of sight so she wouldn't cross his mind.

As I unpacked my things, I turned my attention to the bed—black silk sheets, a large upholstered headboard and footboard, a million pillows. It had Jane written all over it. One side of the bed had his things, a watch, a book, a notepad and pen. On the other side, I noticed a tiny painted dish on the windowsill where Jane's wedding ring and jewelry must have once rested, now covered in dust. It was as if she had died here and he couldn't bear to put her things away, as if they were still frozen in time.

I was overwhelmed by the emotions of being here, with John, where Jane used to live. I was excited to be here with him, just the two of us. But seeing all of this, it was like she was here. Like she would never fully leave. Like it would never just be the two of us together, alone. She would always be present, like a ghost. Haunting the space. I thought this weekend would be easy, free from the pressure to become Jane, but instead, it might've been less painful to just continue stalking her from my desk.

The room closed in on me. The memories that clung to every corner, the scent of something that wasn't quite mine—everything felt foreign, like I didn't belong. My chest tightened, and I could feel my breath quickening. My hands were shaking. The thought of Jane, of her life with him, the life I could never have. It hit me all at once, the panic flooding in. What the hell was I doing? What had I gotten myself into? I squeezed my eyes shut, trying to steady myself, but the world was spinning too fast. I took deep breaths as I dropped to my knees. Breathing fast and heavy.

This wasn't just about John and Jane. It was about my future, my career, my values, the choices I was making. Could I really go through with this? I tried to take deep breaths, in and out, to calm myself down. I couldn't be caught having a full-blown panic attack in his room.

They're not together. They're not together. They're not together, I reminded myself, repeating it until the frantic thoughts started to slow.

When I was with John, I didn't question anything. But as I saw all of her things in this place, a million more questions flooded in. I took another breath, steadying myself. I had to focus on what was right in front of me—on us. As long as I could do that, just me and him, and keep her out of the equation as much as possible, I'd be fine. Being a part of this had been *my* choice, and I wasn't about to let anything or anyone, not even her, take that from me.

———

When morning came, things felt different. We started the day with coffee—John made it and brought it to me in bed. Another night of us sleeping together but not *sleeping* together. I had fallen asleep right after I came down from my panic, and when I woke up hours later, John was sleeping next to me. The light of day made everything seem a little more manageable. Maybe it was the rest, or maybe I was just starting to get used to the idea, but seeing all of Jane's things didn't feel as overwhelming now. It was almost like the room had transformed overnight, the weight of it all softened.

Maybe I had just overreacted because I was exhausted from the flight.

Coffee was followed by two hours of cuddling. It felt good that he wasn't rushing anything physical. Despite his wealth, success, and power, he was surprisingly respectful, not pushing for anything more.

The cuddling turned into a long walk by the water, our hands laced together. Later we went to his gym for a workout, followed by brunch at Urban Eats, the restaurant on the first floor of his building.

The bartender waved as soon as we stepped through the door, like a friend welcoming John home. The ambiance of the bar matched his style—rustic yet elegant, with soft leather seating, black metal beams, and a deep mahogany wood bar. It was warm and intimate, like an extension of him.

We slid onto two stools at the bar. The bartender was halfway through making John's tequila soda with an orange by the time we were seated. Obviously this wasn't John's first time here.

I gave him a look.

His deep laugh made me smile. It always did. "Don't judge," he said, grinning. "I live right upstairs, and I'm a bachelor who doesn't cook." He leaned in and whispered, "Besides, Parker hooks me up—I tip really well."

Parker returned with John's drink. "Parker, this is Sarah," John said, his tone casual. "She'll be staying here for a few days."

Parker looked at me, then glanced at John, then back at me. "She's pretty," he said, as if I wasn't sitting there. "What can I get you, darling?"

I smiled and reached out to shake his hand. "So nice to meet you, Parker. I'll have a mimosa, please." Parker raised his eyebrows at John as he turned to make my drink, a look that was hard to interpret—I wasn't sure if it was approval or judgment. I couldn't help but wonder if he'd mistaken me for Jane, or if John had introduced me in a way that made sure he wouldn't slip up and think I was her. We did look a lot alike, uncannily so. I brushed it off.

John leaned in close. I leaned back into his solid frame. Every touch felt electric, the tension between us building by the second.

"Do you bring women here often?" I asked, trying to dig for a glimpse into his world.

He took a sip from his drink and smiled. "Actually, you're the first person I ever brought here. I don't like to share this place. It's my little escape. I'd rather no one else know about it."

His knee brushed mine under the table and stayed there. "Well then," I said, "I'm honored to experience it with you."

He leaned closer, his arm slipping around my waist, kissing my cheek.

Parker returned with my mimosa. I raised my glass and smiled. "To tainting Urban Eats," I said with a grin.

John laughed, the sound deep and warm. "To enjoying it together." And we drank to that.

———

Once we got back to his apartment and the brunch buzz started to fade, he turned to me. "Since you planned to work this weekend. I figured maybe we could get a few hours in this afternoon?"

"That would be so helpful."

"Great, I have a few projects and accounts I need to move forward as well."

I couldn't help but feel supported. Even though he'd invited me here to spend time with him, he still wanted to ensure I stayed on track with my goals.

An hour into wading through my overwhelming pile of work, I got a text from Izzy.

> Yo, how's Loverville? By the way, I just got
> this message from Willow. What should I
> tell her?

Aria Devi

She attached a screenshot of her text exchange with Willow. The message read:

> Happy Friday! Would you and Sarah like to have dinner with us this weekend? We are thinking Gramercy Tavern.

Shit.

The Gramercy Tavern. I'd been wanting to go there for months. Their burgers were supposedly to die for. I hated missing dinner with Theo and Willow. It was always a great chance to learn from them and get some mentorship and guidance when it came to work.

I chewed my lip, trying to think of a logical excuse as to why I was already busy.

> Hey, it's great. JR is great.

> Can you tell her I have just been really swamped and need some down time? I'm taking the night for myself.

A minute later, Izzy texted back.

> Roger that. Will miss you. Text me any updates. Call me if you need anything.

Me:

> Will do. XX.

I sighed and threw my phone on the table. I had asked Izzy to cover for me, but it felt real now that it had come to it. I was asking Izzy to lie for me. To Willow and Theo! It was like a piece of my good-natured, ethical Midwestern soul had been ripped out and thrown into a burning dumpster. I never imagined I'd be keeping secrets from those I cared about, twisting truths, for some guy. And as I sat there I realized—I had officially broken not only my no-dating rule, but my no-second-date rule. I peeked into John's office, and the guilt within me settled. As if his presence alone were like anxiety medication.

He sat there going through papers on his desk. He wasn't just some guy. He was John Reynolds. And he flew me out here to be with him. I didn't even care that I had broken my rule. I would break any rule to be with this man.

As I stared at him, I realized—this wasn't just a few broken rules and a few white lies.

I was in way deeper than that.

Chapter Twelve

I could get used to this—spending mornings with John, working in separate rooms of his cozy apartment, sneaking kisses between phone calls and work sprints. We'd share dinner and recount our days. For a career-focused woman like me, it was a dream come true.

But it wasn't without its challenges. Not being able to post on social media about where I was, when I was used to posting multiple times a day, finding a blank white wall just to hop on a video call, or lying to some of my closest friends outside of Regent—Emma, Chloe, or Sloan—whenever they asked where I was. I hadn't told them what was really going on yet, and every time they called I had to lie. It felt terrible. Each little white lie gnawed at me. And this was just the first few days. Navigating this for the next ninety days would be . . . interesting, to say the least. I was hyperaware that if I slipped even once to the wrong person, it could risk my entire career.

The one thing I couldn't figure out was how Jane could ever walk away from John. He was incredible—kind, caring, attentive, and supportive. Maybe she knew something I didn't. Or maybe she had just been in search of something shiny and new.

We still hadn't slept together. I wondered if that was a bad sign? I told myself it was because of the marriage situation, that he was a respectful gentleman. But the more primal part of my brain wasn't so rational. *Mate for life*, it whispered. *Have sex with him, and that means you've won. He will have chosen you. You'll be safe, secure, and happy. You'll prove that you're better for him than Jane.*

That same primal part of me couldn't help but see Jane as competition. And John was the prize. Growing up as an athlete, I was naturally competitive. A part of me wanted to prove I was good enough for John to choose me over Jane. And while I cared for John, more deeply each day, if I was being honest, a small part of me saw being with him as a chance to show I could outshine Jane, in at least one area of life.

I glanced at John hovering above the stove, his broad shoulders and muscular back blocking my view of whatever he was cooking. A man was making me dinner.

It took me back. I remembered my father doing the same after my mother left. I was three years old when they split, and my dad became a one-man show. We would be at his house every few weekends, and he would be 'cooking' up bologna sandwiches on Wonder Bread with canned peaches on the side. Occasionally, he'd get creative—white rice with raisins and cinnamon. Ew. My favorite? Buckets of fried chicken, which we'd eat picnic-style on the kitchen floor.

Needless to say, my culinary expectations were low. And when John turned around, bowl in hand, I was glad they were. He placed a bowl of green slosh and a bag of chips on the table. It looked like he had heated up boxed soup. More like my dad than I'd realized.

"Bon appétit," he said, a sheepish grin spreading across his face. "Sorry this is so pathetic. I never cook. I usually eat downstairs."

"This looks great." I smiled and reached for the bowl. And it did . . . look great. Because he'd made it for me. It was sweet, in a way that filled my chest with warmth—a warmth that reminded me of those meals with my father. The meals may have been terrible, but the memories? They were some of the best.

My phone dinged. *I really needed to shut off that noise*, I thought, remembering Jane's advice. It was a message from Willow:

> We will miss you tomorrow. Have fun relaxing.

Willow had this way of being kind yet totally judgmental, like she could see right through me without even trying. Reading her words, I felt totally exposed, as if she somehow knew where I was and who I was with. I was probably just overthinking.

I wished I could tell her everything. I wanted to shout from the rooftops that I was seeing *the* John Reynolds. But, for now, that wasn't possible. I was just so proud to be with him. Despite everything with Jane, he was with *me*. That alone made me feel special. He could be with anyone, yet he was choosing me. In that sense, I'd already won.

I hearted her message and put my phone face down on the table. *She doesn't know*, I reminded myself. *She can't know.* But the thought stayed with me, buzzing in my head louder than my phone ever could.

———

That night, John and I lay on the couch. "Beasts of Burden" played softly, filling the space. John had finished the dishes and poured me another glass of red wine, probably a more expensive vintage than I cared to know. We faced each other, my legs wrapped around his, my feet underneath his back in the way that felt so natural.

"I can't wait to get out of here and move to New York," he said, leaning his head back against the couch's armrest.

I stared at him in disbelief. "Why would you want to leave this place? Look at your view! The natural light in here is amazing. You've got a setup that most people in the city would kill for. This place in New York will cost you five times as much for a fraction of the space."

"I know, I know. But I've been in this building for seven years. Illinois all my life. I'm just ready to move on." His eyes swept across the room. "There's too many memories here. A lot of good ones, of course, but . . . too many bad ones. I want to get rid of all this stuff and have a fresh start." He gestured to the room, his wine glass in hand.

I hesitated. "I can't imagine how hard it must be to still have so much of her stuff around."

"Oh, you noticed?" he joked. "I have been too busy to get rid of all of it. Most of it's gone now. I've just gotten used to having the rest around. I don't even notice it anymore. She grabs a few things when she's in town visiting the office." His expression tightened. I could almost see the irritation at just the thought of her unannounced visits. Shaking his head, he added, "I'm just ready for something new. And what better place than New York?"

"That sounds like a nightmare," I said. "Do you think it'll be weird working in the same office as her?"

"Nah. We're used to keeping things professional. At least I am. We've been doing it for years now. She'll lose it once in a while, but she saves it for our one-on-one meetings. She's good at keeping up appearances when it comes to work."

I took a breath. Should I ask? Was it crossing a line? But curiosity won out. "Can I ask what happened between the two of you? From what I've seen and heard, you seemed like the perfect couple. Successful, happy. High school sweethearts, right?"

He smiled before taking a sip of his wine. "Sounds like you've done your homework."

"I'm thorough. Especially when it comes to my career."

"Oh, is this–us–part of your career?"

"Well, of course it's personal, but yeah, it also is very related to my career."

His smile faded. "Well, your wife cheating with a personal trainer usually does it." His tone was flat, matter-of-fact.

"Oh my God. *Really?*" My eyes widened, but I fell silent, letting the space invite more from him.

He continued, his voice low. "When she first moved to New York, we bought a townhouse there. Lived in it together. But we kept this place too. I'd go back and forth every month or so—maintain the place, get the mail and stuff. Then Chicago started taking up more of my time, and I was here more than I was there."

A knot coiled in my stomach.

"Things started to feel off. She was training two, sometimes three, times a day with our trainer in the city. Phone calls from her became less frequent. When I flew out to surprise her one weekend, I got an email saying she'd ordered wine on Amazon and condoms to the townhouse. The wine made sense. But we were trying to conceive. Or at least, not *not* trying."

He paused, swirling the wine in his glass. "When I got home, I found used condoms in the trash."

My hand flew to my mouth as I gasped. "No. No way."

"Yep." He let out a bitter laugh. "She tried to deny it. Twist the truth. Blame me. Gaslight and manipulate, the whole thing. After that, we avoided each other. For a while I couldn't even speak to her. She's . . . a different person now. The city has really changed her. She used to be so humble, and down to earth. Now she acts like she is some celebrity and like her shit doesn't stink. At first I was happy to still have this place. But now?" He shrugged. "It's been years. The divorce is slow moving, but at least it is moving in the right direction now. It's messy. No prenup. Too many community assets."

"That's terrible. I am so sorry John," I said, anger simmering beneath my words. "I can't believe she would do that to you."

"She's the one who cheated, yet she's dragging out the divorce. I think she's stalling to figure out how to get more money. She has been getting advice from all of her divorced girlfriends. The longer it takes, the crazier she gets."

"Why don't you push her more, not tolerate the misbehavior? Get it over with? She is the one who cheated." The frustration in my voice was sharper than I intended, startling me. Nothing made me angrier than seeing someone I cared about being taken advantage of. The image I had of Jane—this incredible woman I'd admired—was crumbling. Was this real? Could she really be . . . this?

Maybe this was why they cautioned against meeting your idols.

"It isn't that easy. Her cheating doesn't really make a difference when it comes to the legality of everything. Plus she still has some way of making all of it seem like my fault," he said, rubbing his temple.

"She's trapping you, John," I snapped. "You need to stand up for yourself."

"She would only fight harder if I tried to get it done quickly. She would think something is up. I know her too well. I'm not ready to push that button. I am a reasonable guy. But eventually I will get there. She will push me there. But not yet."

I leaned closer and cupped his face in my hands. "I'm so sorry this is happening to you," I said, my voice barely above a whisper. I shook my head and looked away. Everything I thought I knew felt like a lie. Jane—the woman I'd looked up to—was a *cheater*? Everything she preached about integrity on stage at the Gala was a façade.

"Is there anything I can do? How can I support you?" I asked, though the words felt hollow. There wasn't much I could do.

"No. Of course not. I don't want to burden you. I just . . . want you to know the truth." He paused, setting down his wine, then took my hands in his.

"I am glad you told me," I said.

"Honestly? I thought if you knew, you wouldn't want to be . . . involved. With me." His voice almost shy.

"Do you even have the capacity . . . to be involved with me, I mean? Right now? You have so much on your plate. I honestly don't know how you're juggling all of that, plus work . . . let alone this . . . whatever this is," I said, pointing between us.

"Of course I want to be with you. From the moment I saw you, running around with champagne on your coat, I felt a connection. Like I'd known you forever," he said.

"So have I!" I exclaimed, my voice rising a little too eagerly. "It's so weird, isn't it? I was afraid I was the only one who felt it."

"It's really wild—undeniable." His words were calm, so similar to how I felt about us. "Every time we're in the same room, I feel it. I feel pulled to you. I'm always aware of your presence. I feel oddly protective of you, from everything. Always wanting to make sure you are safe."

I nodded, trying to ground myself, though the conversation—encouraged by the wine—felt unexpectedly good. His words sent a thrill through me, but beneath the excitement, lurked fear. Anxiety. This was real. More real than ever. We weren't just caught up in the moment—the feelings between us were mutual. It was like I had strapped into a roller coaster with him, Jane, and their divorce, unsure of where the next drop would take me. I had deep feelings for a married—well, separated, basically divorced—man. A man I worked with. A man whose ex-wife I still might seek mentorship from. And now, I knew he felt the same way about me.

"I know my life is . . . complicated right now," John said. "But I promise it will all be over soon. When it is, we can be out in the open, I can introduce you to my family, I can show you off in the way I want to—with people other than Parker. That is what you deserve."

My cheeks burned. I didn't deflect or laugh it off like I wanted to. Instead, I let the words sink in and wrap around me like a warm hug. "I would love that. I can't wait," I said.

"As soon as the divorce is final, I'll move to the city. In the mean-time, I'll be traveling back and forth almost every other week. We'll still see each other. And when it's all over, Sarah, I want to give you the relationship you deserve. You're amazing—so driven, so full of life. Watching you at work inspires me. Any man would be lucky to have someone like you. I would be honored to be that man . . . if you're willing to put up with this mess a little longer."

His words melted me. It felt so good to be truly seen. Bye-bye, no-dating rule—I'd break it a thousand times over if this could be my reality forever. I could keep things discreet at work. My performance wouldn't slip, and when the dust settled, I'd be senior editor, openly dating John Reynolds. My own version of a fairy tale.

For so long, I believed excelling at work meant staying single. But now, I wondered—had I been wrong? Maybe I really could have both. Maybe I could have it all.

For now, I'd compartmentalize Jane and work. I'd learn what I could from her. But I wouldn't get too close. I would make sure she never suspected a thing. If I stayed professional, avoided drawing attention, and gave her no reason to question me, we'd get through this. The last thing I needed was for her to find out and do something drastic to stall their divorce even more.

As soon as the divorce was final, we would step out for the world to see. Besides, Jane already seemed to be seeing someone new at the office—she'd be too busy to notice or care what I was doing. A pang of fear arrived at the thought of having to face her each day in the office, having to lie to her and Theo and Willow. But John's promise somewhat dissolved those fears. It was just us. Right here. Right now.

"I'll wait as long as it takes if it means I can be with you," I said, the words tumbling out before I could think them over. They were raw, but they were true. Every single one of them.

I could do this. I could wait for him. For us.

"That means so much to me to hear from you." John's gaze didn't waver.

I swallowed hard and forced a smile as Etta James's "At Last" began playing in the background.

He blinked, his lips pulling into a slow, deliberate smile.

"Are you going to ask me to dance?"

He chuckled. "Right now?"

"I'm not getting any younger." I stood and offered my hand, determined to cut through the heaviness. "Come on, aren't you a Midwestern boy? Didn't they teach you to dance in middle school?"

He just stared at me, as if trying to decide if I was joking. Then, with a sigh and a smile, he took my hand and stood.

"All right, Sarah Jones. Let's see what you got."

John's shoulders relaxed. He pulled me close, one arm wrapped around my waist, the other holding my hand firmly. He felt safe. His sheer size made me feel petite—something I had never felt around a man.

We moved in sync, falling into the rhythm, dancing slowly around his living room.

"See?" I said, looking up at him. "Not so bad, right?"

"Not bad at all," he murmured, his eyes on mine. "I didn't know you could dance."

"There's a lot you don't know about me," I replied, tilting my head playfully. "My dad taught me when I was a little girl. He used to turn on music from the seventies and dance with my sister and me around the living room."

"That is adorable. I bet you were the cutest kid." His gaze deepened, his hand tightening on my waist. "I want to know everything about you."

Something shifted between us, a charge humming just below the surface. Like our previous conversation had solidified a new level of trust between us. The song faded, but neither of us moved away. His thumb brushed the fabric of my T-shirt, a subtle caress that sent shivers down my spine.

Our faces moved closer, noses brushing. This was happening. And I was okay with it. I'd known the moment I walked through his door that I would be okay with it. He wasn't really married—not really. They'd been separated for years, their divorce moving at a glacial pace. Like the marriage was already over, a formality hanging on by technicalities. I had justified it over and over in my mind, and tonight, what he had shared about what happened between them finally felt like enough for me to act on it.

"Sarah," he whispered, his voice low.

I locked eyes with him, my heart thundering in my chest. "Yes?"

"Are you sure?" His eyes searched mine.

"Yes," I breathed, tightening my grip on his hand.

The moment hung in the air, suspended between the past we were trying to leave behind and the future that was just around the corner. Slowly, carefully, he leaned down, his lips brushing mine in a tentative kiss. The sensation sent a shockwave through me, and I rose on my toes to meet him halfway.

The kiss deepened, and suddenly, dancing seemed impossible. John's hands slipped into my hair, his grip tight and sure, as if he was afraid I'd slip through his fingers. He pulled me closer, and I followed his lead without question, our steps now an impromptu shuffle that dragged us toward the couch. His mouth found mine again, and everything else—the room, the world—melted away until there was only his warmth, his scent, and the heat building between us.

"Sarah," he murmured against my skin, and I gasped softly as he pushed me back to the arm of the couch. His weight pressed down on me—solid, grounding—and yet I felt like I could float to the ceiling. His lips traveled along my jaw, lingering at my collarbone, and I shivered at how slowly he drew the kisses out, savoring every moment.

"Are you okay?" he asked, his voice low and raspy, a whisper that sent a thrill up my skin.

"I'm better than okay." My voice was steady. I curled into him, running my fingers through his hair, needing more of him, needing all of him. "Don't stop."

He didn't. Instead, he slowed down, as if trying to memorize the map of my body, his touch reverent. His fingers ran up my sides in a feathery touch that burned with intensity. He paused at every inch of skin, every freckle, every curve, as if branding it with his mouth, claiming it. The world narrowed, until all that existed was the rhythm of our breathing, the sliding of skin against skin, and the distant hum of the city outside—unimportant, far away.

He tossed my shirt on the floor, his soon to follow. Our movements were slow, unhurried—as if we had all the time in the world to explore each other, to learn every inch of each other. It was more than physical. It was a conversation in every kiss, every caress—a confession of everything we didn't know how to say.

Chapter Thirteen

John's body curved protectively around mine, his arm draped over my waist. My cheek rested against his chest, and I could feel the steady, reassuring thump of his heartbeat beneath my ear. I closed my eyes and let his warmth seep into me. He absently stroked my hair, his breath evening out as we both drifted toward sleep.

Deep in the back of my mind, a twinge of guilt. Fear of what could happen if any part of this was found out. If Jane ever found out. If any of it went south. But I couldn't think about that right now. I had to focus on what I wanted, which was to become senior editor, and to be with John at the end of it all.

"I meant what I said," I whispered, breaking the silence. He lifted his head slightly and planted a kiss on my temple, his lips lingering. "I'll wait as long as it takes."

He smiled softly, and my fingers traced the line of his jaw, feeling the light stubble beneath my fingertips. For the first time since I met John, I allowed myself to believe—really believe—things might just work out.

"You're sure we can do this without it destroying my career?" I asked.

"That's exactly why we have to be careful. If Jane finds out before the divorce is finalized, she won't just block your promotion—she'll probably try to go after you."

I frowned. "You really think she'd do that?"

He let out a humorless laugh. "I *know* she would. Jane doesn't lose quietly. She has too much influence with the execs—one conversation, and you're off the list for senior editor. And if that's not enough, she'll sabotage you. She'd find a way to make you look bad, convince an author to file a complaint, maybe even spin something to HR about workplace misconduct. If it hurts her ego, she goes to crazy lengths. I have seen her do some pretty extreme things when her pride gets damaged." He shook his head. "She won't come at you directly, Sarah. She'll make it look like you weren't fit for the role to begin with."

I swallowed hard, took a deep breath, trying to process his words. The reality of who Jane really was, hit me hard. I had known she was cutthroat, but hearing it so plainly from John—her husband—someone who knew her better than anyone—made it real. And terrifying.

"Okay," I said, my voice steady but my mind racing. "I get it. She sounds ruthless. But do you think keeping this quiet is enough to stop her from doing all of that?"

"It's our best shot. I am confident she won't find out. I will make sure of it," he said. "I won't let her ruin this for you. But I need you to trust me and play this really carefully."

His certainty steadied me, gave me some sense of confidence that if we kept it secret, we would have no issues. But there was *no* room for error, whatsoever.

We lay there for what felt like hours, neither of us breaking the silence. I felt . . . whole. Safe in a way that felt unfamiliar but right, a feeling I didn't know I secretly longed for all my life. But as the room darkened and his breathing evened out next to me, a stray thought wedged its way into the fragile peace we'd built.

My mother once told me that women cheat when their needs aren't met or to end the relationship. And men cheat for sexual variety.

I looked up at John, his features relaxed in sleep, his guard fully down for the first time since I'd known him. I couldn't imagine John not meeting every need I had ever had—plus some. I wondered what need Jane had that he hadn't fulfilled? And—would I one day have the same need?

My stomach twisted into a knot.

Because if my mother was right, then what had I just done?

John was still married. Separated, yes. Nearly divorced. But still legally bound to another woman. I had spent so much time convincing myself that their relationship was already over, that Jane had checked out long before I ever came into the picture. But was that just a convenient truth I told myself to justify this?

Did this—what we just did—count as cheating?

I exhaled softly, studying his face, searching for guilt in the lines of his features. But there was none. Just peace. As if he had no doubts. No concerns As if, to him, we were already something real and he and Jane had been over forever.

Maybe that was the difference. Maybe cheating wasn't about technicalities or legalities but intention. He wasn't sneaking around behind Jane's back. He wasn't betraying her—she had already done that damage and let him go.

I turned onto my side, trying to quiet the unease. But the question remained, clinging to the edges of my mind.

If Jane had once believed in John the way I did now, what changed? And what if—someday—it changed for me too?

In the dark, with his arm around me and the steady rise and fall of his chest, I tried to tell myself that what we had was different. That I was different. That I would be better for him than Jane.

Just as I was falling asleep, nestled in John's arms, his phone rang, jolting me out of my dreamy state. We both jumped, as he grabbed his phone. It was Friday at 10 p.m. Who could possibly be calling? He looked at his phone, then up at the ceiling, closing his eyes, sighing deeply.

"I'm so sorry. I have to take this," he said, kissing my forehead.

I caught a glimpse of the name on his screen. Jane.

My heart sank.

"Hey," he said as he walked down the hall. "What's up?"

Her shrill voice came through the phone. "Where the hell have you been? I'm trying to get this stuff done before Monday."

There was a brief pause. The last thing he said before he was out of earshot was, "Sorry, I was doing some work on my computer and didn't have my phone."

A lie—so smooth, so effortless—rolled off his tongue without a second thought. He *hadn't* just been doing deep work; he'd been lying next to me in his bed. Their bed. A flash of them in bed together, made me shudder, made my heart start racing.

Part of me wondered if Jane would catch on, sense the lie. I glanced around the apartment they once shared, her things still lingering. This wasn't a hookup—it was real. My feelings for John were real. And now I was in the middle of it. Fully committed. To him. To us. To the mess.

The other part of me noticed how easily he spun the lie, how it came so naturally to him, like it was nothing. Then there was the final part of me that took mental notes, almost clinically, knowing this was just the beginning of a long string of lies I'd have to tell myself and others.

A familiar feeling crept up, like the one I had when I first saw their room. I had just slept with Jane's husband—*in their* apartment. Jane was someone I admired, someone I looked up to at work, someone I wanted to become. How could I reconcile this with the woman I wanted to be? I couldn't believe a human could experience such conflicted emotions.

I tried to breathe but couldn't shake it. I needed a distraction. My feet were freezing. Like my fight-or-flight state had cut off all circulation to my extremities. I needed socks. I got up from the bed and walked over to the dresser. The room felt too quiet now, the hum of the city outside doing little to mask the self-inflicted tension in the air.

I opened the top drawer on the left to find underwear and—yes—socks. I grabbed a fuzzy pair out, and as I went to slide the drawer shut, something caught my eye. I grabbed what looked to be the corner of a frame. A photograph, no less.

Them. It was them. John and Jane, in a frame too beautiful to be accidentally forgotten, captured in a moment that felt like two people in love. They were standing by the Chicago River, the city's skyline sparkling behind them. Jane had her hand on his chest, smiling at him like she was head over heels in love. But it wasn't her that stopped me. It was him.

The way John looked at her.

It wasn't just love—it was complete adoration. Awe, even. Like he couldn't believe someone like her existed, let alone that she was his.

I gripped the edges of the frame until my knuckles were white, the weight of it all sinking in. Had he ever looked at me like that? Would he? Could any man ever fully move on from a woman that he looked at like that?

I wasn't just stepping into a new relationship—I was stepping into the shadow of theirs. Constantly compared to the marriage he had wanted. Years of history, intimacy, and love I may never be able to compete with. No matter how deep my feelings ran, I was the newcomer. And to build a relationship in comparison to the one they had? It would take time. A lot of time.

A sense of competition rose up in me, like I would have to work at it, to make John fall for me like he had Jane. Like I needed to apply the same discipline and work ethic I had with my career into my relationship with John, to ensure that he would one day look at me that way. That was the only way for him to ever truly move on.

And the gnawing question remained—would I ever be enough?

Chapter Fourteen

It was time to head back to New York. Back to Regent. Back to reality. I had done my best to force the image of Jane and John I had found in the sock drawer to the back reserves of my mind. That was the past, after all. As was the lie he had told Jane after we slept together. I told myself that it was all in protection of me.

John and I had a farewell brunch at Lou Mitchell's, an old-school diner, before I caught my afternoon flight home. The thought of flying first class again made the idea of a travel day somewhat bearable.

"So," he began, holding my hand across the table, his fingers caressing my palm. "You're going back today. When will we see each other next?"

"Well, when are you coming into the city next?" I asked.

"The end of next week, if I remember correctly. Maybe I can get a hotel. Would you like to stay with me? The Ritz?"

I choked on my coffee. "The Ritz? As in The Ritz-Carlton by Central Park? Of course!" I narrowed my eyes and grinned. "Does that mean you're too bougie to stay at my place? You don't want to stay in a rat-infested apartment where you can barely stand up straight without hitting your head?" I asked, feigning offence.

"Not at all," he said, holding up his palm in a mock Boy Scout salute. "I just don't want to impose on your roommate. Izzy, right?"

"Oh, trust me. It wouldn't be any imposition on her. She's known about you for years. She's Theo and Willow's assistant, and my best friend. We can trust her. She wouldn't mind having you at our place at all; in fact, I'm sure she would love to have you." I said. "Anyway, that's settled. I'll see you next week at The Ritz."

He gave me a smile and a nod.

"John," I said, squeezing his hand, "I just want to make sure we're on the same page before I head back to the office. We've already agreed to keep things quiet, but I need to know how we'll handle things if we're ever both around Jane. It's complicated, and I don't want any slip-ups."

He nodded. "I know. We agreed: keep it professional with Jane and in the office, no personal talks or hints. She's already been asking about me dating, and she's suspicious of a few others in the office. The last thing we need is her catching on that it is you."

I swallowed, feeling the weight of the situation. "Right. No one at the office can know."

"Exactly," he said. "And if we have to interact with Jane, we act like nothing's going on. Completely professional. I'll handle the divorce stuff, but you need to protect your career until that time comes."

I exhaled. "This is the only way to keep things on track."

He cupped my cheek with his palm. "We'll be fine. Just keep your distance from Jane as much as you can, and don't mention anything to anyone, except Izzy. It's the only way to protect us both." Ironic how the very thing that would help me most in becoming senior editor could also destroy my chances and any potential future I had at Regent.

I nodded, my heart heavy but resolute. "Okay. I'll do my part."

"I will see you next week, Sarah," he said warmly. Remember, we were on the same team. We were in this together.

With that, we shared a final kiss, and I headed off, knowing the plan was set. But the stakes felt higher than ever.

———

I sprinted through the door of the marble-floored office. Shit. Shit. Shit. I'd slept past my alarm—too much fun in la-la land with John. Back to real life.

"Sorry, I held them off as long as I could," Izzy called as I ran down the hall.

The meeting with Gabriel Stone that Jane had invited me to sit in on was starting . . . well, right now. I could not miss this. It was an unreal opportunity to even sit in on this meeting. I couldn't believe I was almost late. How irresponsible of me.

Gabriel Stone. I'd heard about him around the office and been a fan of a few of his books. Gabriel was one of our highest-profile authors at Regent. So high-profile that even after Jane had been promoted to executive vice president, she still maintained the contract to ensure the success of his books. From what I could gather, he was the kind of man whose reputation preceded him, leaving you unsure whether to be intimidated or intrigued. Most likely both.

I spotted Jane down the hall, gesturing for (who I assumed was) Gabriel Stone to join her in the conference room. She caught my eye as he passed her through the glass door and gave me a 'hurry up and get your ass in here' look.

I slowed my fast jog to a walk as he turned and locked eyes with me through the glass. I smiled at him, hoping he wouldn't notice that I was winded and still sweating from sprinting fifteen blocks just to get here on time.

He offered a confident smile, exuding the charisma that had made him a picture-perfect best-selling author. Not only a fabulous writer but oozing with charm, which was rarer than you would think.

Meeting an attractive straight man in a publishing house was like finding Louboutins at a yard sale.

"You must be Sarah," he said, extending his hand.

I tried not to feel self-conscious about my breathlessness. "It is a pleasure to meet you, Mr. Stone. I loved *The Unraveling*. I really enjoyed my first read-through of it," I said with a firm handshake. I couldn't stand a limp handshake—it said a lot about a person, or so my dad had told me growing up. I'd read the latest draft of the manuscript to prepare for the meeting on the flight home from Chicago. *The Unraveling* was about a high-powered lawyer whose life collapsed after a colleague leaked a corporate scandal. I had a few ideas rattling around in my head in case I was asked my thoughts. Otherwise, I planned to observe in silence and let Jane run the meeting.

Gabriel's brown hair was slicked back, accentuating his jawline and sharp, confident gray eyes. His charcoal suit fit like a second skin, perfectly cut to his lean, athletic build. Intimidating. Definitely intimidating. He could have passed for a lawyer himself.

"Nice shake," Gabriel noted with a nod, his gaze lingering a second longer than expected before turning back to Jane. His demeanor changed, now fully in business mode. "Shall we begin?"

"Let's get started," Jane said, gesturing for us to sit. "Gabriel, you mentioned wanting to discuss positioning ideas before we bring marketing in on the project. Let's go over everything you've been considering so we're well prepared."

Gabriel leaned forward, hands clasped together. "The last releases did great overall with the adult market, but the big question is—how do we bring in the younger demographic for future books? It seems like we are missing out on a huge demographic with massive buying power."

Jane paused, tapping a pen thoughtfully against her notepad. "The last release didn't quite hit our expectations. While the adult market came through, we saw a major drop in engagement from our initial expectations in the younger crowd. Only about 15 percent of the sales came from them, even though they represent 40 percent of the potential market for this type of book."

Gabriel raised an eyebrow, his tone sharp and measured. "Exactly. That's a significant gap. My question, and the reason I wanted this meeting, is do you think the issue lies with the content itself—perhaps it needs refinement to resonate better with the younger demographic—or was it more of a marketing flop on our part?"

Jane looked up from her notepad, considering the question. "It's impossible to know for sure, but I believe it's a combination of both."

Gabriel nodded slowly, then glanced over at me. "And you . . . Sarah. You must be in touch with that younger crowd. What do you think? You said you read the manuscript. How do you believe *The Unraveling* would hit with people your age?"

"Sarah is primarily here to listen and learn, Gabriel," Jane said, her voice commanding. "But if she has something to add, then feel free." Jane's eyes were on me—encouraging but cautious.

I blinked, caught off guard. My thoughts? I hadn't expected to be dragged into this conversation so early. But it made sense. My generation consumed stories differently. We were constantly swiping and scrolling—looking for content that felt raw and real. I could help shape the narrative in a way that connected with young people on a deeper level.

"Well, the way you've positioned David's internal conflict is compelling," I said, "especially how it affects his relationships and career. People today face so many pressures—balancing personal expectations with professional demands. It is almost like there is no separation between the two these days. My generation also seems to deal with a lot of betrayal, distrust, and drama—more than previous generations. I blame social media." I paused. "It's raw and human, and it could resonate with a younger audience that values authenticity. The way David tries to navigate the chaos without losing himself— young people will connect with that."

"Good to know," he said, a hint of sarcasm in his voice, as if communicating that he was very well aware of the themes of his books.

"We could market him to my generation by focusing on the raw, emotional aspects of his journey," I said with conviction. "People want something real, not polished or scripted. They resist traditional marketing tactics that work with more seasoned demographics. Young audiences have incredible bullshit detectors these days."

I paused to see if the profanity offended them. Neither of them even flinched. "Sorry for the language," I tried to recover. Gabriel waved me off, like it wasn't an issue.

"Anyway," I continued, "I think we should market from the angle of raw, unfiltered emotion. People are hungry for authenticity these days."

"And what would that look like?" he asked.

"Well, I am not a pro at marketing by any means—my strength lies in editing—but when I think of marketing, I think of Apple versus Microsoft in the nineties. And when I say nineties Microsoft, what comes to mind?"

"Computers," he said flatly, almost unamused. I couldn't tell if he hated me or was just really that serious.

"Right. And when I say Apple, what comes to mind?"

"Steve Jobs," he said, leaning forward, elbows on the chair, folded together, watching me like a hawk. Jane scanned me, listening intently, ready to recover my fumble if I made one.

"Exactly. And when you think of Steve Jobs, what do you think of?"

"Brilliance, innovation, class, simplicity, minimalism, genius . . . black turtleneck."

I laughed. "Right. And what computer do you own Mr. Stone?"

"Apple. Of course."

"And why is that?"

He shrugged, as if to say, *I assume you are going to tell me.*

"The reason people buy Apple instead of Microsoft is because of Steve Jobs and *his* story. He represents everything Apple is about—

freedom, innovation, simplicity, genius. Hardly anyone in the world knows what Microsoft stands for, besides *maybe* Bill Gates."

Jane and Gabriel both let out small laughs, giving each other a look. I couldn't read either of them, their expressions cryptic.

"There's no story behind it, no compelling character for people to relate to. When we market your book, instead of just putting the plot on the back cover, we want readers to feel like they already *know* David. We want him to feel real to them before they even buy the book. Like he is a real person."

Gabriel's eyes narrowed. He nodded slowly.

"We don't want people to buy *The Unraveling*. We want them to buy into the main character. Into David and his struggles and his victories. Into the real and raw emotions. Into the messy human *in* the story. The Steve Jobs of your book."

Silence.

"And how do we do that?" Gabriel finally asked, the corner of his mouth turning up so slightly that anyone else would miss it. Jane wriggled ever so slightly in her seat.

I gestured to him, shrugging my shoulders. "You."

"Me?"

"Yes, you. Look at you. You're dressed like David in the book. Part of the story must be based on your personal experience."

"Sarah," Jane interjected. "That isn't appropriate to assume of Gabri—"

Gabriel held up a hand to stop her. "Sarah, I'm a writer. I get all the inspiration for my books from direct experience. Ideas usually come from somewhere. My own life, mostly."

I glanced at Jane, and she nodded for me to keep going.

"Exactly. But here's the trick: You've been mostly anonymous in the promotion of your previous books and on social media. At least your face has been. We could create a campaign with *you* as the character of David. Involve the audience in David's life and experiences, not just the book. Then, once they're emotionally bought into David, we release the book—and bam, your biggest bestseller yet.

And you'll reach a whole demographic online that you've been missing."

"How are you assuming we get the younger demo?" Jane asked.

"The young BookTok crowd on TikTok will eat it up." I grimaced, crossing my fingers behind my back that he'd like the idea.

"BookTok?" he said flatly.

"It is this thing online where people, mostly young women and men, talk about books on TikTok. They review and suggest them if they like them. Most of these accounts have tens of thousands, if not millions, of followers. We distribute your book to a handful of them, and if they like it, game over in winning that market for life. These readers are cult followers of their favorite authors. If they like you, they will buy anything you put out."

Gabriel gave a slow nod. "Interesting perspective," he said. "You've really thought this through."

"It just came to me once I saw the similarities between you and David. We need to make you the Steve Jobs of your book."

Jane jumped in, trying to recover my comparison. "But David is a messy character. What if Gabriel doesn't want to be associated with David's 'tragedy' in the public eye?"

Gabriel looked back at me, waiting to see what I would come up with.

I paused for a moment, biting my lip. "We could have you use a pseudonym. Yes, David's story is a tragedy, but . . . it's a beautiful tragedy. Once the publicity as David is over, we'll reveal that you're really Gabriel Stone. It will help people relate to you, create intrigue, and keep them guessing which parts of David are real and which are fiction. Most will assume all of it was. Besides, people love to root for a fallen hero. The bigger the fall, the more support you'll get."

There was a silence between the three of us before he spoke. Jane was scanning between me and Gabriel, likely trying to gauge if he thought it was brilliant or idiotic.

"Sarah, this is . . . quite brilliant. I'm hesitant to use my face to sell books, but I'm willing to give it a try. See how it goes."

"I can promise you it will only help if we use your face to sell books," Jane cut in, with a small laugh, somehow making it sound completely professional.

He thought for a moment. "I like it. Let's move forward with it. Let the marketing team know this is the direction I want to go, and they can build out the strategy. Are we still on for the New Year's book release?"

Jane checked her schedule. "Yep. We're all set. I'll have my assistant Jenny reach out to your assistant to make arrangements in the next few weeks once we get this strategy locked in with marketing."

And just like that, the decision was made.

"Great," Gabriel said, closing his leather notepad. "Oh, and I would like for Sarah to sit in on future meetings. Since that was her idea, she may bring a perspective that others won't."

"For real?" I asked.

Jane snapped me a look—what seemed to be disdain for speaking so candidly, but also what seemed like a small hint of excitement for me.

Gabriel grinned. "Yes, Sarah, for real."

"Do you have time with your current workload, Sarah?" Jane asked. "I don't want you to get overloaded."

"I will make it work," I said, nearly interrupting her.

"All right, then," Jane said. "That is settled. Sarah will sit in on future Gabriel Stone project meetings."

They both smiled and nodded at each other. As we shook hands and left the conference room, Gabriel said, "I want this to be our best-selling book yet."

"Let's make it happen," Jane said.

"Thank you for the opportunity, Mr. Stone." I said with as much appreciation as I could muster. "I look forward to working with you on this project."

"Looking forward to it," he echoed.

This was my chance—an opportunity to prove I was ready to

step into senior editor. To add value in different departments even, to prove that I had ideas that could be valuable to our authors. If I could help this project be successful, it would show upper management I was capable of stepping into a leadership role. Theo and Willow had said I needed to prove I wasn't just a great solo contributor. I could not, I would not, do anything to mess up this opportunity.

"Ladies." Gabriel saluted, somehow making it look classy. He straightened his tie, then turned and walked out of the office, heading for the elevator.

Jane and I exchanged glances. Oddly enough, she raised her hands in a soft gesture of approval, a small, reserved smile playing on her lips. "Sarah," she said, her voice warm but not overly effusive. "You were great. This is a big opportunity for you." Her happiness was there, but it was measured, controlled—exactly how I'd expect Jane to show it.

A wave of relief. A small sign of approval from her meant more to me than I would like to admit.

"Did I do okay?" I asked, feeling a little unsure of myself.

Her smile softened, her tone warmer now, as we walked toward her office. "You did well. Honestly, I'm impressed. You did exactly what needed to be done. And handled it like a pro. There were places where your delivery could be more professional. But overall, great job. I'm looking forward to working with you on this project. It's a huge opportunity for you and the senior editor position. It is showing you can go above and beyond your required role. Just let me know what you need." Her voice was confident, laced with eagerness . . . to mentor me, maybe?

Maybe it was because I was still new to all this, still figuring it out, and she saw the chance to help me grow. Maybe she was genuinely excited to help me succeed, or maybe she saw me as someone she could mold into a success. Maybe it was both—she'd win if I did.

"Let's set up a bi-weekly project meeting to check in on progress.

Are you *sure* you can handle all this on top of your current workload? It's basically doubling what you have now."

"Yes!" I blurted out, desperately trying not to show any hesitation. "I can do this. There's nothing I can't handle. This job means everything to me. I'll make it happen."

"Excellent," she said as she sat in her chair and turned to her computer. If she was anything like Willow, that was the sign she was done talking. I turned to leave, eager to tell Izzy about the meeting.

I walked out of her office, filled with excitement. This was my chance to receive mentorship from Jane. Before I was out of earshot, Jane called down the hall, "Oh, and Sarah!"

I turned and jogged back to her door, eager for more encouragement. "Yes, Jane?"

"You better never be fucking late to a meeting again." She didn't even look up from her screen. Her tone had changed, a complete one-eighty, serious, ice cold, as if the conversation we just had, never happened. The same ice queen I had met outside the bathroom at the Gala. It was as if she'd flipped a switch, gone from friendly and supportive to something else entirely. She could have been Dr. Jekyll moments ago, but now she was all Hyde. As if she knew exactly what I'd done with her husband that weekend. The husband I'd slept with . . . several times. The weekend I'd spent at her house.

It was like another person was sitting in her chair.

Jesus. Christ. I had almost forgotten all about the fact that my weekend with John had even happened. I guess that compartmentalization thing was working for me.

My whole body froze, and I barely managed to say "Yes, ma'am, it won't happen again." Then I ran back to my desk, and didn't look toward her office for the rest of the day.

———

Around nine that night, only a handful of the usual late-night working crowd remained in the office. Just as I was about to call it a night and head home, I heard something—someone still in the office.

And I knew just who it was.

Jane.

I stilled, the sound of her voice drifting through the doorway and across the office. I shouldn't be listening. But I couldn't help it. The way she spoke—low, clipped, like when she'd almost threatened me earlier—pulled me in. I leaned in, straining to hear.

"Who were you with this weekend, John?" Her voice was a mixture of ice and accusation. Silence. I could almost feel him searching for an alibi. I tensed in my chair.

"Don't lie to me," she snapped. "You said you were working late every night this weekend, but somehow you've barely touched the projects we agreed on you finishing. What the hell is keeping you so busy?"

Another pause.

"Fine. I don't give a shit who it is." Jane's voice dropped to a steely calm. "But she better be worth falling behind at work for."

The silence that followed hummed louder than any answer he could have given. Did she hang up?

Poor John. That tone. The same one she used with me after the meeting with Gabriel. Frightening. Dark. Manipulative. Scary. Really scary.

She closed the door to her office. I ducked my head as she stopped at Peter's desk before leaving. He was so annoying and immature. In his early twenties like me, but acted like he was twelve. Pompous and arrogant. There was something about the way his team was always goofing off at company events and in the break room that rubbed me the wrong way. Like they didn't take this job seriously at all. I rolled my eyes just at the thought of him.

I couldn't believe there was something going on between them. Major downgrade from John, in my opinion.

Jane arrived at his desk, Peter grabbed his things, and he and Jane left the office together. They might as well have walked hand in hand to Human Resources to announce their workplace relationship. Instead, they seemed to be heading out to dinner—probably some three-Michelin-starred restaurant in Tribeca near her apartment.

The more I learned about Jane, the more her veneer started to crack. On the surface, she had the life I wanted. But something about her felt . . . wrong. She would be great one minute, then terrifying the next. Wanting to mentor me, then seemingly wanting to rip me a new one. What a hypocrite. Five minutes ago, Jane had been tearing into John for potentially being with another woman. Accusing him of infidelity while she waltzed off with her new boyfriend.

A wave of frustration washed over me. I was pissed. I had to hide my relationship with John until this divorce was over. Each day, I feared being caught. Each day, I feared that my career could be ruined if she caught wind of it. That I'd be blacklisted from publishing if Jane found out about me and John. That my secret workplace romance with the man of my dreams would be exposed, leaving me with nothing but a scarlet A ironed onto my three-piece suits.

But Jane—she got to live free with her new boy toy, Peter? Not cool. Not cool at all, Jane. In fact, it was messed up. Messed up, Jane! Fuck you, Jane!

I was jealous. When John moved here, were we going to have to pretend we didn't know each other? Sneak around the office to spend time together? The thought almost split my heart in two. It was plain unfair and a complete double standard.

I didn't know if John knew about Peter and Jane, but I couldn't be the one to tell him. As tempting as it was—to prove I was the better choice—I couldn't twist the knife Jane had already planted in his back. Even if they were over, I couldn't be the one to reopen those wounds. Not yet. I was sure he'd find out soon enough.

Even though they seemed over each other, they had such a long history that it seemed nearly impossible for them to completely sever their ties. I hated to admit that I saw glimpses of the parts of John that still weren't over her. The divorce hadn't been his idea. It was hers.

Like my dad, who fought to make it work even when my mom wanted to leave, time and distance didn't ever fully erase that hurt. It lingered in the cracks, festering beneath the surface. Even now, I still saw it in my dad, every now and again.

After watching them leave, I wanted to say, *Fuck it,* to the whole plan. That we should just be together—publicly. Like Jane and Peter. No one at the office seemed to care about their being together. What would it cost us, specifically me, if we went public? Jane would most likely *destroy* me. She'd tear my career apart, use her position and influence to get me fired, humiliate me in front of everyone. I had no doubt she'd do it. The second she found out, it would be war. She, just like me, hated to lose. And there was no way I'd win that battle. Though it was a total double standard, John said that was how she operated.

Theo and Willow would probably step back too. They'd want nothing to do with this—public image was everything to them. They'd distance themselves from me faster than I could blink, and I'd most likely lose their mentorship too. All the progress I'd made would be gone. They stayed out of drama, *especially* drama involving people in the company. They valued their status above everything else. Plus, they would never be willing to get in the middle of John and Jane.

But it was more than that. If Jane found out, she'd use it to her advantage. She'd leverage the whole situation against John, use it to take *everything* in the divorce. John might be left with nothing. She knew how to manipulate him. She'd strip him of any power or leverage he had left, and she'd use me as a pawn in that game.

It wasn't just Jane's wrath I had to worry about—I had everything to lose. My career, my standing in the company, my future with John. While in a fantasy world, none of this would be an issue and I could be seen out with John Reynolds without any backlash, that wasn't reality. Going public wasn't even an option until all of this was over. And since John wasn't willing to own his truth until his divorce was finalized, we'd have to remain in the shadows, for now.

Chapter Fifteen

A few weeks after my meeting with Jane and Gabriel, my friend Emma invited me out to her bespoke suit shop. Our other friends, Sloan and Chloe, also met up with us. I had met all three girls a year ago at a women's mixer when I first arrived in the city and still had time to try to make new friends. While my calendar was so full these days, I knew I had to squeeze in an hour to see the girls and catch up.

Emma, one of the only female bespoke tailors in all of Manhattan, had a gorgeous shop—sleek marble countertops, plush velvet seating, and tables of impeccably tailored suits displayed like works of art. The scent of fresh espresso and cedar wood lingered in the air, a perfect combination of luxury and warmth. It was the kind of place that felt like a getaway from the city.

The four of us had made a habit of meeting every few months to catch up—our own little tradition of chatting about work and swapping stories over cocktails or brunch. Beyond Izzy, they were the only real friends I had in the city. Between my packed schedule at Regent these days and the whirlwind of being with John every chance I got, I hadn't seen them in months. Not since before I had met him.

"Em, the place looks great. You have done so much since I was here last," I said, sipping on a glass of champagne as she fitted Chloe for another custom suit dress.

"Well, you have been so busy we have barely seen you," Emma mumbled. She was bent over, pinning Chloe's skirt hem, pins in her mouth and marking chalk covering her hands.

"For real. What have you been up to?" Chloe chimed in. She worked as a fashion director at Tom Ford. "We used to see you at least every other month, but you have disappeared since February," she said as she admired the suit in the mirror. "Em, can we make the coat like . . . a quarter of an inch shorter?"

Emma gave a look of annoyance. Chloe always got what she wanted, plus she was a paying client. "Of course." She laughed it off. "But it will take another week or so."

Sloan, the ever-perceptive one, wasn't going to let me off the hook. "Wait, have you been . . . like seeing someone, Sarah?" Her hopeless romantic, and eternal optimist, eyes lit up like a child at Christmastime.

I shooed her off. "Of course not." I couldn't tell them about John. I had promised him I wouldn't say anything to anyone but Izzy. Despite my best efforts, a smile peeked through that I couldn't hold back.

Sloan's jaw dropped. Somehow, her eyes grew even wider. "You are! You are. You are. I can see it. Who is he? Tell us everything."

Emma and Chloe stopped in their tracks, scanning me in the mirror's reflection as I fumbled with some paisley tie on one of the tables. "Okay, drama queens, stop acting so shocked." I rolled my eyes.

"I *am* shocked. You have always been so committed to your work, I can't imagine you actually *dating* someone," Chloe said. "But that would make sense as to why you have been so MIA."

"I have to look him up online. What is his name?" Sloan said, grabbing her phone. She was in PR, and sometimes it was like she knew everyone in the city. She loved nothing more than to stalk all of the guys we would go on dates with, and she was great at it. Truly, the CIA should really consider hiring her. She could track down a guy even if he had no social media and had seemingly been wiped from the internet grid.

"I am not seeing anyone," I said, sipping my champagne. I couldn't tell them, but I wanted to *so* badly. I wanted them to see John and be impressed. I wanted to tell someone other than Izzy that I was dating an absolute dreamboat, who was successful and chose to be with me.

Emma just stared at me. "Come on, Sarah, there is no harm in telling us. Who are we going to tell?"

A long silence filled the space. *Should I just tell them?* I could trust all of them with a secret. Plus their paths would never cross with the publishing house or John, for that matter.

"Sarah, you're either in love or in trouble. Which is it?" Chloe asked.

I sighed, knowing I was about to break and tell them. It was like I couldn't hold it in. Like a dam that had so much water behind it, that it burst open. I had to tell them. I had to tell someone other than Izzy. "It's . . . complicated."

"Oh my God! You are dating someone." Sloan squealed, clapping her hands together.

Both Emma and Chloe stopped what they were doing and came to sit on the couch to listen. I took a deep breath, my fingers tracing the rim of my champagne glass. "Okay, I met someone."

Sloan practically vibrated with excitement. "I *knew* it! Who is he? What does he do? How did you meet? Show me a picture." She was already unlocking her phone, her fingers ready to stalk.

Emma and Chloe exchanged glances, settling into their seats like they were preparing for a show. "Yeah, spill. Now we know why you've been disappearing on us," Emma teased, setting aside her marking chalk.

I hesitated, searching for the right words. "Like I said, it's . . . complicated. No one really knows."

Chloe scoffed. "That means one of two things: either he's emotionally unavailable and it's a hookup thing . . . or he's *actually* unavailable."

Sloan gasped, "Wait, Sarah, *please* tell me you did not fall for some guy with a girlfriend."

I swallowed hard, avoiding their eyes. My silence was answer enough.

Emma's brows furrowed. "Oh my, you did."

Chloe straightened, her fashion-editor sharpness slicing through the moment. "Tell me you're joking."

I let out a small shameful laugh. "I wish I was."

Sloan was already shaking her head. "Okay, but maybe it's not *that* bad. Maybe his relationship is rocky and already over—"

"Actually, he's married."

The words hung in the air like cigarette smoke.

"Well, separated," I clarified. "They have been for years now. It is all just legalities at this point." It was suddenly feeling very hot in here.

Emma exhaled, running a hand through her perfectly straight hair. Chloe crossed her arms, her expression unreadable. Sloan, the ever-hopeful one, looked like I had just told her Santa wasn't real. Then her face shifted to something softer—almost mournful. "Oh, Sarah—" she whispered. "That's . . . I am really sorry. That is so sad. What is his name?"

Emma crossed her arms, a sharp look in her eye. "Sad? Sloan, she just said they're separated. Sarah isn't some homewrecker."

"John Reynolds," I said, and the moment his name left my lips, it felt like a pressure valve had released.

I needed to stop talking, to stop sharing, to stop offering information. But I couldn't. Now that the floodgates were open, I needed to tell them all of it. Like I had bottled this up from everyone in my life except for Izzy, and I had to get it out. "There is something else. . . ." I added.

They all stared, waiting.

"I work at Regent with him. He will be transferring to the Manhattan office in the next few months."

Sloan gasped, but I held up a finger for the real kicker.

"And his soon-to-be ex-wife is an executive at my company." I paused and bit my lip, waiting for their reactions.

Chloe leaned back on the couch, rubbing her temples. "You *met* his wife?" she asked, disbelief in her voice. "Sarah, do you realize what kind of risk that is? If she finds out, it could be a disaster for your career."

"Oh, I am aware. That is why I haven't told you guys yet. And yes, I met her. . . . Actually, I am working on a project with her. She has no idea about us." I sighed but my chest tightened. "I know how it sounds."

Emma scoffed. "Oh, come on, Sarah, it's not your job to protect those people's feelings. If John is ready to date and they are separated, then who cares. Go for it. I am sure she has moved on too." Relief flooded me that at least one of them had my back and didn't think I was a terrible human being.

Chloe exhaled sharply. "I get that, but even so, you all work together. Even if she is over him, if they are still married, she could wreck your name. Couldn't she totally fuck up your career? You have worked so hard." Chloe was often brash in her delivery, but she was right—if anyone at Regent House found out, it wouldn't just be gossip. I could lose my job completely.

"I know the risks," I snapped. "I'm careful. We are careful." Though I could hear the doubt in my voice.

Emma, always the protector, rolled her eyes. "She's not some assistant sneaking around with her boss, Chloe. It sounds like they are separated. And if it is anything like most divorces, the wife was the one to cheat to begin with."

"See, now that's true," I said pointing at Emma.

Sloan sat in silence, looking at her phone, probably doing her routine background check.

Chloe sighed. "I get it, Sarah. But your industry is cutthroat. I would just hate to see you lose all of it for some guy who isn't even able to give you what you deserve."

Sloan finally looked up, I could tell she was trying her best to cheer for love and put her prejudices aside. "I totally support whatever you choose. Just promise me you'll be careful."

I nodded, feeling the weight of their concerns.

Emma gave me a reassuring look. "Don't worry, Sarah. You're not alone in this. We've got your back."

Chloe sat with her arms still crossed. "Yeah, totally." But I could tell she didn't mean one syllable of it. I didn't need her to. I was confident in my choice.

Emma's voice dropped to a near whisper. "Could we see a picture?" She let out a smile.

Sloan held out her phone, and passed it around. "Yes, you can." She smirked, having already found his Instagram account.

Emma's eyes widened as she looked at the screen. "Oh, wow. He's . . . he's stunning."

Sloan giggled, her hand still on my shoulder. "Yeah, no kidding. I get why you're into him now."

Chloe leaned in for a closer look, then sat back, her expression unreadable. "I mean, yeah, he's good-looking. But does that really make up for everything else?"

I sighed, pulling my hair off my face and back in a bun. "It's not just about the way he looks, Chloe. There's more to him than that. We really care for each other."

Sloan raised her eyebrows, "Regardless, I'm starting to see why you're so smitten and willing to risk it. Plus he looks pretty successful, which doesn't hurt."

Emma, still in a trance, staring at his picture, "Jesus. He's got that perfect kind of handsome that's hard to ignore."

Chloe smirked. "All right, all right. He's a good-looking guy. But still, that doesn't fix everything. Do not give your power away to this guy, Sarah. Especially since you work with him. That is all I am saying." She threw her hands up in the air in exasperation.

I shook my head, almost laughing at how this conversation was going. "I know, Chlo. You have to trust that I know what I am doing."

Sloan squeezed my shoulder gently. "Just be careful, Sarah. That's all we are saying."

Chloe leaned forward, eyes now wider with curiosity. "Okay, but what about the ex-wife? Can we see her too?"

I hesitated for a moment before I pulled up Jane's photo. Before I turned my phone to show them, I held it to my chest. "You three have to swear you won't tell anyone about this. John didn't want me telling anyone, but I trust you three. Lips shut, you swear?"

They all nodded in understanding.

I passed my phone around again. Sloan studied it closely. "She's . . . pretty. Not exactly what I expected, though. Lots of visits to her aesthetics lady, I see," she seethed.

Chloe looked at the screen for a long beat before commenting, "Woah. She looks a lot like you, Sarah. Like, a *lot*."

A sick sense of pride twisted in my stomach at the comment, though I didn't want to admit it. It was like a confirmation that I could be just as good as Jane one day. Just as capable of capturing John's attention. I couldn't help but feel a dark thrill at their words, but I quickly swallowed it down.

I leaned in, lowering my voice. "You want to hear something insane Jane did to John a week ago? He told me about it last night." It was like I had to tell them everything, to show them she was the crazy one. To prove to them that I was the better choice. That I wasn't the bad guy in this situation.

Emma raised an eyebrow. "What?"

I couldn't help but smirk, though it was bitter. "She hacked into his email—from her office in New York."

Chloe's eyes widened. "Wait, how does that even happen?"

"She somehow got his login info, got into his email, and started reading through his private emails like it was nothing. When John found out, he was furious. She started to forward him his own emails like she was taunting him, trying to get information to stall the divorce and get more money."

Emma let out a low whistle. "What. A. Psycho."

I nodded, a sick satisfaction creeping in. "When he confronted her, she didn't even flinch. She just said, 'When will you realize you can't escape me, John? I will win this.'"

Chloe shook her head. "Jesus, that's next-level crazy."

I leaned back, letting the words settle in the air. Part of me felt relieved, like I'd unloaded this toxic weight off my chest, but another part of me couldn't shake the guilt. Would John get upset with me for telling them? I told my friends something he'd confided in me, some-thing personal. But the more I thought about it, the more I had to—because if I didn't, they'd never understand just how far gone Jane really was. They would never know the truth, and that I wasn't the bad guy here.

"I really looked up to her when I first met her, but the more she does things like this, the more I am convinced that she's absolutely insane," I said, the words felt strange coming out of my mouth. But they were true.

Emma gave me a long look, her expression a mix of concern and admiration. "I get it. I really do. Crazy ex-wives are some other type of animal."

Sloan crossed her arms. "Yeah. Honestly, that's terrifying."

"You think? Imagine sharing an office with her every day."

Chloe finally gave me a look of sympathy. "You've got us, Sarah. We've got your back." But I could tell she still wasn't fully on board and supportive; she just wanted to be a good friend.

I smiled, sharing Jane's true colors, and having them see that she was the crazy one in all of this, was a small victory. The more I saw of her, the more I realized just how crazy she could be—and I couldn't deny that a small part of me felt like I was starting to win this battle.

I sat at my desk, staring at another email from Jane: *"Sarah, I need these revisions by 4 p.m."* My stomach dropped. The Gabriel Stone project was already behind, and I was drowning under the weight of her and the marketing team's demands.

I had offered to take on the final edits for the marketing material to help lighten Jane's load and get another tick in the "Sarah for senior editor" bucket, but now I was regretting it. I was supposed to keep everything cohesive and on tone for Gabriel, and since I came up with the idea for the strategy, I thought it would be simple. But there were so many pieces of content to work on, it felt never ending. Plus editing marketing materials versus a manuscript was a whole new skillset for me that I was having to learn on the fly.

Another email popped up from Phil in marketing, asking for a final draft. *"Can you get this done by Friday? We really need to move forward."* I read it twice, panic creeping in. Another five pieces of long-form content. I hadn't even finished the first round of content revisions yet, and now they were expecting it all to be completed by this Friday?

My phone vibrated. I glanced at it under the table. I had learned too many times that I should never check my phone with people around. Everything when it came to John had to be careful and calculated, even checking my phone. You never knew who was lurking around. A text from John popped up.

I miss you.

I couldn't help but smile at the message, but it didn't quite reach my eyes. I wanted to be with him. I wanted to leave this office behind and forget about the endless revisions and meetings. But I couldn't. Not yet. I sent him a text back.

Miss you. I'll call later.

But I had no idea when later was. It had been a month since I told the girls about John, and things hadn't exactly gotten easier since then. John's reaction had been mixed—frustrated that I told anyone outside of Izzy about us. He was worried about the consequences, that they would tell someone. But after he cooled off, he could see the relief I felt from getting the weight off my chest.

Every day felt harder. The sneaking. The lying to Jane. The lying to everyone. But while each day felt harder, falling deeper into the web of lies, it simultaneously felt easier over time. Like I could separate the life I had at Regent with the one I had with John. Like the two never existed together. I guess that was the beauty of compartmentalization.

I opened another email—another from Jane. She had attached yet another round of edits. *"Can you get these back to me by EOD?"* Her emails always had that demanding tone, like she was pissed she even had to entertain a written conversation with you. I rubbed my temples, wishing for a break. But there was no time. I had promised to get this done.

I took a deep breath and pulled up a new document to make edits. I couldn't let any of this slip anymore. If I was going to survive this, if I was going to make senior editor, I had to figure out how to manage all of this.

I glanced at the clock—it was almost noon, and I wouldn't have a chance to grab lunch, or dinner. The hours seemed to slip away with little progress made.

This wasn't how I imagined my path to senior editor. Everything I did felt like a step in the wrong direction. I hit *send* on the email to Phil, offering a vague excuse about the timeline, and then shut my eyes for a moment. I couldn't afford to fail, but there were only so many hours in the day.

It was like everything was falling apart. And if I was being honest with myself, I wasn't sure I was cut out for any of this after all.

———

The hum of the engine felt like the only thing keeping me grounded. John's fingers gripped the steering wheel of the Bentley as we drove through Chicago for dinner. He didn't say anything, but the tension radiated from him. Things were off.

"Are you okay?" I asked, but it was more than just small talk. I could feel the weight of the silence between us.

"Yeah. Just tired. Of everything."

I tried not to bring up the divorce topic very often. Every time I did, I could feel his frustration. Like he was a failure. Like he was letting us down for not having it done already. For dragging me into it at all. I found out after the last few months it was easier to avoid the topic altogether.

He kept his eyes on the road, but the way his jaw tightened, he seemed exhausted the last few months. More with each passing day.

"It's been three months, John. You're still trying to act like you're fine, but I know you're not. I can see how much this is affecting you. You have to put your foot down with her eventually," I pleaded for his own sake.

He exhaled. "I don't even know what to do anymore. The divorce. Jane. It's like it will never end. It was supposed to be done by now. . . . Every time I think I'm making progress, she delays it or finds some other crazy thing to drag us back into the weeds."

I acted like I didn't remember that today had been exactly ninety days since he had made the promise that the divorce would be final. And honestly, I didn't know if *any* progress had been made. I looked at him, my voice softer this time. "Has there been *any* progress?" I tried my hardest not to let my complete disappointment come through.

"Yeah . . . a little. She's got this way of twisting things. I try to move it forward, and she comes up with something new—more threats, more guilt, old documents that delay the process. It's like I'm stuck in this loop where she keeps me close enough to control the situation but far enough away to make me feel like I am the reason we are in this mess."

I nodded slowly, feeling the weight of his words sink in. "You don't owe her anything at this point. You've been more than patient. I think it's time to put your foot down and show her you aren't messing around."

He didn't answer right away, just stared ahead, eyes tired. His shoulders were slumped like the weight of it all was breaking him. Crushing him slowly. "Every time I try to lock a date in for mediation, to meet to get things moved forward, she misses the meeting or 'can't make it because of work'—legal threats, money, always bullshit excuses that carry no real weight, but it stalls us long enough. It's just about her keeping control at this point."

"I know." I leaned forward. We had had a few iterations of this conversation over the months. "I can see it. It seems like she has no interest in keeping the marriage going but also isn't fully willing to let it go either, for whatever reason. So instead she is making you feel guilty for trying to move it forward even if it is what she wants," I empathized. "John, I have seen you over the last few months. I have overheard the conversations. You've been trying to do what's right. You are not the villain here," I reminded him. I could see there were times that she had teared him down so much that he forgot he wasn't actually the bad guy. She was.

John looked at me like he wanted to say something, but then he just shook his head. "It's hard not to feel like I'm the one causing all this, though. She has blamed me for everything. I did the taxes wrong, I managed the money wrong, blah blah blah. She turns all of it back on me, without any ownership. To her, I am the reason we can't finish all of this."

I let the silence hang for a beat, then said, "She's playing the game, John. She's using everything she can to make you feel responsible. To wear you out so you eventually give up and just give her everything. But you don't owe her that. You're not the one dragging this out."

"I don't know how much longer I can keep doing this." He stared ahead, eyes unfocused, like the road was the only thing left to hold on to. "I'm just . . . exhausted."

"I know. This isn't the guy I met. You're drained, and you're right —you shouldn't have to keep defending yourself. But don't let her win, okay? Don't let her break you down."

His expression softened just enough that I could tell he was hearing me, even if he didn't believe it all. "I'm trying."

"Just keep going, and don't put up with her bullshit. For you. You deserve to move on from this."

John's grip on the wheel loosened, but there was still a tired edge to his voice. "I'm not sure how much fight I have left, Sarah."

"You don't have to do it alone." I reached over and squeezed his hand. "But you've got to fight for yourself. I'm here to support you." I offered the best smile I could manage, selfishly feeling disappointed that there was almost no progress in us being able to be together publicly.

He looked over at me, eyes now holding warmth. "I don't know how you're still here."

"Because I believe in you. And I care about you. I always will. I am rooting for you John."

He smiled, and we sat in silence for the rest of the drive. The road stretched ahead, endless. I could feel everything back in New York—the pressure of it all, work, Jane, my future with John—all waiting for me. Then I realized that no matter how far we drove, no matter how far from the city we traveled, all of it would always be there, waiting for me.

Chapter Sixteen

My twenty-fourth birthday was just around the corner. John said he had a surprise for me. He flew in a few days early, and after renting a Tesla, we endured five hours of driving and what felt like ninety-two charging and restroom breaks before finally reaching the Finger Lakes in upstate New York. It was the most beautiful place I'd ever seen, narrow lakes cutting through rolling hills, the kind of landscape so perfect it seemed fake.

When we arrived at the Airbnb, I was, once again, in awe. The place was massive—big enough to sleep at least fifteen people. As we walked through the front door, I looked at him in disbelief. "This is all for us?"

"All for you, baby," he said. My heart melted at the gesture.

I walked through the pristine space. With floor-to-ceiling windows, it was a single-story oasis. Multiple pools, hot tubs, a barbecue, even a secluded space for stargazing. I could only imagine the cost. (My later Airbnb research confirmed it was $10,000 a night).

"But . . . Why?" I asked, trying to wrap my head around it.

"You only turn twenty-four once. It's a big year. You deserve to be celebrated," he said, squeezing my hand as I stared out the window.

I tried to let myself enjoy the moment, but it wasn't the grand gestures I really needed—it was something deeper. I just wanted him, not tied up with Jane. I wanted him all to myself. Still, I smiled, "I've never felt so celebrated." I meant it, but as I said it, the tension crept back in—Jane, work, the uncertainty of everything. If this was what he was capable of providing, then I would be grateful for it all. Then maybe I would be that much more grateful when he was able to give me what I really needed. Which was true intimacy, without a looming wife and the risk of losing my job.

"Thank you. Thank you so much," I said.

"It isn't the gift I was hoping to give you, which were the signed divorce papers, but we will make do with what we have and still celebrate you big time," he said pulling me in for a hug.

———

On the morning of my birthday, we lay in our cozy king-sized bed overlooking the infinity pool we'd christened a few times. He looked at me, then tilted his head studying my face.

"Did you get your lips done?" he asked, pulling back a few inches to get a better look.

I instinctively covered them, surprised that he noticed. Despite earlier reservations, I had gotten Izzy to join me to get Botox touch-ups a few days earlier, and the esthetician lady talked me into getting a syringe of filler for my lips. They were slightly bruised. I had planned to keep them covered up with concealer and lip liner since he picked me up yesterday, but in all the Airbnb excitement, I forgot to touch them up this morning. Spending time around Jane at the office, I'd seen how full and plump hers always looked—I just wanted a little more volume. I never thought John would notice. Most men would never even clock botox on a woman. But it seemed when you'd been married to the queen of plastic surgery, you picked up on these things.

I cocked my head and pretended not to understand. I couldn't let

160

him think I was turning into her. I wasn't. "No?" I said, my upward inflection totally giving me away. "No," I repeated firmly. "Why do you ask?"

"They're just a little bruised," he said, squinting to get a better look. "And they look extra . . . plump."

"Maybe . . ." I trailed off, trying to think of an excuse. "Maybe it's from all the kissing we've been doing." I gave him my best sultry look and pressed my lips to his, hoping to distract him from examining my cosmetic changes.

"You know you don't have to do any of that stuff, right?" he asked. "You're perfect and so beautiful just the way you are. Okay?"

I could hear the underlying message in his words—don't go down the same path Jane did before everything fell apart. He was loving, kind, and non-judgmental. What he was really saying was: Don't change for the wrong reasons.

"I know. I won't," I said, my voice steady, but the words felt more like the first lie I'd ever told him.

———

Later that day, John and I were in the kitchen—far too spacious for just the two of us. He was taking a birthday picture of me taking a shot of tequila to kick off the weekend. I was already a little tipsy when, suddenly, two hands squeezed my waist from behind. It wasn't John. My heart stopped.

"Holy shit." I jumped, my mind racing. Was this a break-in? Was I about to be exposed as John's secret mistress lover? Was Jane behind me and this was all some sick set up?

I turned, half ready to run for my life. To where? I had no idea.

Oh. Dear. God.

There, in the doorway, stood Izzy, pulling her hands back from my waist, cackling in pleasure. My brain wasn't registering. Izzy? Here? Five hours from the city? She smiled and moved to the side to reveal Chloe, Emma, and Sloan, who were holding cake, champagne, and balloons—one displaying a 4 and the other a 2. I stood in disbe-lief. My friends . . . were here? With John and me?

"How the? Wait . . . what? How did you all get here?" I gasped, trying to process what was happening. These women were the only ones on Earth who knew about me and John, and they were all together in the same place.

I nearly collapsed, overwhelmed with shock and joy. "How . . . What . . . Oh my God . . ." I blinked, looking between John and the girls. He had brought them here for me? To bring our worlds together. It was the best birthday surprise I could have ever asked for. Tears started streaming down my face—not just from joy but from relief.

Sloan smiled, flipping her hair over her shoulder. "We weren't going to let John steal you and keep you all to himself for your twenty-fourth birthday." She winked at him, then wrapped her arm around me like she was reclaiming me.

I turned to John, still in awe. "How did you even get a hold of them? What is going on?"

Emma stepped forward, rolling her eyes playfully. "He also knows the party's going to be a lot more fun with us here. This place is way too big for just you two," she said, pulling me into a hug before giving John an approving glance.

Izzy jumped in. "It was all his idea. He got my number from the Regent directory, texted me to help him coordinate, and had me put all the girls in a group chat."

I looked at John. His chest was puffed for the first time in months, and I loved to see it. "Thank you, baby," I said to him as we hugged tight.

"I am so glad you all were willing to make the trek up. I hope you enjoy the time here," John said to the girls. "Make yourselves comfy. There are plenty of beds and bathrooms."

Chloe gave a small, forced smile. "I had my doubts. . . ." she admitted, scanning John with a protectiveness that I rarely saw from her. Was that a real smile starting to show through? "But, I can say I am somewhat impressed." She nodded as she hugged me. "You even pulled it off without her having a clue. Good work, John." Chloe was rightfully concerned about my career, but it seemed she may have started to come around to John. This weekend would allow all of them to get to know him and see how amazing he really was, despite all the divorce drama.

John raised his hands for high fives all around. "I have to give credit where credit is due—without you ladies, this party wouldn't be nearly what it is now. Izzy hooked us all up in a group chat and delegated responsibilities. Chloe picked the Airbnb. Emma organized all the food and alcohol. Sloan helped me keep it all under wraps."

I laughed, the tension melting away as I looked at John, then all of my best friends. I felt so loved. So cared for. It was so good to have everyone here. A weekend full of people who could be trusted. I didn't have to lie. Even if not all of them agreed with my choices, for the first time in a long time, I could just be free. I didn't feel like I was living in two separate worlds. No more secrets, at least for the next few days. For the first time in months, I felt free.

Izzy stepped in front of me, "Happy birthday, you gorgeous bitch." Then, they all burst into an off-tune rendition of "Happy Birthday" before handing me another shot of tequila.

"Let the birthday shenanigans begin," John said, as we all cheered.

———

The next day, the girls and I sprawled by the pool, basking in the sun. My pale, overworked skin quickly burned, the kind of burn that was just shy of blistering, but honestly, I didn't care. I was having too much fun. We spent the day lounging with White Claws in hand, chasing them with tequila shots, and hardly drinking any water—a terrible yet sacred tradition of a twenty-something birthday.

"God, I really needed this girl time!" I said, throwing my hands up, feeling lighter already.

The girls raised their cans in a chorus of agreement, their cheers echoing against the rocks surrounding the pool. The trees created a private little cocoon around us, making it feel as though we were the only people for miles. Sloan, Emma, and Chloe sat at the edge of the pool, their feet in the water, gossiping about their latest dating disasters. Izzy and I, on the other hand, took the opportunity to catch up one-on-one—a rare luxury these days with my hectic schedule of work and travel.

"Iz," I started, my voice a little unsteady as the emotions I'd been bottling up came to the surface (damn tequila), "thank you so much for making this happen with John. It really means the world that you went out of your way to come."

"Yeah, of course," she said, her voice too casual, almost distant.

I narrowed my eyes, sensing something was off. "Are you okay?"

"Yeah, I'm fine." Her words were too quick, and her gaze flicked away from me. She rubbed her temples, clearly stressed. "Sarah . . . I have to be honest. I almost didn't come."

"What? What happened? Are you okay?" My mind started to race with a million possibilities—was she sick? Pregnant? Did something happen with her job?

"I'm fine," she repeated. "I just . . . I can't keep lying for you, Sarah."

Her words hit me like a physical blow. My breath caught in my throat as she finally met my gaze.

"Theo and Willow have been on my case," she whispered, lowering her voice even more. "All these questions—asking where you are and what you're up to. You have been seeing John so much it's like I'm covering for a fugitive. You know how they are. They care about you; they feel accountable for your success. That is what you asked for from them." She sighed. "It was fine at first. I could keep up with it all, but over the last few weeks, you are either traveling or skipping out for lunch when John is in town, leaving work early to take his calls . . . It's harder to keep the story straight. It feels wrong, and it's been over three months, Sarah." She waved her hand in the air, her frustration evident. "For God's sake, he can't even be in the photos from your birthday weekend."

"Izzy . . ." I stared at my can, trying to hold back the tears threatening to spill. "I'm so sorry. The last thing I want is for you to feel like you have to lie for me."

Her face softened, but her shoulders stayed tense.

"I know the situation isn't ideal," I said, my voice cracking a little, "but I really think it'll be over soon. John says just a few more months. Jane is—"

"Stalling and being a total bitch, yeah," Izzy interjected. "That's what you keep saying. That's what *he* keeps saying. Do you even know where they are in the divorce? It's been *three months*, Sarah."

"I know," I murmured. "I know. But with all the money involved, and her dragging her feet, it's taking longer than usual. John says—"

"Sarah," she interrupted, her hand gently resting on my arm, silencing me. "I'll lie for you. God, I'd take a bullet for you. But I would hate for this to go on for a year. I don't want you to get hurt. I know John wouldn't intentionally hurt you—he's amazing to you. I just . . ." She exhaled sharply. "I'm scared. Scared that I'll slip up, that TW or Jane will find out, and it'll all fall apart. I know you already know this but . . . Jane could destroy you," she said, her voice barely above a whisper. "You know the kind of influence she has. If she finds out, she won't just take you off of projects and risk you getting the senior editor promotion—she could fire you and shut you out of Regent House, and if she is mad enough, even blacklist you in the industry."

Suddenly, the tequila-fueled haze faded, and I was sober. No matter how many times I faced that potential reality, it was never easier than the last. My chest tightened.

"Thank you for protecting me," I said. "I love you so much for that."

Izzy's concern was still etched into every feature. She looked like she wanted to say more but held back.

"I trust John," I said, my words feeling rehearsed. "I know he's doing everything he can to get the divorce finalized. I hear them talking about it all the time on the phone. I love him, Iz. I love him so much. He's the one for me. And if standing by him during this time is what it takes, then I'll do it. I know he'd do the same for me if the roles were reversed."

She nodded, but it wasn't the kind of nod that told me everything was okay. It felt more like resignation.

"I'll do my best to keep it that way," she said, "if you really think it's going to be over soon."

"It will be," I said, forcing confidence into my voice. "I promise."

But the weight of my words settled in my chest the second I said it. I hated that even my truths were starting to feel like lies.

———

We sat around the fire, eating dinner. John had been working from the Airbnb all day—he didn't want to raise any red flags by both of us being offline. He managed to escape his calls long enough to grill steaks for the girls, throw some romaine lettuce on the grill for a salad, and pour a nice glass of red wine for each of us.

"You girls enjoy. I'll finish my calls and be right out to celebrate with you." He handed me the last plate, then cupped my face, leaning over me as I sat on one of the outdoor couches. Before I could react, his tongue was in my mouth, giving me a kiss I'd remember for the rest of my life. The girls around us whooped and hollered, making the moment feel even more surreal. I was with all of them together, and I didn't have to hide anything. It felt incredible.

My lips were still tender and bruised from the injections—too bruised for me to say that kissing was my cover story. He had to have known I'd lied about it, but he didn't bring it up again. John let me be me, completely. Without judgment. It was one of the things I loved most about him.

As he walked out of earshot, Sloan leaned into the circle, her chest pressed almost to her knees, as if her posture could make her whisper less obvious. "He's a dreamboat, Sarah." She blinked her big doe eyes, her lashes fluttering as if they held the weight of all the love in the world.

Emma, lounging in her yellow bikini, cutting her steak, jumped in, "We *love* him. Handsome, masculine, funny, smart, and he got you this whole place." She waved around the property with her knife. "What more could you want? Where do I find one?" She plunged her fork into the grilled romaine with exaggerated force.

"He's amazing," I said. "The only problem is the goddamn wife." I threw up my hands. "It should be done soon. I'm just getting impatient."

Izzy sat back, swirling her drink, offering a half-hearted smile. She wanted to be supportive—really, she did—but after our conversation, I could tell how much this was affecting her.

"Divorces take time, especially when there's money involved," Chloe added, her tone ever so slightly judgmental, offset by the tequila shots she had taken throughout the day.

"Totally," the group chorused, their voices a unified prayer for the divorce to go faster.

"But in the meantime," Emma said, her tone shifting to mischievous, "the more dick riding you can do, the faster it'll feel like it's moving." By the end of her sentence, she was practically yelling, one arm flailing in the air like she was riding an imaginary mechanical bull.

I slapped her arm. "Emma!"

We all burst out laughing, loud and unapologetic. God, I had really missed girl time.

Emma nudged me with her elbow. 'Maybe you should go in there and, you know, give him a little motivation.' She wiggled her eyebrows.

They all clapped in agreement, their cheers turning into a conspiratorial chant as they pushed me to my feet.

"You're all ridiculous," I said, slapping their hands away as they pinched me like middle schoolers daring me to spin the bottle. But I couldn't stop smiling.

"Okay, okay! But just a kiss," I said, narrowing my eyes at them before spinning on my heels and heading inside.

Their cheers followed me, a chorus of whistles and hoots that faded the moment I crossed the threshold.

I tiptoed down the hall to our room, careful not to make a sound in case John was still on a call. Everything with him required forethought—every step, every move. I always had to be cautious. Not much different from how I'd lived my whole life, I supposed.

As I crept closer, I strained my ears for any sign of his voice. Nothing. Maybe he was wearing headphones? He never used headphones. Unless he was talking to *her*.

My chest tightened. He knew how much it got to me when they talked. He'd say it was about the divorce or work logistics, and I believed him. I tried not to eavesdrop, to give them space to sort it out. But it was hard not to see too much of the woman I once idolized—still did. The woman that I oftentimes still wanted to be.

There was silence for what felt like an hour in tequila time, then I heard John say, "I know. It's really hard."

My plan to surprise him quickly dissolved into a deathly quiet mission to full-on eavesdrop. I blamed the tequila. And those grapefruit seltzers.

Each step was deliberate, my breath shallow, as I approached the door. The floor creaked beneath me, and I froze, my heart pounding louder than it had any right to.

"I miss you too . . . every day."

The words hit me like a slap, stealing the air from my lungs. My mind spun, searching for explanations. Perhaps he was talking to his sister? An old friend? His fucking mom? God I prayed it was his mom.

"It's just been . . . complicated." He sounded sad. Genuinely sad.

His sigh was heavy, filled with a weight that settled in my stomach like a rock. I pressed my back against the wall, hoping it would make me disappear. My heart pounded against my ribs as I peeked around the corner.

John was sitting on the floor in the corner of the room, his back to the wall, hand covering his face, the phone to his ear. He never sat like that, hunched over on the floor—never slouched like that.

"You know this is not what I want, Jane. You're the one making it harder."

That one sentence, the sound of her name on his lips, and the room tilted on its axis, throwing everything off balance. The floor creaked beneath me, and I ducked behind the wall, hoping he hadn't heard it.

Everything—my heart, my love for him, my trust—was shattered in an instant. The air felt heavier, pressing against my chest, choking me.

Chapter Seventeen

The breath I'd been holding escaped in a sharp, heavy rush. Jane. *Jane?* His ex-wife, Jane? The one he was divorcing? The one he called a lying manipulator? The one who, according to him, was just an obstacle—a nuisance to be removed? Not someone *he missed*. Not someone he still talked to in this way— especially not like this.

He fell silent, and I wished I could see his face. Was he angry? Sad? Or—my heart lurched—regretful?

"This challenging season will be over soon," he murmured. "I promise. We'll get what we want."

His words echoed, but it was as if my brain had shorted out. My whole body went numb. What could he possibly be talking about? My legs locked, glued to the floor, as I leaned against the wall, trying to breathe, fighting back tears. My head pounded. Everything narrowed into a tunnel of blackness. My pulse hammered in my ears, drowning out everything else.

Was it all a lie? Did John still *love her?* Was I just a pawn in his game? A temporary emotional crutch, a stand-in, to get him through the divorce?

Then I heard him say, "All right. Take care. Mm-hmm, you to."

You two what? Did she just say 'I love you' to him?

The words pulled me back. I was crouched on the floor now, though I didn't even remember moving. As if crouching would make this less humiliating if I got caught. God, what was I doing?

I stood slowly and tiptoed down the hall, my head spinning, my whole body shaking. At the other end, I paused, pressing my palms against the wall to ground myself. What the hell just happened? What did I just hear? I didn't have time to figure it out, but I felt like everything I had been told, everything I thought I knew, was a lie. Like I had been walking on solid ground only to realize it was quicksand, pulling me under before I could catch my breath.

"Sarah?" John's voice cut through the air.

I turned to find him standing there, looking tired with bags under his eyes. When he looked at me, his smile was immediate, falsely warm, and for a dizzying second, I felt like I was falling.

"Hey, you. What are you doing inside?" He came closer, his hand reaching for my cheek. "Why aren't you out celebrating your birthday with the girls?"

I jumped at his touch. His hand like fire against my skin. But I forced a smile and pushed the reaction down. *Don't overreact. You don't know for sure what you just heard.* "I was just looking for you . . . to see if you were done working," I said, trying my best to force a smile, my voice distant, hollow.

He studied me, his eyes narrowing in concern. "What's wrong?" he asked softly, his thumb brushing my cheek—something that used to make me melt.

"I, um . . ." My throat tightened, the words trapped there. But then I remembered Izzy's warning earlier today. Her worried look. Maybe Izzy had guessed this was happening. Maybe she knew something I didn't. . . . She did have her insider sources around the office. My paranoia started to set it. The puzzle pieces I'd ignored suddenly started to fit together.

"I heard you talking," I blurted out, before I could stop the words.

His eyebrows knitted, his expression shifting to something guarded, unreadable. "To Jane. Um ... you said you ... missed her?"

The silence that followed was suffocating. The truth sat between us like a live wire. Panic rose in my chest, sharp and clawing. Was he pausing to come up with a lie? Even I couldn't tell when he was lying and when he was telling the truth anymore. The lines between the two seemed to blur. If I overreacted in this moment, I might lose him. If I pushed too hard, I would just be another emotional mess he wouldn't want to deal with. Another stressor. I couldn't be that girl. I wouldn't.

I'd given up too much for him, sacrificed too much to make this work. Hiding in the shadows. Protecting us. Letting my work fall behind. Whatever it took. I could get through this. I had to.

I braced myself, ready for him to say something, anything.

He sighed, his shoulders slumping. "Sarah, no, it's not like that. She's just . . . stalling. Playing games. You know how manipulative she is. I'm trying to keep things civil so we can end this without any more drama."

"But you said you *miss her.*" My voice wavered, smaller than I wanted it to be.

He came closer, wrapping his arms around me. I wanted to pull away, to fight the comfort he offered, but I didn't. I needed answers.

"I only said that to keep her calm, to keep things moving in the right direction," he explained, his voice soft. "She was trying to find out where I was, grilling me because I wasn't online this afternoon. She saw charges on our card from out here and was questioning everything. It didn't mean anything. I swear."

A tear ran down my cheek before I could stop it. He caught it with his thumb, holding my face so I couldn't turn away.

"Sarah," he said, his tone calm. "It'll only be a few more months. I promise. I'll talk to my lawyer tomorrow, see if we can move things along even faster. I promise, there's no one else I want. I am here with you and your friends on *your* birthday. There is no one else I care about."

But you were on the phone with her, I wanted to say but couldn't bring myself to.

He leaned in as he pressed his forehead against mine, and for a moment, I let myself believe him. "I know," I whispered, more to convince myself than to convince him. "I trust you."

But deep inside, a small voice stirred. A voice I'd ignored for too long, whispering the question I was too afraid to answer:

Could I ever fully trust him?

———

That night, I let John pull me into his arms, his touch familiar and grounding even as my mind spun. His lips brushed my forehead, then moved down to my neck, each movement slow and deliberate, as if trying to soothe me without saying the words. I clung to him, letting the silence between us say everything I was too afraid to voice—to ask—if he still loved her, if I was just a placeholder, someone to distract him during this difficult time in his life. Or worse yet, if everything we had been through up until now had been a total lie.

I tried to push everything that happened today into the background, but the memories clung to me like smoke in my lungs. I didn't tell Izzy or any of the other girls about the call, especially not Izzy. I didn't want them to see John in a bad light. He didn't need any more women turning on him.

We moved together, not in perfect sync, but in a way that felt like we were trying—trying to hold on, to believe that this—what we had —could still be something. Anything compared to what they had. I focused on every detail: the way his breath hitched when I whispered his name, the soft rasp of my own as I tried not to cry. I wanted to believe that I could still be the one to make him happy. That he would still choose me when all of this was said and done.

Even when the doubts crept in, whispering all the things I didn't want to hear, I pushed them back. I had to. Because no matter how devastated I felt, the thought of losing him—losing him to Jane—was something I couldn't let happen.

If she was the one he missed, then I would become the one he couldn't live without. I didn't know how yet, but I would find a way to be better, to become enough. To replace her. I couldn't give up on him. On us. Not now. Not ever.

"I love you, Sarah. I know what I have put you through is not fair, but I love you."

The words hung between us. I wanted to believe it erased everything, that those three words made it all worth it. That I wasn't just waiting, hoping, holding on to something that didn't even exist.

I swallowed hard. "I love you too." The words came easy, automatic, like breathing. Like a lifeline I refused to let go of.

His fingers tightened around mine, and for now, that was enough.

Chapter Eighteen

The café door chimed as I walked in, my body aching from head to toe from my birthday shenanigans. This café was my favorite spot on the Upper East Side—Recently I had been coming here on the weekends to get ahead on all the projects I had taken on to get the senior editor position.

Over the past months, I had still been putting a lot into making sure I would be a shoo-in for the position, but each week that passed with John's divorce dragging on felt harder and harder to focus on my work. My focus that had previously been all on my work was now being divided, sometimes even completely pulled into his world, the drama between him and Jane. My attention was being pulled in two completely different directions, making it hard to be good at either one. The pressure of having to lie and hide our relationship alone made it emotionally challenging to show up with passion at work, let alone try to go above and beyond for the promotion.

Today, I could barely stand. The long, sleepless weekend, the alcohol, and the conversation I had overheard, had taken its toll. I had no idea how I was going to pull off any of the meetings I had on my schedule today.

I squinted against the bright morning light streaming through the windows, my Chanel sunglasses perched on my nose. They covered most of my face, making me feel like a character from *A Bug's Life*. I wanted an espresso martini, not my usual Americano—anything to take the edge off the pounding in my head. I dragged myself to the counter, my heels clicking loudly on the polished floor.

"Americano, please. Extra shot." My voice was hoarse. I cleared my throat and offered a tight smile to the barista.

"Rough morning?" she asked with sympathy.

I managed a dry laugh. "More like a rough year," I corrected, nervously tapping my red-polished nails on the counter. I used to hate getting my nails done—it took forever, they would always break, and they felt unnecessary. But Jane's hands were always perfectly manicured with long acrylics that made her hands look like claws. Professional. Naturally, I tried them out once and now I was a regular at the nail salon a block away from my apartment.

"Yeah, life has a way of doing that," she said as she typed in my order.

"Wait, make that three," I said, snapping out of my daze. I should at least show up with coffee for Gabriel and Jane for the marketing meeting today. Making a good impression on Gabriel was important, but honestly, just surviving the morning felt like the real goal. Maybe a caffeine offering would make up for whatever I lacked in focus and energy—both of which had been drained by the chaos of my personal life, leaving me feeling more hungover than senior editor material.

"Damn, it must've been a really tough weekend," the barista empathized.

I nodded absently. "You have no idea," I said, then turned to wait, leaning heavily against the counter. The café buzzed around me—the low hum of conversation, the sound of grinding coffee beans, the smell of fresh baked goods that normally made me salivate. Today, though, it just made me dizzy.

When my name was finally called, I reached for the drink, desperate for caffeine. But in my haste, I misjudged the distance and bumped into someone. Hard. *Not again.* Hot coffee splattered every-where, and I looked down at my freshly dry-cleaned blazer—now ruined.

"Oh God," I gasped, falling to my knees to clean up the mess. "I'm so, so sorry."

The man I'd crashed into crouched beside me. "All good," he said, his tone so steady it was like I'd barely brushed past him—never mind that I'd just dumped his entire espresso and my Americano on both of us. His voice was deep, unbothered, like he had nowhere urgent to be. As I frantically dabbed at the mess with a wad of napkins, I finally looked up. He was about my height, all sharp angles and ocean-blue eyes, with a slight gap between his teeth—not in an "I couldn't afford braces" way, but in a "European model who kept it on purpose" kind of way.

"I—uh, no, it's not okay," I stammered, my cheeks flushing with embarrassment. "I should've been more careful. I am sorry."

He chuckled. "I've had worse thrown at me. Trust me, it's no big deal."

I stared at him, stunned at how unconcerned he was, as if this wasn't the most embarrassing thing that had happened all morning. He pulled a neatly folded handkerchief from his pocket and offered it to me.

"Here."

I accepted the handkerchief with a trembling hand. Who carried handkerchiefs these days? Especially men in what I assumed to be in their mid-twenties at most. "Thank you," I said, dabbing at my sleeve. His scent lingered in the air—warm, earthy, like clean linen mixed with something I couldn't place.

"No problem," he said, getting up and offering me his hand. "We've all been there."

I hesitated for a second, then took his hand as he pulled me up. I felt a little awkward but shrugged it off.

"Let me replace your drink," he offered, nodding toward the register.

"No, it is ok—" I started, but the easy smile on his face made me give in. "All right," I said, my lips pursed. "Thanks."

He placed my order with the barista, and I crossed my arms as I waited. The silence stretched between us, not quite awkward, but if the wait had been too much longer, it could have been. I was too drained to make small talk or entertain him, and he seemed content not to push.

"Here you go," he said, handing me my drink.

"Thanks," I murmured again.

"Take care," he added, his eyes lingering on me for a moment.

Then, without another word, he turned and disappeared through the door.

I stood there and watched him vanish into the crowd. Interesting guy—one of those you meet and forget as soon as they're out of sight. The kind who blends in. He wasn't like John, who shook me to my core. This guy? He was easy to overlook, the kind of person you'd never notice in a coffee shop . . . *unless* you bumped into him and spilled your coffee all over him. I had the feeling I'd forget him as easily as I'd met him.

I sighed and glanced down at my coffee-stained jacket. This day was off to a hell of a start.

The barista called from across the room, "You okay? Here are your other drinks."

I forced a smile. "Yeah. Just . . . a rough start to the day, I guess."

Another final smile of pity from the barista.

I stepped out of the café, the cold air biting as I moved down the sidewalk. I dreaded the day ahead. All I wanted was to disappear, to pretend I had no responsibilities, no expectations. Facing Jane—with this hangover, this coffee stain, and the weight of what I'd overheard between her and John—felt like an impossible mountain to climb.

———

Gabriel sat at the head of the table, flipping through his notes, looking as sharp as always. Maya from digital was typing away on her laptop, while Phil, head of marketing, scribbled on his notepad. Jane sat quietly, arms crossed, eyes wide as she took in the coffee stain on my jacket, my first late arrival to a meeting at work, ever.

"Morning, everyone. Sorry I am late," I muttered, handing Jane and Gabriel coffee before sliding into an empty chair. "Had a little coffee mishap."

Gabriel glanced up, offering a tight smile, raising his brows at my stained suit. "Glad you could make it, Sarah. Perfect timing. We're just about to dive into the assets."

I nodded, trying to focus and catch myself up to speed. Maya clicked through the slides on the projector. "Here are the scripts that Gabriel will be using to film content as David for the promotional material."

My heart sank as I skimmed them. They weren't mine. They didn't even look like the original versions I had edited—these were completely different.

I stared at the screen, trying to hide my surprise. These scripts were stiff—too formal. Not right. Not at all what we had discussed. They didn't reflect David's style at all, the image I had pitched as the face of the campaign.

I swallowed hard, my stomach twisting. "Wait, these aren't the ones I worked on," I said, looking at the group, my voice rising a bit. "These . . . they're off. The tone is wrong. David should sound more like the approachable and charismatic character we talked about, not like a corporate executive. If we are trying to capture the younger crowd, this will never work."

Maya glanced at me, then the screen. "These are the final drafts we received after we got market feedback. Did you not see the last email with the updated scripts for you to edit?"

My pulse quickened. "What email?" I asked, scrambling to check my inbox.

Jane looked at me, a flicker of sharpness in her eyes. "The email

179

with the finalized scripts you were supposed to edit. Maya sent them over this weekend for you to complete. You didn't get them?"

There it was. The email sitting in my inbox. I scanned the faces around the table. I hadn't seen the email. I had been distracted—drowning in self-pity following John's conversation with Jane. I hadn't even thought to check for updates over the weekend.

"I . . . I must've missed it," I said, barely above a whisper. "I'm sorry. I didn't know there were final revisions I needed to make."

Jane's brow furrowed in pure fury. "We're already behind schedule. We need these to be aligned with David's voice before we move forward."

I nodded, trying to mask the panic rising in my chest. "I can fix it," I said quickly, my mind was racing. "I'll go through them. I'll get them done as soon as possible."

Phil shifted in his chair, clearly frustrated. "We don't have time to redo everything last minute, Sarah. We're already behind as it is."

My stomach twisted even tighter. I had dropped the ball. This was on me. I hadn't just missed an email—I had missed an opportunity to deliver when it mattered most, all because I was too caught up in John and Jane drama. The pressure suffocated me.

Maya's voice cut through the tension. "We're on a tight deadline, Sarah. We need these finalized today. Can you do that? Then we can all reconvene tomorrow over Zoom to discuss the filming and release schedule in more detail."

I nodded. "Of–of course." Though I wasn't sure how. My work had already been piling up and slipping, and now this. This was at least ten hours of work. This project, the weight of the promotion, suddenly felt heavier than ever.

Gabriel looked at me, "I need you to get this right, Sarah. This is a huge part of the campaign, and your idea. I am counting on you."

The room felt like it was closing in on me. How could I have let this happen? How could I have missed something so critical? I nodded again, swallowing the lump in my throat. "I know. I'll make sure it's done."

The room fell silent for a moment before Gabriel spoke again, his voice kind but firm. "We're all in this together. Let's just make sure we stay aligned moving forward so we don't waste everyone's time."

Jane's gaze stayed fixed on me, cold but calculating. "This can't happen again," she said, her tone as sharp as a blade. She said it quietly, but everyone heard.

I nodded, barely registering the words.

Then a thought started gnawing at me. Was Jane onto me? Had she somehow figured out that John and I were together this weekend? Was that why she'd been calling him, trying to get a sense of where he was? Or had she seen the photos the girls and I posted online? Could she tell I was hungover and realized I didn't see the email because I was partying all weekend? I tried to push the paranoia away, but it clung to me, lingering in the air. I couldn't shake the feeling that she knew something.

As the meeting wrapped up, I was reminded just how far behind I was at work, and in life. And I had no idea how to get back on track.

Chapter Nineteen

John and I sat at a quiet corner table at Carlyle's, an upscale restaurant in an Upper East Side hotel where JFK and Marilyn Monroe once stayed. Oh, the irony—just a powerful man and his mistress of the year. Soft lighting bathed the room in a warm glow, creating an intimate atmosphere. Jazz music hummed in the background. The rich wood paneling and plush velvet seating felt like stepping back in time—classic but modern. Our server, dressed in a tuxedo (*with* a tail), hovered nearby, always ready but never intrusive. I couldn't help but think back to when I first met John, mistaking him for a server. The memory made me almost smile, though the thought of it now carried a different weight, a memory that I once loved to reminisce on now made me sad.

It was the kind of place designed to make you feel special, like you were part of something timeless. But as I sat there, I couldn't quite sink into the illusion. The weight of everything that had happened between John and me made the fancy picture-perfect dinner feel hollow, like I didn't truly belong in this moment or with him—or maybe it was that I believed he was supposed to be at a place like this with someone like Jane, not like me.

"Thanks for having dinner with me before I head back to Chicago tomorrow," John said. I figured this was his way of making up for the birthday fiasco, his way of showing that he loved me and was choosing to be with me over Jane.

I had pulled an all-nighter the previous day, working on the edits for Gabriel's project. My eyes burned from the lack of sleep, but I somehow managed to power through and finish the scripts before the meeting. My mind had been racing with everything, what I'd overheard about Jane and John, my failure of a meeting, but I did my best to push it all aside. The work had to get done, and I couldn't afford to slip up. I'd do anything for the promotion. I'd been running on fumes, and it was all starting to catch up with me.

"A glass of your cabernet and a gin martini, dry vermouth, straight up with a twist of lemon," John said, handing the drink menus to the server, giving me that smile. The smile that used to melt me, the one that made me feel safe, like he really cared for me.

"What if I didn't want a martini this time?"

He gave me a semi-bored look. "Are you telling me you were going to order something else?" He chuckled.

My eyes narrowed, a sliver of levity lacing through my voice. "Okay, fine. I wasn't, but I'd like to at least pretend that I might change it." I said. "Thanks for ordering it for me."

"Of course." He looked down at his menu, likely thinking about the laundry list of items he wanted to order. "So, how are you? How are things at work? How's the Stone project?"

I hated that I felt defensive at his question. "Uh . . . good, I guess. Why do you ask?" Had Jane said something to him about how badly I fucked up in the meeting?

He looked up from his menu, staring as if trying to read my thoughts. "I didn't ask for any particular reason. I just want to know how you're doing. I can see . . ." He trailed off. "I can see how all this is taking a toll on you. All the Jane stuff, your workload. I feel terrible dragging you into it, and I hate that it's gone on for so long."

"John." I put my hand over his, seeing the pain flicker in his blue

183

eyes. "I know you're doing the best you can to make this all go away. It's not ideal, and of course it hurts, but . . . you're worth it." It was the truth. But I was hiding the hurt that I didn't want him to see. I couldn't add more stress to his plate. I couldn't let him see how hard this really was on me. If I did, he may not want to keep me around.

I could see the guilt eating away at his face. Every day he looked a little more tired. More exhausted. "But you have to work closely with her. Lie to your friends, let them lie for you, just so we can sneak away and see each other. I know how much you have on your plate, working to become senior editor. I don't know. I feel guilty for taking you away from your life and your goals. It's not fair to you. The last thing I want is for you to lose yourself in our relationship."

Was he breaking up with me? Was it even possible to break up with someone who was still married? Was I losing myself in this relationship? It sounded like the words someone used to end things.

"Are you . . . Are you breaking up with me?" I breathed. I hadn't given up all this time, broke my no-dating rule, completely exhausted myself, and fallen behind on my workload trying to manage both lives, only to be dumped. I'd spent the last three months lying to Theo, Willow, Jane, and everyone else in the office just to support him and be there for him. *He had to choose me.* He had to choose me. I had been . . . perfect. Perfect in every way. The cool, understanding, sexy, flirtatious, patient girlfriend—I mean, lover. Mistress. Whatever I was. What more could he want? I had been fucking Mistress of Goddamn the Year.

"Oh. My. Gosh!" A shriek carried from across the busy restaurant. Surely a female. My internal alarm went off. Who could it be? What were the chances of John and I being completely exposed right now? My stomach twisted into knots. We both looked at each other, deer in the headlights, as if to say: *We're screwed.*

I looked up, and he turned slowly as the figure emerged from the dimly lit bar.

There she was. . . .

Jane's assistant.

Jenny.

———

For the first time since John and I had been together, I didn't obsessively check social media to see where everyone we knew was having dinner. I was too sleep deprived to have thought about it. As we were seated, I hadn't done my usual scanning of the restaurant to see if anyone I knew was there. I had finally let my guard down. Of course that would be when Jane's assistant would show up at the same restaurant and see us tucked away in the corner. Of the twelve thousand or so restaurants in all of Manhattan, Jenny was *here*. At the same time we were. I briefly wondered if Jane had hired a personal investigator. Or was this just a weird coincidence?

Jenny Thorne was the New York socialite type who didn't quite make the cut. Young—no more than twenty-one—effortlessly chic. The kind of girl born into a brownstone or a six-floor townhouse. Private school, nanny as surrogate mother, and all her friends wore pearls and drank tea. There was a small part of me that envied her, but I could never fully commit to that path of neurosis and polish like she had.

My mind raced to process this and figure out what lie we were going to spin. What would we tell the one person who might even know more about Jane than both of us combined? John was married to her, and I'd stalked every bit of her online content back to 2010 one late night, so it was safe to say we knew a lot about Jane, but Jenny knew *everything*.

John put on his calm-and-collected smile. I followed his lead.

She sauntered over, her Chanel skirt swishing, her five-inch Louboutins clacking on the floor, and Dior sunglasses perched on her shiny, sleek straight brown hair. Thin and petite, she had somehow landed a gig with Jane a few years ago. I had to admit the girl worked hard. She seemed to be a great assistant.

"Thornebush!" John stood up as Jenny reached the table and

pulled her into a big bear hug, the kind I imagined he'd give his three little sisters. He almost lifted her off the floor. I guess it's easy to do that when the girl couldn't weigh more than a buck ten. I assumed "Thornebush" was a nickname. Cute.

"John, it's so good to see you! Your hair is so long. I miss working with you. When are you moving into the office here? Is Chicago trying to keep you as long as possible? They're really losing their best asset. Anyway, I saw your big head over here—can't miss it. How are you?!" She paused to catch her breath, then turned to me, catching my awkward smile, like I was a stranger John had brought to dinner.

"Holy shit, wait . . . Sarah?! How are you doing, girl? I didn't even recognize you. You dress so differently in the office. You look fucking hot."

I didn't know how to respond. I'd recently bought a few new pieces—lace tops, tight leather pants that hugged my hips. Jane's Instagram had been my new Pinterest inspiration board, but I didn't feel nearly as effortless as she made it look. Every time we went out, I wondered if John was thinking about how much better he had had it with Jane.

"Oh, geez." I glanced down at myself, as if I needed to be reminded of what I was wearing. "Thanks, Jenny. What are you doing here? Are you with someone?"

I prayed she wouldn't say, "Oh yeah, I'm here with Jane plotting how to destroy her ex-husband's secret mistress."

"Oh yeah, me, my boyfriend, and some friends from Northbridge Publishing came out for drinks. A little happy hour action. We were just leaving. Isn't this place amazing?" Jenny said, her tone light and cheerful, completely at ease.

It wasn't unusual for people in the industry to mix and mingle, even across companies. The publishing world was surprisingly small, and nights like this weren't uncommon. There was something about the similar schedules and mutual understanding of the industry that made it easier to make friends within the world rather than with people outside of it. There had once been a few whispers here and there about a merger between Northbridge and Regent, though it was unlikely unless there were some big changes at either company.

I nodded, silently hoping that John would jump in soon and explain why we were here together.

"Wait." Jenny started to put two and two together. "Why are you two here? I didn't know you knew each other."

It took everything in me to not throw up on her shoes. A stomach cocktail of fear and guilt. Fear of being found out. Of being outed to Jane and having our whole plan, my career, my life crumble into dust. How could I be so stupid to not scope out the place for someone we knew? We exchanged a look, but before John or I could speak, Jenny snapped her fingers. "Ohhh, it all makes sense now. You two met at the Gala. Jane told me. Duh." She tapped her forehead, as if that little action helped the information click into place. I tried not to show my relief.

"Jane and Sarah are working on a project together. John, you're moving here." She raised a finger and pointed to the sky, as if connecting the dots on one of those detective boards with red string and pins. "Sarah, there is so much you can learn from John. Holy shit. With his help and Jane behind you, you'll be unstoppable. Wait, are you two working on something together? That would be *so* badass."

At least now we had something to work off of. I passed John the invisible talking stick.

"Yes," he said, drawing out the word. "We met at the Gala, and I see a lot of promise in Sarah. As soon as I'm officially in town, I'm thinking of bringing her in on a project. One of our acquisitions, to see how she does. It's on the back burner and hush-hush, actually. In fact, this is the first time I'm telling Sarah about it." He turned to me and smiled. "What do you think?" His asked, palms open.

"Oh my God, this is so cool," Jenny said before I could respond. "My lips are sealed. I don't want to interrupt your business meeting. I'll leave you to it. And Sarah, congratulations, babe. This is going to be huge. Life-changing for you. Working with John is the best experience I've ever had with a boss. He's amazing." Her voice revealed that she missed working with him. I could almost swear there was a hint of, "I wish I was working for you again and not stuck with your crazy ex-wife," but maybe I was biased.

We waved our goodbyes as she ran back to her friends and they left the restaurant.

As soon as they walked out the door, I let out a breath and turned to John. "Well, that was way too close," I said, my voice low but sharp. "For a second, I thought she was going to whip out her phone and text Jane a picture of all of us right there."

John ran a hand through his hair, looking tense. "She won't. At least, I don't think she will. But . . . yeah, we might need to be more careful about where we meet from now on."

I crossed my arms, the uneasy feeling in my chest refusing to settle. "Are you sure she won't say anything? Clearly, Jenny loves to talk, and she seemed . . . excited. If she says *anything* to Jane, we are literally screwed."

His jaw tightened. "I'll handle it if it comes to that," he said, his tone steady but not reassuring. I knew what that meant. More lies.

I nodded reluctantly, but the knot in my stomach didn't loosen. "That was clutch . . . *boss,*" I said, elbowing him, forcing a lighter tone, trying to cut through the tension. "Good call on mentioning it being hush-hush. Without that, Jenny's . . . well, verbose mouth would've definitely spilled the beans to Jane."

He smirked, but a shadow of concern lingered in his eyes.

"How much does she know about you and Jane?" I asked, grasping for some new information.

"She was our assistant when we were together. When Jane moved to Manhattan, she went with her. Jane had a lot more needs than I did. At this point, she knows we're getting divorced. Between all the tax meetings on Jane's calendar and the paperwork that we have to send back and forth, it's hard to hide from an assistant," he said, taking a big sip of his wine.

Then John returned to our earlier conversation now that the Energizer Bunny had left. The one I certainly hadn't let slip from my mind. "To be clear, no, I'm not breaking up with you by any stretch of the imagination. But I can see how tired you are, how behind you are with Stone's project, all the traveling. . . . Is there anything I can do to help with the project load you have?"

I let out a breath. Relief flooded me as I'd just spent the last ten minutes thinking he was going to break up with me.

John had enough on his plate, and the last thing I needed was to give him another reason for the divorce to take longer by helping me with my work. "Don't worry about me. I'm fine. I'll get my work under control. Maybe we can cut back on traveling—at least not every weekend.

Every other week would be more manageable, at least for now. The only thing I need from you is a divorce. Honestly, the sooner the better. I can't keep lying. Every day it's harder and harder to go to the office. Please. Just get the divorce finalized," I said, clasping my hands at my chest. I might be willing to forgo the conversation I overheard if he could prove that he was serious about wrapping up the divorce so we could be together in public.

He nodded, his expression apologetic. "I'm sorry it hasn't happened yet. There's just been so much with the lawyers and Jane. . . . You know how it is. But I'll get it done." His excuses felt hollow now, each one losing its impact. As he spoke, I noticed the numbness settling in. The usual flicker of hope that used to spark when he promised to follow through was now just a dying flame.

"Can you do something for me?" I asked, hopefully.

"Anything."

"Can you just give me a definite date when the divorce will be final?" My voice wavered, exposing my desperation and exhaustion. "I know it might not mean much to you, but I need something solid—something to hold on to. Even if it's not exact, just knowing there's an endpoint . . ." I trailed off, swallowing the lump in my throat. "Even if it isn't ideal, it helps me to know there will be a light at the end of the tunnel."

"With mediation, taxes, and Jane being as easy to work with as a stubborn mule . . . I'm confident it will be done by the end of the year. But I'm hoping to move out here sooner than that. I think it'll be better for us."

Six more months? But he wanted to move sooner? I tried to breathe through the wave of conflicting emotions. Six months was an eternity, but the idea of him being here sooner . . . that stirred something in me. Hope, maybe, but also doubt. Could I really hold on until then?

I took a deep breath, steadying myself. The new timeline felt real now, not just a vague hope. It was something tangible, a finish line I could focus on, but still so far away. If I could just make it through a bit longer, perhaps I could have it all—love with a man who cared for me. Love with a man who chose me.

I had to stay focused. I had to keep pushing forward. But as my workload grew, as the deadlines piled up, I wondered if I could keep up. John's promise of moving sooner had stirred something inside me, but the exhaustion, the constant feeling of being behind at work, the endless balancing act of trying to be there for him—right now, was too much. The hope was still there, but now it came with a lingering, quiet fear that maybe, just maybe, I wasn't as strong and capable as I thought I was.

"Sarah, I can't lose you. You mean too much to me. Please trust me that I am working as hard as I can to get this done for us." John leaned forward, elbows on the table, hands clasped, forehead resting on his knuckles as if holding himself together.

I fought to hide any hint of insecurity, any flicker of fear that this may end terribly. The thought alone was like a nightmare. Instead, I nodded and pushed my hand across the table. I conjured up the cool, unflappable me—the one who didn't need a man to feel whole. The confident girl John had fallen for at the Gala. Not the insecure, desperate version of myself that had emerged over the past three months, anxiously urging him to finalize his divorce so he would finally 'choose me.' I had become the 'pick me' girl. Desperate for validation. Desperate to be selected by the man from the sea of other options. I used to view the woman I had become as pathetic and needy.

I turned off the emotional switch, turned it off like a light. I did what I used to do best. I held out my hand, hovering above the table waiting for a handshake, like a business deal. "Six months? December 31st?" I said, my voice steady. "The divorce will be finalized, and we can tell Jane. Tell the world."

He met my palm with his, sealing the deal. "Six months. I'll do whatever it takes to get it done."

"Then it's a deal." As the words left my lips, a part of me withdrew. I began to shut down, seeking the stone-cold detachment I once wore like armor. I wanted to believe him. I really did. But how many times had I heard a version of this promise? Three more months. Now six more months. Just a little longer. So much of it wasn't even in his hands. Yet, here I was, clinging to a timeline like it meant something. Like it would actually happen.

I went back to picking at our appetizers, avoiding his gaze, though I could feel his eyes on me, sensing the shift in the energy between us —the retreat of the love that once felt secure. The closing off of my heart. To protect myself. I hated that part of me still wanted to hold on tight. That part that was *still* entertaining the idea of waiting for a man who, legally, wasn't free to choose me yet. I had officially become the woman I once pitied.

Chapter Twenty

W hat did you do, get a boyfriend?" Theo asked, half joking but also completely serious. He leaned back in his chair, relaxed and waiting to see if I squirmed.

His office was a perfect reflection of him. Books lined the walls, from Buddhist texts to business manuals. A low couch sat on the floor, as if he wanted to stay grounded while he read. Crystals were scattered across his desk, small objects he fiddled with while on calls.

Quotes were framed everywhere, his favorite being one by Goethe: "As long as one is not committed, there is hesitation, the possibility of withdrawing. . . . The moment you finally commit, then Providence moves. All sorts of things happen to help you that would never have happened otherwise." I read it every time I visited his office.

There were also collages on the walls—astronauts, mushrooms, abstract pictures. I was convinced he was always microdosing. His tattooed arm was usually exposed, despite the office dress code. Theo didn't think the rules applied to him. "Surrender" was inked on the inside of his bicep.

I almost spit out my coffee. "What? No, of course not. Why would you say that?"

Theo had called me into his office without any context. "Come by my office sometime today. I need to talk to you about something," he'd said.

"Anything I can prepare?"

"Nope." And that was that.

My worst nightmare: no clues, nothing to go on, just . . . nothing.

Theo often acted like a father figure—protective not only of my career, but of my happiness, my health. He knew me better than I knew myself at times, which made hiding my life from him nearly impossible. To leave out a huge part of my life, being with John, from our conversations was harder than I had thought it would be over the last few months. I figured my best strategy was to avoid him altogether.

"You used to spend every waking hour plus weekends here at the office. I just haven't been seeing you around much," Theo said. "Is everything okay?"

I leaned back, trying to match his relaxed posture. He could read me like a book, one of the many in his office. He understood human psychology, human behavior.

"I've just been juggling a lot," I said, trying to keep it light. "Trying to keep up with the workload, but also building stronger friendships with my girlfriends here in Manhattan," I lied. "It's a lot to juggle, but it's been great. Good for me." More lies, or half truths. I had to keep it vague—no details to give him room to poke holes in my story. As soon as I started sharing too much, he'd pick it apart. That was his specialty.

His gaze was fixed on me with a familiar intensity. He shook his head slowly, skepticism in his eyes. The corners of his mouth tightened, and I could almost see the wheels turning as he psychoanalyzed each word.

Whoever speaks first loses, he'd once taught me.

But his stare burst the bubble, and before I could stop myself, I blurted out, "Maybe you, Willow, Izzy, and I can get together for dinner soon? Catch up? I miss you guys." I hadn't realized how much I missed them until that moment. There was something about them that was easy to love and fear all at the same time.

He spread his hands, palms up, still leaning back with his elbows on the armrests of his chair. "Sure, if you can squeeze us in. We'd love to," a small smile tugged at his lips.

"Great. Let's plan for next Friday night," I said, locking it in to show him I was serious. Committed.

"Perfect, text us the details." He tossed the ball back into my court. "So, what else?" He left the question open ended. Directionless for me to lead. Dammit. Theo didn't play checkers; he played chess. Always steps ahead. Always strategic.

"You called me here. I thought you had something to say to me," I said, playing innocent.

"Sarah, you know me better than that. I'm not the guy who gives you more work. I'm the guy who makes sure your mind is right so you can be effective at your job . . . and in your life." He said it matter-of-factly. "As I always say—"

We finished the sentence in unison. "Work harder on yourself than you do on your work, and your work will do what it's supposed to do."

"Exactly." He nodded like a proud mentor. "I've taught you well. I just want to make sure you stay focused. Jane told me about the Stone meeting a few weeks ago . . . not like you to completely miss a critical email like that."

"I know. It was a one-time thing. I promise. I had just been buried and missed it somehow." I shook my head. Another lie.

He narrowed his eyes on me. "How is the run going for senior editor?"

"Good, I think. I have been taking on as many projects as I can. Jane asked me to be on the Stone project. It feels like I am doing everything I can, but if you have any suggestions for me to make sure I secure the position, I would love to hear."

Theo nodded slowly. "To set yourself apart, you need to land a major author—someone with high visibility and the potential to hit the bestseller list immediately. Start building relationships with some top authors in the space. Then pitch ideas that align with Regent House's brand. You have a good start by being on the project with Gabriel Stone, despite the slip in the last meeting—I'm sure you'll recover. Use that relationship as leverage to show you can bring in top talent. It's about showing leadership that you can not just work hard, but add actual revenue to the company as well. *That* is real value. Willow is looking for proof that you're the perfect fit, and landing a top author will provide the tangible and measurable evidence that she is looking for."

I nodded, but my stomach twisted. I was already drowning in work, barely keeping up, and now I was supposed to somehow do more? I used to believe hard work alone would get me there, but this —this was something else entirely. Networking with high-profile authors? Pitching their books to the leadership team? But if Theo was suggesting it, I had to do it. If the other senior editors in the office had, I could too.

"Understood." I nodded once. And although I felt a pang of anxiety, I also felt reinvigorated. Like this was a step up from what my competition was doing. Every time I talked to Theo, I was brought back to my goals. I really didn't know what I would do without him.

He softened. "Sarah, you're phenomenal. You're a winner. You're the most driven junior editor I've ever worked with. Hungry. Focused. Capable. You have that X factor that can't be taught. I see a lot of myself in you." For a second, I could have sworn he got a tad choked up. "No matter what path you choose—whether it's this or something else—just know I'm proud of you. Willow and I love you like family."

I choked back what could have been a tear, but I stopped it before it came. "Thank you, Theo. I love you both so much. You've helped so much over the last year. I don't know if I will ever be able to repay you."

"Well, good for you that we've been keeping track. Your bill is somewhere around $500,000. We'll email you the invoice when you make senior editor." He winked.

"Speaking of . . . They are still going to be announcing it at next year's Gala, right?"

"Yep, nothing has changed there."

"Are there any talks about who they are considering?" I asked, knowing he wouldn't tell me, but hey, it was worth a shot.

"Yes . . . but you know I can't tell you that," he said with a big smile on his face. "Now get out there and get to work."

I shrugged. "Figured I'd ask, see if you felt generous today." I smiled.

As I walked out, I waited for his usual sign-off. I approached the door, stopped, and looked back. His eyes met mine, and he grinned, almost as if he'd been waiting for me to notice. "Hey, kid . . . don't embarrass me," he said, grinning from ear to ear—a rare sight.

I tilted my head back and laughed. There it was.

"I would never dream of it. Cross my heart and hope to die. Thanks, Theo," I said.

I sat back down at my desk and worked the rest of the afternoon with a passion and focus I hadn't felt in months. Even though so many things in my life weren't working, Theo breaking down some tangible ways to prove I was the one for senior editor energized me. It gave me a little hope to fuel me a bit longer. I couldn't believe I hadn't considered asking him exactly what I needed to do months ago. I guess some lessons you learn the hard way.

Chapter Twenty-One

I t had been a month since I had seen John, thanks to our new arrangement. I'd mostly stayed in the city, focusing on my workload, while he focused on getting divorced. The idea was that we'd see each other less often—every three or four weeks—so we could each focus on what mattered most, him getting divorced and us being together, sooner. As I sat in my seat on the flight to Chicago to see him, I couldn't help but feel more excited than on trips I'd taken before. The time apart only made me crave being with him more.

Izzy slept beside me on the plane. John had insisted she come out when I told him she didn't have Fourth of July plans. His friend Andy would be joining us as well. John knew how hard it had been on me to keep everything a secret. Having Izzy there to hang out with made me feel like we weren't locked away in our own world all alone. We touched down at O'Hare Airport, and I was starting to feel like a regular here. I knew the Delta lounge attendants by name and even a few of the pilots.

I had been scrolling Instagram, and just as I was about to close the app, I hesitated and typed Jane Reynolds's name into the search bar. As usual, her page was a highlight reel of everything I wasn't—

luxury vacations, jet-setting across the globe, posing with famous authors, and those church photos where she talked about her faith. I had to admit, there was something admirable about how confidently she owned it. I never grew up with religion, so I couldn't relate, but it was hard not to respect how naturally it seemed to fit into her perfect persona.

Then there she was—designer wardrobe, slicked-back hair, unnaturally smooth skin (probably from years of facials and cosmetic work). She seemed flawless in every possible way. Was it even possible to idolize and hate someone at the same time?

I set my phone in my lap, emotions swirling. Part of me resented how she treated John and handled the divorce behind closed doors. But another part of me? I couldn't help but want her life. At work, she was the epitome of success—the corner office, the big clients, the stages. Everything I dreamed of. And yet, outside of work, she made me feel small. Insignificant. How I had to hide my relationship with John just to be around her. It was like I was trapped between envy and disgust—wanting to be her and hating that I did.

Checking her social media started as a way to get work inspiration—tips and motivation on leveling up in my career. But somewhere along the way, it shifted. I started obsessing over every post, checking her profile multiple times a day, studying her outfits, her perfectly styled hair, and her flawless makeup. I wanted to mirror it all. The catch? I was trying to replicate her lavish life on a budget that barely scratched the surface of what she spent. Sometimes I felt like a knockoff version of her. Still, I couldn't stop, hoping that if I copied enough, I might finally feel like enough—like I could even compete with her for John.

Despite the obsession, I hated her. I hated Jane. I couldn't keep idolizing her while knowing she was draining the life out of John. She was the root of his pain, and it killed me to see it.

Her post today: "*New beginnings. Grateful for what's ahead. Life's better when you stop holding on to the past. Cheers to letting go.*" The words stung. She was 'moving on' (at least to the outside world, she was), living her life in a way that seemed effortless, while I was stuck—obsessing, comparing, drowning in resentment. It was like her life was an endless highlight reel I could never compete with, a reminder that no matter how hard I tried, I couldn't measure up.

I couldn't let her control my thoughts. I couldn't take it anymore. I wasn't living my own life—I was too busy wishing I had hers. For the first time, I wasn't just annoyed. I was angry—angry at how much I had let her invade my mind, distracting me from what was important. How much I was losing myself. I could see it happening, but it was like I couldn't stop it. A train that had too much momentum to be slowed.

I picked up my phone, hesitating for a second. The tension in my chest grew, but I wasn't about to let her win. She didn't deserve another follower, especially when she was making John's life hell. I clicked "unfollow," and the button turned from grey to blue, and for the first time in months, I felt free from the constant comparison.

I nudged Izzy awake. "Hey, we're here, Iz."

She pulled off her eye mask like she'd just woken up from a twenty-hour red-eye, blinking a few times before noticing I looked irritated. "What's up?" she asked.

"I just unfollowed Jane on Instagram," I said, watching her face for any reaction.

Izzy's eyes flickered with surprise. "Sarah, that is great. I know that following her has been hard on you. How do you feel?"

I took a deep breath, feeling the weight lift. "A little lighter. Like I can finally breathe again."

———

I got a text from John after we landed.

> Come on in once you get here. I might be finishing a work call, but will try to be finished by the time you arrive. Door code is 0611#.

I couldn't help but notice the code was Jane's birthday. June 11th. Only a few days after mine.

An hour later, we arrived at John's apartment. He had been so busy these past few months, the universe was dumping everything on him, leaving no room for anything but work and dealing with the emotional roller coaster that was Jane and the divorce. Every time we talked on the phone, he'd just finished navigating her latest neurosis, the next mini-drama. But not this weekend. This weekend we were celebrating the Fourth of July all together, and I was determined to have a good time. No slip-ups like at my birthday.

Plus, I was finally going to meet Andy, the first and only person in John's life he was introducing me to. Andy had been his best friend since college. It had been almost five months since we'd met, and he was finally letting me into his circle. With all the overlap between John's and Jane's circles, we'd had to be careful about who knew about us until the divorce was final.

I was excited for the weekend—just some time with the boys and Izzy, lighting fireworks, sitting by the fire, smoking cigars. I was surprised Izzy had agreed to come after the birthday fiasco. She'd been supportive of John and me since, but I wasn't sure if things were really back to normal or if she was just choosing not to say what she really thought about the situation. At this point, I'd decided that the less I told her about the John and Jane drama, the better. I hoped that the more time we spent together, the clearer it would become how great John and I were for each other.

But despite the excitement, I couldn't shake my underlying anxiety. The last trip didn't end well with John and Jane's conversation hanging over us. Part of me was bracing for impact, but I was determined to enjoy the weekend regardless.

I punched in the code to John's apartment and we snuck in so we wouldn't interrupt his meeting. But instead of being in his office finishing a call, he was standing at his kitchen counter, hunched over a large brown box, his hands clasped on either side of it.

"John?" I whispered, just in case he was wearing AirPods and the call was still happening.

He turned quickly, embarrassed, like we had caught him. "Oh, *hey*, you two," he said, trying to hide what seemed like pain. I assumed it was related to Jane's wrath.

My stomach dropped. "What did Jane do now?" I asked, the excitement for the weekend quickly fading as I shifted into protector mode. It killed me to see him like this—such a kind man with a pure heart. She had the nerve to keep mistreating him, and it made me furious.

"Oh, nothing. I'm good. I was just thinking," he said, trying to wipe any emotion from his handsome face. He held my shoulders and looked at me. "How was your flight? Not too long?" He pulled me into a hug and did the same with Izzy. I could tell something was off.

"Sick place." Izzy immediately scoped it out and rolled her luggage into what she declared to be her guest room. "I'll be in here," she said with a yawn and quickly closed the door.

John and I exchanged smiles and rolled our eyes. When we got back to the kitchen, I pinned him with a stare. "John, I can tell something's wrong. Are you okay?"

He looked down and exhaled. I had never seen him like this—stunned, tense. He shook his head slowly. Whatever was in the box must have been something he couldn't process, something that got under his skin. It was too big a box to be divorce papers.

"Honestly, I don't really know," he admitted. "I . . . I just got the strangest package." He stepped aside to let me see it.

"Can I look?"

"Sure." He picked up his water, taking a big drink.

I pulled back the flaps of the box as if a wild animal might jump out of it. But it wasn't a wild animal—it was a bunch of random junk. Toilet paper, tissues, a mirror. It looked like a regular Amazon delivery. I kept digging—diapers, pacifiers.

"Did you accidentally get the neighbors' package?" I asked. They did have a baby. I kept looking. A tool kit and a book called *How to Get Over It*. "What is all of this?"

He didn't answer, shaking his head, eyes fixed on the box, lost in a daze.

I stepped back and eyed it suspiciously. "This is really weird, but it could be anyone's package. Does it say who sent it? Is there a note?" I searched for the shipping label.

"No, it's not from Amazon. The box has my name and my address handwritten on it." He pulled a piece of paper out of his back pocket. "I also found this note inside." He handed it to me.

I unfolded the paper. The typed message read:

John,

I thought I'd send you a little "care package" to help you get through . . . well, whatever's left of this miserable situation.

Some toilet paper. Since you're so full of crap, I figured you might need this to clean up the mess. Good luck squeezing out all that BS you keep carrying around.

Diapers: Since you seem to have trouble dealing with your own messes. Don't want any accidents!

Some Kleenex, for all those late-night cries when you realize you'll never get her back.

Here is a pacifier. Because every big baby needs one. Hopefully this will help with your constant whining and complaining.

A mirror, so you can take a good, hard look at the reason everything fell apart.

Mini Toolkit: To help you repair your broken ego. Might need some stronger glue, though.

"How to Get Over It" Book: Clearly, you need help in this department. Try not to get too distracted by the pictures—I know, the big words might be a challenge for a guy like you.

Anyway, I'm sure you'll find good use for all of this. And hey, cheer up, buddy—there's a light at the end of the tunnel. Just don't block it with your giant head.

Good luck (you'll need it),
XX Daddy

I looked up at him. "What the fuck?" I yelled. "Who sent this?" The longer the months had dragged on, the more protective I'd become of John.

"I think it's from Jane's boyfriend," he said. "His name is Peter. He works in the NYC office."

"You know about that?"

"*You* know about that?" He looked at me, surprised.

My stomach tightened. I hadn't exactly lied, but I hadn't told him either.

"Well . . . no . . . I mean, kind of," I admitted, my voice faltering. "I've seen her leaving the office with him from time to time. I just assumed. But I didn't want to add to your worries if it wasn't real. You've got enough on your plate." I braced myself for his reaction.

John's jaw tightened. "So, you knew about him all along," he said, the frustration clear. "I guess that confirms it." He let out a sharp breath. "You didn't think to tell me?"

"I didn't know if they were together for sure, and I didn't want to add any stress onto your plate," I said, avoiding his gaze. "I didn't want to make things worse for you."

John frowned, like he wasn't sure what to believe.

"I am sorry. I should have told you. I shouldn't have kept that information from you."

He shook his head. "It isn't your fault. I had my suspicions, but every time I'd ask Jane about him, she'd give me the runaround. Denying it. Always trying to turn it back on me—or whoever she thought I was seeing." He let out a dry laugh, but there was no humor in it.

Then, after a beat, he added, "She even threw your name into the mix once. Just to see if she could get a rise out of me."

My breath caught. He didn't look at me. He'd just found out I'd kept something from him, and now he was dropping this—like he was waiting to see how I'd react.

"Wait, she asked about me? Why would she do that?" I panicked.

"Just once. I shut it down right away. Now she's asking about every other woman in the office. She's just throwing spaghetti at the wall to see what sticks. That seems to be her go-to strategy. Probably to justify her own feelings of guilt," he said, his voice calm, reassuring me that our relationship wasn't hanging by a thread.

"Wait." I paused, refocusing. "So you think Peter sent that box?"

"Daddy? Who else do you know that Jane seems to be sneaking around with who talks like that?"

"So true." My mind raced with memories of Peter goofing around with the business development team, throwing around crude, locker-room-style banter. I had never expected John to pick up on it, but I guess with the amount of time he'd come into the office, he had caught a few things that weren't hard to miss.

I reached for the letter again, my blood simmering as I read it once more. It didn't make sense. Why would Peter send something like this out of the blue?

"Do you think Jane knows he sent this?"

The words barely left my mouth before another thought crept in. Maybe this wasn't just about John. Maybe Peter was just as tired of hiding in the shadows as I was. Maybe he felt the same way I did— trapped in a game neither of us could win. And this? This was his way of retaliating. His way of forcing it all into the open.

"I seriously doubt it. She'd be mortified. Besides, this just gives me more leverage in the divorce, and that's the last thing she wants right now." He paused, shaking his head. "Damn, she really knows how to pick 'em, doesn't she?"

I could see the frustration on his face, but all he did was reach into the box, pull out the rolls of toilet paper, and set them on the counter. He grabbed the box, walked toward the office and slid it under Jane's desk, where the rest of her remnants and their bad memories he wanted to avoid collected dust. "Let's just forget about this," he muttered. As he returned to the kitchen, he exhaled sharply, then gestured toward the toilet paper with a forced smile. "At least we're stocked up for the cabin. Nothing ruins a Fourth of July weekend like running out."

I forced a breathy laugh, "I'm so sorry this is happening to you, John," my voice breaking. "You don't deserve to be harassed by some kid at work. And I am sorry for not telling you that I had seen them together a few times. I should have, even if it would hurt you."

He paused, looking back at me, his features softening for a moment. "It's not your fault, babe. It's mine for letting it go on this long." He grabbed my hand, walked me to the couch, and we sat, wrapped in each other's arms.

An hour or so later, Izzy came out of her room, rested and ready to take on the world, blissfully unaware of the box. She immediately brightened the mood. "All right," she said, clapping her hands. "Who's ready to go to the Cabin de la Reynolds?" She strolled over to the counter and grabbed three rolls of toilet paper. "Looks like we're all set in case this Andy character eats too many baked beans this weekend."

We all burst out laughing. John's deep belly laugh filled the room as if nothing terrible had just happened. "I figured those would be handy this weekend. You can never have too much toilet paper in a cabin."

I couldn't tell if he was really good at faking it or if a sliver of his joy had actually returned to him.

Chapter Twenty-Two

As we pulled up to the Reynolds' family cabin, I was in awe. It was not the sprawling estate or polished mansion I expected, but something simpler—humble. The dark wood panels, weathered by time, blended into the wooded landscape. Tall pines swayed around the property, and the soft, earthy scent of moss and pine needles filled the air. In the distance, I could hear the lapping of water, the lake peeking through the trees. A small dock jutted out of the water, and I could almost picture John as a boy, fishing pole in hand, sitting on that very dock. There was a nostalgia here, a rawness that surprised me because it was so different from the carefully curated and glamorous world John lived in now.

It reminded me of the home I grew up in back in Idaho. It was comforting to know he had grown up like I did—humble, quiet, surrounded by nature. No wonder we had such a strong connection. We shared such similar upbringings with similar values.

We arrived at the cabin around four. After unpacking the luggage, food, and drinks from John's G-Wagon (now mostly brown from the dusty drive), Andy rolled up in his old pickup. Moments after he pulled up, we heard him pound on the door as if he'd sprinted from his truck to the cabin. He let himself in like it was his own house. I was sure from how many summers he'd spent up here with John and his family, it basically was.

"Big Andy!" John shouted, running to the door and somehow managing to hug and lift the 280-pound man that made John look small. They did their baboon-boy greeting routine, grabbing each other's faces like two excited kids on the playground.

Then Andy made his way to the kitchen, where Izzy and I were unpacking the food and the booze into an old-school cooler big enough to fit Big Andy inside. I reached out to shake his hand, but Andy slapped it away and bellowed, "Family doesn't shake hands, silly goose." He picked me up off the ground, high enough for my legs to dangle.

"Let me have a look at yeh." Andy pulled back, still holding both of my shoulders, sizing me up. He yelled to John, "She's a beaut, John. She really is, just like you said."

John smiled. "She certainly is," he said before checking his phone, then stepping away to respond to whoever it was, leaving Izzy and me to fend for ourselves for the time being.

Andy turned his attention to Izzy. "And who's this beautiful creature? John said Sarah would be here, but he didn't tell me this house would be filled with *two* beautiful women."

"This is Izzy," I said as Andy walked over to her. She put her hand out between them before he had a chance to do his *Dirty Dancing* routine with her.

"I don't do lifts."

Andy threw up his long, muscular arms in surrender. "I always honor a woman's request. Put 'er there." He opened his palm for a handshake. "I'm Andy." He gave her a devilish smile. He was cute. Masculine. Not Izzy's type. A farm boy who could never stand to live on the tiny island of Manhattan. He wore Wranglers and cowboy boots with a red flannel shirt. His smile took up half his clean-shaven face, and his rich chocolate brown hair was dusted with a little farm dirt. "It is a pleasure to meet you, Izzy."

"You too," she said, sounding impartial.

I caught her eye and mouthed, *"Play nice."*

She blinked, then gave a tight-lipped smile. "So, how do you and John know each other?" she asked, her tone veiled with polite curiosity.

"John and I grew up down the street from each other and played college ball together. We go way back. I'm in real estate here and have a farm about an hour away."

"Can I get you a drink, Andy? You must be thirsty after your drive." I tried to play the role of "housewife" or at least "accommodating girlfriend" as best I could, to impress the only person I now knew in John's world outside of Regent. This might be my only chance to win over one of his friends until after the divorce.

"Sure. What's everyone drinking? I'll take whatever you got as long as there is some alcohol in it."

Izzy jumped in. "We have the usual: gin for courage, tequila for regret, and water for pretending we're responsible adults," she quipped. "But if you're feeling adventurous, I think Sarah brought some I-have-to-impress-the-boyfriend's-friend seltzers." She gave me a sassy look.

Andy chuckled.

"Iz," I said, laughing, "you're giving me too much credit. It's more like I'm-just-hoping-not-to-screw-this-up seltzer. I only get one shot with you, Andy. It's like *8 Mile* . . . but with John's friends."

He laughed like it was the best joke he'd heard all day. "You girls are quick, and feisty. I like it."

John returned from what I assumed to be the bathroom, finishing up a text, having missed the whole exchange.

"John, these ladies are great. You know how to pick 'em," Andy said.

"I'm the lucky one." John finally looked up from his phone in my direction. "Lucky Sarah picked me. Izzy, you're just the cherry on top of the friendship sundae."

I couldn't help but smile.

"I *am* the cherry on the goddamn sundae, aren't I?" Izzy said with a smile.

"All right, folks," John announced, his voice full of cheer. "Now that we're all here and settled in, let the festivities begin!"

We clinked our seltzers together, but as I lifted my can to my lips, my mind started racing. The pressure to impress Andy, my potential only opportunity to meet someone in John's life—I had to make a great impression.

On top of that, with every trip away with John, came the potential of someone noticing I was not posting over Fourth of July. Or worse, if someone else posted and I was caught in a picture. Jane would easily catch wind of it. The stress was endless. It was like I could never fully relax.

Plus, how could I forget work—so behind, so much to do. The promotion still felt so far out of reach. I needed to find time to acquire an author that would wow management, plus stay on top of my current workload, plus the Gabriel Stone project, in which I was drowning. It was like I was being dragged behind a boat, water boarded and barely holding on to the rope. But for now, I forced a smile, trying to push it all down.

Be present, and focus on making a good impression on Andy.

"I am ready for a great weekend ahead," I said, trying to sound more confident than I felt.

The Fourth of July.

Izzy and I slept in the next day. First, because we stayed up way too late playing games and drinking. Second, because we knew we'd be doing it again today. When I finally dragged myself out of bed, it was 11 a.m. My usual 4:30 wake-up time had caught up with me.

As I stretched and yawned, that conversation with Jane, the one John had on my birthday, lingered in the back of my mind. I tried to shoo it away, tried to tell myself I was just being paranoid. But the thought kept nagging me. John had already stepped away to answer a text, most likely from her. I prayed he wouldn't be off talking to her all weekend. He was so distant when it came to her. Distracted with the divorce. He had so much on his plate but hoped that just for this weekend he could let it all fall to the wayside so we could have a fun weekend together.

I mozied into the living room. Izzy followed soon after, her hair standing up in all directions from her peaceful cabin sleep. We made our way to the kitchen where Andy was . . . making breakfast? For us? Plates full of pancakes, eggs, bacon, sausage, toast—everything you could imagine.

The wooden twelve-person table was set for the four of us, with freshly squeezed orange juice and brewed coffee, three kinds of milk and creamers. I was in awe.

"Andy, did you . . . make this breakfast?"

"Of course! I couldn't let our sleeping beauties go hungry when they awoke from their slumber." He said it like he'd been up since four in the morning. He really had that farmer dad vibe down pat. Up with the sun and the roosters.

"Sit, sit, sit. It's all set." He gestured to the table as he brought the last plates of food over.

"I think I just found your dream man," I muttered to Izzy.

She looked at me with surprise. Her eyes went from sleepy to wide in a matter of seconds. The words sank in, and then the corners of her lips turned down, skeptically scanning the table. She nodded slowly in agreement. "Not too shabby, Big Andy." Her version of a thank-you.

"Andy, thank you for doing this. It looks fabulous. So sweet," I added.

"It's the least I could do. I'm so happy to spend time with you both." He took off his oven mitts and a worn apron that said, *Kiss the cook . . . or feed yourself!*

Andy was nothing like the cold, elusive men of Manhattan. There was no guessing with this one. He said what he meant and meant what he said. Maybe I had just been in the city too long, but I had forgotten that chivalry and transparency like that still existed.

I had felt the same about John when I met him. Like I could trust everything he said. But after the call with Jane, the uncertainty started to creep in, tugging at the edges of my thoughts. How much of his sincerity was real? Could I still trust him the way I once had? I did my best to focus on the good moments, but they were there, it was impossible to forget them.

"Where is John?" I asked Andy. He was up and out of bed by the time I woke up. I wondered if he was off somewhere talking to Jane?

"He's been up since sunrise. That guy's always up with the roosters," Andy said, stirring some sort of food in a big bowl. "He's down by the water getting everything ready for today."

"Ready?" Izzy said, her mouth full of syrup-soaked pancakes.

"Hello! It's the Fourth of July, silly goose!" Andy said like a little kid on Christmas. As if we'd forgotten. "We're going to take the boat out, play yard and card games, get drunk, and blow some shit up."

I stood up to look out the window. Out the door was a patio with three flights of stairs down to the dirt backyard where the lake was a stone's throw away. The whole yard was set up for the Fourth. Streamers, lights, what looked like a volleyball net, cornhole, enough chopped wood to last for weeks, several decks of cards, insect repellent, blankets for the evening, and some binoculars (not sure if they were for spying on other people on the lake or for stargazing). The space was totally transformed since last night.

A boat was docked, and there was John, bent over, tuning something, getting it ready. Floaties were already inflated and waiting to be used. I think I fell a little more in love with him. He was . . . such a man. He took care of shit. No questions, no complaints, no waiting for me to ask. He took initiative. Took charge. I loved that. It was better than all the beta guys I dated who couldn't even pick up a bill at the damn restaurant. Maybe that's what being married does to you —educates you. Trains you. I couldn't help thinking about Jane. How could she let this go? How could she not see how good she had it with him?

He must have sensed me staring at him, because he stood up and turned around. He wore baby blue swim trunks and aviator sunglasses that made him look like Tom Cruise in *Top Gun* (the young version). A big smile spread across his face, and he waved at me. He blew me an air kiss and mouthed, *"I'll be right there."*

I smiled and waved.

Then, he ruined the perfectly good moment. He paused, grabbed his phone from his pocket. Read the text from whoever had sent it, and immediately started responding. He tried to recover by giving me another smile and holding up a finger. Seconds later, it was ringing. He rolled his eyes and answered it, turning his back from where I stood. My heart sank. I could feel it was Jane, just from the way he read her name and responded, I could tell. It was like he couldn't keep her waiting or she would get suspicious. I rolled my eyes and turned back to the breakfast table.

Izzy and Andy were getting comfortable, their banter filling the space. Izzy was playing nice, just like I'd asked her to. She was laughing along with Andy, and it actually seemed genuine. It was strange how quickly two people could bond after a night of stupid board games and seltzer.

———

We spent the morning playing yard games. Anyone on a team with Izzy was bound to lose. Her athletic skills left a lot to be desired. John, Andy, and I were highly competitive and sore losers. Somehow we made it through the day without anyone being too devastated by the losses.

John and I couldn't keep our hands off each other. We were in a great place *for now*—being around each other and the people we loved was good for us. But I knew we were both pretending everything was fine, not acknowledging the things we were avoiding. It felt good to get out of the bubble of just the two of us and be around those who cared about us, but there were things we needed to talk about. Unless I brought them up, though, they would probably be ignored.

By noon the heat was unbearable, and we were too hot to be anywhere but the water. We loaded up the cooler and floaties and headed for the middle of the lake. I loved the water. There was something about it that made me like a kid again. I loved floating, my hair wet, possibly risking my bleach blonde turning an ugly shade of pond green—but it was worth it.

Around the boat, we each sat in floaties that John had hand-picked for us. Andy's was a giant inflatable cow—for the dairy farmer. Izzy's was a flamingo wearing sunglasses, mine was a unicorn with a rainbow horn, and John's was a sloth that we named George. Each floatie had a cup holder for our White Claws. It was as if he had thought of everything.

"I'm telling you, pineapple on pizza is a culinary masterpiece. The combination of sweet and savory is unbeatable!" Izzy said to John with complete conviction.

"You've got to be kidding me! Pineapple doesn't belong anywhere near pizza. It's a savory dish! It's like putting pickles on ice cream," John shot back, and I couldn't help but agree with him. But it wasn't my fight. They then moved on to a deeper issue: waffles versus pancakes.

Andy and I lay in silence for a few minutes, our heads back, basking in the sun. It was a comfortable silence. It was the first time in a long time I could just be.

"I never liked her, you know?" Andy said out of nowhere.

"Izzy?" I asked, not sure who he was referring to.

"No, of course not! Izzy's great. Beautiful too. You've got a good friend there," he said.

Did Andy . . . *like* Izzy? "Wait, who don't you like?"

"Jane. I never liked her. None of us did," he said matter-of-factly.

My interest piqued. My buzz almost disappeared at the sound of her name. It was as if my animal brain wanted to retain every bit of information he shared about her to help me later. But I tried to keep my cool, resisting the urge to jump up and shout, "No way, tell me everything!"

Instead, I asked as casually as I could, "None of who?"

"All of the guys. We have a group of buddies, we are like brothers. We all played college ball together, and have known Jane for years."

"Why don't any of you like her?" I asked.

"Have you met her?" He scoffed. "She's a total phony, especially since she moved to the city. The more money they made, the more her head swelled, and now she thinks she is better than everyone. The way she dresses, her house, her cars, the new friends, the new face . . . it's all an act . . . in my humble opinion, of course." He put the pads of his fingers on his chest.

I remained silent, hoping he'd offer more information.

"We all grew up together, you know? The three of us had been in the same class since third grade. John fell in love with Jane the moment he met her. They dated all through middle school and high school. And from day one, I never liked her."

This was a jackpot of insider information. It was nice to hear about her from someone other than John and his limited offerings.

"Really?" I asked. "Why is that?"

"She was always a bitch to him. Always talking down to him, making him feel small to build herself up. Manipulating him and distorting the truth. She came from a tough home life. By the time we got to college, the only real 'break' they had was when she cheated on him and married some random guy."

"Wait, hold up . . . Jane was married before?" I said in complete and utter disbelief.

"Yeah, but it only lasted six months before she came crawling back to John. He has such a good heart, he took her back, and they got married a year later." His hands splashed in the water, his eyes closed, his head still resting on the cow udders of his floatie. "None of his family liked her either, but they accepted her because John loved her. We could always see that she was using him."

I couldn't believe he was saying all this. A glimpse into the dark past of the soon-to-be ex-wife of the love of my life. Her untold story.

"Wow, that sounds terrible. From the outside, they looked like the perfect couple."

"Of course, everything Jane puts out there has to *seem* perfect," he said.

"What happened after they got married?" I asked.

"His career took off, and he built her up. Her career followed. She had no success until John came back into the picture. Her career exploded because of him. They seemed to be doing well for a few years. Of course they had their problems—every couple does. But when she started making real money and moved to the city, we knew things were going to get ugly."

"Do you know what happened?" I asked, keeping my tone as casual as possible.

He clicked his tongue. "John doesn't share much about it, never has. I think he likes to keep his relationships private, and I respect that. . . . Us guys don't need to know everything." He shook his head, and I could see the pain he felt for his friend. "I think the more Jane got into her world of success, money, and popularity, the more she lost touch with reality. She forgot where she came from. She got caught up in her short-term desires and forgot what she had in John. She was getting attention from her trainer when John was home taking care of the house and business. If you live for attention, you'll take it wherever you can get it."

"That's very, very true," I said, my thoughts drifting to my own struggles in that area. "I've been so focused on everything I thought I needed to achieve lately I've started to forget why I was doing it in the first place." I paused, looking down at my hands. "It's hard to keep track of what really matters when everything else feels so overwhelming."

"It is super common," Andy continued. "I heard something once that money only makes people more of who they already are. It

Aria Devi

amplifies them. I saw that happen to her. Her pain, her trauma, the way she treated John . . . it just got bigger and worse."

"I totally agree with that saying," I said. My mind flickered to my own doubts, the creeping thoughts that lingered. I had my share of questions after my birthday weekend. Could there have been more to Jane and John's story? Could there have been things I wasn't seeing? I needed to know. "Did John ever cheat on her?" I asked before I could stop myself. The question hung in the air, unexpected, but there it was. If there was anyone to ask, it would be Andy.

"Oh God no," Andy said confidently. "He was so in love with her. He would never have messed it up. You're the first woman he's even mentioned since her, let alone brought here. That means something to John. It really does. For a long time, we thought he'd never move on." He took off his sunglasses and put them on his head, squinting at me. "But, man, Sarah, he really scored when he found you." His smile was wide.

"Oh, shut up." I laughed.

"No, I'm serious," he continued. "You're amazing. The way he talks about you. From what he has said, you have been there every step of the way supporting him, being there, and still making your own space to grow and work for that promotion. He told me you're not the kind of woman who needs to be saved or taken care of. That's rare." He paused for a moment before his smile returned. "I thought his rebound was going to be some mess of a woman with daddy issues named Cinnamon." He caught himself. "Not that you're a rebound by any stretch of the imagination . . ."

I held up a hand to stop him. "No worries, I know what you mean. And thank you. That is nice to hear. I try my best to support him and not take everything going on between him and Jane person-ally, but it is hard sometimes. I know, because of work, they will always have to be in communication. Sometimes that is challenging to navigate. It's almost like they have a child."

"I am sure it's tough, but you can trust John. If I know anything

216

about John, it is that everything he is doing is for the benefit of both of you."

I nodded in understanding, a sense of determination rising in my chest. I glanced at John and Izzy chatting, the sound of their laughter carrying across the water. It seemed like he had made progress with the divorce, but there was still so much left to go. I had to remind myself that this was the beginning of something new for both of us, not just him.

Andy's voice broke through my thoughts, "Sarah, I know it's hard with him and Jane. But trust me, John's in this for both of you."

I nodded. "I know," I said, trying to sound more confident than I felt. "I just have to figure out how to navigate all of this. Work, their history . . . it's hard not to let it bleed into our relationship."

"Yeah, I can imagine," Andy said. "But he won't mess this up. Not with you. He's been through a lot, and I know he's ready for a fresh start—he wants it with you, Sarah."

His words eased something inside me, but another thought bubbled up, one I hadn't really voiced to anyone before. "How long is too long? I mean, how long should I wait for him to get the divorce finalized? He started by saying it would be three months. Now he is saying it will be the end of the year . . ."

Andy leaned forward, as much as you can in a floatie, "In my opinion, you've been patient enough. You've given him time, and he knows you're in this with him. But don't let him drag his feet. Women like you don't wait forever. Don't let him put this off—put pressure on him, for both your sakes. I know John, and while he is amazing, if things get tough, he can have a tendency to procrastinate."

My chest burned at the thought of pushing John even more. Was John a procrastinator? Or was the divorce just dragging on? We'd been in limbo for so long, and as much as I loved him, I wasn't sure I could stay there forever. Even though I'd promised him months ago I would.

"I know," I said. "This isn't just his fresh start. It's ours too. And I can see the life we could have, once all of this is behind us, if we ever get there."

Andy nodded. "Exactly. You deserve that life. But don't let him drag his feet. You deserve to move forward, not live in the past."

I took a deep breath, a small sense of clarity sweeping over me. Maybe it was time to make sure everything moved forward.

———

Sunburned and seltzer-fueled, we relaxed into the evening. I'd promised myself I'd stay away from my phone today, to be present, but I brought it anyway to listen to music on the dock, my toes dipping in and out of the water, the early summer breeze filling my lungs. It was one of those rare moments alone—the kind I'd been craving.

I sat reflecting on the conversation I had with Andy earlier. I had to find a way to push John to get this divorce finalized as soon as possible. I could not let him procrastinate—if he was—any longer. It was only hurting us.

My phone buzzed against the wooden boards beside me. I glanced at the screen, squinting against the bright light as the sky darkened. My breath caught when I saw who the email was from: Linda McDowell, the director of events at Regent. The subject line made my stomach turn: "Invitation to Present on Panel: AAP Conference." I clicked on it, my heart pounded in my ears. The email had been forwarded by Theo Brooks. His email read:

Hey Sarah,

Forwarding you the invitation to the AAP Conference. Would love for you to join us on the panel in Boston if you're free (was Willow's idea). Linda is reaching out directly to confirm if you're in— let me know what you think!

Theo

. . .

Beneath it was the email from Linda.

Dear Sarah,

We're pleased to invite you to join Theo Brooks, Willow Brooks, and Jane Reynolds as a panel presenter at the upcoming AAP Annual Meeting in Boston, August 23–25. This workshop will focus on innovative editorial strategies, enhancing author relationships, and exploring the future of digital publishing.

The structure will be discussed once all presenters have confirmed their participation. Due to the nature of the presentations, all panelists will travel together on the company's chartered shuttle departing from the New York office on Friday morning.

We look forward to your participation and insights during this exciting weekend.

Best Regards,
Linda McDowell
Events Director, Regent House Publishing

I blinked, rereading the email over and over to make sure I wasn't imagining things. This had to be a mistake. Why would they invite me to speak at the AAP Conference?

I leaned down to touch the water with my hands, trying to steady my thoughts. Jane, Theo, and Willow were all established figures in the industry. But me? Why would Willow suggest me? Was this some kind of favor? Or was I missing something? I hadn't even been in the publishing world long enough to be considered for something like this, right?

I had to admit, the thought of sitting on stage alongside industry veterans made my heart race. I stared at the screen in disbelief. This was it—another huge opportunity to support me getting the senior editor promotion. To be included, to be on stage, to be seen as a leader in the company. This was a dream come true.

Reality dulled the excitement, casting a shadow over what should have felt like a massive career accomplishment. While part of me was over the moon, the other dreaded facing Willow, Theo, and Jane for an entire weekend—trapped in Boston, with no escape.

If Jane had even the slightest suspicion about John and me, could I really lie to her face for three days straight?

I reread the email. Once. Twice. Again.

Sharing an office with them was one thing—I could dodge meetings or hide behind deadlines. But this? Traveling together, stuck at three hour dinners with them? It would be a three-day long interrogation. One slip up with Jane. One misstep and my whole career could go up in flames.

This wouldn't just be me walking into an uncomfortable weekend; I'd be walking straight into the fire.

Chapter Twenty-Three

I ran back to the cabin, bursting through the door, phone in hand. I couldn't wait to show Izzy and John. Despite the fact that I'd have to be around Jane for a whole weekend, it really was amazing news.

"John! Izzy, look." I shoved my phone in John's face.

He leaned back, caught off guard, blinking at the blue glare. "What am I looking at?" he asked, taking the phone from my hand.

"I've been asked to speak on a panel at the AAP Conference this year," I said, bouncing on my toes.

Izzy's smile widened, but for a split second, something flickered in her eyes—something unreadable, quickly masked by enthusiasm. She clapped her hands together. "No way. That is amazing, Sarah."

John scanned the email, "Are you serious?" He jumped out of his chair, pulling me into a bear hug so tight I couldn't breathe. "Sarah, this is huge! I'm so proud of you. Holy shit. It's happening—all the work you've put in is paying off!"

My smile faltered "Okay, so that's the good news," I began, biting my lip. "But did you see who else is on the panel?"

John looked back at the email, his face falling the second his eyes landed on the names. "Willow, Theo, and nooo . . . Jane?" He groaned. He ran a hand through his hair. "I can't help but feel like this is my fault."

"John, it's not—"

"But it is. If I hadn't dragged you into this, you'd be thrilled to share the stage with her. This would be a total career highlight for you."

"It still is."

"Sorry, can someone fill me in? What is AAP?" Andy asked, leaned back in another recliner in the corner.

Izzy jumped in. "The Advanced Authors' Publishing Conference. It is a big deal. It is a yearly conference where authors, editors, agents, and even tech experts come together to discuss trends and what's next in the publishing world. It's like SXSW but for publishing. I have gone the last few years. It's amazing. It's where the industry's big decisions are made. Jane, Theo, and Willow are legends. They're a few of the select people everyone listens to."

I looked back at John to see his expression when Jane's name was mentioned. There was no reaction on his face. I finally looked back at the email. "I'm just . . . not sure why they want *me* there. I'm still trying to figure it out."

Izzy grinned. "Being mentored by Theo and Willow has perks like this. The industry is always looking for young new talent to raise up so that there will be a next wave of leaders. They probably invited you to see how you do under pressure on stage. See if the younger audience resonates with you. Then they can pour more into you and really train you up to become a credible voice in publishing. They want to hear your voice. This is your chance to show them that you belong up there, right alongside them."

"I am so proud of you," John said, wrapping his arm around me. "You'll be sharing the stage with some really skilled and credible people. And honestly, when it comes to Jane, except for the event itself, she'll probably be holed up in her room. She hates being bombarded by people and small talk in the lobby. I doubt you will even have to see much of her."

I laughed, hardly feeling alleviated by his words, but I pretended like I was. "You're right. I can handle that. But dinner with all three of them? That's going to be brutal. They're like professional inter-rogators."

"You can do this, Sarah. Just focus on serving the audience. You don't owe them anything. Your personal life is none of their business," John said.

I exhaled. "Thank you. You are so right."

"We have to celebrate. AAP is one of the biggest events of the year. At the end of August, we'll need a trip anyway. What do you think? After Boston, you and I go to Sedona, Arizona? There is an amazing meditation retreat there, lots of cool walking trails, crystals, sweat lodges, yoga classes. Or even Naples, Florida? It's so serene—I've been dying to take you there too."

My heart leaped, "That sounds perfect. Naples is a quick flight from Boston. Let's do that." A little peace and quiet after the chaos of the event?

John's eyes rested on me. "I am so proud of you, Sarah. Every day with you is an adventure. I want to celebrate all of your wins and victories, and this is one you will always remember."

"Awe, that is adorable," Andy said, gushing. Izzy rolled her eyes and gagged.

John's words melted something inside me, a tension I hadn't realized I was holding. Like some of the trust that had been broken was being mended at the gesture. "I can't wait," I said.

No matter how complicated things got, I wanted to believe we'd face it all together. But a nagging part of me still felt like I was in this all alone, wondering if I would ever fully be able to trust him.

The fire crackled, sending embers into the summer air. Andy and Izzy sat close, their heads tilted toward each other, their laughter easy and unguarded. The scent of burning wood mixed with the scent of lake water, and somewhere in the distance, fireworks popped, their echoes rolling across the lake.

And as if Jane could sense that John and I were finally finding our way back to a good place, John's phone buzzed in his pocket.

I felt it before I saw it. A shift. The way his shoulders stiffened ever so slightly. The way his hand moved with too much urgency, almost frantically, as he grabbed the phone and looked at the screen. His jaw tightened.

I already knew it was Jane.

He stood without a word, phone pressed to his ear before he even stepped away from the fire.

"Yeah, hey," he muttered, voice low. Then he was gone, disappearing down the path toward the dock.

I gripped my red solo cup tighter, staring at the empty space he left behind.

Andy grabbed another beer from the cooler, twisting the cap off with ease. "Another one?" he asked Izzy, nudging her with his elbow.

She laughed, but was looking straight at me. "I'm good for now."

I could feel her eyes on me, so I forced a smile. Pretended it didn't matter. Pretended I wasn't sitting here, waiting. Waiting for him. Again.

Minutes passed. Five. Ten. Fifteen. The fire burned lower, the logs crumbling into glowing embers. Andy and Izzy had shifted even closer, their voices dipping into something more private.

I couldn't sit here anymore. I couldn't do *this* anymore. I was exhausted.

Pushing off my blanket, I stood.

"Where are you going?" Izzy asked with concern.

"Just stretching my legs." The lie left my mouth effortlessly. I was a pro at this point.

I followed the path toward the dock, my sandals crunching

against the gravel. The farther I walked, the clearer his voice became —low. The kind of tone you use when you don't want someone else to hear.

He was still on the phone.

Still talking to *her*.

Fury bubbled inside of me. Something inside me snapped.

"Are you fucking kidding me?" I said just above a whisper.

John turned sharply, lowering his phone, his eyes wide with surprise. "Jane, I have to call you back."

He had to call her back. . . .

Not *I have to go*. Not *Give me a second*. Not, *Sarah Jones is here and she is my girlfriend so I need to prioritize her over you right now*. No, *I have to call you back*.

"Sarah, I can expla—"

"No," I snapped, stepping closer. "Don't give me another excuse. I have been sitting over there for almost twenty minutes while you sneak off *again* to take a call from your *wife*."

He let out a breath, running a hand through his hair. "It wasn't—"

"Don't lie to me." My voice wavered, but I didn't care. "It's *always* her. Every time. You put her first. My birthday, the middle of the night, now *this*. I can't even have one fucking holiday, one day where you're fully *here* with me."

His jaw tensed. "She needed—"

"Oh, she *needed* something? On the Fourth of July? And let me guess, you just had to be the one to fix it, right now." I let out a bitter laugh, shaking my head. "Do you even hear yourself? She snaps her fingers, and you drop everything. No questions asked."

"Sarah, it's not like that."

"It *is* like that! It is exactly like that." My voice cracked, but I didn't stop. "I'm always waiting, always making excuses for you, lying for you, always telling myself I can handle this, lying to myself, but I *can't*." The words tumbled out, unchecked, hot and vicious. "I am drowning, John. I am behind at work, I can't think straight, I can't sleep. And it's all because of *you*. It is all because of *her*. I have put you first since the day we met, and look where that has gotten me. And you can't even choose me . . . put me first for one fucking night. She still comes first."

His brows pulled together. "That's not fair. I told you that this was the situation until the divorce was finalized."

"Fair?" I let out a hollow laugh. "You know what's not fair? Being the other woman. Having to sit there while your *boyfriend* sneaks off to talk to his *wife*. Not to mention that *divorce* was supposed to be finalized months ago."

His mouth opened, but I didn't give him the chance to speak.

I could feel the words swelling, the pressure in my chest rising with each breath, until I might suffocate if I didn't say them. I didn't know where this anger was coming from, but it spilled out anyway.

"You haven't chosen me," I said, my voice trembling. "Not really. Because if you had, you wouldn't be out here, on your phone. If you had, your divorce would have already been finalized, wouldn't it?"

His face was frozen. I could see my words sting him, but I couldn't stop. For a split second, I wondered if Jane yelled at him like this.

"If you really chose me, you'd be ignoring her calls and you would be *with* me, by the fire, with our friends, where you belong. Not holding onto whatever is left of your pathetic past with a woman who doesn't even love you anymore."

Silence stretched between us—heavy—suffocating.

His body tense. He looked down to the ground, as if searching for the right words.

I swallowed the lump in my throat, but it didn't budge. "Say something."

He lifted his gaze, and for the first time, there was something distant there. Something that made my stomach drop. An emptiness in his eyes.

"I didn't realize you felt that way," he said finally.

I let out a slow, shaky breath. "Well, now you do."

And with that, I turned and walked away.

Chapter Twenty-Four

H ere's to Sarah for being invited to speak at her very first AAP panel in two weeks!" Willow announced with pride. Theo, Izzy, and I all smiled at her. We sat at Luigi's, one of our favorite Italian spots in the city.

Luigi's was one of those places that felt so New York City—a cozy spot tucked away in the West Village with dim lighting, exposed brick, wine bottles lining the walls, and wooden beams. Luigi, the owner, greeted us with his usual grin and thick Italian accent, always eager to ask about our latest book projects and dishes that weren't on the menu. We were settled into our usual spot by the window, watching the passersby walk down the cobblestone street. A violinist played in the corner, and a bottle of rich Barolo arrived to pair with our handmade pasta.

"What we hope to be the first of many," Theo echoed. The four of us raised our glasses as Willow continued.

"Sarah, Theo and I are both so proud of you," her voice warm with pride. "It's a huge deal to be asked to speak, no matter your age. We pushed for you to get this spot because we believe in you, and we're excited to see how you shine. We're already looking ahead, thinking about what's next. We see so much potential in you, especially as you work for the senior editor position. This event is just a representation of how far you've come in such a short time. We're honored to be part of your journey." Willow's words settled in, I felt overwhelmed with gratitude.

After Willow's toast, the conversation flowed easily from work talk to weekend plans, and I couldn't help but feel a quiet sense of accomplishment, surrounded by people who truly believed in me. But the upcoming trip with Jane kept creeping into my mind, turning what should have been a pure celebration into a moment laced with anxiety. The last thing I wanted was to spend the weekend constantly on edge around her.

Not to mention, every time Theo, Willow, Izzy, and I hung out, I found myself dreading the moments when Jane or John's name might unexpectedly slip into the conversation. My mind kept drifting back to the fight I had with John at the cabin. Ever since then, things had felt off.Izzy seemed to have softened about the whole situation—less angry about the lying—but I could tell she was more protective after the Fourth of July. I hadn't told her about the fight, but she could sense something was up. It felt like my whole life was spent walking on eggshells.

Tonight, Izzy's smile was a fraction too tight, and I noticed her eyes glancing between me and Theo whenever he spoke, like she was bracing herself for John's name to come up. Being in this environment, surrounded by the people I cared about, only made it harder on her—and on me.

"So, Sarah," Theo began, "have they sent you the questions you'll be answering on the panel at the conference?"

I hesitated—forcing a smile. "They've asked me to focus on how junior editors can contribute fresh perspectives to a publishing house. I think there's a lot of untapped potential in the way we approach new projects—especially when it comes to supporting debut authors. It's about finding creative ways to collaborate and offer a voice that might not always be heard. A lot of the time, it's the younger editors who bring that new energy and fresh perspectives."

"That's a great angle." He nodded. "Your perspective as a junior editor will definitely bring something fresh to the table and support the other JE's in the room, give them encouragement to own their opinions in meetings. There's a real need for new approaches in the industry, especially with everything changing so quickly with social media. We're all proud of you for taking this on."

Shocked that he didn't try to offer coaching, I took a sip of my wine. His approval meant everything to me. I wanted to bask in it, hold on to it forever.

"Actually, I wanted to ask," Willow began. "You know Jane's going to be there, right? How do you feel about sharing the stage with her? The four of us will need to meet and collaborate beforehand. It would be a great opportunity to learn from her even more. I know how much you admire her."

Jesus, was it that obvious?

The question was innocent, but Izzy stiffened beside me. My chest tightened, caught between the excitement of the opportunity and the web of lies I had been spinning for the last seven months.

"Yes I did see that she will be there. I . . . well, it's a little intimidating," I said, choosing my words carefully. "But I'm more excited than anything. Thank you both for championing me and getting me this spot on the panel. I am so grateful to share the stage with all of you, and I am looking forward to learning from her. And you two, of course." It wasn't a lie, but it wasn't the whole truth either.

Willow studied my face, "Sarah, did you get botox?"

I froze, grabbing my forehead, "What? No. Why?" I felt frantic to defend myself. How could she tell?

"Hmm . . ." was all she said as she took a sip of her wine. It was like she could see me slowly morphing into Jane but didn't directly ask. Maybe I was just paranoid.

"Anyways, you're going to be phenomenal." Willow moved on as if she hadn't just asked me such a personal question. "And knowing

Jane, she's probably going to be really immersed in the event—she's not exactly the socializing type, but it'll be a great chance to learn from her expertise and professionalism, even if it's from afar."

"Right, exactly," I agreed. "It's a great opportunity."

Izzy's fork clattered against her plate. "How do you do it?" she asked, her voice tinged with a bitterness that came out of nowhere.

"Do what?" I blinked, completely taken aback. I had never heard Izzy use a tone like that.

"You handle the pressure so well, especially with Jane being there. You face a big challenge with such confidence—it's really inspiring." Izzy's smile was genuine on the surface, but something was lurking beneath. There was still a hint of something in her eyes—was that . . . jealousy? She hid it with an encouraging nod. What was she trying to do?

"Honestly," I said, glancing at Theo and Willow, trying to see if they were catching onto anything. Luckily, they looked oblivious. "I'm just trying to focus on how I can serve the audience and not make it about me. I find the more I focus on that, the less I feel the pressure."

Izzy's lips formed a thin line that could have passed for an evil smile.

"Sarah," Willow said, steering the conversation back. "I know events like this can be a lot to handle, especially with Jane being so well known. But remember, everyone in the audience is rooting for you. We all are. The safest place to be is on a publishing stage."

"Thank you, Willow," I said with a smile, too distracted by what the hell Izzy was trying to do.

"Of course. And if it gets overwhelming," Theo added, "don't hesitate to reach out to us while we're there. We believe in you."

The comment, meant to be comforting, only deepened the pain in my chest. A family that didn't know the full extent of my secrets. A family that, if they did, might look at me differently. Might not look at me at all.

I clocked Izzy rolling her eyes as she took a sip of wine.

I wracked my brain trying to figure out what had gotten into her. Izzy had been at Regent, working with Theo and Willow, for years. I knew she eventually wanted to move into a more important role. Was she jealous that her growth hadn't matched my own? Was that it? Had I been too wrapped up in my own success to notice? Was she angry at me? Was she just pissed at John and me? How could I have missed this?

"Izzy, you will be joining us at AAP as usual," Willow said. "It will be great to have you there to support Sarah, and it is always so helpful to have you around to help keep things running smoothly." In Willow-speak, that meant: "Izzy, please come so you can keep our fridge stocked with bubbly water, check us in for our flights, pull me out of the crowd when I'm ready to go home, and help me organize my stage outfits."

Izzy twirled some noodles onto her fork, "Thanks, Willow. I appreciate it, but it's a lot to manage. With everything going on between Sarah and J—" She shot a quick look at me as she cut herself off. My heart felt like it stopped beating completely. Was she really going to say it? To ruin everything, right now? Was she trying to expose the mess between me and Jane, or—God—me and John? Trying to end my career before dessert came out? I couldn't believe she would do that to me. Anger burned in my chest, and I fought to keep my face neutral.

I was totally blindsided. Had Izzy just taken a full one-eighty turn, or had I been so focused on my own drama that I hadn't even noticed my best friend was angry with me, or worse, jealous?

I could feel the tension in my gut tightening, a knot of anger. What the hell was she trying to do? Did she say that on purpose? To threaten me? Or was it a slip-up? The rift between us was widening. Every second, every word unspoken, driving us further apart. I held my breath, thankful that she stopped herself before something even worse slipped out. But it didn't feel like a victory—it just felt like one more thing I had to fix later.

Willow tilted her head, her eyebrows knitted in concern. "What's going on, Iz? You know we really appreciate you being there. And in case you forgot . . . it is literally your job to be there." Her tone was as brash as ever. A Willow signature.

"I know, and I'm grateful," Izzy said, glancing in my direction. "It's just that with Sarah on stage and . . . you two, and Jane around too, there's a lot of dynamics to keep track of. I just want to make sure I don't drop the ball for any of us."

I reached out and gently squeezed her hand under the table. I needed to say something to keep the peace, even though every inch of me wanted to scream at her for almost outing me. "You've always been amazing at holding it all together, Iz. We couldn't do it without you. You're the only one for this job."

Theo jumped in. "Yeah, and Izzy, if you're not there, who am I going to get late burgers with after the event? I can't walk the streets of Boston alone!" he said, trying to lighten the mood.

Willow rolled her eyes at her husband. "Please. As if Izzy has time, between coordinating speaker schedules and making sure Sarah has everything she needs. She'll have her hands full."

Izzy's smile was more genuine this time, but there was still a shadow behind her eyes. "I'll be there. I just need to prepare mentally, I guess." She flashed me a look, one I couldn't place. Her words were pointed, like she was saying something without saying it, and it hit me harder than I expected.

———

After we left the restaurant, Theo and Willow headed home. Izzy and I headed the other way. I walked ahead, my pace quickening. The anger from dinner was simmering in my chest, I couldn't even look at Izzy right now. She'd almost blown the whole thing—John and me, our mess—right there in front of the two people that could *never* know. She was the one who always warned me of telling them, yet she had almost just sabotaged everything. Why did she have to say that? I wanted to yell at her. Scream at her. Slap her. But instead, I just kept walking, concentrating on the pavement beneath my feet.

"Sarah, wait!" Izzy's voice cut through the summer night air, and I couldn't bring myself to ignore her. I slowed down but didn't stop, keeping my eyes straight ahead. The lights above us flickered as her footsteps came closer and slowed, like she wasn't sure if she should be walking beside me at all.

When she caught up, I shot a nasty look at her. Her shoulders were hunched, her eyes down, as if trying to make herself smaller. "Why would you do that?" I snapped.

"When I first came to New York . . . I thought if I spent a few years working for Theo and Willow, by now I would be way ahead of the game," her voice barely above a whisper. "But everything's moving faster than I can keep up. And I'm just . . . stuck in this job, with them."

As I listened, a small part of me softened. Maybe her frustration, her almost outing me at dinner, the tension that had been emanating off of her, had nothing to do with me and John. Maybe she hadn't meant to slip up at all. Maybe it wasn't about me at all. Maybe Izzy was just . . . overwhelmed. Frustrated by her own career. Her own problems. But that didn't change the fact that she almost just ruined my life.

I raised an eyebrow, not sure how to respond. "Stuck?" I asked. "Iz, you're doing great. Willow and Theo could not survive it without you."

Izzy's laugh was thin. "Sure, I just feel like I'm the one cleaning up everyone else's mess. Like I am a great assistant, and they will never want to get rid of me; therefore, I will never be able to reach my goals. Which means I will forever be stuck doing the bitch work. Being just an assistant. Booking the appointments. Canceling the flights. Keeping the secret. After all these years, I can't believe I am still in the same place. I haven't even had time to build a life of my own. The one I came here to build in publishing."

I stopped and looked at her more closely. I wasn't sure if she was holding back tears or just fed up. "You're more than that," I said. "You're smart. Brilliant. You keep everything running. You are so much more than just an assistant, Iz."

"I know," she said. "But sometimes I look at you—at everything you are doing at your age, working toward senior editor—and I feel like I'm still trying to catch up. And you *just* moved here a year ago. I'm, what, twice your age?"

"Catch up?" I laughed. "Please, my personal life is a complete mess. I am dating a man who is married to my boss. I am behind on all of my work projects. After my mess with the Gabriel project, who knows if I will even get the senior editor promotion at all. The only thing I have going for me is that Theo and Willow were willing to convince the AAP team to have me on this panel, and that was only because it was *before* the Gabriel slip-up."

I couldn't believe I hadn't noticed her frustration. I felt like a terrible friend. I'd been so caught up with John, Jane, and my career that I hadn't even noticed my friend was struggling. Instead, I made it about me. I rolled my eyes and finally turned to face her, grabbing her hands. "Plus, Izzy, you're twenty-nine, not forty-nine. You have so much time."

She let out a strained laugh. "You're moving so fast—killing it at work, with a hot man by your side, while I'm stuck proving I'm more than just The Brooks' assistant. It's hard being in the background. I also blame the PMS. It makes everything worse."

I nodded. I assumed the PMS had a big part to play in this, but instead I said, "Maybe it's more than PMS, Iz."

Izzy shook her head, a tear rolling down her cheek, "It's just silly. I'm happy for you, really. I just have to stop overthinking things. And I really didn't mean to almost slip at dinner, I swear. That was a total mistake, and I am so sorry. It was not intentional."

"That one was for sure the PMS," I joked. "Thank you for saying that. Izzy, you'll be fine. I know it. After all, you know more about the random facts of life than anyone I know. There's no way you won't succeed with all that wisdom in your noggin. Just be patient with yourself. I am right here by your side. I have been a terrible friend with all the John and Jane drama. But I'll be better. I am here for you."

She nodded, though her eyes still held a glint of sadness. "Thanks, Sar."

I tried to change the subject to get her mind off of it. "Speaking of, have you talked to Andy?" I asked. "You two seemed to hit it off in Chicago last month."

Izzy's cheeks flushed a deep red, and she shifted her weight between her feet. "He texts me a couple times a week . . . but I don't know. It's complicated."

"Complicated how? He's great, Izzy. You'd be perfect together. Imagine a double date with John and me." I grinned. Even though John and I weren't in the best place right now, I could still vision cast for our future.

Izzy frowned, and I could see the wheels turning. "I don't know. He's in Chicago, with the whole farm thing, and I'm not even sure how I'd explain how we met." She squinted at the sidewalk as if trying to solve a puzzle. "I met my boyfriend through my best friend's married boyfriend? That's complicated."

Izzy had been covering for me—lying, pretending everything was fine—when she was silently carrying the weight of my secret. "You deserve someone like him, Iz. Don't write him off just yet. And hey, a little shameless flirting never hurt anybody. Remember, you taught me that."

She looked at me, one eyebrow raised. "And look where that got you."

We both laughed.

"Yeah, touché. But promise me, if you ever feel any kind of resentment again, you'll tell me instead of almost sabotaging my relationship and career in one fell swoop. Deal?" I said. "We can talk about it, Izzy. You don't have to let it build up." I looked her squarely in the eye, feeling like I should have taken my own advice when it came to John last month.

"Yeah, I can do that," she said, sniffling.

"All right, let's get home. We both have big days ahead of us. You have an empire to help build, and I have a—"

"An empire to keep from falling apart?" she said with a laugh, and for the first time tonight she felt like the old Izzy.

"Exactly." I wrapped my arm around her shoulders, pulling her into a half hug, and we headed for the subway.

Chapter Twenty-Five

The meeting to prepare for the conference with Theo, Willow, and Jane had gone smoothly—efficient, productive, and free of any major roadblocks. I had listened, taken notes, and even contributed a few points that landed well. It was great to be part of the discussion. As we wrapped up, Theo and Willow gathered their things, exchanging a few final thoughts before heading back to their offices. As the door clicked shut behind them, Jane shifted her focus to me.

"Sarah," she said, her tone a little softer than usual, a mix of concern and professionalism in her eyes. "Do you have a minute?"

My cheeks heated, a chill running down my spine. "Um, yeah, of course." Was this about the meeting, or something else entirely?

"I just wanted to check in on you, especially after the last meeting for Gabriel Stone's project." There was something almost maternal in the way she looked at me today. "You missed the deadline for the edits last time, and I wanted to make sure you aren't too overwhelmed. Are you staying on top of everything?"

Immediate guilt crashed over me like a giant wave. Guilt that she cared. Guilt that she was so nice to me, and I was dating her husband behind her back. I nodded, forcing a smile. "Yeah, I'm all over it. I returned those edits right away. It should be smooth from here on out. I am so sorry for missing those. That was just a really busy week."

She studied me, eyes narrowing just a little, as if she didn't fully buy it. Then she nodded. "Good. Glad to hear it. Just make sure you're not overloading yourself. I know when you are working for a promotion it's easy to get caught up in the big picture and take on lots of projects, forgetting the small stuff. But quality of work is still critical."

I swallowed, feeling a strange lump in my throat. Part of me was grateful for her mentorship. Her concern. I had craved it so badly in some sick and twisted way. She of all people, the women I related to more than anyone in the world, would know about the pressure I was under. Yet she was the only woman in the world I didn't feel like I could go to for support.

"Well, if you are all good there, then I don't think we need to discuss anything else. I am excited to be on this panel with you. It should be a great event." She closed the laptop and headed for the door.

"I'm excited too. Really eager to learn from you up there," I said, forcing a smile to mask the shame gnawing at me. Whenever John told me how rude or manipulative she'd been, or how she was dragging out the divorce, I hated her. But the guilt from the past seven months never left me. Not fully. And when we were face to face—especially when she was kind—it was soul crushing. The reality of betraying her hit even harder in person.

She paused at the door, her fingers resting on the frame. "Sarah," she said, her tone softening just enough to make me lean in. "Be careful who you let distract you. The wrong man can ruin more than just your career. Trust me on that." She raised a brow, then she walked down the hall.

Shit. She knew. She *knew? She knew!*

It was like my body temperature spiked up to two hundred degrees. Suddenly, I was burning hot. Jane knew. Why else would she say that? Maybe not everything, maybe not the details—but enough. Enough to leave that warning hanging in the air like a trap I'd already stepped into.

My pulse thudded in my ears as I replayed and psychoanalyzed everything about the interaction—the way she had looked at me, her words. *Be careful who you let distract you. The wrong man can ruin more than just your career.* As I scrambled to stack my notes, feeling as if the weight of her gaze was still on me. I muttered to myself. "Sadly, I think it's a little too late for that . . ."

I swallowed hard, my hands tightening around the pages in front of me. Had she been waiting for me to slip up? Was this her way of telling me she'd figured us out? Or was she still feeling it out, searching for confirmation? Seeing if I would admit to anything? Then move on to her next victim and repeat the routine?

Either way, it didn't matter. Because if Jane suspected the truth, then I was already in deeper trouble than I'd let myself admit.

———

Two nights before the AAP event, I was sitting alone in my apartment when my phone lit up with John's text:

> Two days until your big event—you're going to kill it. Then it's Florida sunshine and finally moving to NYC. Can't wait. Love you.

It should have been comforting, but instead, my throat tightened

John and I hadn't spoken properly since the Fourth of July, just brief, tense texts, barely acknowledging the rift between us. Yet now, as I read John's message, everything seemed normal again. His words were warm, familiar, but they hit me differently now.

We hadn't resolved anything. It felt like we were pretending everything was fine, but we were both carrying the weight of that night—the hurtful things I had said. Yet there he was, texting me like nothing ever happened, and I couldn't help but wonder if we were just putting on a show, too scared to face what was really going on. The irony was, it was a show no one else was even around to watch. But we kept on playing it.

Jane was there, constantly lingering in the back of my mind—a reminder that everything I'd built, both my career and my relationship with John, could fall apart in an instant. Now more than ever. My chance at senior editor could be shot, or my job at Regent could be taken from me. She hadn't treated me any differently since our last interaction, but that didn't stop me from constantly checking her office, bracing for the other shoe to drop—an email with my termination notice, or worse, wondering if she already knew everything and was just biding her time before making her move to ruin my career. John's too. What a terrible time to have to spend an entire weekend with her, the woman I idolized, envied, and hated all at once.

I had kept my distance the last week as much as I could, but with the AAP prep and Gabriel's project, there wasn't much room to avoid her. We exchanged a few emails and necessary event prep talk, each interaction laced with my paranoia. Did she know? Was she just waiting to confront me? She'd acted like nothing had changed, but after that comment, I couldn't help but wonder if this was her strategy—throwing things at the wall, just to see if they'd stick, like she had with John.

The idea of John moving to New York should have brought me peace, a sense of security, even excitement. But all I felt was anxiety tightening in my chest, pounding in my head. John would be closer, the risks even greater. My job, my reputation, and this thing I had with John felt like they were balancing on the edge of a cliff, waiting for the slightest push to send them over. The stress was wearing on me—sleepless nights, nearly missing my deadlines, and a dull headache that never seemed to go away. I could feel myself slipping, and the worst part was I had no safety net and no fucking clue how to catch myself.

Chapter Twenty-Six

The grand ballroom of the AAP Conference glittered with elegance, crystal chandeliers casting a warm glow over the crowd. Guests gathered in small groups for the welcome party, their laughter mingling with the clinking of glasses and soft chatter. As I walked in, a wave of anticipation washed over me. Tomorrow I would be on a panel, on stage with my mentors and my career idol, in front of all of these people. What should have been one of the proudest moments of my career (and my life) felt overshadowed by the stress of knowing Jane was here, ready to expose me at any moment—her presence looming behind me like a shadow, making it hard to breathe, let alone focus.

I spotted Jane across the room. She moved through the clusters of people with the grace of someone who had been here before, her every step deliberate and graceful. She wore a stunning red dress, the kind that looked very expensive. Everyone around her was vying for a moment of her time, clinging to her like she was the only person in the room who mattered. Jenny was right at her side, a quiet but constant presence, following her every move like a shadow.

I couldn't help but compare—Jane was the picture of composure and class, while I felt like I was stumbling through the night alone, clinging to whatever semblance of control I had left.

Theo and Willow were as inseparable as ever. Their outfits, coordinated down to the smallest detail, as usual. They stopped for photos, answered questions, and engaged with guests in a way that only years of experience could bring. Izzy wasn't far behind. She glanced over at me, our eyes locking from across the room. With a quick excuse to Theo and Willow, she made her way toward me. I couldn't help but feel beyond grateful for her presence.

"Ready for tomorrow?" Izzy asked, tilting her glass toward me.

"I think so," I said, taking a sip of my drink while scanning the room.

"Come on, Sarah. Your first real stage, and you have to do it with Jane. I would be a wreck. Is there anything I can do to support you?" Izzy had been beyond supportive since our dinner with Theo and Willow. I assumed it was out of guilt for almost destroying my entire life.

"No, really, I'm fine." The truth was I felt anything but fine. My hands were clammy; my stomach twisted in knots. I had spent the night before scribbling notes, writing them and rewriting them, then tossing them aside because nothing felt right. It wasn't that I was so nervous to speak in front of thousands of people. I was nervous to speak in front of Jane. I couldn't stop obsessing about how she would be judging my every word. Silently critiquing. I should have been more prepared, but my mind was a mess—flashes of Jane, of John, of everything I was risking, drowning out the words I was supposed to say. I took a shaky breath and shook my head. "I just need to pull it together. I should be ready to go."

She smiled and gave me a side hug, "You're going to crush it up there. Everything will be fine. Don't worry about what anyone thinks of you. Just speak from your heart, Sarah. You know this information."

We sipped our champagne, but my nerves refused to calm. As I scanned the crowd, I noticed Jenny talking animatedly with Theo and Willow. Her warm smile was infectious, but when her eyes fell on me, my stomach sank. Theo and Willow also turned to look at me, their expressions stunned. Jenny turned back to them, and for a split second, I could've sworn I caught the end of her words—something about . . . Carlyle's?

Did she just tell them about running into John and I at Carlyle's? *Fuck. Are you fucking kidding me?* My worlds were colliding. Panic hit me like a freight train. "We have to get out of here," I whispered to Izzy, turning my back on them as if their stares might turn me to stone.

"What's wrong?" Izzy asked.

"I think Jenny just said something to Theo and Willow about that time she bumped into me having dinner with John at Carlyle's."

Izzy looked over my shoulder in their direction. "Relax. They're professional. If they're going to bust you, it won't be here. Too public. They'll wait until later."

"Are you sure?" My voice cracked as I tried to keep it together.

"They're not going to attack you in the middle of a ballroom in front of all these people," Izzy said. I turned back around, and she rubbed my back to calm me down. "Don't worry."

"They're like family, Iz. I cannot lose them," I said, my breath choppy.

"You won't. We'll figure it out." She paused, trying to lighten the mood. "Besides, you don't even know for sure what she said. This is all hearsay."

"Thank God she didn't 'hearsay' it around Jane," I muttered.

Izzy smiled, but the knot in my stomach didn't budge.

This event was going to be the death of me. I was sure of it.

———

The next morning unfolded like a whirlwind. A thousand conversations buzzed in the air, punctuated by the smell of fresh coffee. My pulse pounded in my ears, my stomach twisted into knots.

It should have been exciting—my moment had finally arrived—but instead, all there was, was a sense of impending doom.

Suddenly, as if he knew how I was feeling from hundreds of miles away, my phone buzzed. A text from John flashed across the screen:

> I know you're probably freaking out. Just remember, you're exactly where you're supposed to be. Don't let anyone shake your confidence. You're amazing.

I read the words twice, then once more. For the first time that morning, really for the first time in weeks, I took a deep breath, feeling the weight on my shoulders lift just a fraction. John's presence, even from miles away and despite all the unresolved issues, still felt like my safe harbor in the storm.

Izzy was by my side, another steady presence in a sea of strangers. I scanned the ballroom, and there she was—I couldn't help but admire her, but a sick feeling of comparison twisted in my stomach. Every time I saw her, all I could think was, *I'm not good enough."*

My heart sank as I noticed—we were wearing almost the exact same outfit. Black pants, a tailored black blazer. Hers, though, was something else. It was like the blazer had been made for someone who knew how to walk into a room and make people listen. The cut was sharp, the fabric rich and structured in all the right ways. But it wasn't just the blazer. She also wore a coat, the kind that seemed too perfect to be real, with fur along the collar and delicate jewels along the lapel. She looked like a damned movie star. And her heels—God, they were like weapons.

Then there was me, standing there feeling like a poor imitation. She was power personified, and I was just a girl wearing a cheap ass version of the same thing, hoping it might make me feel as strong as she looked. But it didn't. She wasn't just dressed for success—she was dressed to dominate. And I was just trying to keep up. It was mortifying.

Willow walked by with her usual easy smile, aimed at Jane. "You always look so stylish, Jane!"

"Publishing can be boring sometimes," Jane replied. "You have to make it exciting with clothes. Show 'em who you are." She laughed as her confidence officially crushed mine.

Jane set her purse down before looking at me. Her eyes softened as she scanned my outfit, and her smile widened. Whether the smile came from a place of knowing she wore it better or because she felt bad for me—I didn't know. "Sarah, if you need anything before you go on, just let me know. I remember my first time up there, nerves and all. But once I started, it was like I could finally breathe again."

"Thank you, Jane. That really means a lot," I managed to say, but my words felt hollow, slipping from my mouth like sand through my fingers. She glanced down at my outfit again, that same smile spreading across her face. "Nice style, we're twinning," she said, nudging me with her elbow.

I forced a chuckle, but inside, my pulse quickened. *Twinning?* Was she mocking me? Or was she complimenting my fashion sense? For some reason . . . it felt completely genuine. How could I betray this woman? How could I stand here and act like everything was fine while I was doing what I had been doing behind her back?

No. I had to remember the truth of who she was. Of who John told me she was. *How could I feel guilty when Jane had been nothing but cold and dismissive to John?* The way she belittled him, constantly undermining him, like he didn't matter. She'd treated him as a tool for her own gain, never once offering him the respect he deserved.

I couldn't forget that. I didn't owe her my guilt. She wasn't a friend. She was a master of manipulation, and I'd just been too naïve to want to fully accept that about her.

We stood next to each other in silence, staring up at the stage. *Does she know?* I couldn't shake the feeling that Jane was playing some game–and I hadn't even realized I was a participant. Warm then cold. Nice then terrifying. What if she was waiting for the perfect moment to strike? Was she going to do something unhinged here, in front of everyone on stage? The thought made my skin crawl, but I couldn't tell if it was paranoia or a gut feeling telling me to watch my back.

The four of us were called to the stage, but I could barely hear it. My mind was lost in a storm. A Jane hurricane. This was supposed to be my time, my moment to shine, but all I could think about was the web of lies I had spun. And how Jane, at any moment, could decide that she wanted to burn it all down.

———

The moderator smiled at the four of us as we sat on bar stools up on the stage, Jane sitting next to me, Willow and Theo to our left. "Let's start by discussing leadership and accountability. Sarah, as a junior editor, you've been vocal about encouraging others in similar positions to contribute ideas. Can you share your experience with that?"

I sat up straighter, steadying my breath. This was it. *You've got this.* "Absolutely. I believe that no matter what level you're at, your voice matters. When I first started at Regent Publishing House, I was hesitant to speak up. But I quickly realized that in order to make a difference, you have to push past that fear. Recently, I pitched an idea on the newest Gabriel Stone novel. It wasn't something anyone had considered, but I saw the potential, and that led to me being brought on for the remainder of the project."

I glanced at Jane, looking for some sign of approval. Instead, she barely glanced up from her lap. I cleared my throat.

"The experience showed me that contributing ideas, even as a junior editor, can make a real impact on a project," I continued, starting to feel some confidence.

Before I could go further, Jane interrupted, her polished smile never faltering. "And, of course, as a leader, I recognize potential and believe in giving people the opportunity to grow. That's why I allowed Sarah to step in on the Stone project—because leadership is about guiding others to where they need to be."

My stomach twisted. I blinked trying to get back on track. "Yes, and I—"

"Oh, I'll let you elaborate in a moment," Jane interjected sitting up straight in her chair, her attention already shifting back to the audience. "The Gabriel Stone Project is a major initiative, one that demands precision, timing, and unwavering dedication. It's always unfortunate when unexpected delays occur. As a leader, though, it's crucial to account for those potential hiccups, especially when less experienced team members get involved. You have to plan for those setbacks."

I forced a smile, my jaw clenched. There it was—her way of putting me in my place, of showing me she was the alpha. Reminding everyone in the audience that I was still "learning" the ropes. I tried to stay focused as Theo jumped in.

"I agree with Jane, and that's the beauty of leadership—navigating obstacles, empowering those who are newer or less experienced, and still delivering great work. That is the only way to build truly independent leaders, is by letting them fail so they can fly on their own," Theo said, shooting me a comforting smile.

"Of course," Jane responded, her smile never wavering. "And I do believe Sarah is learning that lesson in real time, aren't you, Sarah?"

The way she said it felt like a challenge. I met her gaze, forcing a calm expression even as my pulse quickened. Was this just frustration over the project? Or was this about something else? I couldn't help but feel the weight of her words—the insinuation that I wasn't quite "there" yet. Like I couldn't ever compete with her.

The conversation moved on, thank God. I had a chance to share some of my story, glazing over the fact that I had only been at Regent for a year. When the moderator asked about innovation in publishing, I jumped in, hoping to try to regain some sense of credibility with the crowd from Jane's earlier comment. "I believe fresh perspectives are vital. The Stone project is a perfect example—when you allow for new voices to be heard, new ideas, you create something extraordinary. It's proof that when younger professionals are given the space to contribute, the industry thrives."

I could feel Jane's eyes on me, but I didn't falter. I spoke with confidence, sharing my thoughts on how important it was to uplift those with fresh ideas. As I scanned the audience, I could see them nodding along. A few were even jotting down notes.

Throughout the discussion, I occasionally caught looks from Willow and Theo. They offered encouraging smiles, and I held on to those moments to remind myself I wasn't alone in this. Jane made a few other snide comments throughout the session but nothing I couldn't handle, it seemed like we would make it out alive after all.

As the discussion came to a close, the audience responded warmly, a mix of applause and thoughtful nods. I felt so proud of how I handled myself even with Jane's digs.

Then, out of nowhere, Jane's arm slipped around the back of my chair. My heart skipped a beat, and I tensed for a moment. Was she trying to act like she liked me? Trying to pretend she hadn't just undermined all my comments? Then, she squeezed my shoulder. There was something about it—a sisterly energy, a quiet support that made me wonder if, despite everything, she was actually proud of me. I shouldn't have felt comforted, but in that public moment, with the applause of industry experts and Jane Reynolds' arm around me, I hated to admit that it felt . . . incredible. And insanely confusing.

We stepped off the stage, and that's when Jane leaned in close, her voice low and sharp, cutting through the hum of the crowd like a knife. "You should be more careful about who you try to outshine up here, Sarah. Some people won't forget it—and it's not worth jeopardizing your promotion, or your career over."

My breath caught. This wasn't just about the project. It couldn't be. She knew. She had to know about me and John. Her arm around me up there had to have been a move to confuse and manipulate me, a public display to show what a great mentor she was, to make me let my guard down. This bitch was crazy.

Jane walked away, perfectly composed, leaving me standing there, stunned. My heart raced, but there was no running from it—I was knee deep in deep shit.

———

The moment I left the stage, my heart was still pounding. The exhilaration was there, but it was muffled, distant—like I wasn't—couldn't fully be in the moment. The group was excused to take a quick bathroom break before reconvening for the next session.

A small group of people, mostly young editors, gathered around me, some nodding and smiling, others offering small words of praise.

"Good job, Sarah. Your story was so inspiring for me as a new junior editor," a young man in his early twenties said.

A young woman in her early thirties tapped me on the shoulder and said, "It is so cool you get to work on Gabriel Stone's next book. That is like my dream."

I forced a tight smile. "Thanks, I appreciate that. I encourage you to keep offering your ideas in big meetings, and I am sure you will get a similar opportunity."

Then, I overheard a man's voice from behind, "Interesting take, but I'm not sure it's as simple as you made it sound. In reality, those 'fresh perspectives' often come with more setbacks than solutions." I turned and gave him a polite smile. I didn't recognize him, my best guess, he was an editor from another company.

I nodded, my pulse quickening. "Of course, challenges come with any new approach. Thanks for your input," I replied, feeling a shift in my energy as doubt crept in. His words weighed heavily on me, and my stomach churned. Did I totally blow it up there?

Then Jane reappeared, her phone held high, snapping photos of me speaking with people, with the focus of someone documenting a victory. As she moved through the crowd, she handed me her phone, her smile wide and practiced. "You should post these on your socials,

Sarah. You look amazing!" she said, her voice bordering on syrupy sweet.

What the hell? She was just putting on a show, using me as a pawn for her public image. To make her look like an award winning mentor. All the while, her backhanded comments were hidden beneath a façade of support. "Great job up there, Sarah," she declared loudly, her voice carrying enough for everyone gathered around us to hear. The words stung, and I realized that her support in front of others was nothing more than a charade, a way to further her own agenda while secretly keeping me in line. This woman may be even more terrifying than I thought.

"Thank you Jane," I said, playing along, checking the photos, my voice catching in my throat. But as I looked closer at her, I couldn't help but notice the strange contradiction in her behavior—either fully supportive or coldly distant, never anything in between. It was like a performance, and I was the unwitting co-star. Her smile was perfect, but there was something in her eyes that made me question her true intentions. Before I could process it, she grabbed her phone, turned on her heels, and walked away, leaving me behind in complete confusion.

Theo patted me on the back with a grin that could've split his face in two. "Thanks for not embarrassing me up there," he joked, pulling me into a tight hug. "I'm really proud of you, honey."

"You were awesome up there," Willow added, only steps behind him, her face glowing with pride. "You fucking killed it."

"Thanks, guys." I was really nervous but glad it went smoothly.

Izzy reached me as Theo and Willow moved on to talk to other attendees. "You were great up there Sarah! Look at how they all reacted to you!" She pulled me into a hug so tight it nearly knocked the wind out of me.

"Thank you. Was it all right? Jane was so intense up there," I said.

She tilted her head. "Are you serious? Jane was acting like a total . . . well, you know. She might have been insane up there, but you *nailed* it. You were calm, collected—she was just trying to push your

250

buttons. But you didn't let her. That's strength." She gave me a nudge. "You did great, Sarah."

I glanced at Jane, still surrounded by people. Leaning closer to Izzy, I lowered my voice. "She said something to me when we stepped off stage. Basically, 'be careful who you try to outshine. It's not worth losing your career over.'"

Izzy froze, her eyes flicking to Jane before returning to mine. "That's . . . fucking creepy. She is trying to rattle you, Sarah. I do not like the sound of that. You need to be really careful, okay?"

I nodded, the concern in Izzy's voice made me that much more nervous. As much as I wanted to believe it was nothing, her warning carried weight. Jane *had* to know about John. She was just waiting for the right moment to use it against me. I couldn't shake the feeling that this was far from over—that the danger to my career was very real— and I might be even deeper in shit than I realized. I am talking neck deep.

Chapter Twenty-Seven

I am so proud of you, baby. Congratulations! Read the note in the bouquet of roses John had delivered to my room. I closed the card and smiled, feeling gratitude for this supportive man in my life.

I slipped the card back into the bouquet, his words lingering in the air. A smile tugged at my lips. I couldn't deny how special it felt that he'd sent them—how seen I felt. He was there for me when I needed it most. He may not be officially divorced, but I knew that much for sure.

But as much as I appreciated his gesture, Jane's comment lingered heavily, puffing away any of the good feelings as fast as they came.

I grabbed my phone and called John, needing to hear his voice. The line rang two times before he picked up.

"Hey, baby! How'd it go? Tell me everything!" His voice was bright with excitement, but I couldn't miss the hint of nervousness underneath—and rightfully so. I'd just spent the last day with his wife.

"It was good . . . I think," I said, pacing the room. "I made it through the panel. Jane, of course, had her moments where she was trying to make me look bad—or make herself look good." I paused, watching my reflection in the mirror. "But I held my ground."

"Thats great," he said.

"Yeah, it is—it's just . . . she said something when we were leaving, something about my career. And I'm not sure how to take it."

"What did she say?"

I hesitated for a second, taking a deep breath, "She told me to be careful about who I try to outshine, that it could cost me my promotion, or my career. And, I don't know . . . does that mean she knows everything about us? Or is that just her trying to see if I admit to it?"

There was a long pause, and when he spoke again, his voice was tight. "Sarah, I really don't like the sound of that. It is one thing for her to ask me about you or any other girl in the office. But if she's making threats like that, we need to be careful, and you need to act like you are completely clueless."

"I know. I just . . . it seemed like she knew everything. I just can't tell if she is bluffing to test me. I don't know what to do. This really could cost me everything."

"We'll figure it out, okay? I'm here for you. Always."

I forced a smile that I knew he couldn't see. The smile was for me. I had to keep playing dumb for now. If I acted oblivious long enough, maybe Jane would get bored and move on to her next target, leaving me out of her crosshairs. But if I slipped up—if I gave her any reason to think I was with John—I could lose everything. My promotion, my career, my reputation. I couldn't let that happen.

———

Bracing myself for the aftermath of Theo and Willow's conversation with Jenny the previous night, I headed down to the hotel restaurant to meet the Brooks for dinner. Izzy had decided to turn in early, leaving me to face Theo and Willow all alone. I just prayed that Jenny hadn't also mentioned our dinner out to Jane.

They both turned their attention to me, smiles wide and genuine.

"You were amazing today," Willow said. "Honestly, I don't think anyone expected you to be that outspoken. We're so proud of you."

Theo nodded. "You really nailed it. A lot of people are talking about you."

I smiled, relieved to hear their praise. Their kindness almost made me forget about the Jane drama earlier.

"Thanks, that means a lot," I said, trying to keep my tone casual.

Willow leaned back. "You handled it all so well. We could tell you were a little nervous, but honestly, you didn't show it at all."

"It definitely didn't seem like it. You looked like you belonged on that stage," Theo added.

I couldn't help but feel a little lighter. Their positivity made it easier to breathe for a second.

"Well, I couldn't have done it without the support," I said.

Willow raised her glass. "To you, Sarah. And to what's next."

As our main courses arrived, the energy shifted and an uncomfortable silence hung in the air. Without giving it too much thought, I grabbed for something to say to break it. Anything to avoid them bringing up Jenny, John and Carlye's. "Ugh, I'm so excited to go on vacation next week."

They both looked at me in complete confusion.

Fuck me. Not that. Anything but that. Why did I say that?

"I m-mean, visit my family," I stuttered, trying to correct myself, shaking my head and holding up my drink as if the martini was to blame. "Man, sometimes I think every time I get on a plane it feels like a vacation because I fly so infrequently." I tried to recover, terribly.

I had told them I was out of the office "to visit my family and my grandmother who was sick." Not to fly to see John and stay in Florida at The Ritz Carlton. I prayed they wouldn't notice my slip.

In true Theo and Willow fashion, they did.

"Sarah, what's going on?" Willow said, glancing at Theo. "We've noticed you've been gone a lot—off almost every weekend. And then

254

there was the whole Stone edit mishap, which was really unlike you. It just feels like your head hasn't been in the game."

"I haven't been away *that* much," I said, more defensively than I hoped to admit. "And I'm still getting all my work done."

"Come on, Sarah." Theo said, "I wasn't born yesterday. You are seeing someone."

My heart stopped. I tried to pull back the deer-in-the-headlights look that I could feel creeping across my face. "No, I'm not," I said quickly. "We agreed, not until I'm a seni—"

"—senior editor. Yes, we made that deal," Theo finished for me. "And yet, you're seeing someone." His eyes narrowed like an investigator trying to break his suspect with assumptions.

"It's okay if you are," Willow added quickly. "You're an adult. You can tell us. You don't have to lie." Her words almost bordered on maternal, which made me feel even more guilty.

The Brookses were masters at playing good cop, bad cop, sometimes switching mid-conversation. They would fire off rapid questions that threw you off and made you feel rushed to answer, usually resulting in misspeaking. It was dizzying. I started to feel hot. Should I tell them the truth? How would that affect my relationship with John? With Jane? With Izzy? With *them*? The walls felt like they were closing in.

I started to breathe harder, feeling sweat under my arms.

"Come on, Sarah. Just tell us," Theo urged, his voice growing more insistent, shifting into the role of the concerned good cop.

"Yeah, how bad could it really be?" Willow chimed in, her tone feigning nonchalance but her eyes probing me like a scalpel. "Is he in college? If so, I bet he won't last more than a month anyway."

"Totally," Theo added.

They circled me, poking and prodding with questions, each one digging deeper, faster. My chest tightened, and the weight of their expectations started to crush me. It was like I was six again, curled up in the corner of my room, terrified of getting in trouble, of being caught. Of failing. Of not being perfect.

The pressure built to an unbearable point. My hands pressed to my temples, trying to steady myself as the truth broke free, spilling out in a rush, sharp and raw. I couldn't keep up the act any longer.

"I've been seeing John," I said with relief.

I crumbled, my face falling into my hands, and the release of ·pent-up emotions hit me like a tidal wave, a weight lifting off me that I hadn't realized I was carrying.

"John who?" Willow asked, as if she couldn't imagine John Reynolds, VP of Acquisitions at Regent, with someone like me.

"John . . ." I breathed in. There was no going back if I said it. "John . . . John Reynolds," I murmured, barely able to get the words out.

Willow gasped, her hand flying to her face.

Theo's mouth dropped open, as if I'd just told him I'd killed someone.

A deafening silence.

"I lied because I didn't want to make a big deal about it if it wasn't serious. Then it got serious. But then I found out about him and Jane. But the divorce has been messy. I was too afraid to tell you. I thought you'd stop talking to me because you're so close to both of them—"

"How did this even happen?" Theo asked, in utter disbelief. "He works in the Chicago office."

"We met at the Gala," I said, swallowing. "I didn't know who he was at first—"

"John Reynolds is dating *you*?" Willow's voice cut through the air, sharp and incredulous. I knew she didn't mean it the way it sounded, but it stayed with me like a scar. A permanent reminder of how she really saw me.

My head hung low. I couldn't make eye contact. The guilt was crushing.

"So every time you couldn't have dinner with us, you were with *him*?" Theo asked, putting it together. "Have you visited him in Chicago?"

"And he visits me in Manhattan. Sometimes we go to other

places," I admitted, my face in my lap, like a dog that had pooped on the carpet and was being reprimanded.

The waiter arrived with another round of drinks—thank God. "So Izzy knows, and she lied for you too?" Willow asked, her words felt so urgent that I didn't have time to process the words before they came out.

"Yes. Izzy knows," I said, barely holding myself together.

"Who else knows?" Theo's voice was as close to desperate as I had ever heard him. He was never rattled by anything.

"Just Izzy. A few friends outside of publishing, but no one else who would care."

"You need to shut this down immediately," Theo said with concern. Warning. "You need to end this. *Now.* Anyone who knows, you need to tell them it's over, immediately. You need to make sure they never tell anyone about this. And if anyone asks, it never happened. This never happened. Do you understand?"

"Uh—" I started, but Willow cut me off.

"It will ruin your career if anyone finds out. Do you understand that?" She paused. "If Jane finds out, she could go straight to HR, accuse you of misconduct, and make sure you're fired. She's got the power to make sure you're blacklisted in this industry, Sarah. It wouldn't just be the end of your career at Regent—it could destroy everything you've worked for. You may never work in publishing again. She doesn't have any idea, does she?"

"No. Of course she doesn't," I snapped. I didn't have the heart to tell them what she said to me in the conference room or after the panel. They might actually die of internal combustion if I told them the truth.

Theo rubbed his eyes. "Jesus fucking Christ. Sarah, John's a great guy, but come on. You want to ruin everything you've worked for for *him*? Anyone but him. Anyone but Jane's husband."

"Ex-husband!" I shot back.

"Are they divorced?" he asked mockingly, his eyebrows raised as if he knew the answer to his question, but he wanted to hear me say it.

"Well, almost. It should be finalized by the end of the year," I said.

"Oh, even better. He's not even fucking divorced yet." Theo's voice was loud enough for the table next to us to hear. "You really think he's going to leave her for you? He can't even get a divorce finalized. What's it been? Two years they have been battling it out? You think it's going to all of a sudden end now because you are in the picture?"

"We love each other," I said, the words coming out flat.

"Is your career still the most important thing to you, Sarah? Is senior editor still on your priority list, or are you throwing any chance you have of that away for a married man? 'Cause if there was a way to throw it all away, this would be it." Willow said.

I nodded, keeping my eyes down, pushing every ounce of guilt, sadness, and shame deep down where it wouldn't see the light of day.

"Then end it. And shut it down," she snapped.

I choked back tears and nodded again. "I understand. I'll end it," I said, knowing it would get them off my back.

I wanted to kick and scream and tell them how I felt. How much I loved him. How much he loved me. All he had done for me. How we had been there for each other. How they were wrong. Instead, I did what I always did: I agreed. I placated. I was coachable. I did what I was told. I couldn't afford to lose them, not now. Not after all they had done for me. If I lost them, I would most likely also lose senior editor.

Willow leaned back in her seat and motioned for the check. And the conversation was over.

———

The next morning, I jolted awake to a loud banging on the door.

"Are you fucking kidding me?" Izzy's voice came through the door.

I scrambled to unlock it, my hands fumbling with the doorknob, still half asleep and disoriented. As soon as the door creaked open, Izzy stormed in, her energy filling the room like a whirlwind.

"Why is everyone yelling at me this weekend?" It was one thing for Theo and Willow to be angry, but now Izzy? Could things get any worse?

"You told them?" Her arms flailed in disbelief.

"Told who what?" I asked through a yawn.

"Theo and Willow about you and John."

"Yes, I did. It's a long story, and I don't know if I want to get into it right now. I can tell you later."

"And you told them *I* knew about it? Now they are angry at me for lying for you. For hiding this from them."

"Shit. Izzy, I didn't even think about—" I stammered. "I'm so . . . I don't know what to say. I didn't think telling them that you knew would even be a problem."

"Well, it is." She snapped. "They have just found out I've been lying for the last seven months, keeping this a secret, and now they don't trust me. I could lose my job over this, Sarah."

I couldn't lose Izzy too. She was my rock. "Please, Izzy, let me expla—"

"Save it." She threw her palm in my face to stop me. "This was fine when we were only risking *your* career. That was your choice. But now it's affecting mine. I can't go down with your sinking ship." Her arms fell to her sides, defeated.

I fought back tears, feeling every inch of my heart breaking. "Izzy, please, John said the divorce will be final soon. For real, this time—"

"You know what?" Izzy scoffed. "I think Theo and Willow were right to react the way they did. If Jane finds out, you're absolutely fucked." She paused. "She'll ruin your life. You'll never work in publishing again. I hope it's worth it and that it all works out, for your sake. But honestly, I don't see it happening."

"Izzy . . ." I stood, frozen, as she stormed out without another word.

The sound of the door clicking shut echoed in the space.

Aria Devi

I sank onto the edge of the bed, my heart pounding. I had always known the risks of being with John. Until now, I had managed to push them out of my mind, or at least tell myself that it would all be worth it if it meant I ended up with him. But now, with Theo, Willow, and Izzy knowing, it was real. And I wasn't so sure that he was worth losing everything. Losing my friendships. Losing the life I had built. Real people were aware of the mess I'd gotten myself into, and it wasn't just an abstract danger anymore—it was a ticking time bomb. If Jane really knew and decided to act on it, she could destroy everything with the snap of her fingers. Suddenly, the stakes weren't just theoretical. They were tangible.

Theo and Willow knew. Izzy was furious. My career, my friendships, my reputation—everything felt fragile, like it could shatter with one wrong move. Like everything I had done at work to get ahead could become completely obsolete. It was like I was living in a nightmare that I couldn't wake up from.

I couldn't live like this anymore—the hiding, the lying, the waiting for the inevitable fallout. The fear of losing my job—everything I'd sacrificed. It was all slipping through my fingers.

I couldn't do this anymore.

I couldn't live like this anymore.

I had to tell John it was over.

Tears blurred my vision as I reached for my phone. My thumb hovered over his name. I had to stop this before everything fell apart. But the thought of losing him, of walking away from the one thing that made me feel alive, tore me apart just as badly.

I took a deep breath to try to calm myself. The guilt, the fear, the shame—it had to stop. With trembling hands, I pressed "Call John Reynolds."

The phone rang once, twice. When he answered, before he could even say one word, I cut in. "We need to talk."

Chapter Twenty-Eight

I finally landed in Florida. John planned to arrive the next day.

I checked into the Ritz in Naples, where everything was flawless—the marble gleamed, and the scent of ocean breeze lingered in the air. Normally, a place like this would have felt like a dream. But today, it was empty, hollow. The beauty around me only highlighted the void inside. It was as if excitement for life had packed its bags and left without me.

As I finally made my way to the room, I dropped my bags, took off my shoes, and sank into the chair by the window, staring at the water. In the solitude of my room, my mind reeled from my conversation with John.

"What exactly did you tell them?" His question was soft, more controlled than I had expected.

"The truth." My voice was hoarse, the words coming out fast, like I was trying to outrun them. "About the affair. About everything. I had to tell them, John."

There was a pause on the other end. His exhalation was audible, and it sent a shiver down my spine. "You told Theo and Willow?" he repeated, slower this time like he was trying to believe it. "What were you thinking, Sarah?"

"I couldn't lie anymore. They pressured me, and not telling them was eating me alive. I told them everything. They deserved to know."

His reaction wasn't exactly angry—I had never seen John angry—but this was definitely the closest I'd ever seen him. "Sarah, why would you do that? You know how much power they have in the company, right? What if they say something? What if they tell someone else? What if they told Jane?"

"They won't," I said, trying to reassure him. "Theo and Willow . . . they won't tell anyone. The last thing they wanted was for anyone to know. They made that really clear. They just want it to go away. They're on our side."

Lately, I was the only person John trusted. But now that I told Theo and Willow, that trust felt fractured—just like mine had been after hearing his call with Jane.

"Sarah, we cannot let Jane find out about this. There's a reason I asked you not to tell anyone. The second she hears anything, she'll go nuclear. Especially if someone else tells her and it makes her look like she had no idea. She's already making this divorce hell—freezing accounts, dragging negotiations, threatening to fight me for things she doesn't even want. But if she finds out about us? She'll make sure I walk away with nothing. She'll bury me, Sarah."

He was right. Everything was at stake—for both of us. If Jane found out, she wouldn't just make the divorce harder; she'd make it her mission to destroy him. And by extension, me.

I had to talk to him—in person. I couldn't end things over a screen. It needed to happen face-to-face. I needed to shut it down, like Theo and Willow said. "John," I said, "I just . . . I didn't want to do this over the phone. I want to see you. I want to talk in person."

I paused, a wave of realization hitting me. Despite planning to end it when he arrived, there was a small, desperate part of me that secretly hoped we'd find a way to push through it. Maybe speed up the divorce, or find some way to stay connected—at least until we could be together. Maybe we would find some sort of loophole or workaround. The idea that it was really going to be over, the idea of losing him—felt unbearable. I couldn't imagine losing John . . . losing him to Jane.

Despite the trust that had been shattered after I overheard that call with Jane, the truth was—I loved him. As much as I felt betrayed, the thought of losing him felt like losing a part of myself, a part I hadn't even known I needed until he came into my life. For as long as I could remember, my career had always come first. I had built my life around that, protected it, prided myself on it. But with John, it was different. The idea of losing him made everything else—my success, my independence, my promotion—feel trivial. It was like a piece of me I never even knew was missing had found its place, and now I couldn't imagine my world without him. I was willing to sacrifice everything I had worked for if it meant I could keep him. And that terrified me more than anything.

He was quiet for what felt like an eternity, like he knew the conversation that was coming. Then he said, "I understand. We'll talk when I get to Florida. Let's not make any more decisions until we're together."

It was a small relief, a brief moment where I could finally catch my breath. But, the more I stayed on the phone with him, the more I desperately needed to see him in person—I needed to feel him close to me—before I could make any decisions. Without that, everything felt uncertain, like I was about to step into something I wasn't sure I was ready to face.

———

Later that night, standing in front of the bathroom mirror, I barely recognized the woman staring back at me. The woman with the frozen forehead, the full lips. The bleached blonde extensions that flowed down to my butt, and the clothes that looked like a cheap imitation of Jane.

She wasn't me.

She was . . . foreign.

She was . . . a Jane lookalike. A knockoff

Everything about me felt like a costume, something I put on to fit in, to be someone else. To be like Jane. I used to love my sharp, tailored suits. Now I wore things I'd seen Jane wear—things I only bought because they looked like something she would wear. It had become a game, a race to be like her. To be more Jane than Jane herself. To fill the void she left with John. I'd never wanted to admit it, but the idea of slipping into her life . . . pretending to be her . . . was all I could think about. I had become compulsive. Obsessed.

I ran my fingers through my hair. *God, who had I become? When did I stop being me?*

Hell, I had no fucking clue who I even was anymore.

I was chasing something—someone—who no longer existed. Not just the "Jane" I had tried to become, but the version of myself I had crafted to make John feel less heartbroken about losing the love of his life. Before all of this, before John, I loved who I was. But after months of molding myself into the woman I hoped John would learn to love more than Jane, I no longer recognized myself. The only thing I knew for sure was this:

I didn't fucking like her.

I dragged myself out of the bathroom, glancing back at the hotel room. The bed, with its crisp white sheets and heavy curtains drawn tight against the Florida sun, should've felt luxurious, but it was just a cold, empty shell, holding my suitcase.

A wannabe Jane Reynolds—that's who I'd become. Someone who had slept with her idol's husband, lied to everyone I cared about, and lost sight of who I once was. The Ritz, in all its opulence, felt like a sleazy Motel 6, with me playing the role of the mistress. The other woman. It was like the life I'd built—shiny on the surface—nice vacations, a sexy boyfriend—all of it was hollow underneath. Cold. Lonely.

I collapsed onto the bed and closed my eyes. As I lay there—the realization that something had to change washed over me. I couldn't stay in this version of myself any longer, but I had no idea what the next step was. All I knew was that I couldn't keep pretending.

———

I spent the next morning preparing for John's arrival: a shower, makeup, the usual routine to become the woman he had fallen in love with. But even as I stepped into one of the hotel's robes, I couldn't shake the feeling that something was off. I hadn't heard from him all morning, not even a *'Can't wait to see you'* text.

I had wanted to create some space, though. Let him miss me a little. Even though I knew what was ahead—the difficult conversation we had been avoiding—I couldn't help but feel that familiar flutter of excitement in my chest. I wanted him near. His presence made everything seem easier, even the hardest conversations.

A few hours later, I checked my phone, the screen lighting up with a familiar name.

It was John. Video calling me. I sighed with relief that he was okay and that I would see him soon. He always called me just before his flights took off.

"Hey, are you about to take off?" I smiled, trying to sound casual, but as I got a better look at him, I realized he wasn't on a plane. He wasn't at the airport at all. He was sitting in his apartment; the leather chair was too familiar to miss.

A pit settled in my stomach, and I checked the time, confused. Maybe I'd messed up the time zone difference.

"Hey, how's it going?" John's voice came through, strained. He sounded . . . distracted, like he was here but a big part of him was somewhere else entirely.

"Why aren't you on your flight?"

John paused. "I'm sorry, Sarah. Something came up."

A lump swelled in my throat. "What happened? Are you okay?" The words tumbled out, panic rising in my chest. I was suddenly aware of how vulnerable I was. Was he really missing his flight? I was going to be here alone? At first, I was concerned about whether he was okay. But if he was fine, and he is missing his flight for no reason . . . then I would be pissed.

"Yeah. Yeah, I'm fine. Um . . ." He trailed off, as if gathering the courage to say something heavy. I braced myself.

"Jane's here."

The world tilted. For a moment, I couldn't process the words. Jane. She was . . . there? In Chicago? Why?

The silence stretched on, the space between us growing wider with every passing second.

I took a breath, trying to steady myself. "Why is she there?"

John sighed, almost as if the weight of what he was about to say was crushing him. "It's a long story, but . . . the IRS showed up at my house yesterday. They're auditing us."

My head spun. The IRS? Audits? Was he in some sort of financial trouble? How did I not know about this? My stomach flipped as I fought to make sense of the news. "John, what are you talking about? Are you okay? What's going on?"

"I'm fine," he said. "But, yeah . . . the IRS came by. I've been going through the last five years of receipts all morning. Apparently our accountant fucked up pretty bad on our taxes once we started making a lot of money, and we underpaid."

"By how much?" I asked. Were they about to lose everything?

"It's not good, Sarah. We owe about four hundred thousand dollars in back taxes."

Four hundred thousand dollars? I'd known about his financial issues with the divorce, but this was much worse than I imagined. Could *this* be the cause of all the divorce delays?

"Who was responsible for all the money?" I asked. My stomach twisted into knots. "Is that . . . is that something you can handle? I mean, can you pay it?"

"I was. That is why Jane is blaming me for everything. I'll figure it out. I have that much in savings but not much more." His voice was tight. "Anyway . . . Jane flew straight here from Boston. She showed up unannounced this morning. We've been dealing with this all day."

A chill ran down my spine. Jane. They were in their house *together*. And I had nothing to do but sit here, waiting. My mind raced, trying to wrap itself around the fact that he hadn't even bothered to tell me he wasn't coming until *now*. Not a word, not a hint of what was happening, not even a fucking text. As if I didn't even deserve the courtesy of being informed.

"Are you saying you're not coming to Naples?" I forced the words out, bitterness slipping through my words. Of course. Jane came first, once again. It stung more than I cared to admit.

"I'm so sorry," he said, his voice full of regret. "I didn't want this to happen. I had no idea she was coming—or the IRS, for that matter. I was dealing with them all yesterday and today. This was the first chance I had to call you."

I wanted to shout, to demand that he choose me, that he come to Naples to be with me like he promised. I was drowning—drowning in anger . . . frustration . . . sadness. The relief I had looked forward to on the other end of our conversation was long gone, replaced by the suffocating weight of reality.

"So, you are choosing her." I said. This wasn't just about the IRS or the timing. It was about her. About Jane being his first priority, every single time.

"I am not choosing her," he protested weakly. "I swear, it's not like that. I don't want this, Sarah. I want to be with you." A lie. All I could think of was him there, with her, the woman who still had a hold on him—physically, emotionally, mentally, financially, and however else someone can have a chokehold on another person.

"If you wanted to, you would have, at the very least, texted me. Not called me as your flight is about to take off and you aren't on it." I paused. I had to do this now. I couldn't wait until his schedule allowed us to have this conversation. If I waited for that, it may never come. "John, I can't do this anymore," I said, my voice quieter than I expected, a finality hanging in the air. "I thought . . . I thought we could make this work, but I can't keep fighting for something you're not willing to fight for too. It will leave me with nothing. It will leave me with less than nothing."

It wasn't what I planned to say. If he'd come to Naples, maybe we could've had a real conversation, worked through the mess, found a way to still be together. I'd been holding on to the hope that he'd come around, see the value in what we had, and be willing to risk it all like I had. But that was just wishful thinking, naïve and foolish. Even so, it didn't stop me from hoping, even now, with every word, that we could still make it work. That he would fight for me. *Please fight for me.*

"I understand," he said, his voice hollow. Even now, I'd been expecting him to say something . . . different—to fight for me. Even fake fight for me. But there was nothing. No pleading. No promises. Just complete resignation.

I wanted to scream. Rage bubbled up inside me. I wanted him to tell me he loved me, that he needed me. That he would risk it all if it meant he could be with me. I wanted him to choose me, damn it. But all he said was, "I understand"? He was too scared to stand up for me. To be honest. To own his truth. To move on. I couldn't help but believe that it was because, underneath it all, he still loved her. He still chose her. And he always would.

The silence between us was deafening. I couldn't even cry. I felt numb, like a part of me was already gone. Dead.

"I love you," I said, my voice catching. "But I can't keep doing this. Not like this."

"I understand," he said again.

And with those words, all the hope I'd been clinging to shattered into a million pieces. He had given up on us, just like that. Too afraid to choose, to act. This wasn't about Jane or his marriage. It wasn't about Theo or Willow or Izzy or the promotion. It was about me, my value, and how much longer I was willing to let him keep me waiting in this uncertain space.

There was nothing left to say. I swallowed hard. "Goodbye, John."

I ended the call before he could say anything else.

I threw my phone into a pillow and stared at the empty room, numb. Empty.

An hour passed.

Then a deafening scream came out of me.

Another hour passed.

Then, without warning, the tears came.

And came. And came. And no matter what I did, no matter how hard I tried, I couldn't stop them.

Chapter Twenty-Nine

I tried calling Izzy, but she sent me to voicemail every time. I needed to talk to her. To someone. I had spent the entire day crying. I woke up throughout the night, tears soaking my pillow.

Today hadn't been off to the hottest start either.

I wrote to Theo and Willow in our group chat:

Me:

> It's done.

Willow:

> We're so proud of you.

Theo:

> Good.

I couldn't stand to stay at the hotel all week. I couldn't walk around the gorgeous grounds and eat at the fancy hotel bar without the constant reminder that John was supposed to be with me. But, I figured I could handle staying for one night. I deserved to let myself get some rest and a good meal before heading back to the city. Back to reality. Back to all my problems.

It was strange how someone could go from being such a big part of my life to completely absent in the blink of an eye. Before they show up, they're just a name, a face you haven't seen before. Then suddenly you're talking to them every day, sharing thoughts, jokes, little pieces of your world.

They slip so seamlessly into the fabric of your life that you don't even realize they're becoming a part of you. And then, when they leave, nothing feels the same. You can never fully go back to the way things were before. They've *changed* you, woven themselves into your routine, your thoughts, your heart. Every day was different with them there, and now that they're gone, it's like something in you has gone. Like something in you has died. You keep going through the motions —eating, working, doing laundry—but it all feels different, wrong, a little off. Like life is happening, but now there is something missing from it.

I had a college professor named Nick. He was in his late thirties, and was so laid-back that we called him by his first name. He was way too cool to be a physics teacher. One day, he taught us about quantum entanglement—a concept in which particles are so linked that the state of one directly affects the state of the other, even across vast distances. Millions of miles, even. The change that happens to one, happens instantly to the other, regardless of the space between them.

One day I was sitting in his class, my first love had just cheated on me. With my best friend of course (is there any other way to make someone hurt at the deepest level?). My heart was so raw. I could barely hold it together when I raised my hand.

"Yes, Sarah?" Nick called on me, his trademark pearly smile lighting up his face.

"Does quantum entanglement explain why when someone breaks

your heart, it feels like physical pain?" I asked, sounding so pathetically hopeless. I didn't care how it sounded to the entire junior class. I needed to know why my heart hurt so badly.

I remember the way Nick looked at me. Knowing. With empathy. "When two people form a deep bond, it's often described as an 'entanglement' of their energies. Scientifically, it's linked to neural pathways and mirror neurons—cells that activate when we experience emotions or witness them in others. These neurons help us connect on a deep level. So, when that connection is broken—such as in heartbreak—the brain and body actually feel real, physical pain because the neurons that had been entangled are literally ripping apart.

I felt so seen and understood that tears welled up and ran down my cheeks.

"But the hopeful part is that humans are incredibly adaptable," Nick continued. "Over time, these pathways begin to rewire themselves. Think of them like hiking trails or lines in the sand—the more you walk them, the deeper they get. The more grooves you make, the easier it is to walk them." He paused, letting the class process. "For a while, it will feel like your heart is being ripped from your chest. But soon those old paths will fade as the new paths are trudged enough times. It will be as if the old never even existed."

At the time, I wanted to believe in that hope he talked about—that the pain would one day feel like a distant memory. When I was in it, it felt endless. Like I'd never find my way out of it.

Though I had, eventually. Eventually and with time, the pain in my chest didn't hurt as much. Eventually the grooves faded. I formed new ones. My heart healed. Unfortunately, I felt like John had found that same scar that had seemed to be healed—the one on my heart—and stabbed a knife into it, exposing the same damage as before.

But, if I could hold on to anything in this moment, it was hope. Hope that one day it would heal again. Hope that my career would survive this. My friendships would survive this. And hope that I would be able to survive my life without John Reynolds in it.

I had to remember this. Today, with John, I had to remind myself that all this pain I was feeling, this heartbreak . . . while it felt real and never-ending, it wouldn't last forever. It couldn't. Eventually, the weight would lift, even if it was hard to see how right now. Eventually, it would go away. And even though it was crushing me now, I had to hold on to the belief that one day I'd be free from it. With enough new grooves. With enough time.

That reminder was my only way of surviving this moment.

———

Before checking out of the hotel and heading back to Manhattan— back to reality, to the life that had slowly slipped away since February —I realized the full weight of what I was returning to. I had let everything unravel, and now I had nothing to show for it. *Nothing.* No John. The thought was terrifying. This was exactly why I made the no-dating rule in the first place—I was such an idiot. I sat at the hotel bar, drinking and eating, just as I would have done with John if he were here. But that only made it feel more sad, more pathetic.

I wasn't thinking about my future today. I didn't have the energy for plans or goals. All I wanted was to make the present a little less painful, even if it was just for a few hours. I couldn't stay this way for long, no matter how much I wanted to sulk and sit in my apartment with ice cream for months. I would have to go back to work and pretend I was fine, at the very least, and refocus so that my career wouldn't completely fall apart.

I checked my phone—no new texts from Theo, Willow, Izzy, or John. I scrolled through Instagram, hoping to see if Jane or John were online (yes, I had unfollowed Jane on the flight before the Fourth of July, but it hadn't stopped me from stalking her page on the regular). To get some insight into what was going on between them. My mind went to the only obvious thing they could be doing, realizing how much they loved each other and wanting to call off the divorce and get back together. My heart dropped when I pulled up Jane's page.

She had posted just one picture. It was from last night's dinner.

Jane, glowing in a dress that screamed sophistication, sat across from the person taking the picture at . . . Urban Eats. The photo had to have been taken by John . The same place he'd sworn he had never taken another woman to, the place that had been ours. And there they were, sitting in the same intimate lighting we'd shared on my first trip to Chicago. Parker stood in the background behind them making cocktails.

I could feel my heart tighten, the anger rising in my chest. He had lied to me. This was the place he had promised was special. And now, there they were, acting like it was just another night out. I stared at the photo, rage twisting in my stomach, the truth hurting even more than I had imagined. Her caption should have been: *Dear Sarah, If you're trying to get with my ex-husband, take a good look. I'm still here, and he's letting me back into his life.*

I couldn't believe it. Was this the plan all along? Lure a naïve young woman in, make her fall in love, and then crawl back together? Was this some twisted divorce foreplay before calling it all off and living happily ever after? It probably wasn't the case, but it didn't stop my mind from spinning there.

I didn't know what was real anymore. Part of me wanted to screenshot the post and send it to John with a sarcastic 'Looks like you are really focused on getting those taxes done' message, but I stopped myself. We'd broken up less than twenty-four hours ago. Reaching out now would make me look pathetic. Besides, he had enough on his plate with taxes and that woman at his house all week.

I couldn't keep looking at Jane's photos. Each one tore me apart for different reasons—whether it was her success at work or how she seemed to outshine me in every way—looks, clothes, wealth. I couldn't take it anymore.

As I finished the last sip of my martini, I realized I had to block her in order to keep my sanity. This woman had been unknowingly tearing apart my life for the past seven months. She was that good.

I Googled 'How the hell do you block someone on Instagram?' read the directions, then headed back to the app. Just as I was about to click "Block Jane Reynolds," my phone buzzed with a new message. My head spun. My fingers hovered over the screen as my mind, clouded by the martini, couldn't quite process what was happening. Why now? Why in this fucking moment? I didn't want to look, but I couldn't stop myself.

A message from none other than . . .

Jane. Fucking. Reynolds.

Fuck. Shit. Fuck.

Chapter Thirty

Immediately ordered another martini from Ted the bartender and prepared myself for what I was about to read. First of all, Jane still wasn't following me, so she had to go out of her way to find my profile to message me. Second, fuck her for still not following me.

"Hey Sarah, I've been thinking about you and . . ." The message preview taunted me, leaving the rest a mystery. My drunk spy instincts kicked in. If I opened the message, she would know I saw it. I wanted to document everything—just in case. Just in case what, though? Divorce court? The thought was almost laughable. I didn't know the first thing about how divorce legally worked, but better safe than sorry. I screenshotted the message. Then doubt crept in. What if I showed someone and they tried to say it could be from a fake account and I fabricated the whole thing? What if it was all a setup? I didn't trust anything or anyone anymore.

I figured it was best to screen record, starting from my home page and going straight to her profile to prove it wasn't a fake account, then opening the message. I needed to make sure no one could say it wasn't really her.

My God, I had become so paranoid.

I took a deep breath and told Ted, whom I had told my whole life story to last night, to wish me luck. He responded with an overly enthusiastic "You got this, girl!" followed by a high five. Bless his heart. I needed more gay bartenders in my life.

I closed my eyes and opened the message.

Hey Sarah,

I've been thinking about you, and I just couldn't keep quiet anymore. As a sister in Christ, I feel it's my duty to warn you. You've always struck me as someone with strong morals, a true daughter of Christ, and I know deep down you want to do the right thing.

I want you to know the truth about John—my STILL husband. He's not who you think he is. He's manipulative, cruel, narcissistic, and incredibly deceitful. I've lived through it for years, and I can't stand the thought of someone as pure as you being caught in his web of lies.

Despite everything, he is STILL my husband, and the things he's told you, they're twisted, I imagine. Please, from one woman of faith to another, be careful when it comes to him. He isn't who he says he is. I don't want to see you hurt the way I have been.

Xoxo, Jane

The words knocked the wind out of me.

My hand trembled as I slumped back on my bar stool. This bitch was crazy. I'd heard the conversations they'd had. She was the manipulative one trying to blame him for everything. She was the morally bankrupt one, cheating on her husband. I heard it from John; I confirmed it with Andy. She was the one sleeping with her trainer, leaving used condoms in the trash. And don't even get me started on her new boyfriend Peter, who sent John that vile package of hate mail. *She* was the villain here, *not* John. It was too much evidence to refute it. And now she was texting me that John, the man who had never as much as raised his voice at me, was the one pulling all the strings and *she* was the victim? Crazy. Fucking. Bitch.

I should have known this moment was coming. She must have been waiting for the right moment to confront me. Now, she was finally taking her shot. But why now? I screenshotted the message.

And why the religion card? I wasn't religious—never had been. But Jane, with her unwavering faith, seemed to assume I was. I could almost admire how neatly she tied in her beliefs, but she didn't know me. She didn't know a thing about where I stood on any of this. Sorry, Jane, but I learned in Psych 101 that those who accuse others of being manipulative are usually the manipulators themselves. It's called gaslighting. She really was a pathological liar.

I read the message again. And again. A hundred times over. Each time, the words started to feel heavier, like they were sinking in. But the more I read, the more I started to analyze everything. Every word. Every sentence. I couldn't help it. I was an editor—it was what I did.

And then, somewhere between the eightieth and ninetieth reading, a thought hit me. It scared me more than anything she'd said.

Was it possible . . . that she was telling the truth?

My mind went into full freak-out mode. I replayed every single moment with John. Every interaction. Every word he said about Jane. I went over it all like I was retracing my steps in a maze. No stone unturned.

But I came up empty. He'd always been genuine, kind, loving—never cruel. He wouldn't even stand up to Jane, let alone be the one pulling the strings behind the scenes. There was no way. Not with me, at least. Andy even said how amazing he was.

But the more I read Jane's message—my idol, my muse, the woman I wanted so badly to become—the more I considered that maybe I had been too trusting, too focused on what I wanted to see. How well did I really know him?

Now, I was left trying to piece everything together, connecting dots that didn't make sense. The truth was slipping away, blurring more with each passing second. I had no idea who to trust anymore. The truth was a moving target, constantly shifting and never staying still long enough for me to aim.

I didn't respond to the message. I wanted to. God, I wanted to. But I didn't. I still felt like I needed to hear it from John first—his side of the story, his truth. I had to give him a chance to explain this. I needed him to tell me, to look me in the eyes and finally tell me the truth. Without that, I couldn't move forward.

Chapter Thirty-One

Sitting at my desk the next week felt . . . wrong. Like putting on a sweater that had been washed too many times and didn't fit right anymore. No more texts from John. No more daily updates. That tiny, perfect bubble we created—just us—popped. And the strangest part? No one even noticed. Because to them, it never existed in the first place.

At home, Izzy would brush past me, almost daring me to say something. When I tried, she'd stiffen, mumble an excuse, and retreat to her room. The air between us was thick—she was still furious that I'd told Theo and Willow about the lies she had told to protect me and John. I'd broken her trust, I would be angry too.

At work, it was no better. Every glance from her was laced with coldness. She avoided me in meetings, her tone sharp like knives when we were forced to speak. She was still holding on to that anger, and it made every interaction feel like I was walking on eggshells. The silence between us felt like the real punishment.

It was just as awful with Theo and Willow. Willow was polite but distant. When I spoke to her, she was dismissive. Theo didn't even bother to pretend—his focus remained glued to his laptop when

I would stop by his office, the conversation over before it began. They were keeping their distance because, despite doing what they asked and ending things with John, I'd still broken their trust. They didn't want to get tangled in my office love-pentagon drama, and now they were doing everything they could to stay out of it—keeping their distance from the inevitable fallout.

Meanwhile, work had piled up into an insurmountable mountain. I was falling behind on Clara Hawthorne's final round of edits—each page hitting harder than the last, her entire book felt like a gut punch, a reminder of how love and the choices we make can destroy everything. Willow had asked for the edits two days ago, and here I was, still nowhere near done.

I was keeping afloat with the Gabriel Stone project, but that was only because marketing had fully taken over at this point. I only had meetings to attend and sporadic edits for marketing material. I still had to find a new author to bring to Regent, someone who would impress management and help me secure a senior editor role (though I doubted after everything that I was even in the running anymore), and I had made absolutely zero progress there. And I couldn't help but see, more clearly now than ever, if I hadn't stepped away from John when I did, there was a very real possibility I would have lost my job by now.

On the other side of the office, Peter hummed along like nothing had changed, while Jenny kept giving me guilty looks, as if she somehow felt responsible for the mess, like she knew more than I thought. Jane was still gone, and the rumor was she'd be out for weeks. Part of me was relieved—at least I didn't have to face her right now. The other part of me knew it was all a matter of time before I would have to face the music.

At home, I unraveled. The apartment felt colder, quieter. I threw myself into anything I could to avoid the silence—work, loud bars, even mindless TV. But even as I tried to drown out everything else, the questions crept in. Had I just been a substitute for Jane? Did John ever really love me?

I used to be unstoppable, driven. That fire in my belly that burned my whole life—it was gone, crushed by the weight of everything I would never get back. The fire in me reduced to ashes.

I needed a break from the pressure, from all my work. I couldn't face it all right now. I'd give it until the start of the week—just until Sunday. I'd let myself feel bad—guilt, confusion, all of it. I'd sit in it. Then? I'd flip the switch. After that, I was going full throttle—pushing through the Clara edits, finding the perfect new author for Regent, and getting back to the grind like nothing had changed. Becoming a senior editor was all that mattered now. It was the only thing left to prove I hadn't completely fallen apart. Maybe I could still get there. I had to.

Because if I didn't, I didn't know what was left.

Because if I didn't, I would have nothing.

Because if I didn't, I would be nothing.

———

The next week, I got a text from Gabriel Stone with the address to his office, 388 Greenwich Street.

Our monthly meeting with Gabriel had arrived, but this time, I was flying solo. Jane's absence meant I had a chance to meet with him one-on-one to discuss the progress we had made on the marketing campaign. I'd offered to meet Gabriel in his office this time, partly to escape the minefield of Theo, Willow, and Izzy back at Regent, and partly to try to win him over.

The last time I had seen him was the meeting where I'd completely wasted his time, missing the edits on all the marketing material because I had been too busy at my birthday party in the Finger Lakes. His frustration had been clear, and though he tried to be diplomatic, there was no hiding his annoyance. It was a mistake I couldn't erase, but as I walked into his office alone, I hoped I could redeem myself before he lost any more faith in me.

I'd offered to meet in person this time. I owed him that—an

opportunity to show I was serious about getting this right. I couldn't afford to lose this project.

Walking into Gabriel's office was like stepping into another world. Modern and borderline sterile, the room was flooded with light from floor-to-ceiling windows as the sun set behind the Hudson River. His desk was disturbingly perfect—papers lined up with military precision, as if he weren't months away from a book release.

Seeing him here, in his element, was jarring. It was like meeting someone outside the context you'd built for them. Like running into your high school teacher at a nightclub—it just felt wrong. Gabriel belonged to my world of conference rooms and manuscripts, not this gleaming, curated fortress. He stood to greet me, his hand outstretched.

"Thank you for coming all this way, Sarah." His voice wasn't unfriendly.

Gabriel was dressed in a sharp three-piece suit, the kind you'd expect to see a lawyer wear, not a writer in his office. Who wore a suit to write books? Most of our clients tended toward Stephen King chic: jeans and a rock band T-shirt. Gabriel was polished, almost unnervingly so. My best guess was prep school in Connecticut, maybe. Tennis lessons as a kid. And there was probably a family crest above his parents' fireplace.

He gestured for me to sit down as he leaned back in his chair. "Is Jane not joining us today?"

"Jane won't be here this week." I smiled. "She's in the Chicago office tying up some . . . loose ends." Like her divorce from my ex-boyfriend. "She'll be back for our next meeting. I hope that's okay with you."

"Sure," he said. There was a brief silence. "That makes sense as to why you're here," he continued. "Jane would never come to a client's office for a meeting. Nice touch, Jones. That kind of initiative has got to help with that promotion you're after."

Had Jane told him about the promotion I was working for? How else would he know about it? I nodded, not sure what to say.

"I guess it gives us a chance to discuss things more candidly," he continued, leaning back again with a small shift in his tone. "Without her keeping things so . . . serious." It was clear he didn't exactly warm to Jane's style.

I gave him a smile, then I grabbed my computer and pulled up the marketing assets. As I did, I noticed writing trophies and awards lined the walls behind him. The bookshelves held an intimidating array of literary greats. Gabriel didn't look like an ordinary writer; he looked like someone who would legally represent one. The suit, the mannerisms—maybe he was into method writing, where he dressed like David. After all, he was writing about a lawyer.

"Here are the final cuts of the marketing materials you filmed as David," I said, tapping the mouse to start the video and rotating the laptop so he could see. "The editing team did an incredible job, and I think it really captures the essence of your book and David's internal struggle. I really think my generation will resonate with him."

Gabriel watched intently as the video played, his eyes never leaving the screen. When it finished, he gave a slow nod. "Yeah, I love it. This looks great," he said. "Funny thing, watching this . . . I didn't realize how much of David was based on my own life until I saw it put together like this. It's all there, right in front of me. Like I am talking about my own life. Kind of surreal."

I smiled, knowing exactly where he was coming from. "Life's beautiful tragedies," I said softly. "Sometimes the stories we write are the ones we need to heal from the most, and we don't even realize how much of the story is ours until it is laid out in front of us. We're so wrapped up in the act of telling 'someone else's' journey that we forget it's often our own. But that's the magic, right? It's like we're uncovering parts of ourselves we didn't even know were buried there."

Gabriel raised an eyebrow, a hint of surprise in his eyes, as if he hadn't expected me to say something so profound. "Exactly," he said slowly. "I think that's what makes it so real—David's story, the struggle . . . It's very personal. Hence why I was hesitant to be the face. I'm sure, as an author, you can relate."

The way he said, "as an author," made me pause for a moment, a small smile tugging at my lips. I was in no way an author. But I said, "It's funny how much of ourselves we pour into our characters without realizing it," anyway.

Gabriel chuckled. "Yeah, it's like you're telling someone else's story, but if you are really honest, it's your own." He leaned forward, crossing his arms, his focus returning to the computer screen. "Next steps?"

"Just need your review and final approval on these assets," I said, feeling a little more confident. "Once you confirm, we can start rolling out the promotion. And, of course, we'll need to keep pushing forward the book release plans, and set a meeting with marketing to lock in the release event logistics."

Gabriel gave a quick, approving nod. "Sounds good. Let's get this locked in."

I smiled, feeling a sense of relief that everything was moving smoothly. "I'll send you an email with the review notes, and we'll take it from there."

Gabriel's eyes met mine. "Looking forward to seeing it all come together."

"Anything else you wanted to discuss today?" I asked.

"That's all for today. But since you came all this way for such a quick meeting, how about a walk? Or we grab a drink?"

"Are you sure? I don't want to take up too much of your time." I checked my watch. He *was* my last appointment of the day.

"Of course," he said easily. "We can talk more about the book if you want."

"I would love that," I said, a little too excited. Another opportunity to win him over and stay on this project. "No espresso though, I'll be up all night."

He smiled as he opened the door for me. "A walk and a drink it is," he said, his hand hovering just over the small of my back as we walked out. It felt professional, respectful. But for the first time, I saw something different in him—something open, friendly even. Maybe I had won him over after the marketing meeting flub after all.

"Just so you know, I'm not an author," I said to Gabriel as we sat down for drinks at Dante's in the West Village. It was one of my favorite places, a quaint, dimly lit bar with velvet banquettes and old-world charm. It was like the rest of Manhattan, and all my problems melted away.

"What do you mean?" he asked, sipping his drink.

"In your office, you referred to me as an author. But I'm not."

"Yes, you are," he said matter-of-factly. "Whether you like it or not. I recognized it the moment we met at Regent. You think like an author, but you've got business sense, too. It's a lethal combination, if you know how to use it. You may not officially have a book out there, but you will one day."

"I wanted to be one when I was younger . . . but I never pursued it. Told myself it wouldn't pay the bills. But after seeing your nice office in Tribeca, I'm starting to wonder if I made the wrong choice," I said, nudging him, half joking.

His suit jacket was off, and the sleeves of his crisp white shirt were rolled up. There was something about him that felt different—more relaxed, more approachable. It was like seeing a side of him that was hidden behind the formalities of his professional image.

I looked away and pursed my lips. "Who knows, maybe someday." I raised my glass. "To life's beautiful tragedies and all the inspiration that comes from them, Mr. Stone."

Gabriel looked sideways at me, smiled, and raised his glass. "And to our best selling book yet." It was the first time I had ever seen him smile—really smile—with teeth. It was a beautiful sight.

"So, what beautiful tragedies are you navigating these days, Ms. Jones?" he asked.

"Me?" I almost choked on my wine. "Uh . . . what?"

"Come on," he urged, a small grin creeping through his serious demeanor. "I need a muse for my next book. If *you* don't end up writing a book about your life, maybe someone else will."

I shook my head and let out a big breath. "Let's just say my whole life is one big, beautiful tragedy right now," I said.

"That's perfect." He elbowed me. "Sounds like you would have a lot of material to work with."

I changed the subject. "Why do you always wear suits? Authors don't wear suits."

Gabriel threw his head back and laughed. "Why do *you* always wear suits?"

I looked down at my outfit. I was wearing a suit.

"But I'm not an author, so that doesn't count!" I pointed at him with an 'I got you' look.

He chuckled. "I guess I hadn't really thought about it. I worked in marketing here in New York in my early twenties, went to law school, practiced law for a while before I started writing books. I always wore a suit as a lawyer. I guess it just stuck."

I knew he'd been to law school.

"I like it. I think more men should wear suits these days. It's a lost art," I said, doing the quick math. Based on his background, I guessed he was in his early to mid-forties.

"What about women? I don't think I've ever seen a woman actually rock a men's three-piece suit," he scanned me from top to bottom. "It's cool."

"Why thank you. They're so much more fun than women's clothes. I have a friend who is a great bespoke tailor on the Upper East Side. Her name is Emma. She's incredibly talented. I can't afford her, but she gifted me a few pieces for my birthday last year."

"Nice, I will have to check her out. I have never heard of a woman making men's bespoke suits. Most women don't wear them because they could never pull them off." He said, taking a sip of his whiskey.

It hit me then that I was having a drink with Gabriel Stone. I'd been a fan of his books for years, but now that I was having a drink

Aria Devi

with him. This was surreal. I wanted to know more about him. "So why did you leave the law to become an author?"

"You really want to know?" he asked.

"I mean . . . I think so?"

He laughed. "It's a pretty anticlimactic story."

"Most real stories feel anticlimactic to authors," I said.

"Touché. Well, I was working as a lawyer on Wall Street. I met a woman—"

"Oh, here we go. The greatest tragedies always start with a woman," I teased.

"Totally. Right?" He laughed. It was then that I missed John's laugh. For a moment, sitting here with Gabriel, I'd completely forgotten about all the drama—Jane, John, everything. It was like being with someone who, for a fleeting second, made me forget how much of a shit show my life had become. Gabriel's presence had a way of shifting my focus, pulling me out of my own head and reminding me what it was like to just *be* in the moment.

"So I met this woman. Do you know Harper Blair?"

"The jewelry mogul, Harper Blair? Of course, who doesn't?" I said in disbelief. Harper Blair was a total tycoon in the jewelry space. Starting with only $5,000 and building her net worth to over $500 million (aka richer than Beyoncé). From jewelry. Insanity.

"Exactly," he said, gesturing with an open palm. "Well, I met Harper. We fell in love and decided to get married. She was doing so well in her business that she asked me to leave my law firm to help her company with legal and marketing."

Jesus, another married guy? I glanced at his hand. No ring.

"While I was helping her, I had a lot more time than when I was doing one hundred billable hours a week. So, I started writing. Stories came pouring out of me. I sent my first manuscript out to a few agents, got picked up, and signed with RHP. Six years, eight books, and one messy divorce later, here we are."

"Wow," I said in surprise. "I'm sorry about the divorce. That must have been really hard to go through."

"Yes, divorce is one of the most difficult life events a person can go through. But everyone is usually better off on the other side. In the long run, at least."

"That is good to know," I said, sighing. "I just hope I never have to go through that myself. I have witnessed one too many divorces."

"You're still super young, Jones," he said, tilting his head like he was fishing for my age. "I wouldn't be worrying about that any time soon."

"I guess." I shrugged. "I'll be twenty-five next year."

"You're only twenty-four?" he said, clearing his throat. "Holy shit. You may be the most impressive, focused twenty-four-year-old I've ever met. When I was your age I was snorting coke and god knows what else."

"I don't know," I said, raising my eyebrows as I took a sip of my wine. "I haven't been too focused these past few months." I shook my head, thinking about the chaos of my life north of 14th Street.

"What do you mean?"

Gabriel seemed familiar, trustworthy. Like I could tell him anything, but I wasn't about to unload my dirty laundry in front of a client. "Let's just say I have gone through my form of divorces this year. And I'm in the midst of a complicated relationship with my career as well. It feels like I'm dating my job and it's just not that into me."

"Wait, *you're married?*" He almost spat out his drink.

"Don't act like that would be so hard to believe." I punched his arm.

He threw up his hands in surrender. "I just don't know how anyone who works as hard as you do would have time for a relationship, let alone a husband."

"No, for your information, I am not married, nor have I ever been. A story for another time."

"I respect that," he said. "I love a good cliffhanger. Keeps me on the edge of my seat. See, I knew you were a writer." He gave me a knowing look. "Maybe next time you can tell me all about it."

"I wouldn't want to keep you waiting for material for that next book," I joked.

Gabriel chuckled. "Sounds like you're juggling quite a bit at work then?"

"There is a senior editor promotion I am working toward. I need to find a distinguished author who would be interested in signing with the Regent team. I haven't had time to scout for new talent. I just don't know if I am going to be able to make it happen by the end of the year with all the other work I have."

Gabriel raised an eyebrow. "What type of author are you looking for?"

I paused, considering the question. "Ideally, someone with a strong history of writing women's literary fiction, one who has demonstrated both critical acclaim and commercial success. Their work should resonate with younger audiences, an author that can be as close to guaranteed profitability on the first book they publish with us as possible."

He thought for a second. "Hmm, I may have someone in mind. Let me talk with them and see if I can make an introduction."

"Seriously?" My heart skipped a beat.

"Of course, what is the use of knowing all these authors if I can't make introductions that are a win-win for everyone involved?"

An introduction to an author in Gabriel Stone's network could change everything. If I was able to pull it off, I would be that much closer to securing the promotion.

"Thank you, Gabriel. I can't tell you how much this means to me."

"No problem at all," he replied with a grin. "Happy to help out." Then he stared at me for a second.

I smiled, masking the flutter of excitement that stirred within me from his look alone. "I should get going. I have a lot of work to do to make sure your book is your biggest success yet." I winked at him as I stood. "Thank you so much again."

I held out my hand to shake his. He stood, his eyes locked with mine. Before I could react, he reached out and pulled me into a tight embrace. Not sexual. Friendly. For a moment, I was caught off guard, the warmth of his embrace lasting longer than I expected. When he pulled away, his expression was unreadable.

"See you at our next meeting, Jones."

I gave him a polite smile, walked out of Dante's, and caught a cab to the Upper East Side.

The meeting left me feeling grateful. It had been a much-needed break from my personal chaos, and it was refreshing to talk to someone who didn't know about my personal relationships or office drama. Gabriel had been unexpectedly kind and helpful, offering to introduce me to potential clients—something that could make all the difference for my promotion. I could hardly believe he was willing to help me, but his support could change everything for me profession-ally—or at least be a huge reason I get back in the running for the promotion. Or at least don't lose my job.

The week after my meeting with Gabriel, I was able to fully focus on my work. I was still heartbroken over John, but after several days of not talking to him, my mind finally felt clear enough to give some of my attention back to my work.

I had seen earlier today on Instagram that Jane was out at a football game with her friends in Chicago, meaning John was finally alone. So, I took the chance to send him a screenshot of the message she had sent me while I was in Naples, hoping to give him a chance to explain himself. Along with the screenshot, I added a note:

Hey, I know we aren't supposed to be speaking, but I thought you should know Jane sent me this message.

I sat on my bed, laptop open, surrounded by paperwork. My phone buzzed on the nightstand, interrupting the silence.

It was John.

I hesitated before picking it up, knowing exactly what it would be about.

I finally answered, and before I could say hello, he jumped in. "What the hell? She really sent you that?"

"Hi, yes. Right after the event, when she got to Chicago," I replied.

My heart pounded a little harder, the old familiar ache surfacing as I waited for him to say more. Explain it. It had felt like years since we last spoke, and hearing his voice, even this irritated version of it, brought back a flood of memories. It blew apart all the cracks I had been trying to glue together, opening them all over again.

I hadn't expected him to react so harshly. Part of me wanted to demand an explanation, but I forced myself to stay calm, to not let his frustration pull me back into the whirlwind we'd left behind. "I didn't know how to handle it," I said quietly. "But I figured you should know."

I paused, trying to steady myself. Was he going to address what she'd said about him? The accusations? Was he going to explain himself or deny it all? My stomach twisted in anticipation.

"I can't believe she threatened you with that message."

"Neither can I." Was going to address the elephant in the room— the slander she threw at him. Was it true?

"I'm so sorry you got dragged into this. This crosses the line for me." His tone was full of smoke.

"Can I ask you something?" His lack of defense made me feel like none of this was true, but I had to ask.

"Of course." His voice was calm, grounded.

"Is what she's saying true?" I began. "I know you. I love you. I don't want to believe it's true. We have been through so much together. But she seems really convinced. You are getting divorced, right?"

"Oh, Sarah." His voice softened, not patronizing. "Of course it's not true. She'll say anything to get what she wants out of this divorce. She's looking for any way she can. All of her friends are divorced, and they're giving her terrible advice on how to screw her husband for all he's worth."

He was right. I *knew* this man. He wouldn't do this. He was the most honest, sincere man I'd ever met. I couldn't let her manipulate me too. She'd shown her true colors time and time again.

"You're right. I'm sorry I even suggested it. How did she find out?"

"I honestly don't think she knows for sure. I didn't say anything. She's probably just testing you, seeing if you crack. Trying to isolate you, get you to confess while she's here. Turn you against me. More throwing things to see if they stick." He continued after a pause, "She has been getting scrappy and will try anything right now. You've heard her on calls with me. She grabs at anything. Goes from cold to hot. She won't stop until she gets what she wants or is ignored long enough to bruise her ego. You didn't respond to the message, did you?"

"No. I didn't want to until I spoke with you first. What was I supposed to say?"

"The thing you need to understand about Jane is that she was raised by a single mother. Her father left the day she was born. Her whole life has been about men leaving her, abusive situations, leaving stable things like our marriage to chase something more exciting, risky, and unstable. Then when she gets it, she blows it up and goes back to what she is used to. When she finally has something stable, she doesn't know how to act. Her reaching out is just her trying to control things, to make sure she's the puppeteer for her next move. I get it. If my dad had left the day I was born, I'd be super manipulative to keep control too."

I had no idea. But it made sense. It explained why she was so intimidating at work. She loved being the boss. That way she couldn't be taken advantage of. That way no one could hurt her.

"The only way to defuse this is to give her zero energy."

I nodded, even though he couldn't see me.

"Has she said anything since?"

"I'm not sure. Let me check." I pulled her name up on the app, but the message she had sent me . . . it was gone.

"Wait, no, the message is gone. I swear it was right there." I had checked it at least a hundred times. I closed the app and restarted it. I checked Jane's thread again. No messages.

"She may have thought it was evidence I could use in the divorce and deleted it," he said. "She probably sent it during one of her outbursts and regretted it now that she is heading back to the office."

"So I just pretend it didn't happen?"

I felt a strange sadness now that the message was gone, cutting off the one thing I needed to talk to John about. Now we had no excuse to stay on the phone.

Before he could respond, I asked, "Well, now that she technically knows . . . couldn't you just tell her? It seems like she already knows. And she didn't fire me. We could just tell her the truth, right? The worst part is over."

I tried to sound logical, but even as I said it, I knew it wasn't possible. Was I really prepared for what would happen if we were fully out in the open? Jane had already proven she wasn't above playing dirty. If she was this vindictive when she only suspected, what would she do if she had confirmation?

Still, I wanted to believe it would be easier this way—cleaner, somehow. And ultimately prove that I was important enough to John that he would suddenly be willing to risk it all for us to be together. No more sneaking around. No more waiting. Just the truth.

"I really wish we could, Sarah, but you don't know what she's capable of. Seriously, that message was full of manipulation and gaslighting. She didn't even have a reason for sending it. She could've sent it to ten other random women she suspected."

"You could tell her that, out of respect, you won't be together until the two of you are officially divorced. We can all be adults about it, like we are with her and Peter."

"I'll think about it," he said. His words carried a flicker of hope, but I knew better. He wasn't really considering it—his mind was already made up.

"It would mean a lot. I'm just so tired of lying. I don't want her to come back to the office and have this unresolved. The more open and honest you can be, the more she'll respect that. I think it's the lying and the dishonesty that's probably the hardest part for her, being kept in the dark about what's really going on. Especially if she loves control. That is how I would feel, anyway." Why was I suddenly empathizing with her?

"Totally. You're right. And so mature. Thanks for that, bab—uh, I mean Sarah."

The hardest part of all this was that neither of us wanted to be apart, but some outside force was pulling us apart. It was like holding two opposite ends of a magnet together, but not letting them fully join. It was impossible if they got too close.

"How's everything else going?" John asked.

"Um . . . fine. I guess. Izzy hates me and avoids me like the plague. She's hardly ever home, and when she is, she's in her room. I hate being home now, so I try to work as much as I can. It's for the best. I'm so far behind. Even though I told Theo and Willow that you and I are done, they basically act like I don't exist unless they have to. I am sure they don't want to risk their own PR crisis if anything gets out. So yeah, you could say I'm doing fabulous," I said.

"God, Sarah, I'm so sorry. I miss you. I miss your voice."

It was like my heart opened wide again, undoing in seconds all the new neural pathways I'd worked so hard to form without him.

"I miss you too. I hate not talking. It sucks." A tear slid down my cheek. I couldn't let myself start crying again.

"I feel so bad for dragging you through this for so long. You didn't deserve any of this. I really want you to know that," he said.

"I know. But I chose to stay. You didn't make me. I told you I'd wait as long as it took. I want to be with you, John. Forever."

There was a long pause.

"Hello?" Did the line go dead? Or did I just tell John that I basically wanted to marry him?

Another pause.

Then, "When is your lease up?"

"Not until February 1st," I said.

"Would you like to move into my apartment in the city? It's available in early December, but I can't leave Chicago until all this is done, especially now with the IRS on my back. No one will be there. You could stay there until you get things straightened out with Izzy," he said.

My jaw practically hit the floor. "Are you serious?" I blurted out. "You're offering me your apartment? After everything?"

It was sudden—too sudden. I had been the one to walk away, the one who chose to cut things off. And yet, here he was, handing me a key to his life like nothing had changed.

"But . . . we're not even together," I added, my voice quieter now, laced with confusion.

"I know, but I got you into this mess. I want to help you in any way I can. Even if we aren't together right now. I love you, Sarah. I want you to be happy. It kills me to see you like this. It's the right thing to do. You need a place. I have one I can't even live in. You can decorate it however you want, make it yours. And when this is all over, we can figure it out."

I hesitated. The offer felt too good, too easy. Did he really want nothing in return? Maybe he felt this guilty for dragging me through everything the last few months and this was the only way he felt he could reconcile.

"Holy shit." My breath hitched, my emotions tangled between gratitude and hesitation. "This is . . . the nicest thing anyone has ever offered me." I exhaled. "But I can't afford to furnish a place like that right now."

"Don't worry about that. I have to fill it with furniture anyway. I've got it covered. Just make it your home. I can't give you the life I want right now, so this is what I can offer to take care of you, Sarah. To make up for everything I have dragged you through."

I searched his face, trying to read between the lines. What did he expect from me in return? "So we're just going to keep not talking until this is over? Or . . . ?" If I said yes, what would it really mean?

"Yeah. I mean, whatever works for you. I respect that you want to wait to be together until it can be in integrity and out in the open. I can get this all wrapped up, and we can start fresh once this is done. Plus, knowing that you'll be sleeping in my bed every night and I'll be missing out will light a big fire under my ass to get this done." He chuckled, his laugh splintering my heart a little more. Oh, how I missed it, hearing his voice, his laugh.

He must really love me. I felt it more than ever. But love had never been our problem, had it?

To open his home to me, even though we were not together, felt like something beyond words. But was it really a solution, or just another way to stay tangled up in something that would never work?

I swallowed hard. This wouldn't fix anything—Jane was still in the picture, my job was still on the line, and moving into his place would only make Theo's and Willow's disapproval worse if they ever found out. They already thought my choices were reckless when it came to him. What would they say about this?

And yet, despite all of that, I wanted to say yes. Maybe it was foolish. Maybe it was naïve. Maybe it would only make things harder in the end. But there was a chance—a small, fragile chance—that this meant something real.

I couldn't shake the feeling that John's offer, the apartment, was a sign. It had to mean something, didn't it? Maybe this could lead some-where. And no matter how many times I told myself I should walk away, a part of me was still holding out for him.

I was willing to take that risk. Plus, no one needed to know.

"I don't even know what to say."

"Just say yes," he said.

I paused, my heart racing. "On one condition . . ."

"Okay," he said as if it was already a done deal.

"Just don't let me sleep alone for too long in the huge bed I'm going to get. I might get used to it and not want to share," I said.

"This is the best deal I've made all year," he laughed. "And I make a lot of deals."

I smiled through my tears. "Thank you, John. Thank you so much. You literally just saved me a few months of agony, having to cohabitate with Izzy while she is this mad at me. I am so grateful."

"You are more than welcome, Sarah. It's the least I could do. I owe you. You're welcome." His voice softened. "I'll talk to you soon."

"I'll talk to you . . . soon," I replied, having no idea what soon meant. There was a long pause before I added, "Oh, and before I forget . . ."

"Yes?"

"Happy birthday, John."

I could hear the smile in his voice, "Thank you, Sarah. You have no idea what that means to me."

We ended the call, and for the first time in what felt like forever, the weight that had been sitting on my chest, lifted.

Chapter Thirty-Two

I'm going to the grocery store. Do you want me to get you anything?" I shouted toward Izzy's room, where she'd been hiding away for the last month, avoiding me.

No answer. This woman was stubborn. I knocked quietly on her bedroom door, opening it a crack. "Izzy?"

"What, Sarah?" Her words cut through the air like knives. Thank goodness I had decided to move out at the end of the month. I really thought Izzy would have gotten over this by now; she wasn't usually one to hold grudges.

But things were worse than I imagined they could ever be. Izzy was still furious with me for telling Theo and Willow that she knew about me and John all along. I hadn't bothered telling her that I'd broken things off with him; I didn't want to talk about him anymore, knowing the sound of his name alone could set her off.

Jane was still in Chicago. With her gone, I didn't have to brace myself for her wrath or wonder if today would be the day she confronted me about John. Or worse, fire me. It was a relief—like a storm had been delayed, even if I knew it was still coming. For now, I could focus on work without the constant stress of her looming presence.

Then there was John—or, rather, the absence of him. After everything that happened, we hadn't spoken in weeks. The only communication had been about moving arrangements, but even that felt mechanical, like we were just going through the motions. He hadn't bothered to respond to my last message. The silence was deafening.

Work was the only thing that didn't feel like it was completely crumbling anymore. Well, not completely. I had finally managed to get my head above water on Clara Hawthorne's edits, focusing on making Gabriel's project a big success. I still hadn't been put in touch with his author contact, though, and while I had been doing some recruitment of my own, I hadn't had any luck signing a new author. The senior editor promotion would be announced in just a few months at the Gala. Despite all my efforts, I wasn't sure it was enough to secure the position. Had I not been distracted with dating John and traveling to romantic getaways the last eight months, I was sure I would have secured it by a long shot. That regret was enough to drive me crazy.

"I was just checking to see if you wanted anything from the store," I said.

Izzy looked up, then back down to the paper she'd been concentrating on. "I'm good, thanks."

"Izzy, I know things have been weird between us. It's all on me, and I'm so sorry. I'm sorry that I let a guy come into my life and blow everything up, that I let that affect you and our friendship. That I asked you to lie for me to Theo and Willow. It wasn't my intention to drag you into any of this and put your career at risk. At the end of the day, I love John, and I know his character, and if that's—"

Izzy cut me off, just as I predicted, the sound of his name alone setting her off. "But that's the thing, Sarah. This situation has nothing to do with John. This is about you and me. And your choices. But John seems to be all you can talk about. A guy who can't even be fully with you. A guy who can't take you out and show you off on dates unless he's wearing a disguise. A guy you can't even post on social media. A guy who doesn't even live in the same city, who has to pay in cash and sneaks around every five-star hotel you visit. A guy who only knows me and, what, three other people in your life? A guy who can't even meet your family. A guy whose family doesn't even know you exist." She took a breath, her words leaving a thousand paper cuts on my heart, but I let her go on.

"While we're on the subject . . . It's been almost a year. A *whole year* of your life, spent trapped in that hellhole, hiding from Jane and the world. It has changed you. It has affected your career a ton. Some of your friends might let it slide, but I can't. You're too talented to waste away like a princess locked in a castle, hidden from everything and everyone. You deserve to be with someone who treats you like a queen. Who can actually tell the people in his life about you. Right now. Not when he becomes available . . . *now*."

I did everything I could to stay silent.

"And the craziest thing? *Jane* has moved on. She's out there gallivanting with Peter, and everyone, including your boyfriend, knows it. But he's still not ready to say, 'You know what? I've moved on to someone absolutely fucking amazing: Sarah Jones!' He's too scared to completely let go of Jane and move on with his life, so he's dragging you along. He doesn't even want to accept the harsh reality that Jane is *over him*. And it's affecting you. I can't support how he is handling things, or be dragged into it anymore."

I went cold, unsure if I should say anything at all, hoping maybe if I stayed quiet, she'd calm down and this could work itself out. I couldn't bring myself to look at her, overwhelmed by the feelings she had—about me, about him, about everything. She had kept all of this bottled up, never saying any of it. I had been so focused on venting about my problems with John all year, and I had no idea that this was how she truly felt all along—silent, stewing in it.

I swallowed hard, knowing this was as good a time as any to tell her I'd be moving out. At this point, I was sure she wouldn't care.

"I get it," I said finally. "I'm sorry for dragging you into this. I never should have." I stared at the door handle, trying to gather myself. "I'll be out of the apartment by the beginning of December. I'll still pay rent until the lease is up, but you can have the place."

I took a breath, forcing myself to keep going. "Also, I ended things with John after Naples. We haven't been together all month. I didn't want to bring him up to you again. But just so you know, it's over." Saying it out loud for the first time since it happened made it feel real. Tears welled in my eyes.

"Wait, what?" she called as I closed the door behind me. "Sarah, wait!" Her voice was sharp, but I had to get out of there. I couldn't have her listen to me cry in my bedroom, and I couldn't cry at the store. I opened the window to the fire escape. Before I stepped out, I grabbed the pack of cigarettes and a lighter from the cabinet under the sink—the ones Izzy and I kept for houseguests when we had parties. Sometimes I'd take a few puffs while we were drinking. Now seemed like a good time to have my first real cigarette, out in the chilly fall air. An escape to my fire escape. Feeling more alone than ever before.

Had I been so focused on John, trying to salvage what was left of him, of us, that I hadn't seen how much I was losing Izzy . . . was losing everything in the process? As I sat alone on the fire escape, I wondered . . . maybe John wasn't the man I thought he was. Maybe he would never be able to fully move on from Jane. But I couldn't stop myself from holding on to the possibility that one day, when he finally let go of the past, we could be together. I still hoped it wasn't over yet. That once the divorce was finalized, all these problems that seemed so big now would feel small. There was still a glimmer of hope, faint and fragile as it was, that he would come around and it would all be fine. I couldn't let go of the small part of me that believed in us—believed in him.

———

As soon as I lit the cigarette, the tears started to fall. Tears streamed down my face, my stomach burned, my hands froze. The constant battle between holding in my emotions and letting them pour out had reached its peak. I struggled to breathe, every breath heavy. Another love, another heartbreak. Not only had I lost John, but I had lost Izzy. My neuropathways were shattered in the wake of my choices.

Choices woven with threads of desire and fear.

Clara Hawthorne was right. My choices, born of desire and fear, had slowly destroyed me, and I was so tangled I wasn't sure how to free myself.

Had Izzy been right? Was John just a coward, clinging to his wife while leaving me alone? Had I just been strung along all this time? No. No. No. I had too much evidence to the contrary. The private conversations with him. Andy, the walking testimony. Jenny, who loved him as a boss. Almost a year with John, and not once had he said anything unkind. Not to me. Not to anyone. Not even in the conversations I'd overheard with Jane when she would be screaming at him.

I was angry—first at John, then at Jane, and finally at Izzy. I couldn't lose her too. She was my rock. She didn't know John like I did. She was just mad about me telling Theo and Willow.

I had seen the distance between Izzy and TW at the office, the trust broken in ways that killed her. She hadn't lost her job, but Theo and Willow no longer trusted her like they used to. I hadn't seen them invite her to lunch in weeks, and the way they asked her for favors had become curt, with no explanation. Things were different now, and that fear of losing it all was making her lash out at me. And truth be told, I deserved it.

Tears. Tears. Smoke. Tears. Inhale. Repeat. The only thing I could do was cry and breathe, the smoke filling my lungs, somehow grounding me. I grabbed my phone, scrolling through contacts, looking for the one person who could make it right, who could help me recover whatever I still had left of my dignity and relationships. I hesitated, taking another drag, feeling the buzz, then I hit "Call Dad."

As he always did, on the first ring, he answered, "Well, hello there, young lady! How's everything going out there in the big city?" My dad's cheerful voice boomed through the phone.

I hadn't been a good daughter this year. I'd only called once or twice a month, caught up in my own mess with John and the chaos of my schedule. When Dad couldn't take it anymore, he'd break down and call me. Every call would start the same way: "I know how busy you are. I just thought I'd check in on my daughter in the city, to make sure she's still alive."

Hearing the sound of his voice made me cry even harder. The best dad in the world. The one who *lived* for being a dad. The one who was at every sporting event, every concert, and every recital. The one who played with us in the yard for hours every night when we were little. The one who answered my calls on the first ring, even if I hadn't called him in months.

"Hey, Dad. How are you doing?" I asked, trying to steady my breath.

"Oh, good. Just working, surviving over here, you know. Nothing new, just living life. How about you? Haven't heard from you in a while. The city hasn't swallowed you up yet?"

"Yeah, things are good. Great, Dad," I lied, then paused. "Actually . . . things are terrible," I said, choking on my words.

"Oh no." I could almost hear his brow furrow. "What's going on, sweetheart?"

Between heaving breaths, I told him everything. John, Jane, work, Izzy, Theo and Willow. I filled him in on the Gala, the months of hiding, of sneaking around. It all poured out, like I had to get it all out in one big breath, all that I had been holding in for months. It felt almost as good as that second cigarette I had lit up mid-story. I needed an outsider's point of view, someone who knew me but wasn't involved in this world. Not a friend who would tell me what I wanted to hear. My dad was the straight shooter I needed.

When I finished my rant, there was a long pause. A whistle. "Whew, Sarah. This is one hell of a mess you've gotten yourself into."

I shook my head. "I know," I said with a huff and a little chuckle. Saying it all at once made it real. It was like I'd just vomited out all my problems, laid them out in front of me. And now I had to face them, and it was disgusting, to say the least.

I waited for his wisdom, for him to tell me what to do. *Please help me.*

"What I know for sure is that I raised you to make the right choices. You're smart. You're strong. You'll figure this out. And that's why I raised you to never be financially dependent on a man, right? You never know what might happen with these guys out here, especially in today's world, so plan for the worst and hope for the best, darling," he said.

It was the phrase I'd heard since I was three years old: Plan for the worst; hope for the best.

"Dad?"

"Yes, sweetheart?"

"What happened between you and Mom? Why did you get divorced?" I had never asked. The answer was never freely given. I had assumed my own version of the story. But all my life I never really knew why it hadn't worked out between them.

Another pause. This one longer.

"Well, she may remember it differently, but my version goes like this . . . after you were born, your mom's postpartum depression was pretty bad. No one talked about it back then, so she didn't have much support. I sure as heck didn't know what to do to support her. One weekend, the four of us went camping at Shoshone Falls Park. Remember that place? You girls loved to play in the Snake River there. Well, when we got back that weekend, she sprung it on me, saying she wanted a divorce." His voice cracked.

A tear rolled down my cheek. I lit another cigarette, muting the phone so my dad wouldn't hear, while taking a big inhale.

"I suggested we wait a while, let the emotions settle, but she insisted. I tried to fight for us for years. . . . I think she'd met someone at the gym. I'm not saying she acted on it, but I'm pretty sure he promised her everything if she left." A belly laugh escaped him. "Actually, I confronted him once. Scared the shit out of him. I think it made him reconsider."

I had hardly ever heard my dad get emotional. But his voice cracked as he spoke, the raw emotion he'd been holding back for years still present. "Since she wasn't working and had been staying home with you girls, I offered to let her stay for six months to get back on her feet. I even offered to buy her an apartment, pay her living expenses for a while. I let her take all the furniture. Except your beds. I kept your beds, so you girls would have somewhere to sleep when you came to stay with me. But other than that, I gave her everything so you girls would have a comfortable life when she took you," he said. I could hear the pain in his voice. "I didn't—" He choked on his tears. "I didn't even have a mattress after she left. The whole house was empty except for you girls' beds."

My heart cracked. I had no idea. I was only three when it happened.

He continued on, "The day she left for the new house, I cried, sitting in the empty living room, in an empty house, alone. It was the hardest day of my life. I could barely function for years. When we finally signed the divorce papers, we were in the elevator leaving the court, and she turned to me and said, 'I think I made a mistake.'"

My mouth flew open. *Mom, are you serious? What a dick move.*

Then, it all became clear—John and Jane were just like my parents. Jane, like my mom, had already left in every way that mattered. And John, like my dad, was still holding on, unable to accept the truth of the relationship.

I had spent my childhood caught between two people who were no longer together, watching my dad try to fix something that had been broken long before he was ready to admit it. And now, here I was again—stuck in the same story, only this time I wasn't a bystanding child. As a child, I had no power, no way to change the outcome. But as an adult . . . maybe I did.

Maybe I could help John move through it. Help him see what my dad never could—that holding on to something already gone would only break him more. If I could just be patient, if I could show him that there was a way forward, maybe he wouldn't have to stay stuck the way my dad did. Maybe I could hold out hope that this time the ending could be different.

"Anyway, honey, it was for the best. If I hadn't married your mom, I never would have had you and your sister. You're the two best things that ever happened to me."

After we both said, "I love you," I hung up, mascara streaked down my cheeks, my last cigarette burning out. A shiver ran down my spine. What my dad had shared stirred something deep inside me.

Maybe walking away from John didn't have to mean giving up on him completely. Maybe I could still help him, in the way no one had helped my dad. I had seen firsthand what it looked like to be left behind, to keep reaching for someone who had already moved on. I knew how much it hurt. If there was even a chance that I could help John see the truth—help him find a way forward instead of staying stuck—I had to try. Maybe it wasn't over, not in the way I had thought. Maybe I could still make a difference, even if we weren't together.

Chapter Thirty-Three

A few days had passed since my blowup with Izzy. I hadn't expected it to affect me like this, but it did. The words we exchanged still burned in my chest, and every time I tried to get my head in the game with the Clara project, I found myself thinking about it. And about everything else.

I was sitting at my desk, trying to focus, but my thoughts kept slipping—bouncing between Izzy, John, Jane. The Clara project was important, but right now, it was a distraction from the real mess I couldn't seem to escape.

"Want to grab lunch?" Theo's voice startled me so much that I nearly fell out of my chair.

"Jesus!" I gasped.

"No, just call me Theo." He laughed, full of himself, as usual. He jerked his head toward the door. "Come on. My treat."

"You're the worst," I said, laughing. "But okay, deal."

I grabbed my coat, suddenly aware that he hadn't asked me to lunch since I broke up with John after the AAP Conference. Maybe he heard about Jane being in Chicago. Maybe since I had actually broken things off, it was a peace treaty.

It was a strange relief, feeling like he finally wanted to talk to me again. He hadn't exactly given me the cold shoulder, but there had been distance. I was was grateful—grateful that he was here for me again.

It wasn't really lunch. More like a walk. We grabbed coffee at Bluestone Lane and headed to Central Park.

"Things seem to be going better since AAP?" Theo asked.

"Um, yeah. I guess," I said, trying to play it cool. And things had been better—sort of. I had been in the office more, finally catching up on work. Without constantly traveling to see John, there was a little more stability. If that's what Theo meant, then sure—things were better.

Neither Willow or Theo had spoken to me much lately, and now, here he was—alone, without Willow. That almost never happened.

As if reading my mind, Theo smirked. "I know Willow and I together can be . . . a lot."

I nodded slowly, still trying to figure out what was happening. What exactly was he fishing for? And why now?

"Things with you and John?"

"I told you already, I ended it," I said looking at the ground, kicking a rock.

"Oh, you meant that? I thought you were just saying that so we wouldn't give you a hard time." He nodded and looked ahead.

"I wasn't lying. I ended it right after that." What I didn't mention was I'd done it after flying to Florida for what was supposed to be a romantic vacation with him. I also conveniently left out that I would be moving into his apartment in a few weeks.

"Well, I'm proud of you. I can tell you are more focused since you ended things." He paused, studying me. "You doing okay?"

"Yeah, I'm fine," I said, forcing a smile.

"Sarah, come on. You know what it means when a woman says she is fine, don't you?" he asked.

I kept my face blank.

" Means she is freaked out. Insecure. Neurotic. And Emotional," he said, poking his elbow into my ribs.

We both laughed.

"That's a good one," I said, rolling my eyes.

His tone turned serious. "I know I joke about it, but it was obvious you really liked him."

It's like the words suddenly activated up my tear ducts. God, how could one person cry so much in a single lifetime? I stared down at my coffee, picking at the sticker on the lid, desperate for something—anything—to keep the tears from spilling over. But the first one slid down my cheek anyway, followed by a deep, shuddering breath that felt like it was going to turn into a full-blown sob.

Before I could stop it, Theo turned to me. The way men do when they stumble into emotional territory they never intended to enter.

"Oh, sweetie." Theo's voice softened, carrying the weight of genuine concern. He rarely used that term unless it was serious. He led me to a nearby bench, his hand on my elbow as if I were blind—and honestly, I may as well have been, given the sheer volume of tears streaming down my cheeks.

"It's just so hard," I finally choked out, my voice trembling. "I regret even telling you because ever since I did, everything's fallen apart. You treat me like I'm radioactive or something—like even being friends with me is a risk." I swallowed hard, the words tumbling out. "And Izzy hates me now. Work feels impossible. This job is hard enough as it is, but on top of that, the man I love—loved . . . the only man I've ever really loved—is married to the woman in the corner office. The woman I wish I could be. Now, I'm stuck working on this project with her—a project that should be a dream come true. I should be learning from her, being mentored by her. But instead, I resent every second of it because the part of me that hates her for hurting John can't stand to be around her. I don't even want to work on this project anymore. I just . . . can't stand being near her. And, I'm so tired. Tired of lying."

My voice cracked. "And the worst part? I didn't even get anything out of this mess! I went through all of this for what? To be with John. And now I don't have him. I don't have you, or Willow, or Izzy. I can't stand Jane, and I could lose my job if she ever found out." I wouldn't dare tell him that Jane most likely already knew. She had to. I couldn't bring myself to tell Theo—he'd probably distance himself again. The last thing I needed was more people on Jane's side. A bitter laugh escaped my lips, a desperate attempt to keep from breaking down completely. "So yeah, Theo. That's how I'm doing."

Theo clicked his tongue, letting the silence last just long enough to make me uncomfortable. "I get it. I really do. This sucks for you. But Sarah—you chose this. You chose to date the married man. You're not a victim here. Nobody forced you into this."

His words hit me like a slap, and I shot him a glare sharp enough to cut glass. That wasn't fair for him to say. "First of all, he's not 'with' Jane," I snapped. "And second of all, we don't choose who we love, Theo. You of all people should know that."

"You're right," he conceded. "We don't choose whom we love. But have you ever stopped to think how hard this situation might be for Jane? Have you ever considered what this has been like for her?"

"She's got a new boyfriend in the damn office!" I threw up my hands and gestured toward Jane's window in the building behind us. "Jane is not the victim here."

"It doesn't matter," he countered. "I'm sure she senses something's going on between you and John. And yes, maybe she's seeing someone else, but losing someone you love—however it happened—isn't easy. And for her to suspect that someone she thought she may be able to mentor is in love with her not-even-official ex-husband? Sarah, that must hurt. Even if she doesn't know for sure, it can't be easy."

I stared at him, stunned. "Did you bring me out here to scold me even more? To make me feel worse about myself than I already do? I'm doing my job. I'm not dating anyone." I held up my hand in a mock Boy Scout salute. "I feel bad enough already, Theo. I broke it off. I don't know what else you want from me."

"I'm not trying to make you feel worse," he said, his tone calm. And somehow I believed him.

"Then what are you trying to say? And what's your problem with John now? I thought you were friends."

"Sarah." He turned to face me fully, his expression steady. "My job is to help you get what *you* want. To keep you focused on your goals. But this?" He gestured to me. "This isn't you. You're a shell of the person you used to be. Before John, you were unstoppable. Focused. Driven to excel and make a real difference at this company. You had that light in you—that spark. And now?" He scanned me and shook his head. "It's dimmed. You don't look like yourself. And I can't just stand by and watch. You're too talented for that. What kind of mentor would I be if I didn't say something to the mentee I saw driving toward a cliff?"

His words stung, but I couldn't argue. Instead, I looked down and tried to absorb what he was saying. He didn't understand. He'd never understand. No one would. No one would ever understand what John and I have—had.

"And hey," Theo added, "I love John. I've been friends with him for over a decade. Hell, if he was available, I would have been the one to try to set you two up."

"Then what's the problem?" I glared at him.

He held up his hand, silencing me. "I would set you two up *if* he was fully available. If he was willing to be with you—fully, publicly. Emotionally. But he's not. You can see he still loves Jane. That he is still holding on. And you deserve someone who gives you 100 percent of himself, Sarah. Not 99 percent, or in John's case . . . 10 percent or less. You deserve nothing less. If I wasn't fully available—emotionally or otherwise—I would never have let Willow be with me. She's worth more. And so are you."

I swallowed hard, my throat tightening. "I know John. He wants to give me everything. He will, as soon as he can."

Theo sighed. "I hear you. But right now he can't, and nothing will change that." A pregnant pause. "Sarah, have you ever considered that you've only heard one side of the story? I know Jane. I've heard things from her that would probably shock you."

I raised my head. "I've been there, Theo. I've heard the conversations between them. I've seen it all. I've been there for it all."

"And yet you've only heard John's side. That's all I'm saying. There's always more to the story. I'm not saying Jane is right or wrong." He elbowed me, a faint smile tugging at his lips. "But let's face it—no one's good enough for you anyway. Willow and I both know that. We're proud of you, Sarah, no matter what. We just don't want this to be something you look back on and regret."

I bit my lip, fighting the urge to argue. Deep down, I knew he was trying to help. Even if it felt like he was physically ripping my heart out.

"I hear you," I murmured, though I wasn't sure if I believed it. What John and I had was something real. I knew it. He knew it. And when the time was right, everything would fall into place.

"Do what you want with this," Theo said, standing up and holding out his hand. "We love you, Sarah."

"I love you too," I said, letting him pull me to my feet. "But can you please stop acting like I murdered someone and just be normal around me again? I can't stand the cold shoulder."

"You got it." He chuckled and shook my hand. "Just don't do any more stupid shit."

"Fine," I said and stuck out my tongue at him.

We walked back to the office together, and no matter how badly I wanted to, I couldn't unhear his words.

———

I had Theo to thank—no matter how painful that conversation had been, it had woken me up. I hadn't realized how much of myself I'd lost, how much I'd been swallowed up by the weight of John and Jane and the tangled mess that came with them. The distractions, the constant pressure, the emotional toll—it had worn me down. But now? There was a clarity I hadn't felt in a long time. Determination to become a senior editor, no matter what. It felt good to throw myself into the work again, to lose myself in the project, my mind sharp and focused. I could feel it—the spark was back.

I sat at my desk, chewing on the end of my pen, my mind drifting to John and Jane for the first time in days. It was strange to think I'd be moving into his apartment in two weeks, but still not speaking to him—or Izzy, for that matter. She hadn't said a word to me since our blowup, and I wasn't about to be the one to break the silence. I didn't even know what to think about Jane at this point.

Then, it was as if my thoughts made her appear.

Jane walked past my desk, a little too composed, like she hadn't just disappeared for a month. She had casually mentioned in an email to the team that she'd been gone on "time-sensitive" projects. Translation: dealing with her divorce. She'd been gone so long that part of me thought, or hoped, she might never return, but now here she was, strolling through the office like nothing had changed.

She reached my desk and offered a bright, almost rehearsed smile. "Good to see you, Sarah. Thanks for handling the Gabriel meeting while I was away," she said, her tone light, as if everything was normal. As if the message she'd sent—and unsent—had never existed.

I blinked, my mind racing, trying to piece together what I was feeling. What the hell? Was she embarrassed? Was she pretending it didn't happen to save face? Maybe she realized we were over after visiting him? Or was she clinically insane?

Was this the "nice" version of her, luring me into opening up so she could strike later? Or was this just another game, one where she would remind me—without saying a word—who really held the power in this office? My throat tightened, and all I could do was force a smile, my insides twisting with a sick mix of frustration and dread. Was this her pretending it all went away, or was she setting me up for something worse?

"Welcome back, Jane," I called after her.

She disappeared into her office, but her smile still haunted me.

I'd spent the past month wondering if John had told her—or if she had somehow found out about us. The thought of them being room-mates for a whole month gnawed at me, twisting my insides. Just imagining them in the same room made my stomach turn. Sure, I told myself he probably slept in the guest room and gave her the bed, but that didn't make it any easier for my mind to go to my worst night-mare, that they were back together.

———

Later that day, the weekly all-hands publishing meeting came to a close, and my calendar was brimming with the upcoming holiday commitments. Book release parties, holiday events—each day seemed to fill up faster than I could keep track. I headed back to my desk, and out of the corner of my eye, I saw a figure standing there. For a second, I thought it was John. My heart raced, my stomach tighten-ing. Why would he be here? It couldn't be him. He hadn't moved yet. But as I approached, it was very clearly John.

I raced back to my desk, smoothing my face into a neutral smile. "Mr. Reynolds, welcome to New York. How was your trip?" The words felt rehearsed, but I had to pretend this was just another day with someone I hadn't made out with for a majority of this year.

His handshake was firm, too normal, professional. It was as if he'd never laid next to me in bed just months ago, never traveled around the country with me, never said, "I love you," to me. As if we'd only met at work, as if that was all we'd ever been. Strangers.

"Sarah . . . Jones, right? Always a pleasure," he said, his smile a little too casual, but his eyes told a different story. They were soft, full of unspoken things. I hated how much they tugged at me.

I pulled my hand back, trying to ignore the electricity. I had to pretend it didn't matter, that I felt nothing. "Can I get you some water? What can I help you with?"

His smile was more gorgeous than I remember. "I'm meeting all the big bosses today," he said. "Conference room F. Can you show me the way?"

Why was he asking me? He *knew* the way. Was he trying to make an excuse to talk to me? To be near me?

"Sure? I can show you the way back," I said, gesturing for him to follow.

He was wearing black, of course, the color that made my knees weak. It was like he knew what he was doing to me. His blond hair was slicked back perfectly trimmed. He looked good. Maybe that's what happens when you go cold turkey on the man you love. They become that much more tempting.

"I'd like that. I'll be moving into this office soon, after all. I need to learn the way around," he said with that grin. His voice was just low enough that only I could hear, but I couldn't shake the feeling the nearby employees were watching us.

I led him down the hall, past the bullpen. "How's Manhattan treating you?" I asked, loud enough that anyone listening would think we were just talking shop.

"Loving it," he said, staring at me. As we stepped into the hallway out of earshot of everyone, his tone completely changed. "It's good to see you, Sarah. God, I've missed you."

"Are you allowed to say that? Aren't we supposed to be broken up?" I whispered.

He looked at me, his demeanor calm. "I know we're not together, but that doesn't change how I feel. Do you really think I can just turn that off?"

I could feel the heat rising in my cheeks, the old feelings bubbling up. I missed him too. So much that it hurt. But this wasn't the time for this conversation. We were steps away from walking into a room full of people who had no idea what was going on between us. And I hoped to keep it that way.

"Will you see me tonight?" he asked, pleaded, as we approached the conference room.

Luckily, this room had solid walls without windows, because my jaw was on the floor. Would I *see* him? I thought we weren't even talking? Now he was talking about us seeing each other? Even him being here and having this conversation felt like dishonoring our breakup.

We rounded the corner before I could respond, into the room filled with eight executives, including Theo, Willow, and none other than Jane. Each of their stares threatening, in different ways. Theo, protective. Willow, judgmental. Jane, God only knew what she was sending through her piercing daggers. Eyes wide, scanning between us as if she'd caught us in the act. Red-handed.

I was an idiot. An idiot for taking him to a meeting with 'all the bosses,' and for what? Ten seconds of thrilling conversation that only made me more confused and my heart crack all over again? Distracting me from the focus that had finally returned to my life?

"Here is conference room F, Mr. Reynolds. Enjoy your meeting," I said, gesturing him in, trying to recover my reason for being with him.

I turned and started to make a beeline back to the bullpen, my desk, my safe harbor, hoping when I got there I could sink into the floor and disappear forever. But before I could make it even two steps, I heard someone calling my name.

"Sarah?"

I knew that voice all too well. Jane.

Great.

I turned slowly, cringing. She curled her finger and motioned for me to come back for a quick 'chat'. Just us girls talking in the hallway. Kill. Me. Now.

I shuffled quickly back to her, her energy giving me full on Miranda Priestly in *The Devil Wears Prada* vibes. I didn't dare move slowly and make her wait.

"Yes, Jane?" I said with the most genuine smile I could muster.

"I wanted to let you know that I won't be needing your help with the Gabriel Stone account anymore."

I froze. "Um, wait . . . what?"

"Send me all your notes from the project by the end of the day. Thanks." She touched my arm as if she'd done me a favor. I stood there in shock. She just took away the most important project that was going to be the turning point in my career. Like it was nothing.

"That is all," she said with a smile before she stepped back into the conference room.

It was like the wind had been knocked out of me. She'd just taken the one thing I had going for me—the project that was supposed to be a huge contributing factor to the promotion. She just took it away like it was nothing. In five seconds. As if she wanted to prove how quickly she could take everything away from me and ruin my career. As if she wanted me to know that she was the alpha. That I was just a pawn in her little chess game.

Had she been waiting for the perfect moment to take me down a peg, and seeing me walk her husband to the conference room had what? Confirmed something? After seeing me with John, it seemed she finally saw her opportunity. She was putting me in my place, making sure I'd never get any closer to becoming senior editor.

I was too stunned to be pissed. I couldn't even think quickly enough to fight back. It was like she had already won. My jaw may as well have been dragging on the floor as I turned and dragged myself back to my measly desk, feeling the weight of everything she'd just taken but too paralyzed to do anything about it.

———

Jane had just taken the one thing that mattered most: Gabriel's project.

I sat down at my desk, my fingers hovered over the keyboard, but I couldn't get myself to type anything. Like all the focus I had gained from my conversation with Theo evaporated instantly with the return of John and Jane. I had been sucked right back into their drama in a matter of minutes. All I could do was stare at the blinking cursor on the screen, my mind racing.

I needed a minute—hell, I needed more than that.

I didn't even notice when Jenny walked up to my desk.

"Sarah," she said, her voice soft, apologetic, "Jane wants to see you after her meeting with the execs."

I blinked up at her, confused. "Um . . . yeah, okay. I will be there."

She gave me a sympathetic look before walking away.

An hour after the conference room catastrophe, I was still at my desk, staring at my screen. What more could Jane possibly want from me? The thought of skipping the meeting with her crossed my mind more than once. But against my better judgment, I got up and headed to her office. May as well face the music now.

When I arrived at Jane's office door, I didn't need to be invited in. It was wide open, and she was sitting behind her desk with that same poised, unnerving smile on her face.

"Come in, Sarah. Take a seat." Her voice was calm, too calm. I didn't trust it.

I walked in slowly. I had no idea what this conversation would entail, but I had a pretty good idea that it wouldn't be good. Not after what had happened.

I took a seat across from her, doing my best to maintain a neutral expression, but my heart was pounding so hard I was convinced she could see it. Jane didn't waste time with pleasantries.

"I've told you I don't need your assistance anymore on the Gabriel project," she began, folding her hands on the desk, her eyes never leaving mine. "But I thought you should know why."

"What?" I managed, my voice cracking. "What do you mean?"

"I've reassessed the direction of the project, and it no longer aligns with your skill set," Jane said. "Gabriel agrees with me. He would prefer a more senior employee on the project. I need someone with more senior-level experience to take it forward and make it a real success."

More senior-level experience? Gabriel said that? I couldn't believe it. Was she insinuating I would not be getting the senior editor position? Or was this just her way of punishing me for things with John? I wished she would just come out and say what she knew rather than playing these horrible games.

"But Gabriel *asked* me to be on this project. Plus the entire marketing strategy was my idea," I said, my voice trembling.

Jane tilted her head. "It *was* yours, Sarah," she said, as if indulging a child. "But now, it's no longer in your hands. And I am sure you'll understand why."

My pulse quickened. This had to be about John. The way she said it told me everything I needed to know. She was doing this to make a statement, to remind me that she still controlled the game.

"Jane, is this really about the Gabriel Stone project, or is it about something else?"

"I have no idea what you are talking about, Sarah," she said, leaning back in her chair, her gaze unyielding. "This is about the project being done by the best person for the job. And that person is no longer you." I noticed her glance at my lips for a split second, and I instantly felt self-conscious, suddenly aware of the filler I'd gotten months ago. She raised an eyebrow slightly, a subtle roll of her eyes. Even she could tell. She could see how much I'd become obsessed with becoming like her. I was mortified.

Speechless. I was speechless. There was no winning this conversation. If I fought her, she could fire me or ruin my career right here and now. Arguing with Jane was not an option. I had no leverage. "Jane, this was a huge part of me getting the senior editor promotion."

"I'll have Jenny send you an email later to reassign the work," she added, her tone dismissive. "Any history of your involvement with this project will be revoked moving forward. Since you didn't bring it to completion, it's only fair to make it clear you weren't part of the final success."

I nodded slowly, my jaw clenched. I didn't say anything more. What was the point?

"Good. I knew you'd understand," her voice was laced with satisfaction. "That will be all, Sarah."

I stood up, my body feeling heavy as I walked out of her office. As I passed Jenny on my way back to my desk, she didn't say anything, but there was pity in her eyes. I wasn't sure how long I stood there, trying to process everything, but the silence only made the sting more intense. Jane had made her move, and I had nothing left to do but accept it.

I stepped into the bathroom, hid in a stall, and cried. My chances of getting the promotion were gone. And now, I was officially left with nothing. I pulled out my phone, and found Jane's profile on Instagram. I couldn't take it anymore. With a single click, I blocked her, hoping somehow that would stop the pain, even if just for a moment. It was a small victory—cutting her out of my life, even if only in this small corner of the digital world.

Chapter Thirty-Four

Fueled by fury and the sting of Jane's betrayal, I texted John:

> Meet me at The Mark. 6 p.m.

I should have been strategizing how to recover after Jane ripped the Gabriel project away from me. I should have been focused on my career, on my shot at senior editor. But I was too angry. And as long as Jane was involved, it felt like a hopeless cause.

John had wanted to meet at the office today—fine. I'd make him do it on my terms.

When I arrived, he was already there, standing, waiting.

"Hello, Sarah. I've missed you."

His voice was a welcome distraction from the storm inside me. I didn't want to think about Jane's smug smile, about how she had played her game and made me a pawn. I didn't want to think about the mess I was walking into. I just wanted to take back control—even if it was only for tonight.

Two drinks in, and it was like no time had passed. Laughing, kissing, touching. We both knew it was wrong, knew nothing had really changed—but neither of us cared enough to stop.

Jane had taken everything from me. My project. My dignity. Maybe even my promotion. Potentially my job. My sense of control. My Love.

So tonight, I would take something back.

I knew where the night was headed—another hotel room, another escape. But this time, it wasn't just about pleasure. It was about drowning out the pain, about feeling something other than defeat.

I had nothing left to lose.

————

I sat across from John the next morning, reflecting on everything that had happened last night. The restaurant hummed with quiet conversation, but all I could hear was the echo of my own thoughts. I had told myself I was done. I had promised myself I wouldn't go back.

And yet, here we were. Here I was.

John reached for my hand across the table. "Sarah, I messed up. I hurt you. But losing you—God, it's been unbearable."

I exhaled slowly, pulling my hand back. "John, I don't know if I can do this again. We've been through this cycle too many times. I don't want to be that woman who keeps making the same mistake."

His jaw tensed. "You're not making a mistake. This—us—it's real. I wasn't ready before. I was too caught up in trying to manage everything, but you make me want to be better. I want to be better. For you."

I studied him, my pulse steady but my mind racing. How many times had I let myself believe that before? How many times had I told myself that if I just loved him harder, if I just waited long enough, he'd finally become the man I needed him to be? He would finally be able to choose me. To be with me. Fully and completely.

"And Jane?" I asked, my voice careful, though I already knew the answer.

John sighed, running a hand through his hair. "The divorce will be finalized at the end of the year. We just have to sign the papers."

"So couldn't you get that done like . . . today?" I said, hoping it would show him I was serious.

"Well, technically yes, but she has to fly to Chicago on New Year's and we will sign them together."

I nodded, avoiding his gaze, avoiding the thoughts pressing at the edges of my mind. Jane's trip to Chicago—I still hadn't asked what had happened between them while she was there. The lingering ache in my chest from her taking away the Stone project resurfaced. I didn't want to think about any of it. Not now.

I should have walked away. I had every reason to. And yet, a quiet, stubborn part of me whispered that maybe this time, if I had the strength to demand more, if I didn't just sit back and let things happen to me—maybe this time, we could get it right.

"If we do this again," I said slowly, "it has to be different. I won't just wait around for you two to figure things out. I need to know you're actually choosing me. That you're ready to be the man you keep promising to be."

John leaned in, his voice quiet but certain. "I am. And I'll prove it to you."

I let out a breath I hadn't realized I was holding. Maybe I was making a mistake. Maybe this would all end in disaster. But if there was even a chance that this time could be different, that we could be together, I had to take it.

Just one last time.

Chapter Thirty-Five

December 31st. I was finally settled. After a month in my new apartment (aka John's new apartment), it finally felt like home. The large windows flooded the living room with light. There were dark oak floors, and the place had a modern feel to it. Everything looked sleek: the gray sectional, the glass coffee table with brass accents, and the abstract art I picked out for him. Polished. Classy. Just like him.

I had decorated the entire apartment, down to the last detail, so that when John moved in after the divorce, it would feel like home. His kitchen gleamed with marble countertops and untouched top-of-the-line appliances. I imagined him cooking there, me sitting on a barstool sipping wine. I had made it perfect for us. Everything was waiting, ready for him to come home. To our home.

Most days, especially when I was all alone here, I missed living with Izzy. I missed Izzy, period. Sometimes it was like I was a rich widow, surrounded by everything I ever wanted—everything she would want—but empty inside. I hated to compare it to my small, old shoebox on the Upper East Side. But sometimes I wondered if I was happier in that tiny place with Izzy than being in his massive home, alone. Waiting for John. But at least here, I had someone that loved me, even if he was seven hundred miles away.

The holidays were the hardest. On Christmas morning, I sat on our gray sectional, wrapped in a blanket, and stared at the tree I had decorated, alone. A fancy display of tinsel and glass ornaments. With no one to share it with. John was in Chicago with his family. Since they still didn't know I existed, it was hard for him to come to the city when his family expected him to be in Chicago. I imagined what it would be like when John and I could exchange gifts one day, laughing, drinking champagne together. But instead, it was just me and the hum of the refrigerator. I just hoped next year would be different.

I FaceTimed my family in Idaho on Christmas morning. They were all smiles, waving at the screen, so joyful, the whole family together. I couldn't bring myself to tell them how lonely I was. How I had spent Christmas Eve on the couch with takeout and a bottle of rosé, scrolling through Instagram, watching everyone else's perfectly curated family-time joy.

As I swiped past post after post of people celebrating, I felt a tug of curiosity. Wondering what Jane was up to? How was the queen herself spending her holidays? I hadn't been able to see her profile since I blocked her, but in that moment, it was as though the distance between us felt like it could be bridged if I just saw what she was doing.

Without giving it a second thought, I unblocked her. A quick click, and suddenly, I had access again. Or so I thought. My stomach churned as her profile picture appeared in front of me, but nothing else. There were no recent posts. No stories. No updates. Nothing.

I refreshed the page, thinking maybe something had gone wrong. Maybe my wifi was out. But as I went to see if I could send her a message, a notification popped up.

This user has blocked you.

My heart sank. She had blocked *me*? She had blocked me back.

I stared at the screen, disbelief settling in my chest. She had blocked me. After everything, I never imagined this. I thought I was the one pulling away, protecting myself from her. Not the other way around.

Can you imagine what this has been like for Jane? Theo's voice rang out in my mind.

Maybe all of this had affected her more than I even knew.

I sat there, unsure of what to do. After she kicked me off the project last month, everything changed between us. We didn't speak anymore. We weren't working together; it was like an invisible wall had come up between us. She was as icy as ever to me, distant and cold. It was like a mutual agreement to ignore each other had been in place. I did my best to stay out of her way, hoping that maybe if I just kept my head down at work, I could avoid the drama and at the very least stay on track and not lose my job.

I'd sent Izzy a text a few days ago, telling her the truth: that John and I were back together. She hadn't responded, though. I hadn't expected her to, not really. But I felt like I had to tell someone, even if she and I weren't technically friends right now. She was all I had. The only person I could really trust.

I couldn't shake the curiosity about what Jane had been doing for the holidays. I knew, though, exactly what she and John would be doing tonight.

Tonight would be different. Tonight would change everything.

It was December 31st—otherwise known as the day the divorce papers would be signed, sealed, and delivered. John and Jane Reynolds should be at the courthouse signing their divorce papers now.

I'd given John space all day, trying not to overwhelm him with the weight of it all. I just wanted him to be focused on finalizing everything. We didn't need any more delays. I hadn't heard anything from him since last night. He told me he would be out with Andy, probably pre-celebrating the divorce. I could sense how emotional the last few days had been for him.

I had sent him one last text last night before bed:

> Thinking of you. Can't wait to celebrate with you and have you here in our new home.
> I'm cheering for you. I love you.

The day stretched on, and as the evening rolled around, I still hadn't heard back from him. I didn't want to seem too eager by reaching out to him again, but I couldn't wait any longer to celebrate. This was it—he was about to be mine.

What a perfect way to start the new year. The new decade. 2020.

———

Later that evening, and still no word from John, I was getting ready for Gabriel's book release party that kicked off at nine. I tried calling Izzy to see if she wanted to join me, but there was no answer.

Even though Jane had removed me from Gabriel's project without warning, I still wanted to attend his book release to show my support. He'd reached out a few times, asking why I was no longer involved, but I kept my distance. I didn't want Jane to see me talking to him and misinterpret it. The last thing I needed was to get fired or have her take the rest of my projects away. Still, the idea of going to the event tonight stung. This project was supposed to be the turning point in my career. The entire marketing strategy, including making Gabriel the face of David, had been my idea—and from what I could tell, it was set to be a record-breaking pre-release for the company.

I checked my outfit in the mirror, touched up my lipgloss, and checked my phone one last time before heading to the party. Still no reply from John.

I sighed and tried not to think about it. He'd text me soon. Soon. Once the papers had been signed. Once he was no longer married. I should hear from him any minute.

I grabbed my coat and headed to Gabriel's party.

———

The event space was buzzing with hundreds of guests, champagne flutes catching the light as they glimmered under the dim ambiance. Waiters moved through the crowd, balancing trays of hors d'oeuvres; all of them, I couldn't help but notice, had coattails. The venue exuded a classy, speakeasy vibe, with black drapes and polished elegance—the kind of event New York does so well. But this felt like something more, the grand finale to a string of holiday parties that everyone had been attending. One last celebration before the new year. It had to be something special to pull people away from their own plans and get them to show up for a book release party.

I was dressed for the occasion—a skin-tight black dress with draped chiffon that hung off my shoulders and trailed behind me. It was something Jane would have worn.

"Jones! Welcome. I'm so glad you came." Gabriel smiled and shook my hand firmly. As he pulled me in for a hug, he said, "You look stunning."

The shock shot straight to my stomach, and I prayed it didn't show on my face. My breath caught. Stopped. "Well, thank you," I managed, keeping my tone as natural as possible. "You look fabulous yourself. How are you feeling? This party turned out great." I gestured around the room, lit by the glow of the candlelit tables.

His tux was gorgeous, accentuating his broad chest and arms, more defined than I remembered. It must have cost at least ten thousand dollars. I noticed his initials, GS, embroidered on the sleeve. That was an Emma special.

"Wait," I said, grabbing his arm. "Did you go to Emma's shop and have this custom made?" I almost screamed with excitement.

A grin spread across his face, and his eyebrows wiggled. "I sure did, I tracked down the only female bespoke tailor on the Upper East Side, told her I knew you, and she cut the delivery time in half," he said, grabbing the lapels to show off the jacket, taking a spin.

I smiled, so excited he was having Emma make his suits. "It's absolutely perfect." Our eyes locked, and something inside of me . . . missed seeing him? I missed our monthly meetings. Something about him felt comfortable. My heart skipped a beat as I focused back on the room of guests around us. All for Gabriel. "Amazing turnout, Mr. Stone."

"All thanks to you. Your marketing strategy killed it. More pre-orders than any book release in Regent history. Or so I am told."

"Everyone is singing your praises, of course," I said, doing my best to remove any semblance of resentment toward Jane from my voice.

He looked at me, with his grey eyes. "What happened to you being on the project, Jones? I'm really disappointed that you couldn't finish it with me. Your ideas were inspiring—literally the only reason we broke the record. And I really enjoyed working with you."

My brow furrowed as I scanned the room for Jane, before I remembered she wouldn't be coming. She was busy getting divorced.

"What do you mean?" I asked. "Jane pulled me off the project one day without much of a warning. She told me that you asked me to step down from the project, that the two of you wanted a more senior person on it." I grabbed two mini tacos and a glass of champagne from a passing server's tray and stuffed them into my mouth to calm my nerves.

"*That's* what Jane said?" Gabriel's tone turned cold, his eyes narrowing as he stared across the room at nothing. Thinking? He shook his head, laughing dryly.

I shrugged and sucked air through my teeth. "That was all she said. I thought our last meeting while she was out of town must have turned you off, maybe you hadn't really liked the end result of the marketing materials I showed you, but then you used them anyway. I was confused, to say the least."

"Are you kidding?" Gabriel's voice sharpened. "Those were some of the best marketing materials that Regent has ever created, and you aren't even on the marketing team! I wish you'd been around for my first several books—my career could have been ten times what it is now." He downed the rest of his champagne in one gulp, placing it on a cater-waiter's tray as they passed. "Jones, I would have preferred to work only with you on this project. I can't stand working with Jane. Keep that between us, of course." He raised his hand to his face, running his fingers down his jaw.

"Really?" I blinked, surprised. "You don't like working with her? Why not? She's the best of the best."

"She may be the 'best,'" he admitted, "but she's never come to my office in Tribeca in ten years of working together. That went such a long way that you were willing to come all the way to meet. She rarely pushes back on my decisions, never gets down in the trenches with me. She's cold, Jones. She cares about the bottom line, not the client. You, on the other hand?" He paused and looked at me with startling sincerity. "You're amazing. You have something special—a secret sauce."

I tried to stop the blush from creeping up my cheeks, but the champagne had other plans. Gabriel's words warmed my entire body down to my toes.

"But more than that . . . you have this." He reached out, his fingers tapping the hollow of my chest, just above the fabric of my dress. His touch sent a pulse through me, down my spine, straight to my pelvis. My breathing quickened, and I knew my face was now bright red. I didn't overthink it.

"You have heart, Jones," he continued. "And that's something you can't fake. And when you have heart, you win every time."

I held out my hand to shake. Gabriel took it, his grip firm. "Well, Gabriel Stone, the next book you write, I am all yours." If Jane could cut me out of a deal, I could do the same with her, especially if that was what the client wanted.

A waiter came over, and Gabriel grabbed two more glasses of champagne.

"Let's make it official," he said.

We raised our glasses.

"Cheers to your next best-selling book," I said.

Gabriel leaned in slightly, lowering his voice as if the crowd

331

around us had suddenly faded. "I want you to meet someone. Remember how I told you about that author who may be interested in signing with Regent?"

He motioned to a woman standing a few feet away, her posture slightly stiff, but there was something almost uncertain in her eyes as she glanced around the room. When she turned to face us, I immediately sensed a quiet strength, masked by a hesitancy. Nothing new for an introverted author.

"Sarah," Gabriel began, "this is Nora Edwards. She's a best-selling author who's worked with some of the biggest publishing houses out there. Nora, this is Sarah Jones, the editor at Regent House I was telling you about."

Nora offered a tentative smile as she extended her hand, almost as if she was unsure whether I'd want to shake it. "Nice to meet you," she said softly.

I shook her hand. "You too Ms. Edwards."

"Gabriel has told me so much about you," Nora said, her voice quiet. I had to lean in slightly to fully catch everything she was saying. "He mentioned your marketing campaign for his book. Super impressive. I've been thinking about switching publishers for a while now, but I've been hesitant. I'm not sure if . . . Well, I'm not sure if it's the right time." She paused, uncertainty lacing her voice. "But hearing about you. I'm very curious."

This was it. This was the opportunity I'd been waiting for.

"What are you looking for that you don't feel like you are getting with your current publisher?" I asked, keeping my voice steady even though a rush of excitement was building in my chest.

"I just need someone who gets it," Nora said. "Someone who knows how to make a project shine, especially in today's world, who isn't afraid to push me when it comes to my narrative, my characters. I don't need anymore 'yes men.' I need someone who will tell me when my work is shit and be honest. Anyway, Gabriel tells me you're the one."

"I'd be honored to help."

"Good," she replied, giving me a small smile. "I'll have my assistant reach out to schedule a meeting next week. Let's see if we can make magic happen together."

As Nora turned to speak to another guest, Gabriel leaned in again, his voice low. "Don't let her fool you, she already told me she was sold when I told her about you and the Regent team last week."

I nodded, still in shock, but every nerve in my body was on fire. This was what I had been working for. This is the thing that could save my career and help me secure the senior editor position.

And it had just been handed to me on a silver platter by Gabriel Stone.

"Thank you, Gabriel," I said. "This means more than you know. I'm truly grateful for the opportunity. And I am pretty sure you just saved whatever chance I have left at getting that promotion." I crossed my fingers and smirked.

"Good, I am happy to help." He smiled. "I have to entertain my guests to make this a record-breaking bestseller; otherwise, I'd talk to you all night. Help yourself to food and drink, of course. Thanks again, Jones, for everything. I can't wait to work with you." He gave my shoulder a brief, appreciative squeeze before excusing himself to mingle with the guests.

I called after him, "Gabriel, where's Jane?" Of course, I already knew where she was, but I wanted to make sure he knew she wasn't here tonight.

He shrugged. "Don't know. Don't care." He winked again. Jesus, he was sexy. There was something about men in tuxedos. They were just . . . hotter?

As I turned to head to the bar to set down my empty glass of champagne, I saw Izzy standing there with a drink in hand, a handsome man chatting her up. My stomach churned. I had to apologize. I had to make this right. We were at a stalemate, and I knew she'd never be the one to give in. I couldn't live like this anymore. Since we were in public, she couldn't yell at me. I figured it was as good a time as any to confront her.

She caught my eye as I walked toward her. Then she looked back at the tall, well-dressed man and said, "Thanks for the drink, but you'll have to excuse me. I have a friend coming over that I need to talk to," and she shooed him away.

"Hey, Iz," I said with the proverbial tail between my legs. "It's so good to see you."

"You too. How's John's apartment?"

It killed me that the first thing she'd said to me in a month was about John.

My lips turned down, shrugging my shoulders. "Eh . . . I mean, it's fucking beautiful, and massive, but it's nothing compared to living in a shit-hole with my best friend."

She smiled—the first smile she had shown me in months.

"I'm so sorry, Izzy. I never meant to drag you into this. But on the bright side . . . his divorce is final today!"

"Great!" she said, in a dry tone. "I'm happy for you, Sarah. I really am."

There was an awkward pause before I broke the silence. "Izzy, can we please be friends again?" I asked, channeling full puppy-dog energy.

"Bitch, I never didn't want to be friends with you! You just went rogue and tried to screw up your life and take me down with you on your sinking ship." She laughed.

"I know, I know. I never should have said anything to Theo and Willow. I guess I was so caught up in the lie, it slipped out, and I didn't consider the ramifications it would have in your life. It was so wrong and selfish to mention that you were involved."

"Well, thank you. Your apology means a lot." She acted like she was considering my request. "Yeah, we can be friends again." She smiled.

"Why the hell have you been icing me for the last few months?" I laughed.

"I was pissed off because TW started treating me differently after they found out about you and John," Izzy said. "I was being punished for something that wasn't even my fault. I mean, I get that I was in the middle of it, but it started affecting how I was treated at work. I couldn't tell if it was all in my head or if they were actually pulling back from me because of it." She paused, running a hand through her hair. "Honestly, I was scared it would hurt my career. I can't afford to have that kind of fallout right now."

She leaned back against the counter, taking a deep breath. "But I'm over it now. Just don't make me lie for you anymore."

"That's fair." I felt such relief. Finally someone in my corner again. "Luckily, after today, neither of us will have to worry about that ever again."

"Thank God. Come here." She pulled me into a hug. "So where is the Wicked Witch of Tribeca?"

It felt good to have my partner in crime back on my team.

"She should be in Chicago signing divorce papers with John as we speak." I glanced around the room and saw Peter, networking with his usual salesman charm, but he kept darting glances around the room. Even he seemed puzzled by Jane's absence.

Izzy shot me a sidelong glance. "No way. She is heading this entire project. She should be the first one here and the last one to leave tonight. God, she really is the worst. I guess if she doesn't show up, it makes you look even better. She can't even fucking show up to her client's release party. Ridiculous." Izzy shook her head.

I looked at her as she continued to scan the room, a smile spreading across my face. "It's really nice just to be talking with you again, Izzy. I missed you so much."

"Same. By the way, what was going on with Mr. Man-of-the-Hour when you came in?" Izzy raised an eyebrow, gesturing toward Gabriel. "God, I didn't think it was possible to top John Reynolds, but that guy . . ." She whistled, then shot me a knowing look. "He might take the cake. You two seemed pretty *friendly*. What's up with that? Aren't you all in with John now?"

"Izzy . . ." I warned, my voice low, trying to shake off the sudden unease that crept up my spine. "It's not like that with Gabriel. Actually, he just told me he wants to work on the next project together—without Jane." I looked at her wide-eyed, waiting for her reaction.

"Oh shit! Go for it, girl," she said. "That would be huge. Having you as sole editor on the next Gabriel Stone novel? That would fucking kill Jane." She cackled.

"Yeah, well . . . she killed a big part of me, including nearly ruining my chance at senior editor, so she'll have to deal with it," the words slipped out before I realized how bitchy they sounded. "And he introduced me to an author that is interested in working with Regent."

"Whoa, what a score. That could be huge for the promotion. No other junior editor has brought in an author since they announced the promotion. Honestly, if you can close that, you might be a shoo-in. Plus, if things don't work out with you and John . . . Gabriel is a great second choice," she winked. "Gosh, that would be so cruel. You steal Jane's husband, then you steal her number-one client," she said, clicking her tongue.

"I would *not* do that. Besides, I have no doubt that John and I will be together. For God's sake, I moved into his apartment." I laughed at the fact that she would even suggest it.

There was nothing between Gabriel and me. Right? I shook off the thought.

Two hours later, Izzy and I left, eventually making our way to the Bathtub Gin for a nightcap. The night we never had—the night I met Jane . . . and John, the night that changed everything. I wondered how my life would have been different if we had gone to the Bathtub Gin that night instead of staying at the Gala, if I hadn't arrived early and met Jane or John in the way that I had. If Willow simply would've introduced me to them in the group, if I hadn't bumped into Jane, mistaken John for a cater-waiter.

Maybe I would've made a better first impression. Maybe then I wouldn't have fallen for John, maybe Jane would be my mentor, and maybe none of this mess would've happened. Life was certainly easier then. Life was definitely more fun then. Everything wasn't weighed down by the weight of the Reynolds drama, and this goddamn divorce. My life could have been completely different.

But tomorrow. Tomorrow the divorce would be finalized. And all of this would be behind me. I would finally be able to move forward.

To move on.

Izzy and I drank and talked and caught up on life as the night wore on. We gossiped, laughed so hard we cried, and by the end of the night, it was like none of the drama between us ever happened.

I checked my phone one last time before heading home. Still no text from John. As I slipped my phone back into my bag, the weight of his silence became heavier. No text. No call. Nothing. I assumed everything was going to plan and he was celebrating his divorce. But a part of me couldn't shake the feeling that something was very wrong.

Chapter Thirty-Six

The next morning, Izzy and I woke up in John's (aka my) bed at eleven, hungover and craving coffee and croissants. I checked my phone, hoping for a text from him. Nothing. It was 10 a.m. his time, and he almost always texted me by now. I tried not to overthink it. I told myself he was probably still celebrating. Maybe even still sleeping depending on how much celebrating he did last night.

That evening, worry started to creep in. My mind wandered, wondering where not only John was, but where Jane was too. Since Jane blocked me on Instagram, Izzy had been checking her profile for me, while I monitored John's. But there was nothing—no posts, no check-ins, just unusual silence from both of them. Something didn't feel right.

"How long before I can send out a search for a missing person?" I asked Izzy.

"Forty-eight hours," she replied. Izzy with the random facts, finally being put to good use.

I could wait forty-eight hours.

One minute, I was worried about his safety. The next, I was

trying to remember if he had said anything that might explain why he was still off the grid. And then, absurdly, I found myself thinking about if he were dead, would I even be invited to his funeral? Unless, of course, Andy remembered to invite. Of course, he wasn't dead, but the thought still crossed my mind. Then, without warning, I was pissed. If he *was* alive and was ignoring me like this . . . I'd kill him.

If I hadn't had Izzy to distract me today, I might have gone insane.

"I'm sure he's fine," she reassured me.

But I wasn't so sure.

———

Jane wasn't at work the next day. My worry had now shifted to mild panic. I walked past her office and saw Jenny, sorting through a stack of papers with an energy that could only be described as a puppy waiting for a treat.

"Hey, Jenny, how are you?" I asked as I paused by her door, slipping in with the perfect amount of casualness to make it seem like I wasn't trying to find out where Jane was.

"Oh my God, thank you for asking! I'm doing great, Sarah. How are you?"

"Great. You really nailed that Gabriel Stone event. Super classy. It seemed like a big success," I said, knowing how much assistants put into events like that, especially ones that the project lead doesn't show up to.

"Awe, thanks! That really means a lot coming from you. You know, I just have to say how much I look up to you, especially after everything you've accomplished this year. It's inspiring to see how you've been climbing your way up. I mean, you spoke at the AAP Conference and helped lead the Stone project. I hope to be able to do the same one day. I can tell that Jane and John admire you as well. They had similar successes when they were your age. They see a lot of themselves in you," she said.

She leaned forward and lowered her voice. "Don't say I said anything—but I think it's really messed up what Jane did to you on that project. I saw how hard you worked on it. You pitched that marketing strategy, and you were clearly the one who should've been leading it all the way through. Then, she just cuts you out right before it has success, after everything you did to help that book have potential. I can't believe it." She gave me a sympathetic look.

A small sense of satisfaction came over me. To get pity from Jenny, Jane's assistant, of all people? It was as if the universe had given me further confirmation that Jane was as untrustworthy as I assumed her to be. Even her own assistant thought she was a piece of work.

"It's no big deal. It'll all work out in the end," I said, brushing it off, knowing my future plans with Gabriel wouldn't be an issue after his release party. "I noticed Jane wasn't at the event. It's kind of weird for the main editor of a project to skip the release party. Is everything okay?"

Jenny looked over her shoulder, then leaned in closer, her voice dropping to a whisper. "Well, you know how it is . . . things are getting a little complicated with her and John." She gave me a look, like I should have already known what she meant.

My stomach tightened. "Complicated how?" I did my best to look clueless.

Jenny shrugged and stared at the pile of papers as if they held all the answers. "I probably shouldn't say, but . . . let's just say they still have a lot to sort out. From what I understand, there are a lot of loose ends to tie up. . . . " She gave me a knowing, tight-lipped smile. "But you didn't hear it from me."

I blinked, trying to process. I wanted to scream, *Wasn't their divorce finalized on the 31st? Yesterday?* But I still hadn't heard from John.

"So . . ." I actually said, "they're still in touch? Like, beyond just getting divorced?"

"Ha! In touch? Please. They're married, for God's sake," Jenny

340

said with a grin. "I figured you'd know, what with you and John being so close. Anyway, some people call it a 'vacation to clear the head,' but we all know what that really means."

My heart sank, and my throat went dry. Loose ends? Vacation? What was she saying? "From what I heard, they were getting divorced. . . . Isn't that true? Isn't Jane with Peter?"

Jenny rolled her eyes. "Let's be real—we all know they're not getting divorced. If anything, this is just a pause before they're back to playing the happy couple."

I couldn't believe what I was hearing. I had planned my next steps, counted on it—John was supposed to be mine after December 31st. Today. Today he was supposed to be divorced—able to be with me. He promised. My hands clenched into fists at my sides as heat burned in my chest. If they *were* still sorting things out, what the hell did that mean for me?

Jane and John were never signing divorce papers? They were on vacation. Together? That trip wouldn't be about separation—it was about reconciling. Rebuilding. Everything John had told me, every promise, every assurance that it was over, had been a lie?

No. That couldn't be right. Maybe Jane had spun a story, knowing Jenny would tell me the office gossip as soon as I came around asking. Maybe this was some twisted game, her way of keeping me on edge. Maybe John had told me the truth, and this was all just a misunderstanding.

God, I hoped it was. It had to be.

I forced a smile, hoping it didn't look like I was about to set Jane's office ablaze. "I see," was all I could manage, my voice uneven. My world was turned upside down. How could he not tell me the truth? Did he think I would never find out that he wasn't actually getting divorced?

I could feel Jenny's eyes on me. Seeing straight through me. My lies. I had to get out of here before I let more panic slip through the cracks. The last person I needed to know about this was Jenny. "Well, thanks for the heads-up," I managed, my voice strained. "I'll catch up with you later."

"Sarah!" Jenny called after me, a small smile crossing her face, more sympathetic. "Let's hang out soon."

I nodded, already knowing it was one of those things people say and never actually do. "Sounds great," I said, but we both knew it would never happen.

As I turned to leave, my mind raced. I swore to God, if John wasn't hurt, harmed, kidnapped, or dead. If John was with Jane right now . . .

I would fucking kill him.

———

It was the fifth day without a word from John. *Five days* of silence. Five days of pretending his absence didn't feel like a heavy weight on my chest.

Every hour, my emotions swung wildly between certainty and doubt. One moment, I was furious—convinced he had played me, that every word he'd said had been a carefully crafted lie. The next, I was desperate for there to be an explanation, like John would say something that made this all just one big misunderstanding. Had Jane twisted the truth? Had Jenny misinterpreted? Had I? At this point I had no idea what to believe.

Each morning would bring resolve. I'd tell myself I was done, that I had my answer. By afternoon, I'd be spiraling, rereading old texts, searching for proof that John wouldn't—*couldn't*—do this to me. By night, exhaustion would take over, but sleep never came easy. The uncertainty gnawed at me. Not knowing. The possibility that at any moment, I could wake up to a message from him that would confirm everything. That everything I waited for would collapse like a house of cards.

I never did call the cops. I didn't know what I would have said. *Hi, I think my almost-boyfriend is missing, but he also might be with his wife on a vacation. I would love some help in finding them. Do you think you could help me out?*

Yeah, that wasn't going to happen.

And as for Jane, she hadn't shown up at work either. Like the universe was playing some sick game, leaving me to stew in my confusion. I had so many unanswered questions. Where the hell were they? What was going on? What was the truth?

Around four that afternoon, there was a soft knock at the door. Izzy poked her head in. She had been staying with me since John disappeared.

"Sarah? I brought you ramen from our favorite place. . . . Are you hungry?"

I didn't answer right away, just stared out the window, my gaze empty. I curled up with a body pillow as if it were my only companion. The apartment felt cold, and foreign. The kind of space where you'd think you'd feel free, but instead, I felt like I was slowly dying. Locked in a torture chamber. Red, puffy eyes from crying all weekend. Wine stains on my sheets. His old T-shirt was still clinging to me, as if his smell in the fabric could keep me from remembering that my life wasn't falling apart.

"Any news?" I finally murmured, still looking out the window, my voice like gravel. Deeper than usual, cold, the kind of cold that seeps into your bones when you've been frozen out by someone you trusted. Someone you loved. I had put Izzy on social media watch duty. Since Jane had blocked me, I couldn't see what she was up to. And since John was ghosting me, I couldn't bear to trust myself with my phone. I might unleash hell's fury on him and regret it later.

Izzy hesitated, putting the steaming bowl of ramen on the nightstand before sitting down on the bed next to me. "Um . . . yeah, actually," she said, biting her lip. "I checked Jane's Instagram this morning."

My stomach dropped. But I was too numb for it to really affect me. This was probably why she blocked me. So she could post with John on their vacation. "Tell me," I said.

343

Izzy bit her lip, narrowing her eyes. I held my breath, unsure whether what she'd found would be helpful or just another knife to the gut. "She posted about being in Sedona, Arizona. I don't know if they're . . . together. But, uh . . . yeah."

"Show me." I held out my hand. "And bring me my phone. I want to check, just in case he texted me."

Her lips pursed, but she pulled my phone from her purse and handed it to me. I opened my text thread with John. Still nothing. Nothing from him. Just the fifteen messages from me—each one more desperate than the last.

> How did things go with the paper signing?
>
> Hey, I haven't heard from you?
>
> Are you okay?
>
> Hello?
>
> John, I am worried about you. It has been two days.
>
> Are you dead?
>
> Please give me a sign that you are okay . . .
>
> Please, John.

And so on and so forth. It was officially pathetic. But again, I was too numb to care.

"Did she write anything about him?" I asked.

"Not directly," Izzy said, reaching for her own phone. "But he also posted something today."

I wanted to get excited, maybe get a shred of clarity. At least he was alive. But I couldn't get my hopes up. Izzy found the post and handed me her phone.

The picture seemed innocent enough—a walking path, one sign pointing left to 'Crystal Shop,' the other signs to the right said, 'Sweat Lodge,' and beneath it, 'Spa.'

As I zoomed in, Izzy offered, "It kinda sounds like the place John talked about taking you on the Fourth of July."

I froze. My fingers clenched around the edges of the phone, as if it might slip away. She was right. The signs—crystal shops, yoga retreats, sweat lodges, hiking trails—everything pointed to one place: Sedona. The place John had once talked about taking me instead of Naples.

Are. You. Fucking. Kidding. Me?

This confirmed several unfortunate things. On a positive note, he was alive. But on the other hand, he was ignoring my texts. He seemed to be on vacation with Jane. Not signing divorce papers.

And yet, despite all of the proof, that small part of me was *still* holding out for him to be a good guy. An honest guy. The guy I knew he could be.

That thought—that realization—fueled a surge of anger so intense I could barely breathe. I wanted to throw the phone across the room, but instead, I gripped it tighter, my pulse pounding in my ears. All of it—lies? Lies, lies, lies. And that pathetic part of me still couldn't believe it, keeping alive a shred of hope that it wasn't what it seemed to be.

Who was I really up against? What did I even know about John, beyond what he'd told me? His side of the story. Was he the crazy one pulling all the strings?

I went back to Jane's profile on Izzy's phone. Full investigator mode now. I clicked through her stories. Then, there it was—her lunch spread, innocent-looking enough to anyone else. Perfectly arranged, zen and effortless. But I wasn't looking at the food. My eyes were drawn to the corner of the picture.

And there it was. *The* proof that they were together.

John's sunglasses. The ones *I'd* bought him this summer, the ones he'd said made him feel like an Italian movie star. The ones that he was so grateful for when he unwrapped them after one of our vacations together.

My breath caught in my throat. I couldn't look away. The reality of it hit me all at once, crashing through me like a wave.

I sat back and stared at the picture like it was going to bite me. "Are you fucking kidding me?" I yelled, my voice cracking. I wanted to smash the phone against the wall.

Izzy jumped. "What? What happened?"

I buried my face in the pillow, the fabric muffling my scream as I let out all the pain, the anger, the disbelief in one fowl shriek—at the top of my lungs. A noise that wasn't human. That I didn't even know I could make.

Then I lifted my head, wiped my face, and said through gritted teeth, "They're together. I knew it. I fucking knew it." I slammed the pillow down next to me with all my might.

"Are you sure?" she asked, her voice small despite her attempt to sound supportive. She grabbed her phone to check.

"I'm 100 percent sure, Izzy. Look at those damn sunglasses. I got them for him. I knew he'd go back to her. No matter how much he said he was done, how much he swore he wanted something real. I fucking knew it. He would never leave her."

I swallowed hard, the words tasting bitter. Just like how my father couldn't leave my mother, no matter how much she'd already *been gone.* How much she had already moved on. This would always be John's life. He saw his future with her, that would never change. He would never let her go. I was just . . . temporary. I was just some . . . rebound. Some distraction while their shit was rocky. All this time, all he really wanted was her. And I was just a knockoff version he used to distract him when she threw him out like an old outfit she was done wearing.

John Reynolds was a spineless coward. He was *never* going to leave her. He lied to me, lied to himself. Or maybe he wasn't lying. Maybe he just liked having me around—an ego boost, a distraction. God, I had put up with so much. The sneaking around. The endless excuses. The bullshit promises he never intended to keep. For nothing.

No matter what happened between John and me, she would always be there. They shared a history, a business together. He would never be able to say no to her. He would never be able to stand up to her. He would never be able to fully move on from her. And she would just keep him around forever, using him for her own sick needs.

Sympathy was etched into every inch of Izzy's face. "I'm so sorry, Sarah. I can't believe he did this to you. I mean . . . to not even tell you? This is terrible. Maybe John's not who I thought he was. Or who you thought he was. It's just . . . it's really fucked up, Sarah."

I didn't answer. Instead, I did what I knew I had to do. The only thing that would make me feel better. I took a deep breath, my fingers shaking, as I grabbed my phone. I typed the words:

> Are you fucking kidding me, John? We need to talk.

I attached the picture with his sunglasses circled, the evidence of his betrayal staring back at me.

And then I hit *send*.

———

I got to the office late the following morning. I had to go to work. I'd called in sick for a couple of days with everything going on, but I had to go back. The atmosphere felt oppressive. Everything in the building reminded me of her—of him—of what I'd lost and what I was about to lose.

I'd tried reaching out to John a couple more times, but of course, no response. Not a word. I figured I was about to get kicked out of my apartment—hell, it was almost unbearable to even be there at this point. But I had nowhere to live. I'd probably have to sleep on someone's couch until I could figure it out. Izzy had a new roommate so I couldn't move back in with her.

With my current performance at work, plus Jane's ability to pull

347

the rug out from under me at any moment, I was fully preparing to be fired. If that happened, I couldn't afford to live alone. I wouldn't be able to afford to move at all. Especially not in the city.

My eyes were swollen, red from crying the night before, and I wore my oversized sunglasses all the way to my desk, hoping no one would notice the mess I was. I passed Peter, hunched over his desk, deep in whatever project he was obsessing over. I wondered how this was affecting him—if he even knew what was going on, or if he was just as clueless as I had been, blissfully unaware during his time spent with Jane.

As soon as I sat down, Izzy appeared, her breath coming in short gasps.

"Where the hell have you been, Sarah?" she panted, leaning against my desk. "You're late for your meeting with Clara Hawthorne. You're supposed to be in there today, remember?"

I stared at her blankly. "That's today?" I almost choked on my words. "Shit."

I tore off my sunglasses, wiped under my eyes, and scrubbed away the mascara I hadn't bothered to remove from crying earlier. I scrambled for a pen and my notebook and sprinted to the conference room.

Ten minutes late—it felt like I'd committed a cardinal sin. Being late made me feel like the world was falling apart around me, completely out of control.

I dodged abandoned coffee cups and neglected office plants in the hallway. As I sprinted for the boardroom, I could hear voices, including Clara Hawthorne's unmistakably calm tone.

I opened the door quietly, hoping to slip in unnoticed. Clara was sitting at the head of the table, back straight, in the middle of a sentence. Her book, *The Choice of a Lifetime*, that I had been working on for the last several months, was the focus of today's meeting. Clara's presence exuded the quiet authority of someone who had made more than her fair share of life-changing decisions. I scrambled to grab a seat in the back, pulled out my notebook, and did my best to blend in.

Clara's eyes flickered in my direction for only a second, but I had the feeling she could see right through me. The rest of the team—Phil from marketing, Maya from digital, and a few others—didn't seem to care that I was late. They were deep in discussion, the kind of talk I usually preferred to stay out of and observe.

I was one of the junior editors on Clara's book, tasked with smoothing the final stages of the manuscript. This meeting was supposed to be the handoff from editing to marketing, where Clara's work would be positioned to the world..

"Now that the editing phase is complete, we'll be focusing on marketing," Phil said, flipping through his notes without so much as a glance at me. "Clara, you've been very vocal about how we should position this. It's your most personal work to date. I'd love to hear your thoughts."

I stayed quiet, observing. Clara was historically particular in our meetings, she knew what she wanted and wouldn't settle for anything less. Everyone was hoping for a smooth handoff—no mistakes, no missteps.

Clara nodded, her face composed. "This book is about pivotal decisions—those moments when we face our fears and make choices that shape the rest of our lives. It's not just a story of change—it's a story of confrontation. The characters must face themselves, face the truth, and decide what kind of future they want."

I scribbled down the last part of her sentence, but her words hit me like a freight train. Crucial choices. Confrontation. I had run away from both when it came to John—until last night, finally, when I told him we needed to talk. But even then, the words had come out without confidence. They had been laced with fear. Fear of him not responding. And still, radio silence from him.

The image of him and Jane, looking so perfect together on their blissful getaway, resurfaced like a nightmare I couldn't escape. The irony of discussing life-changing decisions for Clara's book while failing to confront my own with John wasn't lost on me.

Phil leaned forward, seeming eager. "We need to hit that theme hard in the campaign—life-changing choices. People love stories where characters are forced to make tough choices, especially when it comes to love, friendship, and their career."

Clara remained calm, her voice steady, her chin high. "It is not *only* about tough choices—it's about recognizing when something is no longer serving you. That is the hardest part. They say awareness is the first step. Admitting that what you've invested in—time, money or energy, whether it's a relationship or a career—may be the very thing holding you back."

Was she talking about the book? Or me? The words hung thick in the air. Like the whole room knew something—some truth about me and John that I hadn't come to terms with yet. I shifted uncomfortably in my seat, my eyes darting from face to face. The rest of the team nodded along, absorbed in the campaign talk, while I could barely keep it together.

As Clara spoke, I realized: I had edited this book—read it a thousand times, dissected every paragraph—and I had never seen it before. The theme of avoidance, of running from confrontation . . . How had I missed it? Now, with everything unfolding in my own life, the parallels were undeniable. *I was living the book*—running from the truth, avoiding the hard choices. All that time spent editing those words, and it was like I'd been blind to the very thing I was doing in my own life.

I swallowed hard, the irony almost suffocating. The book had been about a woman avoiding the hard truths of her life, unwilling to see people for who they truly were—just like I had been with John. Maybe I hadn't wanted to see it, but now, it was impossible to ignore.

Maya jumped in next. "I think we can emphasize that emotional rawness in the campaign. The audience will really connect to the fear of having to make an impossible choice. What if we gave them a few different painful options to choose from? Like, 'Would you choose to lose everything you've worked for or the person you love?' Or maybe, 'What if you had to walk away from your dreams to save your relationship?' See how people answer. People love those hypothetical *would-you-rather* questions that make them reflect on what they'd sacrifice if it came down to it"

"Exactly," another person from marketing agreed. "Clara's readership will eat that up. They expect more than a simple love story— they want that gut-wrenching choice of reckoning."

It was difficult to stay focused. My mind was spinning, racing through my own decisions. Letting go. Choosing between what's safe and what's necessary. I was stuck in the loop of my own difficult choices.

Clara's voice broke through again, sharp and deliberate. "The main character's journey is about recognizing her *own* power— learning that sometimes the most important choice is leaving both options, and walking away completely. Even if it's something or someone you've invested everything in."

I swallowed hard. I didn't want to walk away from John. But wasn't I already losing him? It was like the choice was being made for me. He hadn't responded last night when I told him we needed to talk, and nothing today either. The silence from him felt louder than any words he could have said. My eyes fell to the agenda in front of me, but the words blurred together.

The meeting continued, ideas flying around the room about campaign angles, social media tie-ins, and influencer collaborations. I had to snap out of it. I forced myself to focus, pushing John, Jane, and everything else to the back of my mind—just for the rest of this meeting.

Then, an idea clicked—maybe it was Clara's words about tough choices and the power of walking away that triggered it. I raised my hand. "What if we created a social media campaign inviting readers to share their own difficult choices they have made? The ones they were afraid to make, terrified to, but once they did, it changed their lives for the better?" I asked. "We could use a hashtag—something like hashtag YourChoiceYourLife. It could encourage people to think about their own defining moments, the moments of impact in their life. The choices that changed everything for them. It could connect the themes of the book to real visceral experiences. It would allow the readers to become emotionally invested into the book."

Clara turned to me. "That's a powerful angle, Sarah. Engaging readers on a personal level can increase the impact of the book. It gives them a way to interact and share their own vulnerability, which is the most powerful buying tool."

Phil clapped his hands. "Great idea, Sarah. Let's add that to our strategy." He leaned back in his chair, a smirk tugging at the corners of his mouth. "Sarah, are you sure you don't want to be on the marketing team? You have a real knack for it."

I smiled politely and shook my head.

As the meeting ended, I couldn't shake the feeling that the choice I'd been avoiding was finally catching up to me.

As everyone packed up to leave, Clara's eyes met mine again, holding my gaze for a brief moment as she walked toward me. Her voice was calm, but there was something else—something deeper. "Just remember, in the end"—she put her hand on my shoulder. Her touch was nurturing, kind. Exactly what I needed right now—"the choice of a lifetime is about choosing yourself. Even if it feels impossible."

Our eyes locked for another second, and it was as if she'd stripped me naked. She smiled, and her eyes wrinkled. She gave my shoulder a gentle squeeze, and that motherly touch brought tears to my eyes. Then she turned and left the room without another word.

Chapter Thirty-Seven

Clara's words echoed in my mind for days: "The choice of a lifetime is about choosing yourself. Even if it feels impossible." Every fiber of my being screamed to keep fighting for John, to hold on to the remnants of what we had, but deep down, I knew it was time to make the impossible choice. I had to walk away—not just from John, but from the twisted situation I'd let myself get tangled in. It hurt, but I had to choose myself.

I needed to tell John that whatever was left between us was over. Done. But more importantly, I needed to tell Jane. I needed to tell her the truth. I needed to tell her everything.

Nine days had passed since John disappeared, and by now, I'd completely written him off. Still living in his house, I figured I'd have to hear from him eventually. But let's face it—if the person you're dating hasn't reached out in nine days, you either assume you're broken up, or they're dead. Since the latter had been proven false by his social media presence, I was coming to terms with the former.

I pulled Jane's name from the directory at work, my fingers trembling as I navigated through the list. The moment I clicked on her name, her phone number appeared on the screen, and a wave of determination rushed through me. I had to reach out to her. I had to tell her everything. Even if it meant risking my career. I couldn't hide anymore. It was killing me inside. I couldn't wait any longer.

With the number now saved in my phone, I closed the browser on my desktop, grabbing my things to head home. I couldn't stop thinking about the text I was about to send and the repercussions it may have. Would she freak out? Would she refuse to meet me? Would she fire me? As I made my way out of the office, I was already mentally typing the message. I knew exactly what I had to say. I would send it as soon as I got home, before I chickened out.

When I got back to my apartment, I stood frozen in front of my apartment door, unable to move. My finger hovering over Jane's number. The knot in my stomach twisted tighter as I stared at the screen. I had to do this. My heart pounded in my chest, and I forced myself to breathe through the panic rising inside me. I typed out the message:

> I know everything. We need to talk. - Sarah

I stared at the message for a moment longer. I was so scared to do this, but there was no turning back now. This was my choice of a lifetime. I had to face the truth. I had to right my wrongs. No matter how much it terrified me. No matter how much I had to lose.

With a shaky exhale, I hit *send*.

Without waiting to see if she would reply, I shoved my phone in my pocket, put the key in my door, turned the handle, and stepped inside.

When I crossed the threshold, I froze.

There, sitting in my living room, was Jane Reynolds.

My heart stopped. The room seemed to shrink, everything else fading away until it was just the two of us, suspended in the silence of what was coming next. I was shocked that she was in my apartment, and terrified that she really did know everything.

Somehow, despite it being my apartment, she looked right at

home, in a way I never had. This was *my* space—John's and mine—the place I had decorated and made my own. But now, it felt like I was the foreigner, like *I* was the intruder. She seemed to belong here, while I didn't feel like I belonged anywhere anymore.

Jane raised her phone and held up the message I had just sent. "Yes, we do need to talk." she said. She was sitting on my couch, her posture relaxed, her voice calm, though the air between us crackled with tension.

"Jane," was all I could say, my voice weak. I shook my head as I stood there, the silence stretching on for what felt like an eternity. "Um . . . how did you get in my apartment?" I finally stammered.

"Well, technically, it's my apartment," she replied coolly. "Since John and I aren't officially divorced, it wasn't too hard to get an extra key from the landlord. John's name's on the lease. I could see on our credit card statements that he'd been paying for this place. But I didn't expect *you* would be living here."

The words hung between us, heavy with unspoken accusations. I couldn't bring myself to look at her directly, but I had to. I had to face the consequences of the choices I had made.

"How long have you known it was me?" I whispered, more to myself than to her. I joined her in the living room, sitting across from her on a chair.

"Well, I didn't know for sure until today. Not until after I got this text and you stepped through that door," Jane replied, her voice steady, though the hurt beneath it was undeniable. "I had my suspicions. I was just trying to figure out who John was seeing. My best guess was between you and a few other women at the office, but I couldn't be sure. I was just waiting to see if any of you would tell me the truth."

"Jane, I *never* wanted to hurt you," I said, my voice barely audible. "This was never part of the plan. John had said that keeping things quiet was the best way to protect everyone—so no one would get hurt, and so you wouldn't be blindsided. He made me think it was for the best, for all of us."

"How long has this been going on? How did it even happen?" she asked.

I couldn't believe this conversation was happening. I swallowed hard, my fingers trembling slightly as I collected my thoughts. This was impossible. I wasn't sure how much I should say. Would this cost me my job? My entire career in publishing?

"I . . . I don't know how to answer that without it sounding like an excuse," I said. "It wasn't something I planned. It just . . . happened. At first, it felt harmless—just something between us. But then, as things escalated, I kept convincing myself I could control it. That it would work itself out. That I wasn't doing anything wrong. But I'm just as guilty for letting myself get involved with John."

Jane exhaled slowly, her expression softening. "Sarah, look. This isn't your fault," she said, her voice more gentle now. "This isn't the first time something like this has happened with John. John is the one who's been pulling the strings, manipulating *both* of us. You didn't ask for this, and you certainly didn't deserve to get wrapped up in it. He's the one who needs to be held accountable here."

I stared at her in near shock. Could this actually be the truth? Was she seriously not furious with me? Did she really just say it wasn't my fault? This isn't the first time *this* has happened? *This* what? Did she mean he had done this before? It was surreal hearing her speak this way. I had never expected her to speak so openly, let alone nearly absolve me of blame completely. I was in complete and utter shock.

"You can tell me everything, Sarah," Jane continued, her tone reassuring. "I may have been angry—hell, I was furious when I was sure I had figured out it was you. And I didn't handle things well. Taking you off the Stone project was very wrong, and I regret it. But now, with some space to think, I see it clearly: John is the one who's at fault. Not you."

The weight of her words hit me like a wave, and for the first time in months, I felt a breath of relief. She wasn't going to destroy me over this. She wasn't going to ruin my career. At least I didn't think so.

"You didn't have to keep quiet, Sarah," she affirmed again. "I don't want you to feel like you have to hide anything. Your career is not at risk here. None of that will be affected by what you tell me here today, I promise you. Whatever happens from here on out, I'm on your side. John's the one who's been lying to both of us, and I'm not going to let him manipulate the situation anymore."

Theo's words came back to me with sharp clarity: "Imagine how hard this must be for Jane. Imagine her side of the story." I hadn't been able to see it before. I'd been so consumed by my own pain, by the web of lies John and I had spun, that I couldn't even fathom what Jane had been going through. That this affected her too. She deserved the truth, even if it felt impossible to say the words.

John had been the manipulative one—making me feel like I had no choice but to play along with his version of reality. He'd turned me into someone I didn't recognize, someone complicit in his lies. But Jane? She deserved better than that. She deserved the truth.

I looked at her, really looked at her for the first time, and it was like I was staring into a mirror. The woman I idolized and admired, the woman I feared all year, was now sitting in front of me in a peace treaty, asking for the truth. I couldn't keep hiding. Even if she hadn't been perfect in their dynamic. Even if she had her moments of hurting him. I had to tell her my side of the story. All of it. Even if it made me look crazy. Even if it made everything harder than it already was. Something in me knew she was telling the truth, that she was on my side.

I was done protecting John Reynolds.

Taking a breath, I finally spoke, my voice shaky. "You're right," I said softly. "I can't keep hiding it anymore. You deserve the truth. All of it." I took another breath, deeper this time. "It all started at the Regent Gala last year. . . . Actually, I don't know if you remember, it was after I bumped into you outside the bathroom."

"That was *you?*" she said incredulously.

I raised my eyebrows, "Yeah . . . "

I shared everything. All of it. How we met at the Gala, how I'd

357

mistaken John for a cater-waiter, the first date we went on, what he told me at each stage of our journey together. What he told me about the divorce. The months of traveling to see each other, the trips we'd taken. Overhearing his call with her on my birthday. I explained why he had me move into this place. I shared my suspicions. I shared how he painted her to be the bad guy in all of this. Overhearing their fights. I told her about our own fights. The pain of being kept hidden.

Her jaw hung heavy as I spoke. She covered her mouth with her hand, shock painted across her face as she listened. But I had to get it out before I second-guessed myself. His repeated promises that the divorce was just around the corner. I spared no details. I shook my head in disbelief as the words tumbled out.

"I can't do it anymore, Jane. I've been dragged along for long enough. I have let myself be dragged along," I corrected. "I've hidden my entire life for long enough. I have feared losing everything every day of my life all year. I've lied more times than anyone should in a lifetime." I sighed as I completed my last thought, and it was like all the lies I held inside were released with that last breath out.

After a long silence, Jane shook her head. My heart pounded in my chest as I braced myself for her wrath. I expected her to flip the table, scream at me, maybe even fire me on the spot—honestly, all of it would've been deserved.

"Sarah," she said. "Thank you *so much* for sharing all of this. You have no idea what your honesty means to me." She touched her heart with her hand. "And I am so sorry you've had to go through this alone. I can't even fucking believe him."

"You aren't furious at me?" I asked incredulously. I couldn't believe this was her *only* reaction. John really had spun her to be a horrible person. Instead I suffered fearing her for a year.

"Oh my god, of course not!" She scoffed. "First of all, I can't blame you for falling in love with someone. None of us decide who we love. It can suck at times. I get it." She let out a small laugh, something I hadn't expected. Was she referring to Peter? "You know, I've had my suspicions for a while, but not *that* long. Since the Gala? Wow."

"Here is the thing," she continued. "All along, all I have wanted was for John to tell me the truth. To own *his* own truth. To be honest if he had moved on and was happy with someone else. But he wouldn't. I gave him plenty of chances." Jane's face softened, almost sadly. "Of course, I wasn't innocent either. I am the one who cheated. I am the one who tore the marriage apart. I wasn't happy anymore. I wanted him to meet my needs, and when he didn't, I found a way to fill that void. I'm not proud of it." She looked down in her lap, a look of . . . shame? I didn't know Jane could feel shame. It made her . . . human. Like I could see behind all the cosmetic surgery, designer clothes, and Botox, a real vulnerable woman.

She went on, "Here is the thing, at the end of the day, I want John to be happy with someone. I had been honest with him about my moving on." Her voice became bitter. "I told him I was with Peter." I raised my brows. I couldn't believe she had admitted that in front of me. "And he just couldn't move on. He wouldn't tell me the truth no matter how many times I asked him. And each time that I knew he was lying, it made me more and more angry. Because I could tell he was with someone new. And I was pissed he was hiding it. For his sake and whoever he was dating's sake. Jesus, I can't believe him. Keeping you hidden like that . . . He's such a coward." Her words were sharp.

"I'm so sorry, Jane," I whispered.

She shook her head, a tear welling in her eye, though she seemed to fight to hold it back. "You don't get it. I was not angry because of you. I was angry because John couldn't just be honest with me. I kept telling myself maybe it's because he doesn't know what he wants. Maybe he's confused, and I let him lie to me more and more. Eventually I . . . I snapped. I was angry at him but never at you, or whoever I thought he was with. I just wanted the truth. Even though I took it out on you with Gabriel's project. Again, that was so wrong. I am going to put your name back on it as a sole contributor and make sure

Aria Devi

it is accounted for when the senior editor position is being decided for."

A weight lifted off me, like hundreds of pounds that had been pressing on my chest for months. Gone. Why couldn't he have done that? Told her the truth. Saved me months of pain? It wasn't so hard, was it? Why couldn't he have just told her the damned truth? Was it worth losing me over, John? Clearly, it had been.

She was never going to ruin my career. He just made me believe that to keep his secret. And for what? So he could have the best of both worlds? So he could hang on to her a little longer? I didn't know what to think anymore. "Why do you think he didn't tell you?" I asked.

Jane hesitated for a moment, as if she was deciding whether to reveal more. Finally, she spoke. "Over the last year, he's been trying to get back together with me. Multiple times. I told him candidly I was with Peter and unavailable, that I had moved on, and he should to. But he kept pushing. Trying to save our marriage, making excuses to get me to go back to Chicago, to come out to New York, claiming we needed to deal with the divorce paperwork—but really, he just wanted chances to fix things between us." She paused, her eyes softening as she added, "He's terrified of his family's judgment. Being seen as a failure. They're very traditional. He still hasn't told them we are close to being divorced."

Her words hit me like a meteor, shattering my heart into pieces. He'd been trying to get back with her this whole time? I knew he may still feel things for her, but I thought he loved *me*. I couldn't cry here, not with her. I couldn't let her see the pain. I mustn't have done a good job of it because her voice was quieter when she spoke again.

"I'm sorry for telling you this, Sarah, but you need to know the truth. No man should ever hide you away like this. You deserve to be with someone who's proud to be with you, who can't stand to keep you a secret. It's disgusting what he's done to you." She shook her head and looked out the window.

I nodded. "No, of course. Thank you for sharing that. It helps a lot, actually. I appreciate you telling me so I can move on. Can I ask, though, if this is all true . . . then why were you in Sedona? He told me you were supposed to be signing your divorce papers on New Year's. Then we could be together. I haven't heard from him since."

Jane sighed deeply. "Jesus Christ, I can't believe him," she mumbled. "We went to Sedona for a hard reset. After everything we'd been through—the lies, the back-and-forth—I thought it might help us clear our heads. I still care for him after all. We were married. It was supposed to be to get some last-minute end-of-the-year business stuff done, but I figured why not do it at a place we can recharge as well. I am bougie like that," she said with a laugh. I was glad she could still find humor in this. It was a good sign. "But I think he took the trip as us getting a fresh start. But it was not that way at all for me."

She rolled her eyes before she met my gaze again. "But the truth is I am done and moved on with my life. I have no interest in this man . . . but the divorce isn't anywhere near being finalized. He is still hanging on, Sarah. It is really sad."

"How far from over?" I asked, swallowing hard.

"It's not even close," she continued, her voice hardening. "The papers aren't signed because of his negligence. For years, John's mishandled our taxes, underpaid by hundreds of thousands of dollars. It's one mess after another, and he's been stalling to get everything in order. He is the definition of procrastinator. If I am not holding him accountable, he never gets anything done. Truly one of the laziest people I have ever met. It is like trying to get a toddler to do things. That's what's holding everything up." She let out a sigh, her fingers tapping against her phone. "And on top of that, he's been investing money in hidden accounts. It's like he's planning to stack everything in his favor when the divorce finally happens, trying to get as much as he can and leave me with nothing. That's why I've been on his case about it to get it done. He's stalling to figure out where to put the money. There's been so much shady stuff going on behind the scenes, and I only found out about it recently."

She shook her head, frustration thick in her voice. "I don't know how much longer it's going to take. It could be another couple of years before everything's settled. He's done everything he can to drag this out, just so he can come out on top, or end up back together. Honestly, he is a pathetic, sick man. Not the man I married."

I couldn't believe my ears. But I could tell every word she spoke was true. It was like a fog had lifted and I could finally see John, for who he truly was. All his lying, manipulating, gaslighting. All of it. I couldn't believe I had been so blind to it until now.

Everything he'd accused her of was exactly what *he'd* been doing all along. The room felt smaller as I processed her words. His lies, his excuses, his entire mess of a life—all of it had been created behind the scenes while I unknowingly played my part in his manipulative game. The pieces were falling into place, but the puzzle was still too big to solve in a single conversation.

"I'll tell you this much, Sarah," Jane said. "John will do what he does. . . . But it's so strange. There's something about our dynamic, you and me, I mean. Maybe it's the Gemini twin thing—our birthdays are right next to each other. I don't know if you know that or not —or maybe it's something else, but ever since I met you, I've always felt like we're sisters. Like you are a version of me from years ago. Like we're the same person. Is that weird?"

Her words hit me like a truth I knew but had never let myself recognize. It may have been one of the only things she could have said in that moment that would make me feel a little better about everything she had shared with me. I'd felt the same way but never thought she'd notice, never thought she'd see me like that. I was stunned that she knew our birthdays were just a few days apart—though, of course, there was an eight-year age difference.

"That's really wild you sense that. I have felt the exact same way. I feel so connected to you." I smiled. It was like we'd known each other forever. "I've always looked up to you so much. It killed me all year, betraying you like that. It felt like I was betraying myself. And even worse, he made you out to be the villain the whole time. And I am sorry to say, but I believed it." I shook my head, still struggling with how much I'd been played by him.

"Well, here is some advice. Don't repeat what I did and marry the guy and get stuck in his shit show of a life." She scoffed. "And don't blame yourself for getting sucked in, in the first place. John is a master manipulator. He plays the innocent victim and martyr better than anyone I've ever met. He's not all bad, though. At least that's what I want to believe."

It was like an older version of myself had stepped in and was giving the current version of myself advice. And some damn good advice, at that.

"Yeah, I think he's a good person deep down . . . just making really fucking terrible decisions," I offered, trying to make sense of it all.

"Exactly. He is a coward," she agreed. "But we've got to be on each other's team now, Sarah. We can't let guys like this win and take our power away. We can't let them manipulate us and tear apart our lives. We both have way too much going for us."

"Agreed," I said firmly.

"I'm so glad we finally had this conversation," she said. "I'm here for you, okay? Anything you need, I've got you." She hesitated for a moment. "And I owe you an apology. Showing up at your . . . his apartment like this was out of line. I thought it would be empty, honestly. I didn't expect you or anyone to be living here. I was just trying to get some answers and figured his vacant apartment in the city would be a good place to start."

"All good," I replied, a sense of calm washing over me. "I probably would have done the same if I was in your shoes. Plus it forced us to have this conversation. So, I'm grateful. All I can say for sure is this year is going to be so much better than last year."

"Yes, ma'am, it is," she said, grinning. "Cheers to a killer next year together at Regent where we can actually collaborate in the office without all this bullshit John drama." She stood as she stepped in to hug me and added, "Let's just keep this between us, okay? No need to stir up any more drama. You and I have already been through enough."

I nodded, smiling as our eyes locked. It was like I was looking at myself "I was hoping you would say that," I said, relieved, as I returned the hug. And for the first time in a year, I felt light. I felt free. I felt like I could do anything.

My phone buzzed. We pulled away as I checked to see who it was. The name sent a jolt through me.

John Reynolds.

I hesitated for a moment, then turned the screen toward Jane.

She glanced at it, her eyebrows furrowing. "Ugh, really?" she muttered, her voice thick with disdain. "What does he think this is—some kind of game? What a fucking asshole, not reaching out to you for days and then calling you now."

I swallowed. "I don't know if I want to hear anything he has to say."

Jane grabbed my shoulders. "You don't have to answer it, Sarah. Whatever he has to say is not worth the energy. Besides, you have a promotion to secure." She winked.

I nodded, feeling the pull to pick up the phone, but her words, that calm assurance in her voice, made me realize I had the power to walk away from this. I didn't need to give him any more of my time or emotions. Not right now. Not until *I* was ready.

With a steady breath, I pressed "decline." The phone fell silent, the screen dimming. For the first time in a long while, it was like I was finally back in control of my own life.

Jane gave me a knowing look. "Good choice. When you're ready for that conversation, you'll have it on your terms. Not his."

I nodded again, a small smile tugging at my lips. She was right. I didn't owe him anything, not anymore. I couldn't help but notice that maybe there was a chance of her becoming my mentor after all.

"Not today," I echoed softly with a smile. And we hugged again, this time for several minutes.

————

The next morning, I was lying in my huge bathtub—big enough for three people—when I opened Instagram, still feeling the lightness and relief from yesterday's conversation with Jane. As soon as the app loaded, a message from Jane of all people popped up. I tapped it, my heart beating a little faster. She had unblocked me?

It was an image—bold, simple, and to the point. The words read, *"Never be someone's secret."* She had forwarded it to me with a heart emoji attached.

My eyes welled with tears, reminding me of everything Jane and I had talked about, everything I had come to terms with. I was worthy of being seen, of being with someone who could be fully with me, and not be hidden in the shadows by a cowardly man.

I sat back, absorbing the message. A tear slipped down my cheek. But this time, it wasn't out of sadness—it was out of something else. Something that felt like another small step toward taking control of my life again.

I typed back:

> Thank you. That's exactly what I needed to hear.

As I hit *send*, there was a sense of release. Jane had given me something important in that moment—validation, strength, and the reminder that I deserved to take up space in the world.

Since last night, John had texted me nine times, and called twelve times. I ignored each and every one of them. After the clarity I'd gained in my conversation with Jane, the mere thought of him disgusted me. The idea of hearing his voice felt like it would turn me to dust; if he touched me, my body might reject him outright.

As if the universe wanted to test me just moments after the message from Jane, John's name appeared, once again, on my phone screen. "John Reynolds is FaceTiming you" . . . his name alone was enough to piss me off. I stared at it while debating. Something about this call felt different.

I was ready. I felt strong enough to talk to him and not be pulled back into his game. I took a deep breath and clicked "accept," my face a blank slate. My eyebrows arched slightly, waiting for him to speak.

"Hey," he said casually, as if nothing had happened. *Nothing.* Like he hadn't just ghosted me and failed to tell me the truth for a year of my life. As if he hadn't made me feel insecure, humiliated, and alone. His apathy just made it worse. "How are you?"

I narrowed my eyes into a death glare. "How am I? Are you fucking kidding me, John?" I exclaimed. "How am I? How am I? I'm terrible, John."

He dropped his eyes, silent. Here we go again. Me yelling, him playing the victim. Just like he did at his cabin on the Fourth of July. Just like Jane did so many times over the phone, and I believed she was the bad guy. Little did I know he had been playing the martyr all along. I'd feel guilty for being angry, for making him feel bad. But not this time. Not anymore.

I couldn't stop. Fire rose inside me, consuming everything I was and had ever been. My vision blurred red as the words poured out like lava. "You fucking left me! Days of silence, and then I find out you're with her? On a fucking vacation? A romantic getaway? You told me you were getting a divorce. You said you were done. And then you abandoned me. Ghosted me."

His silence was gasoline on my fire.

"For the first five days, I thought you were fucking dead! Do you have any idea what that was like? I called and called, and you just *ignored* me. I couldn't even find out if you were dead because I don't even know one person in your family. Because you were with her. You chose her . . . over me. Again. You lied to me about where you were and what you were doing. You chose a woman who literally does not even want to be with you over the person who's been there for you. Every single day. Day in and day out. For a year. Supporting you. We share an apartment, John! You left me in your house without a single explanation, without a single word of communication!"

My voice cracked, but I went on. The words I'd been swallowing for months came pouring out, unstoppable. "Do you have any idea what that was like for me? What this whole year has been like for me? Do you even care? Did you even sign the damn divorce papers?" I had to act like I hadn't learned what I did from Jane. We had agreed not to tell him we talked.

I paused, forcing myself to breathe, to hold back the rest of the anger bubbling up inside. I needed an answer—just one.

"There was . . . another delay. With the taxes," he said flatly. His voice was lifeless.

"That's really all you have to say?" I asked.

"I'm sorry, Sarah. I'm so sorry that I did this to you. I wish there was something else I could do."

I let out a bitter laugh and shook my head. "You could've fucking texted me. Five seconds. That's all it would have taken. Five goddamn seconds to let me know you were alive."

He rubbed his forehead, his expression pained. "We didn't plan for the trip. We were both so stressed, and we just . . . left. It all happened so fast. I didn't have time to text you."

"Are you serious? You didn't have *time*? A text of 'hey Sarah, I am going on vacation with my wife, I have no intention of divorcing anytime soon' takes what . . . a total of ten seconds to type and send— maybe? You just . . . left. Without a word? And now you're telling me this after weeks of radio silence? You didn't care enough about me to step away for ten seconds for days on end to let me know you were alive?" I couldn't keep the anger from seeping into my voice. "You think that's okay? Is that how you treat the women in your life?"

He chose not to text me. He chose to lie and hide. He chose not to tell Jane about me. He chose not to do his taxes. He chose not to get divorced. He chose all of this. And now he chose to be a coward. He chose to lie to me again and again and again.

At the same time, my heart was whispering something I hated: *Don't forget. You love him.*

And God help me, I did. In spite of everything, I still wanted him to choose me. I still wanted to hear him say the words, "You're the one, Sarah. I'll tell Jane the truth. You're worth it—all of it." But now I knew better.

I didn't want this life anymore. I wanted more. I deserved more. I deserved the truth. I deserved to be shown to the world, not hidden away like some secret. I deserved to have someone put me first. More importantly, I deserved to put myself first, not wait for a man to do it. Because if I waited for this man to do it, I would be waiting my whole fucking life.

Tears streamed down my cheeks as I stared at the screen. My chest felt hollow, as if my heart had been ripped out and replaced with nothing. Minutes passed. It felt like years. Our entire year together flashed before me—every good moment, every shitty one. Laughing. The lying. The pain. The love. The fights. The endless cycle of betrayal and reconciliation.

I thought about who I was before John. I was alive. I was full of joy. I loved my work. I never cried. I was confident. I spoke up. I took risks. I had courage. I trusted myself. I was . . . free.

But now? Now I was a shell of my former self. A bottom-shelf knockoff version of Jane Reynolds. My face, streaked with mascara, reflected on the screen. My eyes were dull, lifeless, as if someone had stolen the light from them.

John had spent the whole year building his life and left me without my own. It was like my real life had completely slipped away from me. I had trained myself to stay small, to not draw attention, so the lies wouldn't catch up with me. But even that wasn't enough. I had lost everything I loved about myself, even how I looked, all so I could become the woman I thought he would love. The one that looked like his wife. But I would never be more than the wannabe. The mistress. The other woman.

Clara's words echoed in my mind—*the choice of a lifetime is about choosing yourself.* I had to stop hiding, to stop letting fear dictate my every move. It was time to choose me, even if it meant walking away from everything I thought I wanted. Even if it meant walking away from John. It was time to reclaim what I had lost—not for anyone else, but for myself.

"I can't do this, John. I can't anymore. I am done."

His face fell, and he started to cry. "Please don't do this. This is all just a mistake. I promise I'll make it up to you. I am so sorry I didn't reach out to you. I didn't want Jane to catch me on the phone and have her put your career in jeopardy."

He looked so hurt, so vulnerable, and for a moment, I almost felt sorry for him. But as I stared into his eyes, really looked at him, I finally saw through the mask. The show he'd been putting on—his charm, his apologies, his "poor me" act—it was all starting to crumble. I couldn't unsee it now.

How in the hell could I have fallen for him? For so long, I had justified his actions, convinced myself he was just lost or confused. But now, the truth was undeniable. The pieces were all there, laid out before me, and I couldn't pretend any longer that I didn't see the bigger picture. I could no longer pretend I couldn't see him for who he truly was.

A liar.

I knew deep down that he *could* be a good man. But anybody *could* be anything. But good people can still make bad choices—choices that hurt others, choices that don't align with who they really are or who they claim to be. He wasn't the man I thought he was. And I had been living in his illusion, blind to it all. The realization stung, but it also set me free.

"I can't trust you anymore," I said, my voice cold and unwavering. "This is over. There's nothing left to fix."

"Please," he begged, "give me another chance to make it right. I'll prove it to you."

I wanted to believe him. I wanted to believe every word. But I didn't. I couldn't.

"John–"

"I'm going to announce it," he said desperately. "At the Gala. Next month. A year from the day we met. I'll tell everyone. Including Jane. I will say it from the stage, that we are together."

I laughed bitterly. "Yeah, right. That could ruin both of our lives."

"Everything with Jane will be over by then. No one will even care. And I don't care. You're worth it to me."

I studied his face, looking for the man I had once loved, finally saying the words I had wanted—waited—needed him to say, all year. But he was too late. "You'll never do that," I said.

He looked so sad, but I didn't care anymore. "Sarah, I want to make it up to you. I want you to trust me again."

"John, I will never trust you. Ever again."

"I understand. I don't like it, but I understand." He sounded disappointed. Like a victim.

"Goodbye, John," I said with a sharp edge.

"Sarah, I love you," he said, his voice breaking. "I promise I will do it!"

I ignored him and let out a bitter laugh. "Oh, last thing, John. I'm leaving the apartment. I won't be staying here and pretending everything's fine. It's over."

And with that, I ended the call.

Chapter Thirty-Eight

As the Gala approached, I found myself finally able to focus not on the drama of the past year but on moving forward. Jane and I had managed to find our way to a professional, even enjoyable, working relationship. And as for John—I had ended it for good. No more half-hearted attempts at something that wasn't meant to be. And I was sticking to those guns.

Walking out of our monthly all-hands meeting that Thursday, Willow stopped me. "Sarah, can we talk for a minute? Come into my office."

I followed her, the door clicking shut behind me. Willow wasted no time. "You seem better," she said plainly. "You've been much more focused and on track since you broke things off with John."

I nodded, offering a small, appreciative smile. "Yeah, I guess I'm getting there. I'm finally back ahead of my workload, and Jane and I have mended things. I'm feeling more like myself."

Willow leaned back in her chair. "Good. I can see it. But I wanted to talk to you before the Gala. Whoever I ultimately select to promote to senior editor, I need solid, tangible evidence that they're the obvious choice for the promotion. I would love for you to be that

371

person, but I need to show the board that you're the one by the Gala. I can't just hand you the role because I like you. They need to see if you can bring in revenue and recruit authors to support in making the company profitable."

I nodded.

"Have you had any opportunities to bring any new authors to Regent?" Willow asked.

I straightened in my seat, feeling a surge of pride. "Actually, yes. I didn't want to jinx it by telling you before it was official, but Nora Edwards is interested. Gabriel introduced me to her, and we have a meeting set for tomorrow."

Willow's eyes lit up, and she leaned forward. "That is perfect. If you can lock her in, that could be what I need to give you the promotion. Signing Nora Edwards would be huge, Sarah. That would be the tipping point to push you across the finish line. None of the other junior editors are even considering bringing in an author, let alone have a whale like Nora Edwards on the line."

I couldn't suppress a smile. "I'll do everything I can to make it happen."

Willow gave me a reassuring nod. "Do you feel prepared for the conversion? I suggest having Jane sit in on the conversation."

"Way ahead of you. She already agreed to it," I said confidently. "I feel prepared as well." And I did. I had prepared for weeks.

"I have no doubt you will make it happen. If you secure her, that's your ticket."

It finally felt like the senior editor position was within reach. I just had to lock in this meeting. This was about proving to myself that I was capable of more than I had ever imagined. And I was grateful to have Jane on my side for it.

———

The meeting with Nora Edwards was set for the following afternoon in a small conference room on the top floor of Regent House. I'd spent the morning preparing, going over every detail of our potential partnership, rehearsing what I wanted to say—but no amount of preparation could stop the nerves that gnawed at me as I sat at the polished table, waiting for her arrival. Jane would be there too, of course, which only added to the pressure. This was my chance to prove myself—not just to Nora, but to Jane as well.

When Nora walked in, she gave me a small nod. "It's nice to see you again, Sarah," she said, her voice soft—a far cry from the boldness the world had come to expect from the Nora Edwards brand.

"Thank you for taking the time to meet with us," I said, leaning forward slightly, trying to match her calm energy. "Your time is valuable, Ms. Edwards, and I really appreciate the opportunity to talk about how we can work together. Mrs. Reynolds will be with us in a moment."

She nodded, her fingers tapping the edge of the table. "Of course," she said in a voice that was kind, reserved. "I've heard good things about the company . . . and you. And of course, through Gabriel. I've been thinking about taking this step for a while. I've just been waiting to find the right home."

My heart was racing, but I kept my voice steady. "I am confident you'd be a fantastic fit for Regent House. I've read all of your works and have been a fan since I was young. Our company is growing, and we're eager to bring in writers like yourself—writers who have an established voice, who are looking for a supportive but dynamic environment to bring their next project, or many, to life."

Nora's eyes met mine. "I've worked with a lot of publishers over the years, but I've always believed that the right fit is crucial. I've been watching Regent House from a far for a while, and I think there's potential here. The team seems strong, and you seem to put your authors first. That's really important to me."

"Your work speaks for itself, but I want you to feel supported here. We're not just about pushing books out into the market; we're about creating long-term partnerships with our authors. Whatever you need to succeed, we'll do our best to provide."

The conference room door opened, and Jane stepped inside, her heels clicking against the marble floor. Her presence filled the room, but for once, I didn't feel intimidated by it. It was like there was finally a signed peace treaty between us. We were on the same team.Her gaze met mine — she wiggled her eyebrows as if to say, *"Here we go!"* She sat down across from Nora and gave her a small smile.

"It's good to see you, Nora," Jane said. "We've been hoping this conversation would happen for a while now."

Nora leaned back. "I've worked in environments where it was more about the bottom line than the creative process. I'm not sure I can do that again. It's challenging as an artist to work under those conditions."

Her words struck a chord with me. "I completely understand. It's about making sure you're seen, heard, and respected as a creator—not just a commodity."

Nora paused, then, with a look between Jane and me, she asked, "How do you handle creative control? I need to know that my voice won't be diluted in the process, especially by the editing team. I've been burned before."

I opened my mouth to answer, but Jane spoke first. *Let her do her thing. Learn from her,* I reminded myself. "At Regent House, we believe in collaboration," she said. "You'll always have a seat at the table and a hand in final decisions. Your vision remains intact—that's non-negotiable."

I nodded, feeling gratitude toward Jane. "Exactly. This is your book; we're just supporting you in bringing that vision to life. Not controlling it. We want you to feel like a partner, not just a client."

Nora studied me. Finally, she spoke again. "And the contracts . . . Are they flexible? I need to feel like I'm making the right choice for the long term, not just for the immediate book."

Jane slid a leather folder across the table. "It's straightforward," she said. "We can tailor it to your needs. And we offer separate contracts for each book you write so you won't be locked in for years under the same agreement. This gives you freedom and flexibility. It's designed to protect you, not trap you."

Nora picked up the contract, running her fingers over the paper as if she were weighing the decision in her hands. The silence between us stretched for a moment before she looked up at me.

"If I'm being honest, Gabriel sang your praises so much that I made my decision before I came in here," Nora said quietly, almost to herself. With a deep breath, she picked up the pen and signed her name at the bottom of the page.

Relief flooded me. I had to fight to keep my expression neutral. Was it really going to be that easy? It felt like I was cheating the system. No way signing an author like Nora Edwards would be this simple.

"I'm thrilled to have you with us, Nora. I'm confident this will be the beginning of something great," I said.

Jane smiled at me, the kind of smile that told me she was genuinely impressed. My chest swelled with pride.

Maybe after a year of suffering, the universe was throwing me a bone—making my final push to senior editor easier than I could have imagined. Thank you, Gabriel Stone.

Nora offered a small smile in return. "I hope so," she said. "I'm looking forward to seeing where this goes."

As Jane stood to leave, she extended her hand to Nora. They shook, and then Nora turned to me. I offered my hand, and she took it.

As the door closed behind her, Jane turned to me with a warmth in her expression. "Nice work, Sarah."

"Couldn't have done it without you," I said.

Jane walked over to me and whispered. "You were ready for this. Me being here was just a formality," she said with a wink before turning to leave.

As she walked out of the room, I sat down, feeling shocked at what just happened. We signed Nora Edwards. We actually did it. This wasn't just about landing Nora—it was about proving to myself, to Willow, to Jane, and to the board that I was capable of more than just editing and contributing ideas every so often. I had just brought a huge player through the door—a move that would generate millions for Regent House.

The position was almost mine. I could taste it.

Chapter Thirty-Nine

Days before the Gala, I was getting ready to leave the office when Jenny walked by, her expression unusually serious.

"Hey, Sarah," she said, her eyes searching mine. "You got a minute?"

I looked up from my desk, raising an eyebrow. Something about her tone felt off.

"I just wanted to leave you a little note," she said, pulling a sticky note from her bag and slipping it onto my desk.

I stared at it as she walked away.

It read: *John's been acting weird. Be prepared before the Gala.*

I couldn't help but wonder. Was John really going to announce that we were together? That could ruin everything now. Did he find out about Jane and I resolving things, so he wanted to sabotage me? Was he planning to ruin my chance of getting the promotion?

I stared at the note, anxiety swirling in my stomach.

———

Izzy was stretched out on my bed, a slice of mango in her mouth. She was helping me choose an outfit for the Gala, though "help" mostly meant moral support while she lounged and I informed her of the Jane and John Reynolds updates. Izzy was going to the Gala too, though as usual, she waited until the last minute to get ready. I could already imagine her throwing on a dress in a frenzy with wet hair, ten minutes before the festivities started.

She had been offering support and listening to all the updates I had, but when I mentioned Jenny's ominous warning, her posture shifted. She sat up.

"Sarah, you need to be careful," she said, after swallowing the mango slice. "Men with bruised egos can do some crazy shit. And the last thing you need, especially if they promote you to senior editor, is for John to ruin it with some crazy PR stunt. At this point, I don't think he is above making a scene. Especially if he is the one losing everything now."

My stomach sank. She was right. I had no idea what extent John was willing to go to. Or what he knew. But would he really sabotage me? At the Gala? It was all starting to feel like one big, chaotic mess again. Hadn't I put all this to rest by ending things with him and righting things with Jane?

"I am sure everything will be fine, but we will keep an eye out for him doing anything crazy. Worst case, I will distract him. I'll throw my drink at him and boo him off stage," Izzy assured me. Before I could respond, she asked, "Dress or suit?"

I was sure it would all be fine . . . or at least I hoped. I took a breath and focused on my outfit once more. I stood in my walk-in closet—the one room alone was bigger than our last apartment. I hadn't moved out of John's apartment yet. I was looking for a place, but the rental market in New York was terrible, and since he hadn't mentioned it, I figured I could stay for a few weeks. I ran my fingers over the suit I'd worn to last year's Gala. The same suit I'd worn when I'd first ran into Jane. The suit I had worn when I first met John, the cater-waiter with the handsome smile and the champagne-soaked napkins. I brushed my fingers over the lapel where the champagne stain had been.

"I know exactly what I'm wearing," I said with a small smile, turning away. I'd chosen myself over the drama that had surrounded me for too long, and tonight, my outfit would reflect that.

I pulled out a sharp, tailored black tuxedo that Emma had made for me for my birthday last year, holding it up. The sleek lines and structured silhouette felt like armor—a statement of power. The fabric was elegant, and the subtle sheen of the material hinted at something more expensive than I could afford. I threw it on.

Izzy got up from the bed, her fork hovering midair as she stared at the suit. She blinked a few times before a slow grin spread across her face. "Whoa, look at you," she said, her voice tinged with surprise and approval. "That suit screams . . . 'I am a fucking senior editor a Regent House Publishing, and you'd better take me seriously' energy. I love it."

She moved closer to inspect the suit. "And John will feel like an idiot for letting you go."

I laughed, feeling excited and nervous all at once. "I'm not doing this for him," I said, smoothing the fabric over my arms. "I'm wearing this for me. But funny you should say that," I muttered, pulling a package out of the spare room. "This came in the mail yesterday."

Izzy frowned. "From who?"

I held up the package, biting my cheek, "John," I said, raising my brows.

"No . . . Let me see."

I sat down on the bed, the package in my lap. I peeled back the tissue paper. Inside was a dress—or rather, a masterpiece.

It was emerald green, jewels all over the bodice. The fabric was gorgeous silk. Tiny crystals glittered along the straps and mesh over-lay, catching the light and reflecting it back like stars.

Tucked inside the train was a handwritten note in John's unmistakable handwriting:

. . .

Sarah,

    I saw this dress and immediately thought of you. I can't wait to see you in it at the Gala. You deserve to shine as brightly as you make my life feel. Remember, this is where you belong. I'm so proud to be by your side and for the whole world to know it.

    All my love,

    John

"Holy shit," Izzy breathed. "That dress has gotta be like five grand. And is that a fucking threat in his note?"

I grabbed the note, crumpled it in my hand, and threw it in the trash. The audacity. After everything he'd done, he thought he could just step back into my life and make a public spectacle of it all, *now?* My anger rose, again. But alongside it, doubt began creeping in. Jenny's warning echoed in my mind—this gala could be his stage, and I needed to be ready.

But I wasn't about to let him dictate the night, and especially not what I wore. Not now. Not after everything I had been through.

I hung the dress in my closet and looked at it. It would probably fit perfectly. And yes, it was gorgeous. But . . . it wasn't me. And the fact that he thought it was me showed how he never even knew me at all. He only knew the woman I created in the hope that he would leave his wife for her.

I straightened, forcing some conviction into my voice. "Well, I'm not wearing that dress." I considered throwing the dress away. But instead I let it hang there as I put on my tux.

Izzy grinned as I put on my bowtie. "Now that's the badass future senior editor Sarah Jones right there."

I took one last look at the dress. And rolled my eyes.

"So what's our plan for the Gala, then?" Izzy asked. "If John tries something crazy, how are we going to handle it? I hate to say it, but your career's on the line. I will still throw my drink and boo him if you want."

I stood there for a moment, I had worked too hard to let John's mess jeopardize everything I'd worked for. My career was mine to protect, and I wasn't going to let anyone—especially him—derail it.

"I'll handle it," I said. "If John tries something, I'll confront it head-on. I'm not backing down. Not anymore. No one is going to take this promotion from me." I paused, glancing at the dress again. "I'm not going to play his game. I'm going to play my own."

I took a deep breath, mentally steeling myself for whatever the night might throw my way. Whatever happened, I was going to walk into the Gala with my head high, and if John tried to pull any stunts, I'd be ready to face it with everything I had.

Chapter Forty

The grand ballroom for the Regent House Literary Gala buzzed with New York's authors, agents, editors, and executives—all mingling under extravagant chandeliers, champagne in hand. This event was even more extravagant than the year prior.

I couldn't believe it had already been a year. A year since that same event shifted the course of my entire life. It hit me then—so much had changed, but in ways I didn't expect. My career was back on track, far beyond where I had been a few months ago. I'd mended things with Jane, settled into my role at Regent House Publishing, and put to rest the drama that once consumed me. Ending things with John was the final piece I needed. Even though I wasn't sure what he might do tonight—I was ready.

Then there was Nora—signing her had solidified everything. A huge step, and one that meant I had a very real shot at senior editor. And by the end of the night, I would know if I secured the position or not.

As I looked around the Gala, I felt it—a shift. Everything was coming together. Finally, I was in control, and tonight would be the start of the next chapter.

As Izzy and I mingled. Theo and Willow looked sharp, as always branded together—this event was all black with accents of baby pink. Jenny was at Jane's side, and Peter lingered nearby. Everything seemed . . . normal.

As I scanned the room, I caught a glimpse of Gabriel. I walked over to him, offering a quick smile and a nod. "Hey, just wanted to thank you again. Nora signed on at Regent, and I really appreciate your help in making that happen," I said.

Gabriel's smile was warm. "I knew you had it in you, Sarah."

"Plus, I am pretty sure it secured my position as senior editor. I literally couldn't have done it without you. I'm not sure if I can ever repay you."

"Let's just make sure my next book is a bestseller and we can call it even," he said with a gorgeous grin.

"Thanks, Gabriel. That means a lot." We both excused ourselves, moving on, mingling.

As the event unfolded, there was a surge of anticipation within me—not for John, not for some grand declaration of love, but for the moment that could finally solidify my place as senior editor.

Tonight was supposed to be about my career. About stepping into the role I had worked so hard for. But beneath the excitement, a hum of anxiety coursed through me. Because John was here. And I knew what he was capable of.

Would he really do it? Would he finally say the words I had once ached to hear—only now, it would ruin everything? And if he did it . . . were his actions genuine or malicious? Some ulterior motive driving him.

If he did, the whispers would start. My name would become office gossip, not for a reason I would prefer. And after all the progress I'd made, after finally getting out from under his shadow, would be gone. I couldn't let that happen.

I swallowed hard and straightened my shoulders. No. I wouldn't let him take this from me. Not tonight.

I scanned the room, searching for John. Maybe I could stop him before he did something stupid. But how? What could I possibly say to change his mind if he had already decided to burn it all down? I had to be prepared for whatever came next.

John finally arrived, looking every bit the charming, polished man I had fallen for a year ago. But I saw him completely differently now. He moved through the room with ease, exchanging handshakes and smiles, his presence potent. Compelling. But this time I knew it was all a façade. When he reached Jane, he greeted her with a gentle smile, touched her arm briefly, but didn't linger. My stomach twisted.

The accents of his jacket matched the deep green of my dress—the one I had deliberately chosen not to wear. A flicker of something unreadable crossed his face when he saw I wasn't wearing it. Disappointment? Resignation? I forced myself to look away.

"Are you going to go talk to him?" Izzy asked, touching my arm.

"I will, I just need to wait for the right moment. And I prefer Jane, Theo, and Willow to be distracted when I do."

"Let me know what you need from me, Sarah. Happy to be a distraction," Izzy said.

"I won't ask you to do that, but thanks, Iz. You are a great friend." I smiled at her.

I watched as John made his rounds. Eventually, he stopped just several feet away, standing near the bar, swirling a drink in his hand. His gaze was unfocused. If he was about to do something reckless, I had to stop him before it was too late.

I looked at Izzy and gestured to him. "Time to make my move."

"You got this," she said with a thumbs-up.

I pushed through the crowd, my pulse hammering. "John," I said, my voice low but urgent as I reached him. "Don't do this. Whatever you're thinking of doin—"

Before I could finish, a hand clapped over John's shoulder. One of the event coordinator. "John! Time to get up there."

No. Not yet. Not like this.

He gave me a final look—one I couldn't quite decipher—before he let himself be pulled toward the stage.

I froze, breath shallow, as he stepped into the spotlight.

Izzy grabbed my elbow, grounding me.

"Whatever happens," she murmured, "you're going to be fine."

I wished I believed her.

John stepped up to the microphone, and the room fell silent in anticipation. "I want to thank you all for being here tonight. I want to congratulate and celebrate the writers, editors, and teams that make everything we do at Regent possible." He gestured around the room. "Give them a round of applause." He began to talk about the future of Regent, the future ahead. The coming year. His usual charm was on full display. I scanned the audience—captivated, hanging on every word. But the longer he spoke, the more tense I became. So far, no mention of us. Thank God.

Izzy shot me a sideways glance, "You okay?"

I forced a smile and nodded.

He continued speaking, every muscle in my body wound tight. When his eyes met mine, my breath caught—but his expression gave nothing away. He spoke with the same practiced ease he always had, as if our year-long affair had never happened. Every word felt like a tightrope walk, balancing between professionalism and personal disaster. My pulse pounded in my ears. Any second now, he could say something, and ruin everything I'd worked for.

Izzy's fingers pressed lightly against my elbow, grounding me. I barely registered it. I was too busy holding my breath, waiting for the moment my fate was sealed.

I scanned the room for a way out. Jane and Peter were standing nearby, both smiling up at John as if there had not been a problem between them the past year. Jane glanced at me for a split second before returning her eyes to the stage, no real change in her face. Man, they were pros at maintaining a public persona.

No lifeline out in the storm. I turned back to John as he cleared his throat, the microphone amplifying his voice.

"Ladies and gentlemen, it is my honor tonight to make a very special announcement." *Oh my fucking god.* Every cell in my body tensed as I braced for impact. "Someone who has been a pillar not only of this company, but of my life." He paused and looked around the room. My heart pounded in my throat.

"And that person," John continued, "is my incredible wife, Jane Reynolds—I am so honored to announce her as this year's Woman of the Year!"

My heart stopped. Then it plummeted into my stomach. The room erupted in applause, but all I could hear was the rush of blood in my ears, the weight of everything that could have gone wrong settling in my chest.

John hadn't said anything. He hadn't dragged our mess into the light.

Relief flooded through me so fast it almost made me dizzy. I nearly fainted. But beneath it, buried deep, was something else—something I hated to admit. A part of me that still had been waiting. Still believing, against all logic, that, maybe . . . just maybe he would have proven me wrong. That he would have followed through on the one last promise he had made. That he would have been truthful. That he would have chosen me. For once.

But he hadn't.

All of the hope that I carried with me, washed away completely.

As Jane took the stage, her eyes met mine, a knowing look passing between us. It wasn't filled with malice, but something more understanding, sympathetic.

I wanted to look away, but I didn't. Instead, I stood there, frozen, as John and Jane stood together under the spotlight. The applause around me seemed distant, like I was watching from the outside, a part of something but not truly in it.

I exhaled, slow and steady. For the first time, seeing them

together up there, I didn't feel the sting of jealousy. Instead, I felt . . . peace.

"He was never going to choose you," Theo's voice murmured behind me. "He will never stop loving her."

I didn't flinch. I didn't turn. I didn't breathe. I just kept my eyes on the stage, on the man I had once believed would upend his life for me. Choose me. But didn't. Wouldn't. And this time, I wasn't devastated by it.

Tears welled up in my eyes. Not sad tears. Tears of relief. Tears of freedom.

I looked at them. Jane and John. The elaborate show they were putting on for the world. John clapped behind Jane as she continued to smile and wave to the audience as she accepted her award.

She then stepped up to the microphone, her presence commanding the room's attention. It was almost as if the air itself held its breath as she prepared to speak. Her voice was smooth and measured, captivating everyone in the room.

"Ladies and gentlemen," she said, her eyes scanning the crowd with confidence. "Tonight isn't just about awards, promotions, or accolades. It's about what they represent. Excellence. Integrity. Perseverance. These aren't just words we use; they're the very core of who we are at Regent House Publishing. But I believe excellence is truly defined by how we rise when the world around us pushes us down. By how we hold ourselves to a higher standard when it's easier to do just the opposite. And by the strength it takes to continue to show up—no matter the challenge."

She paused, letting her words settle over the room. Her gaze, now softer, swept over the crowd before landing on me. My heart skipped a beat as our eyes met again, and a lump formed in my throat. She wasn't just speaking to the room anymore; she was speaking directly to me.

"Over the last year, I've had the privilege of working with countless talented individuals," Jane continued. "But one individual, in particular, has exemplified what it means to be truly exceptional. She has faced challenges most would never dream of, yet she has never wavered in her pursuit of excellence. In her pursuit of integrity. I've watched her face moments of uncertainty, moments when it would have been easy to walk away, moments when it would be easy to sway in her values to get ahead, but she ultimately stayed true to herself. She didn't just stay—she rose. She grew. She fought."

I could hardly breathe as the weight of her words settled in. She was speaking about me—but not just about the work I'd done, or the tasks I'd completed. She was speaking about who I had become.

I could feel the tears pricking at the corners of my eyes, but I held them back, every word a reminder of how far I'd come. How much I'd fought for this moment.

"Sarah," Jane said, her voice softening, "you have proven not just to us, but to yourself, that no matter how many times life tries to knock you down, you can get back up. And win. You can prove yourself in any room, you can build something from nothing, and you can lead with humility, integrity, and a fierce heart."

Something inside me cracked—finally, I felt seen. For who I had become over the last year. The seemingly impossible choices I had made. The journey hadn't been easy, but hearing Jane's words, feeling the pride in her voice, made every hardship worth it.

"And so," Jane said, a smile tugging at her lips, "it is with the utmost pride, admiration, and respect that I announce the newest senior editor of Regent House Publishing . . . Sarah Jones."

The room erupted in applause, but it felt like I was in a different world entirely. The sound of the clapping was distant, drowned out by the thudding of my own heartbeat. Tears streamed down my face, but this time, they weren't from fear or uncertainty. They were from a place deep inside me—a place of acceptance, of knowing that I had finally arrived at a place I had worked so long to reach, and for a long time, thought I had lost completely.

As I stood there, trying to process it all, I met Jane's eyes once more. Her smile was genuine, full of pride, and there was something else in her gaze that I couldn't quite place—respect, perhaps. I wasn't just being given a promotion. I was being given recognition from her, the woman I respected and admired. That felt like a victory over everything that had ever tried to tear me down.

I had earned it. I had earned *this*.

As I stood in the audience smiling, everyone clapped for me and giving their looks of approval, I glanced at John. *"I'm sorry,"* he mouthed from the stage.

But I didn't react. I simply turned away, my gaze drifting toward the crowd, focusing on the moment that had just changed everything for me. The moment I'd earned. And for the first time since last year's Gala, I didn't need John's validation anymore to feel whole.

———

Izzy reappeared after the event resumed—I hadn't noticed she'd left —with two glasses of wine and a tray of pigs in a blanket. She handed them to me, the familiarity of the gesture a small comfort. "Congratulations, Sarah. I am so proud of you, newest senior editor."

I took a deep breath, the alcohol burning as it slid down my throat. "Thank you, Izzy. I couldn't have done it without your support."

She pulled me into a hug, an unexpected warmth wrapping around me. I stood stiff at first, unused to the affection from her, but it felt nice. After a few seconds, we both laughed and pulled away.

Izzy grabbed my shoulders. "You're a fucking star. You are a senior fucking editor of Regent House Publishing, for Christ's sake. You're fabulous. Just remember, there are plenty of men out there— plenty of time for that—better ones, available ones," she said, touching the lapel of my suit. "But for now, focus on yourself. The right one will come along."

"Thank you, Izzy. You're such an amazing friend."

She grinned, her eyes twinkling. "One question, though . . . as a great friend." She winced before asking, "Do you mind if I go out with

Andy? We've been talking more, and I really like him. But if it's weird because he and John are friends, I won't touch him."

"Oh my goodness. I have been waiting for this. Of course you can go out with him!" I hugged her again, tighter this time. "You'd better give me all the details later. I want to know everything."

"Done," she said, a grin spreading across her face.

I was genuinely happy for Izzy. She deserved something good, something easy. But as I watched her, a small pang settled in my chest. I thought I had found love too. I had imagined that, at some point, it would be enough—that maybe the love I shared with John would carry me through the hard times. But now . . . it was gone. Forever. Like it never even existed at all.

I had achieved what I'd been working for, but there was no one to share it with. The thought of ending up alone—something I'd feared from the very beginning—now felt real. The thought crept in, making everything I had worked for seem a little less bright. But as quickly as it came, I dismissed it.

Over the past year, I had learned that I didn't need anyone else to validate my worth. I was enough, just as I was.

"I have to pee. I'll be back," I mumbled, making any excuse I could to slip away from the crowd. I needed a moment to collect my thoughts. I needed a minute to breathe.

Izzy nodded and went to join Theo and Willow.

My eyes slid past her, landing on Theo and Willow. They didn't say a word, but when our gazes met, they both gave me a small, knowing nod—an unspoken acknowledgment, a silent approval. I had done it.

As I passed Jenny, she lit up like a Christmas tree. "Huge congratulations, Sarah. I am so happy for you."

I gave her a small smile but kept moving. My feet moved faster and faster, my eyes fixed on the bathroom door. As I neared it, a memory flashed—a year ago, I had walked out of this very bathroom and collided with Jane Reynolds, completely unaware of who she was or how much she would affect my life.

A smile tugged at my lips. How far I'd come since then. Even if not all of it had been sunshine and rainbows, I was proud. I had faced the storm and stood tall through it.

I grabbed the door to the ladies' room, but before I could pull it open, there he was.

John, standing, waiting for me. My chest tightened.

I scanned the room, searching for Jane, Willow, Theo, anyone who might see us.

"Hi, John. Congratulations on everything this year," I said, my voice flat and professional—distance in my tone.

"Sarah, I'm so sorry," he said. His words felt rehearsed, empty. As if I was on a merry-go-round of "I'm sorry, Sarah," over and over. The same thing with no new action. In fact, John was the boy who cried, "I'm sorry, Sarah." After a while, it didn't have the same effect.

I raised a hand and tucked my hair behind my ear, the movement somehow steadying me. "Forget it, John. It's okay. Really."

He frowned, obviously confused. He was waiting. Waiting for me to have some kind of reaction. To break down? To beg? To yell at him? To scream? But I wouldn't give him a reaction. I refused.

"Can we talk later?" he asked, his voice low, pleading.

"No." I stepped back, shaking my head, feeling the sharp edge of finality in my bones. I'd seen him for what he was—a coward, hiding me, stringing me along. "There won't be a later," I said. "When I said we were done, I meant it."

"Sarah, don't do this now—"

I cut him off. "No. I should have done this a year ago."

His face changed, realization dawning. I was really done. But before he could say anything else, I turned to walk away. He grabbed my arm to stop me.

I pulled my arm back, glaring at him. "John, I am done. I am done with all of this. I gave up my whole life for you. My career was in shambles. My friendships were damaged. You couldn't even tell the people closest to you, your family, about me. I lost all sense of who I am. Because you are a coward. And a fool for holding on to a woman who was clearly done with you. Ironically you turned around and treated me the exact same way. You couldn't just own your truth. You left me with nothing. I have given you too many chances. I. Am. Done."

The finality of my decision pulsed through me, powerful and certain.

There was pain in his eyes, but I didn't care. I narrowed my eyes on him. "Goodbye John," I said, then turned and walked away.

I stepped back into the ballroom, and my eyes met Jane's. Her gaze was steady, like she had watched the whole interaction. She looked right into my soul. We didn't have to say anything. We already knew. A quiet understanding passed between us—one that needed no words. We were on each other's teams.

The room buzzed with energy, glasses clinking, voices rising in celebration—but I felt detached from it all. Gone was the overwhelming sensation. Everything I'd worried about and worked toward for the past year had come to a resolution. I was a senior editor, at peace with Jane, and done with John. And for the first time in a long time, I didn't feel like I had anything left to prove.

I moved through the crowd, stopping by Izzy, Theo, and Willow. "Hey guys, I'm going to head out. Thanks for everything."

They all offered quick congratulations. "So proud of you," Theo said with a grin. "You've earned this," Willow added. Izzy gave me a wink, her smile full of pride.

The air outside hit me like a slap, cold and sharp, and I took a deep breath, feeling it all, a whole year, slip away.

I pulled my phone out of my coat pocket, my thumb hovering over John's number. I stared at it for a long moment—his name, the thread that had kept me tied up for so long. Then, with a single, decisive swipe, I pressed *delete*.

A wave of freedom washed over me. It was real. It was done. I was done.

I was free.

And I was officially the newest senior editor of Regent House Publishing.

As I left the Gala, the city around me felt different. I was different. There was hope in the air.

———

As I walked down the street, each step seemed to lift the weight of the past year, as if the layers, the lies, the hiding, were peeling off, leaving me lighter. I didn't need to hurry. For the first time in a long time, I was not running toward or away from anything. I was just moving forward—finally. And it felt right.

The city was buzzing with life, but inside there was a stillness I hadn't felt in a year.

My phone buzzed in my coat pocket, but I didn't check it. Whoever it was, whatever they needed, it could wait. The corners of my mouth turned up.

I was no longer waiting.

I was no longer waiting for someone else to choose me.

I had finally chosen myself.

Acknowledgments

I never imagined I would be writing the acknowledgments section for my debut novel this early in life... but here we are (and I'm so grateful). As I have learned, writing a book truly takes a village. I could not have done it without the incredible individuals who have supported me along the way.

To my editor, Allison Lutz — this book truly wouldn't have been possible without you. I am so grateful to the editing angels who made sure we crossed paths. The work and time you poured into this novel means more to me than you will ever know. I couldn't have asked for a better blend of critique partner and cheerleader throughout this process.

Alexander Ryker — my love. Thank you for standing by me through it all and encouraging me to follow my dreams. You saw me for who I truly am from the very beginning and supported me until I could see it too. Your unwavering support is something I once only dreamed of, and for so long, I didn't know if I would ever find. I truly believe I went through all the difficult relationships so that when I found you, I could appreciate you even more. You are my support system, my rock, my visionary, and my strategist. I wouldn't want to do life without you. I love you.

To Mitch — Oh, Mitch. You have been one of the most pivotal reasons this book exists (and a huge reason that there will be many more). From holding space for me through hours of tears and breakups, to talking through the smallest of decisions with me (like what font to use on the cover). You have been a steady and eternal reminder that divine guidance is with me every step of the way. You are the reason I found my way back to writing, and there will never be enough thank-yous for that. Writing has become the greatest gift of my life. Thank you. Thank you. Thank you. (times a million)

To Ramy, thank you for sharing your wisdom. Going through this process with you was incredibly empowering, and now I'm officially addicted to the publishing game.

To my family — Dad & Dana, Mom & Dennis, Randi, Levi & Camber — I am endlessly grateful for your unwavering support in every venture I pursue. When I told each of you I was writing this book, you all cheered me on without hesitation. That support means more to me than you'll ever know. Thank you for always believing in me, no matter how wild or unconventional my dreams are.

To my girlfriends — Marlys, Chelsea, Jessika, and Nafsika. Thank you for cheering me on as I wrote this book. I hit the jackpot when it comes to supportive friends. I love you.

To the past relationships that didn't work out — thank you. Because of you, I've grown in ways I'm deeply grateful for today.

And finally, to you — the readers. They say the artist must stand alone to observe the crowd. I'm truly grateful to have any crowd to observe (and if you are reading this, then I have at least one). I pray that this book brings you a sense of empowerment to choose yourself, to fall back in love with yourself, and to know that you truly can 'have it all.' And if 'having it all' for you, includes finding your person... Just be patient. He's on his way.

Thank you for allowing me to share this piece of my heart with you. My hope is that these words meet you exactly where you are and remind you that you are never alone.

About Aria Devi

Aria Devi is the bestselling author of *The Other Woman* and *Wanter Dynamics & The Love We Are*. *The Velvet Clover* is her third novel. She lives and writes in Austin, Texas.

You can find more from Devi at www.AriaDeviBooks.com.

Your Next Read by Aria Devi

Don't miss Aria Devi's next novel, *The Velvet Clover* - a magical, heart-wrenching holiday romance where PR executive Ava Hawthorne stumbles into a 1925 speakeasy and an impossible love that will test everything she thought she knew about fate, family, and the risks we take for love.

Thank you for reading The Other Woman

If you enjoyed this book, please consider leaving a review on Amazon.

To learn more about Aria Devi and her upcoming releases, visit www.AriaDeviBooks.com.

Follow Aria on Instagram, TikTok, and Substack @AriaDeviBooks for the latest updates, news, book releases, and behind-the-scenes content.

www.ingramcontent.com/pod-product-compliance
Lightning Source LLC
Chambersburg PA
CBHW030336120726
47901CB00007B/1812